The War of Gods

A Welcome to the Underworld Novel

Book 3

Con Template

Also by Con Template:

Welcome to the Underworld, Book 1
The Fall of Gods, Book 2 of Welcome to the Underworld

Cover Photo by: Con Template

Cover Illustration Design by: Dorothy Duong

Dedicated to My Sister,

Because it is my biggest honor to call you my sister.

ACKNOWLEDGEMENTS

The publication of The War of Gods could not have been possible without the unwavering love from my family. Thank you for spoiling me every single day with your love, affections, and your unending support. Thank you to my mom for being so awe-inspiring, to my dad for being so amazing, and to my sister for being my "Holy Trinity"—my best friend, my mentor, and my partner-in-crime.

Kevin N., every time I work on the Welcome to the Underworld novels, I am reminded of you and how much I miss you. Thank you for that majestic card that you sent us—we love it so much. Stay strong, stay safe, and please come home soon. We miss you.

To all my friends—thank you for all the laughs, the heartfelt memories, and all our silly adventures. It is an absolute gift to have you in my life—you're all wonderful!

A massive "Thank You" is owed to my beloved beta readers: Jocelyn H., Anita Law, Anna Chanthakhoun, Annie Park, Ghetty Hilaire, Jamie Lee, Kim Tong, My-Trinh Nguyen, Vivian T. Hoang, Melanie, Yanny Zhang, Maria L. Loo, Joules, Tiffany H., Cindy Thi Cao, Julie Doan, Shirley L., Theresa, Grace Suh, Sandra, Kix Choi, and Vicky Chow. This book couldn't have come this far without all your time, dedication, generous help, and genuine love for the story. Thank you so much again!

As always, thank you to my graphic artist, Dorothy Duong. I could never express enough gratitude for all that you've gifted to me. Thank you for *always* giving me something better than I could envision and thank you for being an amazing friend in the process. Your masterpieces leave me in awe every single time, and I cannot wait to finish the final cover with you. Thank you a million times over again.

To Solangel—Publishing a book can be a whirlwind journey. There are the really outstanding moments, and then there are the really frustrating moments. Thank you for constantly being there for me during all those whirlwind moments, for lending an ear of support, for giving me so much encouragements, and for always being such a positive force. I feel unbelievably lucky to have your kind support, and I cannot wait to share in more whirlwind journeys with you!

Last and never least, thank you to all my wonderful readers for opening your hearts to Welcome to the Underworld. I can't believe we're already on the third book. Every single day, I find myself humbled by your unending support, awe-inspiring messages, and kind encouragements. I never feel like I deserve so much love from all of you—but I'm grateful for it everyday. None of this could have come to fruition without you. Thank you for taking part in this journey with me—I can't wait to finish it with you in the final book!

CONTENTS

Acknowledgments

"Our world isn't a society where love conquers all."

00: Fallen Gods

He remained quiet while he stood atop one of the tallest buildings in the city. His dark brown eyes watched as a young woman sped away in a silver taxicab. His eyes moved over to the King of Serpents. The infamous King stood quiet, dazed, and broken. It looked like someone had just ripped the heart out of the Underworld Royal.

A gust of wind rippled over the roof, blowing away the snow that once layered the silent observer's hooded black jacket. His face was obscured by shadows. His only visible feature was a gold ring piercing on his lower lip and a scar of the number "57" that covered most of his left cheek.

He balled his fists as he watched the taxicab disappear out of sight. Coldness seeped into his eyes. He extracted a silver flip-phone from his pocket and dialed. As the phone rang, his eyes strayed downward to the barefoot King of Serpents sitting on the hood of a snow-covered car. He looked miserable with his face buried into his hands.

"What is it?" a female voice answered over the phone, snapping the man from his stupor.

"She's alive," he whispered, getting right to the point.

"Who?"

Hatred saturated his voice. "The Queen."

A short, uncomfortable pause came over the line. "That's . . . That's impossible. She died in Taecin. In the fire . . . she died. No one could have survived the fires we set."

"Somehow she did survive," he stated firmly. His voice pulsed with scorn. "And she's back in Seoul."

"Why . . . Why are you calling about this?" she stuttered. "Why aren't you going after her?"

"The King of Serpents was with her."

His eyes returned downward when he heard the sound of shattering glass.

6

The Underworld King had punched his fist into the window of a parked car. Blood oozed from his clenched fist. He did not appear to be affected by the physical injury, but his face still reflected pain from a different source. Perhaps from the one who just left him.

There was a long pause on the other end at the mention of the King of Serpents. "And he isn't anymore?"

The man withdrew his eyes from Kwon Tae Hyun.

"Just gather everyone," he said instead, absently running his fingers over his scar. The thirst for vengeance seared in his eyes. "We have unfinished business to take care of."

Apprehensive silence occupied the line. "But boss—"

"I'll personally deal with him," the man assured, cutting the woman off. His jaw clenched as he cast one final glance at Tae Hyun.

"Right now, all that matters is making An Soo Jin pay for what she did three years ago."

"It is a cruel world..."

01: Enjoy Your Coffin

When faced with the adversities of life, most people turn to the likes of alcohol to take them unto a world where the pain becomes numbed, nonexistent.

Always a firm believer in maintaining control, Choi Yoori opted out of the "get-my-ass-drunk-because-my-life-sucks" therapy and gravitated toward something healthier. In lieu of wallowing in a bar somewhere, Yoori chose to immerse herself in a world where there were stories that were bigger than hers, stories that could con her reality and momentarily shield her from her problems. A local library proved key to this therapeutic endeavor.

It had been three weeks since the altercation between herself and her former crime lord boss, Kwon Tae Hyun. After months of being together, she discovered that he purposely sought her out, blackmailed her into being his assistant, and used her because of her resemblance to the Queen of the Underworld, An Soo Jin. Though it turned out that Yoori was indeed the missing Queen who somehow acquired amnesia, it did not lessen the blow of the discovery. She had fallen for him—hard. To find out that he had used her like a fool since the beginning was a difficult pill to swallow. Needless to say, their breakup was as volatile as an exploding car.

Since the dispute, Yoori returned to her cramped apartment and did her best to get some semblance of her life back. Regrettably, Tae Hyun made such an attempt difficult for Yoori. Instead of disappearing from her life, he continued to make his presence known by ensuring that she was well taken care of. It was likely because of a guilty conscience, but he not only made sure that her bank account was stocked with enough money to last her for years, he also sent over a messenger days later with the key to his black Mercedes convertible.

Yoori was initially too pissed off to even look at the car. Once she calmed down, she rationalized that it was safer for her to be at the library late at night with her own car as opposed to taking any public transportation. She may be stubborn and prideful, but she wasn't stupid. Aware of the dangers around her, she knew that having the car would decrease the amount of trouble she could find herself in. Though she had more than enough funds to purchase a brand new car, Yoori convinced herself that she should keep the Mercedes because she wanted to save money for emergencies. Deep down, she couldn't deny the warm feeling that came over her whenever she was in the car. She chose not to examine why she felt that way. She merely convinced herself that it was because she was in love with the car, not the previous owner.

Yoori made her peace with accepting Tae Hyun's car, but adjusting to the other aspects of her life proved to be difficult. She hadn't realized how comfortable she had grown in Tae Hyun's apartment until she started to feel like a stranger in her own. She also couldn't stop thinking about how her best friend was raped because of her, how she singlehandedly killed eleven men, and how she found out about Tae Hyun's betrayal. It didn't help that she had no one to vent to. Her only saving grace was the library and the escape she found in the stories living there.

In the midst of adjusting into her new life, her best friend Lee Chae Young, was discharged from the hospital. When Yoori visited her, Chae Young's boyfriend, Jae Won, was there with her. Jae Won, who was in Tae Hyun's gang (and An Soo Jin's former right-hand man), had been by his girlfriend's side since she left the hospital. While Yoori was able to refrain from having another guilt-stricken breakdown, it still tore her apart to be in Chae Young's company. As absurd as it sounded, she didn't feel worthy enough to breathe the same air as her best friend. Despite this torturous feeling, Yoori didn't show it externally.

Yoori's thoughts drifted from the fictional book she was reading to a memory of what took place the last time she visited her best friend.

"Is everything okay? You look thinner than before," Chae Young had observed during one of Yoori's visits. Her face was also pale. Unlike Yoori's though, Chae Young's face was still marred with healing bruises and scars.

"Everything is okay," Yoori lied with a forced smile. It agonized Yoori that even in her own state of misery, Chae Young was still watching out for her. "You know me, I suck when it comes to dealing with cold weather. I'll be better soon."

Chae Young nodded, her sad eyes detecting the lie in Yoori's voice.

Yoori kept a reassuring smile on her face. Standing at a modest 5'3" with big eyes and plump lips, Yoori was a force to be reckoned with when she smiled. She had the ability to make people feel reassured, like the heartless world was actually a safe place. It was a power that, for the good of everyone around her, Yoori used and exploited daily.

Jae Won was busy preparing dinner so she had some alone time with Chae Young. During the course of their conversation, Chae Young wasn't inclined to talk about the details of what happened to her in the diner. Yoori respected this and played along. They spoke about nonchalant things that meant nothing to either of them. While they spoke, Yoori also decided it would be better not to update Chae Young on the situation with Tae Hyun. It was an odd thing that two best friends couldn't confide in each other. One was traumatized while the other was consumed with guilt. Yoori wished she was stronger for Chae Young, but she knew if they even mentioned Tae Hyun or spoke about what happened in the diner, then she would likely have an emotional breakdown that would push Chae Young over the edge. Yoori couldn't do that to her best friend. She'd rather suffer in solitude.

It wasn't until Chae Young left to shower that Yoori was snowplowed into talking about Tae Hyun. The force behind this ambush was Jae Won. Yoori had been ignoring Jae Won the whole time she visited her friend, and she was not happy when he finally confronted her.

"I know that things are over between you and Boss Kwon, but why are you ignoring me too?" Jae Won confronted with frustration.

They could hear the showerhead running as they stood in the hall.

Jae Won, looking like a refined aristocrat with a rugged quality to him, eyed the bathroom door. He towered over her. He was dressed simply in a khaki jacket and jeans. Had Yoori not seen his fighting capabilities firsthand, she would venture to say that he looked like a spoiled rich boy who had too much money and too much time on his hands. In reality, he was far from the spoiled rich boy. He was a formidable figure in a powerful Underworld gang. He may have served Kings and Queens, but to the rest of the world, he was a deadly royal in his own right.

When Jae Won determined that Chae Young wasn't within earshot of their conversation, his attention returned to Yoori. He, too, knew that it was best to keep all the drama away from Chae Young. She needed time to heal; she didn't need to be hounded with other worries.

"You knew he was using me all along, and you didn't warn me," Yoori answered irritably. She clenched her fists in resentment. "You just watched as he played me for a fool—you *and* your brother."

She'd had time to mull over everything and a big realization came over her: Jae Won, along with Kang Min who was his younger brother and part of Tae Hyun's gang, knew all along that Tae Hyun was using her. *That* was why they told her in the limo they weren't sure if Tae Hyun could be trusted. It was because they knew that her relationship with Tae Hyun had been forged on lies. They knew and never told her. She loved the brothers, but her pride—her hatred for feeling betrayed—was all consuming. As far as Yoori was concerned, cutting off ties due to the betrayal didn't end with Tae Hyun. It extended to the brothers too.

"Why the hell would we tell you since we all knew you'd run off because your damn pride means more to you than your own life?" he snarled. For the first time since she had known him, Jae Won's face contorted in anger while speaking to her. He was beside himself with fury. "We knew he used you to get me, to get my gang to merge with his. That was why I hated him in the beginning. *That* was why I told you not to trust him. But as time went on, it became obvious that he fucked himself up because he fell for you. We took back our uncertainty and told you that we thought he could be trusted because we both knew that he would take care of you, regardless of the decisions he made in the past when he didn't even know who you were to begin with."

Yoori snorted at his last sentence. "You're siding with him?"

Jae Won made a rude sound as well. "Boss, do you honestly think that Kwon Tae Hyun is the type of guy who brings girls to lake houses, creates personal made Winter Wonderlands for them, and decorates his apartment for their birthdays? Do you think he did all that just to get into your pants?" He shook his head. "He did all of that because he felt guilty for bringing you into this world. He wanted to take you away from the cruelties of this world and allow you to temporarily live in a dream world." His eyes became aggrieved. "He may have dragged you into this world for his own selfish needs, but he's paying for it now. He's fucked up his status and power in this world. He's paying for it now, and he protects you more than you'll ever know. I told you that I trusted him—I still do. I'm not siding with him; it's just that I empathize with loving someone who suffered because of the world I brought them into."

It was only then that Yoori saw guilt devour his eyes. Jae Won understood Tae Hyun because he related to him. Jae Won blamed himself for what happened to Chae Young; he blamed himself for bringing her into this world. Yoori breathed in painfully. The guilt he felt was something she wanted to relieve him of. It wasn't his fault that Chae Young was raped. The burden rested on her and her alone.

When she was about to muster up the courage to tell him that none of this was his fault, the bathroom door opened.

Chae Young came out in her white sweater and pink pajama pants. The outfit dwarfed her normally tall figure. Chae Young used to emanate the most vivacious aura but for the past few weeks, as the weight came off her like the falling water from her newly washed hair, she looked like a shell of her former self. The very sight broke Yoori's heart.

"Are you guys ready to eat?" she asked meekly.

Dread assailed Yoori as she stared at Chae Young. She no longer found the valor to voice her guilt. She became a coward again and wanted to run away.

"I actually have to return some books to the library," Yoori shared with a smile that hid the storm brewing inside her. "We'll have dinner together another time, okay?"

As Chae Young nodded in confusion, Yoori walked over and gave her a huge hug. She pulled out, gave Jae Won a stiff nod, and left without another word. As she exited the building like the coward she was, Yoori belatedly realized she didn't have her keys.

Damn, she thought.

Rushing back, Yoori quietly reentered the apartment. Chae Young and Jae Won were no longer outside. From the mumbled voices coming from the hall, she deduced that they were in Chae Young's bedroom. Yoori slowly inched in to look for her keys when she froze like ice. She was taken aback when she heard soft sobs emit from Chae Young's room.

Chae Young's cries spilled over her like acid rain, sending aches to eat at her heart. It was then that Yoori realized Chae Young had been holding in her tears this whole time, waiting for her to leave. Yoori wanted to rush into the bedroom to comfort Chae Young, but she resisted the urge. She couldn't see Chae Young at that moment without breaking down as well. God help her if she broke down again. Her chest tightened while she suppressed her own tears. Unable to withstand it, Yoori quickly grabbed her keys and left before anyone found out she was there. She trusted Jae Won to take care of Chae Young, holding and comforting her as a boyfriend should . . . as Tae Hyun once held her when she needed a shoulder to cry on.

Yoori chewed on her lips.

She had never felt more alone.

Heaving a quiet breath as she thought about Chae Young and what happened that night, Yoori flipped the next page of her library book. It had been days since she last saw Chae Young, and the pain was still fresh within her.

"Shh! Go outside if you want to make a call."

Yoori lifted her gaze from her book when she heard murmuring from the other corner of the library. The source of the sound came from three men. All were dressed in dark puffy jackets, jeans, and beanies. They were three of the many men who had kept her company in the library for more than three weeks now.

Although Tae Hyun hadn't made an appearance in her life since their fall out, that did not mean that Serpents gang members hadn't appeared in her world either. After moving back into her apartment, Yoori noticed that there were Serpents watching over her and following her everywhere she went. If she hadn't recognized some of them, then she wouldn't have even suspected she was being guarded. She hadn't complained because they had all been very quiet. She also wasn't a fool. She knew her life was in danger. Regardless of where it came from, she would accept all the protection she could get. Lastly, she felt alone so it was nice to know that wasn't actually the case.

"Miss, we're about to close in fifteen minutes," a library assistant informed Yoori, smiling warmly at her as Yoori's gaze averted from her unofficial bodyguards.

Yoori nodded at the young college girl, thanking her for the notice before the girl went to inform other library patrons that it was time to pack up.

It was closing time again.

Another day gone by . . .

Snow was pouring when Yoori walked out of the library. She pulled the white hood of her jacket over her black ponytail and raced to her car. She peered at the rearview mirror after she started the engine. Like clockwork, three Serpents got into their black BMW, ready to follow her.

Yoori drove in silence, thinking about nothing in particular. She parked a block away from her apartment and was running home when she suddenly felt a pair of eyes on her.

She stopped in her tracks and looked around.

Countless people walked around her in the drizzling snow. Yoori looked across the street. The Serpents were in their car, drinking coffee while looking all around to make sure no threats were present. The feeling of someone watching her became more prominent, and she knew it did not come from the Serpents in her company. Yoori surveyed the street again. Though people surrounded her, the sensation of being watched did not appear to be coming from those who stood in her direct line of vision. It felt like it was coming from above.

Her gaze gradually climbed up to one of the taller buildings on the block. Her heart jolted to a quick stop.

What the?

Was it her imagination or was someone standing on the roof of that building?

Yoori blinked the snow off her eyes and continued to keep her focus on the silhouette above. She began to walk toward the shadow when the sound of tires screeching distracted her.

"Watch out!"

She averted her eyes in a panic, thinking a vehicle was coming for her. Her breath steadied when she saw that a red truck had skidded to a stop in front of a young couple jaywalking on the street. Luckily, the truck stopped in time. The couple waved their apology to the driver and ran off into a nearby apartment building. The truck resumed driving and everything returned to normal on the street. Yoori took her eyes off the scene and looked back at the top of the building. Surprise met her when only an unoccupied roof greeted her eyes. The mysterious shadow was no longer there.

Yoori blew out a relieved breath. It was nothing after all. Shaking her head at her overactive imagination, she wasted no more time and hurried up to her apartment. She stepped in, flicked on all the lights, and locked the door. She was about to step into her bedroom when she heard the sound of someone breathing.

Yoori straightened like a cobra on the attack.

She moved back into the hall. Slowly, she started approaching the living room. She stopped cold once she spotted the silhouette of someone hiding behind the bookshelf in her living room.

"Shit!"

Wasting no time, Yoori made a beeline for the door when a second intruder sprang out from the kitchen and kicked her away from the exit.

"Ugh!"

Her body slammed into the back of the living room sofa. Pain from the impact detonated inside her, and she scrambled to escape. She was merely inches away from the door when the man, who was previously hiding behind the bookshelf, locked a powerful arm around her neck and held her prisoner.

"Always so good with your hearing," he whispered with amusement.

Yoori looked at him and the other man by the door. They wore gray suits and had dark hair perfectly slicked back. They looked like they belonged in a business meeting rather than in an apartment ambush.

"What do you want?" she said breathlessly, attempting to get oxygen into her lungs while in a chokehold.

They were either here because of her relationship with Kwon Tae Hyun or because she was the Queen of the Underworld prior to her amnesia. Either way, Kwon Tae Hyun and An Soo Jin had a lot of enemies. Being attacked for either reason would never end well for her.

"To bury you in your coffin," he growled, confirming her worst fears. He eyed the other man by the doorway. "We have five minutes to get her down. Will the Serpents downstairs be a problem?"

"No," answered the second man. "We're taking her through the back exit."

"Let's go."

Survival instincts overtook Yoori. She would be damned if she made it easy for them to kill her. If she was going down, then she wasn't going down without a fight.

"Fuck you!" Yoori shouted, grabbing a lamp from the table and hitting the guy holding her across the head. Taking out all her pent up anger on him, she hit him continuously, drawing blood as the light bulb flickered into darkness.

"Fuck!" the guy screamed, stumbling back while holding on to his assaulted head.

In that instance, the man by the door rushed to Yoori. She attempted to hit him with the same lamp, but unlike the other man, he avoided her strikes with ease. In her state of panic, Yoori resorted to chucking the lamp at him. While he was distracted with batting the lamp away, she seized a dining room chair. She raised the wooden chair and broke it over his head.

Boom!

The wood shattered over his skull. He screamed as he crumpled to the floor.

Using this as her opportunity, Yoori unlocked the door and sped out into the hall. She bounded down the stairs, huffing and puffing for air.

"Help!" she called out, hoping a neighbor or one of the Serpents would hear her. "Help me — *Ah!*"

Yoori nearly toppled over the stairway railing when a third attacker snatched her off the stairwell and hauled her through the back exit. Snow pelted her at full force as he dragged her into the quiet back alleyway of the apartment complex.

"Get off me!"

Adrenaline still pumping through her, Yoori used the wall of the apartment complex as her crutch. She jumped on it and pushed herself backward, slamming the man against a parked red car behind them. He cursed and loosened his hold on her.

Screech!

Yoori whirled around. A black, unmarked limo sped toward her. It stopped right in front of her, its bright headlights blinding her eyes momentarily.

Car doors slammed. Two other silhouettes sprinted toward her.

"Shit!" she screamed.

Yoori tried to make a run for it, but was stopped when the two men who attacked her in the apartment dragged her into the limo. They roughly threw her in. The back of her skull hit the window, nearly causing her to black out. The first attacker from the apartment pulled her down to the floor. He pinned her to the ground by jamming his knee into her neck. Yoori struggled to breathe as she watched the rest of the men pile in. Like the two from the apartment, the other three were also dressed in gray suits and had their hair slicked back.

They closed the door as the limo sped off like a runaway train.

"An Soo Jin," said the one pinning her to the ground. "Do you remember us?"

Yoori groaned. She knew it was only a matter of time before someone from Soo Jin's past caught up to her. She just didn't think it'd be this soon. Anger inundated her. She was still reeling from how fucked up her life was; she was not going to allow these assholes to make it worse.

"Get the fuck off me!" she shouted.

Fury filling her, she grabbed the hand of the one pinning her to the ground.

She flicked his wrist back.

A loud crack suspended in the air.

"Ahhhhhh!" He screamed bloody murder and recoiled from her.

Yoori surged up, gasping for air. She crawled on her hands and knees, and moved to the farther end of the limo, trying to put as much distance between them as possible. Yoori almost reached the end when someone seized her legs and tugged her back.

"No!"

She kicked against the one who grabbed her. He collapsed back on to the seat, taking two other men down in the process.

"I don't think so, Soo Jin," said the one who pulled her off the stairwell. He lunged for her, pinned her to the ground, and started punching her in the face.

Pain engulfed her before she started seeing stars.

"You piece of shit!" she shrieked.

A monster awakened inside her, and she no longer felt fear. All she felt was the thirst for blood. Blocking his hit with her arm, she punched him hard in the neck. He let out a scream and released her. She drew up, snatched his head and banged it against the limo window. After that, she threw his body to the ground and stepped on it before lunging for the rest of the men.

Everything that followed was a blur for Yoori.

All she remembered was punching necks, slamming skulls against windows, and cracking bones. Her fists bled from the assault she was bestowing on to her kidnappers, but she could hardly care.

"Who the fuck are you to attack me?" she hollered at the top of her lungs. "I am not someone to fuck with!"

One laughed and elbowed her chin, causing her head to collide against the window. Soon after, a large hand grappled her neck and pinned her against the highest part of the window. The crown of her head touched the limo ceiling. Once again, she struggled for air.

Yoori opened her eyes to see the rest of the men wipe blood away from their mouths. Her eyes strayed to the one who held a syringe in his hands.

"Seriously?" she struggled to say, knowing the purpose of that needle was to sedate her. "You guys can't take on a girl without that?"

The one restraining her against the window chuckled, blood from his forehead trickling down his face. "We all know a simple girl cannot beat the hell out of us like you just did."

The one holding the needle came closer to her. He pricked the needle into the side of her strained neck.

She screamed when the syringe pierced her.

"Always a pleasure, An Soo Jin," he whispered as darkness engulfed her world. Yoori blacked out when he said his final words to her. "Now enjoy your coffin."

"Where the heartless and vengeful..."

02: The Coffin Throne

Darkness surrounded her when she opened her eyes. At first, she did not know where she was. However, as she reached out blindly, she began to realize where they had laid her body.

Sobs overtook her.

"No . . . no . . . not again," she whispered, sobs wracking her body as her unsteady hands touched the tight walls that imprisoned her. She could hardly move.

Her hands struggled to find anything in the confined space. Her fingers grazed over an object. She quickly grabbed it in the darkness. She touched it and recognized that she was holding a lighter. Her breathing was becoming erratic as she struggled to light it. Light illuminated the space she was in, and her heart stopped cold.

Her worst fear was realized as she stared at the sight above her.

The coffin.

She was in the coffin again.

The putrid smell began to fill her nostrils and bile rose through her. She moved the lighter to the side to determine the source of the disgusting scent. Horror clutched her once she made out what else was in the coffin. The light spread over severed legs, broken fingers, and ripped off ears like a wave from the ocean.

Body parts.

She was sleeping in a coffin with amputated body parts.

"No! Not again!" she continued to cry. She started pounding on the coffin lid, using all her might to push it open. It would not budge. "Please . . . Please let me out!"

The rancid smell grew stronger as her panicked body moved against the decaying body parts. Air was becoming scarce and it felt like the world was closing in on her.

All she wanted was to get out.

All she wanted was to die . . .

Yoori opened her eyes in terror.

She attempted to calm down by focusing on slowing her breathing. When the disgusting cadaver odor from earlier was nowhere near her nostrils, she placed a reassuring hand over her frantic heart. To her great relief, she concluded that what she experienced was not real at all.

It was just a dream.

Her relief was short-lived when she found a lighter sitting atop her chest. Yoori picked it up and stopped breathing when she realized she was holding a similar lighter to the one in her dream.

Her hands fumbled in the darkness until she was finally able to light it.

Light bloomed around her, running over the walls surrounding her and the lid above.

Her pulse quickened in fear.

She was indeed inside a coffin.

She moved the lighter, afraid that her reality would reenact the awful dream. To her relief, there were no decaying body parts inside this coffin. It was only filled with her presence, along with a lighter and a white bandage wrapped over her injured hand.

Yoori calmly stared up at the coffin lid. She furrowed her brows when she noticed distinct markings on it. She lifted her lighter and moved her fingers over the fingernail marks. There were so many markings that she wondered how often this coffin was used to trap a living person.

She gulped.

Yoori did not intend to be the last occupant of this coffin.

She flicked the lighter off and pushed the coffin cover.

Creak.

The lid easily lifted, permitting fresh air to enter her lungs.

Yoori shielded her eyes from the bright light that suddenly assaulted her after being surrounded by darkness. Once her eyes acclimated with the bright stream of light, she looked around the room. The entire room was pitch dark. The spotlight was on the coffin.

She struggled out of the coffin, her legs feeling like jelly. She nearly crashed to the floor after she jumped off the table the coffin sat on. Once her muscles started working properly again, she stood up.

She appraised the coffin in a newfound marvel.

Yoori had expected to see an ordinary black coffin. What stood before her was a coffin fit for royalty. The outer surface of the coffin was made of pure gold. With the light beaming down, it illumed like a golden casket meant to bask in the heavens. The grandiose of this coffin astounded her. Who would lock her in something worth millions of dollars?

Her eyes perused the mysterious room to unearth the answer.

"Hello Soo Jin," said a voice from somewhere above.

Yoori moved to the end of the room where she noticed stairs that led to the upper portion of the estate. She climbed up, vigilantly grazing her fingers over the railing. Her breath hitched when she saw a familiar face.

"You," she whispered incredulously.

Shin Jung Min, one of the Underworld's three elder Advisors, stood on the balcony in a dark gray business suit. He was a middle-aged man whose hair was a mixture of blonde and gray. He had an upper mustache of a similar hue. Her attackers stood close to him, their hands respectfully behind their backs. Behind them was a projector with a grainy video reel of a group of people fighting in an enclosed space.

Yoori growled under her breath. It made sense that the one who arranged her kidnapping was an Advisor of the Underworld. She evaluated the room again, the extreme coldness bringing forth an unpleasant memory. She had been here before. Yoori hypothesized that this room was part of Seo Ju Won's massive estate. The meeting room where her initiation was held was just one small part. The other rooms were what held all the Underworld secrets.

"My name is Yoori," she corrected crossly. She stood up straighter, refusing to appear weak.

Jung Min smirked patronizingly. "My mistake. Hello Yoori. How was your nap?"

She stared at the men behind him. They were all cleaned up. Despite the souvenirs she left on their skin from the fight, they still looked like a million bucks. "They're yours?"

Jung Min's voice became warm in the air-conditioned room. "You may not recognize them, but they were all Soo Jin's trainers. They were a part of everything that made Soo Jin legendary."

"Why did you have them attack me?" Yoori looked at the grainy video recording. She belatedly realized that it was a recording of the fight in the limo. She turned to him, anger revving inside her. "And you had the audacity to record the whole thing?"

Jung Min did not even blink at her accusation. "Look closely," he directed calmly.

Yoori faced the screen again. Her eyes widened when she discovered something strange about the video. She moved to examine the faces more closely. What she saw surprised her; it wasn't her just a few hours ago in the video recording. It was a younger version of herself: a younger version of herself fighting all five men in the limo and a younger version of herself who looked like a God doing so.

What the hell?

"You are strong, but you are weaker than your twelve-year-old counterpart," Jung Min stated, staring at her in a chastising manner. "How do you expect to wage war against the favored King if you cannot even stay conscious on the ride here?"

Yoori looked at him sideways. The disbelief she felt from seeing a younger version of herself was eclipsed by his statement. Heat infiltrated her voice at the implication behind his words.

"I am *not* waging a war against him," she grated, feeling like she was back at the teahouse holding a similar conversation. He had done everything in his power to turn her against Tae Hyun back then, and as it appeared, was far from giving up.

Jung Min laughed patiently. "Which is why you received a limo instead of a town car."

Yoori smirked coldly, grasping what was happening here. This was Jung Min's punishment to her for discounting his advice when they had tea. This was his way of punishing her disobedience.

"Are you that bored with your life that you have to find entertainment in screwing with mine?"

Yoori barely had time to scream when Jung Min viciously kicked her in the stomach and sent her flying across the room.

Bam!

Pain exploded inside Yoori after her head hit the railing of the stairs. She was barely able to hang on to the railing when she stumbled down, her flesh slamming against every hard step of the stairs. Every impact rattled her bones, making it hard to breathe. Her world spun, nothing but agonized groans marring her existence. Mercy was only granted when she landed on the ground floor.

"Ugh."

She laid motionless on the bottom of the stairs, breathing in agony.

Soon after, she heard sounds of footsteps descending peacefully down the stairs. She peered up and saw that Jung Min's men, Soo Jin's former trainers, were coming down the stairs in a single file line. As she regained her bearings, Jung Min's men merely stepped over her unmoving body and walked out of the room, leaving her alone with the Advisor.

Seconds later, Jung Min descended down the stairs.

"Amnesia does not give you the right to disrespect your elders, my child," he whispered, calmly walking down toward her. His left hand smoothed over the railing as he took step after step. "That is the primary difference between you and Soo Jin. No matter her status in life, she would never forget respect. You have a lot to learn if you hope to fill her shoes."

"She can fucking stay dead for all I care," Yoori gritted through her teeth. She pushed herself up into a sitting position and leaned against the wall for support. It took all her control to not lose consciousness. She did not want to give Jung Min the satisfaction of blacking out from his assault.

Jung Min chuckled when he strode off the last step. "So much anger since the last time I saw you. Did things not work out with the King of Serpents?"

Yoori remained quiet. The reminder of Tae Hyun's betrayal hurt more than the aches in her body.

Jung Min's expression became all knowing. Her silence was a deafening confirmation to his assumptions.

"I warned you," he stated simply.

"I know you did," she whispered, looking down at the floor in shame. Despite the fact that it had been weeks since it happened, she still felt embarrassment (and hurt) resonate through her. He had. Jung Min had warned her about all of this. But like a fool, she didn't listen. Now she had to pay for her foolishness.

"This is your own fault."

"I know it is," she concurred again.

"Good," he said, moving back up the stairs. "Remember this moment. Remember how pitiful he made you feel." He stopped midway up the stairs and stared down at her. "Let this feeling sink in and when you are ready, stand up."

Yoori regarded him with inquisitive eyes. She wondered what he had up his sleeves. Did he want to punish her more for disobeying him? Did he want to rub salt in her wounds?

She tried to read his face, but he merely stared at her while waiting patiently on the stairs.

Although she did not trust him, Jung Min did not feel like a threat at the moment. He felt like a mentor. At a time like this, she needed a mentor.

Yoori stared back down at the area where she landed. She allowed the humiliation to inundate her, to remind her of how much she resented Tae Hyun. If she had never met him, then she would not have been in this dreadful place in life. She would not feel this broken and she would not feel less than human. After Yoori was done despising her own existence, she did as Jung Min commanded and stood up. As if she had done this countless times in the past, she followed after Jung Min, leaving behind her pitiful state.

"Do you want to know the wonderful gift of your training?" he asked as she stepped back on the stairs and climbed toward him. "You may have fallen as a God, but the beautiful thing about falling is how powerful you are when you rise again." His lips spread into a smile when she reached him at the middle of the staircase. "Have you ever wondered why Soo Jin had three Advisors?"

"Why?" Yoori asked, genuinely curious.

"Although Ju Won knew that he could turn you into a God, he also knew that the human in you needed to be strong as well. This was where my brother and I came in. Dong Min was your political Advisor. He was your sounding board in matters pertaining to influence, politics, and business." Jung Min motioned her to walk with him up the remaining portion of the stairs. "Do you know what I was?"

She shook her head.

"I was your spiritual Advisor." He chuckled at the skeptical look on her face. "I may seem far from someone you'd turn to, but while you were growing up, I was the one you turned to when your human self got the best of you. I was the one who reminded you of your greatness, and I was the one who would never let you fail." They reached the top landing. Slowly, they returned to the circular balcony. "The beauty of being more superior than human is our resilience. Once we fall from grace, we stand stronger every time." They moved toward the railing of the balcony that overlooked the spotlighted coffin. "You will rise again. No matter how hard you fall from your throne, you will always rise again."

Yoori couldn't take her eyes off the gold coffin as she listened to his last words. "Whose coffin was that?"

"Soo Jin's."

Yoori gazed at his profile. She recalled the "dream" she had before rising out of the coffin. She wondered now if it was truly a dream or a memory from the past. "You made her sleep in that coffin?"

"Yes," he said without guilt. "Every night she failed as a God, we would throw her in that coffin and make her sleep there for the night."

His confirmation unsettled her. "Why would you do that to a young girl?"

"So her weaknesses would not become a habit."

"Why the coffin?"

"So she could be reborn." Jung Min faced her, his expression purposeful. "We all fall as Gods. No matter how invincible we may appear, at one point or another, we have all fallen as Gods. The coffin was to remind Soo Jin of her fate every time she fell from grace."

"Where did she sleep when she succeeded as a God?"

He pointed to an area adjacent to them. "On that throne."

Surprise entered her eyes. She hadn't realized there was another balcony up here.

Yoori followed him on to the other balcony.

There, she saw something that made her heart hammer. Standing alone on that balcony was a regal looking throne. Like the coffin below, it was made of pure gold. Elaborate gold carvings swam over the throne, protecting the red velvet cushion with a sense of valor and richness. There was not a single scratch or malady on this enticing chair. The throne looked grand, powerful, and divine. It was, simply put, perfection.

A sense of longing filled her when she approached the throne in a hypnotized state.

"Soo Jin loved this throne. She was the most peaceful when she slept here."

Yoori's eyes ran over the elaborate embellishments on the throne. She could sit here for days examining every individual carving and never get to the "end" of the story this throne was trying to tell. Legends before her sat on this throne, and as it appeared, their secrets would die with it.

"You used this to remind her of her fate if she was better than human," Yoori provided. She swallowed uneasily and reverted her attention back to the coffin. She came out of her hypnotized state. In place of awe came incredulity. Everything came together in the most horrific way. "And you used the coffin to remind her of her fate should she fail as a God."

The Advisors had conditioned Soo Jin to seek nothing but power. If she succeeded, then she was rewarded with this throne, thereby meaning that she would not have to suffer. She would be above all the suffering—figuratively and literally. Yoori peered down at the coffin. But if Soo Jin failed, she would have to be punished like the rest of the humans; she would have to endure what humans feared the most in life—a glimpse of death.

Yoori recalled the horrific scene she dreamt about. She wished it wasn't reality, but she had a distinct feeling it was.

Almost apprehensively, she voiced her speculation. "What else did you put in there with her?"

"The body parts of the people she killed."

Any magnificence she saw from the golden coffin evaporated. Her stomach heaved with nausea. Yoori felt like she was going to be sick. "You're all sick."

"Perhaps, but that did not mean our tactic did not work." Jung Min pointed at the screen. The younger version of Soo Jin was still fighting her trainers in the limo. Although the film was grainy, it was clear she was winning. "Look at how perfect she was. Look at how much power she exuded by simply existing on that screen." He turned to her. "Now look at *you*. Look at how pathetic your current state is. Do you think Soo Jin would ever be in this appalling state? Do you think she would ever be as pitiful as you?"

Yoori lapsed into a thoughtful silence. She knew the answer as clearly as she knew the sun would dawn once morning came. Despite her hatred for her past self, Yoori knew that Soo Jin would never be in this disgraceful condition.

And if she was, Soo Jin would not only conquer this pathetic affliction, she would also punish those who brought her down this road to begin with.

Doing her best to keep Soo Jin's mental state out of her own mind, Yoori moved the conversation along and asked a question she had been curious about for the longest time. "Why did you choose her out of all the Underworld children?"

"What do you mean?" he said, patronizing her.

Yoori gazed at him, knowing well that he was playing with her. He knew exactly what her question meant. Nevertheless, for the sake of getting the answer, she patiently elaborated. "There must've been countless Royals for all of you to choose from. Why did you choose Soo Jin? She was the second born heir and a female. As much as I like the idea of equality, it doesn't take a rocket scientist to see that this is a male-dominated society. Why her?"

"Because you have Royal blood."

Yoori blinked at Jung Min in confusion. "I thought all the heirs have Royal blood."

"Your blood also belongs to that of the Royal family in Japan. Your mother isn't like Tae Hyun's mother or Ji Hoon's mother. She is not an outsider; she is a Royal from the Japanese Underworld. No matter how powerful Tae Hyun and Ji Hoon's blood may be, your blood will always be more powerful than theirs."

"Soo Jin's brother has the same blood as her," said Yoori. "Why wasn't he chosen?"

"Because he was already chosen by the eldest Advisor in the Japanese Underworld." Jung Min smirked. "Plus, he and Ju Won did not see eye-to-eye. Ju Won has always favored you over your brother." He sighed before bringing them back on topic. He no longer had the patience to waste time with her. "How much longer will you continue to deny your fate?"

Yoori sighed as well. Her patience with this subject was quickly dwindling. "If I have already failed as a God, why do you insist on trying to resurrect the dead?"

Jung Min permitted himself a small smile before he touched the armrest of the throne. "Do you know how Gods rise again after falling?"

"How?"

"They wage war against those responsible for their downfall."

Yoori clenched her jaw and shook her head. After all this time, he was still trying to pit her against Tae Hyun.

"I will not let you resurrect her nor will I wage a war against Tae Hyun," she told him adamantly. "I am done with them—both of them."

"Is he really done with you?"

Yoori didn't miss a beat. "Yes."

"Then why are his men with you every second of every day?" he asked, causing her to freeze in place. "Why are you driving his car and why are you pining after him?"

"I am not," she whispered, only able to answer the latter part of the question.

"You are." He smirked knowingly. "You have broken free from him physically, but not emotionally. It will only be a matter of time before you go back to him and be at his mercy again."

"I am done with him," Yoori repeated through clenched teeth. The pain ached inside her. It felt like she was attempting to convince herself more so than Jung Min.

"He is not done with you," Jung Min pressed on without mercy. "You are his favorite toy, and Kings like Tae Hyun do not let go of their favorite toys easily. He will figure out a way to win you back, and when he does, the next time he breaks you, you will not be able to rise from your fall." He tilted his head. "Follow my advice as your past self once did. I did not steer her wrong. Look at what she became in this world."

"She died," Yoori said tightly, fighting to keep the emotions buried deep inside her. She could not show it; she could not show Jung Min her weakness.

"She became an immortal in this world," he corrected immediately. "She is now a crowned jewel in this unforgiving society." He stood closer to her. His voice became softer, more mentoring. "Do you really not see how incredible that type of power is? How can you choose this shameful state in life when you can have all the power in the world?"

"I do not yearn for power."

Jung Min grinned, gesturing a hand to the throne. "Sit on the throne."

Yoori shook her head, refusing to budge even though deep down she wanted nothing more than to sit on that throne.

"It's not for me," she said with difficulty.

"It doesn't belong to anyone right now. Sit."

Yoori could no longer deny herself. The throne was beckoning her and she no longer had the strength to deny its enticing call. Slowly, she moved towards it and sat. At once, this surge of euphoria came over her. The tightness that once plagued her body eased. After weeks of feeling like a lost soul—like a pathetic soul—everything in the world finally made sense.

"Close your eyes."

She closed her eyes.

"Imagine a room filled with the most powerful men and women in the world. Imagine the ones who have the power to control a city, dictate the laws of a country, and shift the fate of a world any which way they like. Imagine all of them packed into this room. Now imagine them falling to their knees when they see you sitting on this throne. Imagine how euphoric that feeling is, to know that the most powerful Kings and Queens in the world are kneeling before you because you are their God—because you are their Lord. There is no feeling greater than power; there is nothing more desirable than this throne."

Yoori agreed.

As much as she hated to admit it, she agreed.

It did not matter how much she had fallen in life, how pathetic she had become. It did not matter how badly she had been treated. None of that mattered, for everything had led her back to this throne, to this blissful state. This was her remedy from all the problems in the human world. No one could touch her on this throne. When she sat here, she was above all the troubles of the world. She was better than human; she was finally a God again—

"Tae Hyun."

Yoori broke out of her trance when she heard his name.

She unsteadily stared out at the world below. Her eyes immediately fixated on the coffin.

Jung Min continued, relentlessly spewing poison into her mind. "Imagine all that divine power and imagine Tae Hyun wanting that power too. Imagine him fighting you for your throne."

Territorial anger sparked inside her.

She clenched her hands on the arm handles.

Jung Min fed off this territorial emotion. "You have played dead for long enough. There is only room for one God on this throne, just as there is only room for one failed God in that coffin. Would you really choose to lay in that coffin for Tae Hyun?"

Yoori stood abruptly. The conflicting emotions were suffocating her. She no longer had time, or strength, for this. She moved past him. "Let me out of here."

"I know that right now, you do not want to fight him," Jung Min persisted, slowing her in her tracks. "I know that you still have feelings for him, but do you remember what you said to me when you were younger?"

Yoori stopped by the landing on the stairs and awaited his answer.

"I asked Soo Jin why she kept fighting, and she told me that she was fighting for the one who would be worth all this hell. She was fighting for the one who would make her an immortal God. She spent her life training and perfecting her skills to prepare for her war against another God who would immortalize her in this world." He walked over to her on the landing. His eyes were piercing, poignant. "You have found him, Soo Jin. You have finally found the one you spent a lifetime training for. *This* is the epic war that you've always dreamed of; *this* is the moment you've been waiting for all your life. Wage a war against him, kill him, and only then will you finally know true immortality."

Yoori lost all semblance of control when Jung Min said, "kill him."

Akin to a monster awakening inside her, she lifted her leg and kicked him hard on the stomach.

Boom!

Jung Min was sent flying down the stairs. His groans echoed throughout the estate as he fell over every step.

As he made his way down, Yoori started to calmly walk down the stairs.

"My name is Yoori," she declared as she followed his falling body down the stairs. Her voice was calm, yet her eyes blazed in anger. She had enough of Jung Min's poisonous instigations. "I am not An Soo Jin. I am not your advisee, nor am I your puppet."

Jung Min finally landed on the ground. Breathing painfully, he gazed up as she continued down the stairs. Her eyes were on him every step of the way.

"I may not be your beloved Queen, but I am still a force to be reckoned with. *I* singlehandedly killed those eleven bastards in the alley, not Tae Hyun or Soo Jin. *I* am the one who is standing before you alive and breathing, not Soo Jin."

She stopped at the last remaining step and stared down at him with unforgiving eyes.

"If you ever pull another stunt like this and have those bastards kidnap me again, I will show you how powerful I can be. Soo Jin is not here, but you do not want to test me. Her wrath will never match mine. If I am truly a fallen God, then I have nothing to lose. Soo Jin did not have the guts to bury you in that coffin, but I do. And trust me, if I bury you in that coffin, you will never come out again."

That said, she strode over his body and made her way out of the estate. Never once did she look back.

Long seconds later, when she was finally out of sight, Jung Min smiled like he just witnessed the return of a long lost Queen. Yoori's reaction was *exactly* what he wanted from her all along.

"Welcome back to the Underworld, child," he whispered with a cruel smirk. "I hope you enjoyed your fall. Now it's time for war."

"Are revered like Kings and Queens..."

03: A Royal Run-In

"Shin Jung Min literally kidnapped you?" Kang Min asked incredulously the following night.

Yoori nodded, uncomfortably playing with the edges of the book she was reading.

After she returned from Ju Won's house of horrors, Yoori was immediately greeted by horrified Serpents who were shocked that they had not only failed to protect her last night, but that she also had battle wounds to show for their failure. They had asked her what happened, but Yoori, who was still fazed by Jung Min's instigations, refused to talk to them.

It wasn't until Kang Min, who had been absent since her fight with Tae Hyun, appeared at the library did she relent. At the offset, she was intent on giving him the cold shoulder. Much like her bitterness toward Jae Won, Yoori was also pissed at Kang Min.

Despite her cold treatment, Kang Min persevered, telling her that he wasn't trying to trick her; he only had her best interest at heart. He explained to her that he had to choose between trusting Tae Hyun to watch over her or trusting the Underworld to "take care" of her. Given that the former was the lesser of the two evils, Tae Hyun was the best option. Although Yoori still harbored some resentment toward Kang Min, she also needed someone to talk to about this. Even if it was an abbreviated and very shortened version of the true story, she had to at least let something out.

"Yeah. He literally kidnapped me," she confirmed. "He still thinks I'm Soo Jin in disguise and he was trying to 'resurrect' her. He had these guys beat me in the limo, and he even locked me in a coffin at Ju Won's mansion. It was horrible and creepy. I'm glad it's over."

"That old bastard," Kang Min muttered to himself before saying, "How did you make it out? The guys said that they saw you walking back to your apartment. No one dropped you off. You just literally walked. How did you escape from Jung Min?"

"I gave Jung Min a piece of my mind," she said softly. *And I kicked the shit out of him*, she amended in her mind.

"And he let you go just like that?"

"Yeah," she confirmed with a shrug. "I mean, I told him again that I'm not Soo Jin. I told him that Tae Hyun and I are over and that I'm done with the Underworld. I guess after all of that, he got tired of me and decided to let me go."

Kang Min shook his head again. Although he was only eighteen and had a face that resembled an innocent angel, the current hardened features on his face told another story. He looked pissed beyond measure. "I can't believe he had five men beat you in a limo. That old bastard is sick."

"I handled myself," Yoori hinted to him vaguely.

Kang Min was not paying attention.

"I know who the five trainers are," he assured her, anger still radiating from him. "I'll take care of them for you."

"There are five of them and one of you," she reminded. "And they were the ones who trained Soo Jin."

"I was trained by An Soo Jin *and* Kwon Tae Hyun. I think I'm good—"

Kang Min stopped talking when he saw the light change in Yoori's once emotionless eyes. She had been spreading so many lies about being "fine" with her current predicament, but her anchor to this world would always be Tae Hyun. He was always the one who reminded her that she wasn't fine, that she was broken.

Kang Min shifted uncertainly. After a long minute of silence, he asked, "Do you want an update on him?"

"No," Yoori said at once. Even though secretly, she did. But she would not torture herself. He was out of her life for good. She did not need to be curious about his well-being.

"Okay," said Kang Min. He looked around uncomfortably again. "Well, I'm really glad you're okay. Jae Won and Hae Jin will be relieved too once I update them."

Yoori looked at Kang Min. She pushed her book closer to her chest. "They know I was kidnapped?"

"Yes." He glared at the Serpents at the other end of the library. "Our fellow Serpents over there told us about your . . . bruised state last night. They didn't know what happened, but they knew it was bad, which was why I decided to brave your wrath and make an appearance today."

"Brave my wrath?"

Kang Min swallowed, looking more like a fearful teenager rather than a badass in a black leather jacket and dark pants.

"I know you're mad," he reiterated. "And I wish you didn't find out the way that you did, but please know that Jae Won and I only wanted the best for you. What Tae Hyun did was wrong, but he really fell for you—"

"It's done," Yoori interrupted. "I have moved on. Your boss has moved on, and it's time for you and Jae Won to move on as well. I was upset with you, but I'm not pissed anymore. I want to forget everything and not dwell on all this useless stuff."

He nodded. "Then does this mean that you'll return Hae Jin's calls soon?" When Yoori went still, he plowed on. "She truly didn't know anything. She only found out recently when she noticed that you had been avoiding her. Out of the whole group, she was the only innocent party."

Yoori ran her fingers through her hair and tried to conceal her frustration. "I have to move on, Kang Min. That means I have to let go of things—and people—who will prevent me from doing so. I can't be friends with Hae Jin anymore. I have to move on."

"Excuse me, we're closing in ten minutes," the female library assistant reminded Yoori and Kang Min as she made her rounds through the library.

Yoori and Kang Min gave a polite smile. "Okay, thank you."

They stood up.

Yoori slung her black wristlet over her wrist and pulled up the hood of her forest green hoodie. She then gathered her books and stacked them on a box to be shelved.

Yoori smiled softly at Kang Min. "I'm going to call it a night." She paused before saying, "It was good seeing you."

"You too, Yoori," he said quietly.

"Have a good night."

Without waiting for him to reply, she rushed out of the library. She was afraid that if she spent a second longer with Kang Min, then she'd want nothing but her old life back.

Yoori bid goodbye to the librarian and the library assistant closing up at the front and sped outside to where the Mercedes sat. The winter cold spilled over her as she ran to her car. There was no snow or rain, but the night was still relatively cold enough that she was thankful she had her hoodie covering her head. As she was about to open the door, the call of her instincts had her frozen in her stance.

The sensation of being watched washed over her again.

Instinctively, her eyes veered up to the building down the street. She was greeted with the sight of a silhouette standing on the roof. Yoori squinted her eyes. She was about to move closer to determine if her eyes were playing tricks on her when she heard her Serpents bodyguards running out of the library. They rushed to their cars, ready to follow her to her next destination. She returned her eyes to the roof. The silhouette was no longer there.

For a paranoid moment, she wondered if it was one of Jung Min's men stalking her and waiting to kidnap her again. She pondered it further for a second, and then dismissed it as nothing. After the ass kicking she gave Jung Min, she doubted he would send anyone after her anytime soon.

There's no one on that roof, she attempted to convince herself. It was just her imagination.

Her eyes returned to the library. There, she caught sight of Kang Min standing beside one of the windows. He gave her a small nod as he watched her from above. She smiled tentatively at him, waved goodbye, and got into her car. She breathed in deeply, doing her best to recollect herself. Now that Kang Min was no longer in her company, she finally felt like she could return to her numb state. It was a state that she preferred and one she was grateful to get back into.

As she was not too keen on whipping up another bowl of instant noodle for dinner, and because she was craving some burgers and fries, Yoori decided to head over to one of her favorite restaurants. When she reached the restaurant, she was floored by the crowd. The street was packed with people; there did not appear to be a close parking spot in sight. After circling the block a few times, she was thankful that she managed to find street parking a little further out. She was also thankful that she had placed her order on the phone beforehand. This allowed her to quickly run into the restaurant, get her food in a white to-go box, and make her quick exit within a moment's notice.

"Excuse me," Yoori uttered.

She dodged around a group of fancy looking girls. They were dressed in sparkly dresses with their makeup done to perfection. After that, she moved around a group of well-dressed guys who were meandering around the sidewalk.

Yoori was in one of the upscale neighborhoods in Seoul. It was an area where the most high-class restaurants were available for people who had the money to afford the more extravagant dining in life. All around her were people who wore clothes and jewelry worth thousands of dollars. Truth be told, Yoori felt like an eyesore on a Christmas tree that had many beautiful ornaments. She was simply dressed in a forest green hoodie and blue jeans. The hems of her jeans were tucked into her black suede boots and that was the extent of her creative "fashion" sense. It was an understatement to say that she felt out of place. Yoori just wanted to get home as quickly as possible before someone started to think she was a mugger.

Yoori hopped off the curb. She was standing in the space between her Mercedes and a black Jaguar XF-R when she heard someone call her name.

"Yoori?"

She whirled around. She restrained a gasp when she saw who had called out to her. There, in front of one of the most lavish restaurants in town, stood Lee Ji Hoon waving at her. He was dressed in black slacks and a navy blue dress shirt. He couldn't have looked more like the ideal clientele for this restaurant. His black jacket hung off his hand as he advanced toward her. His black hair was slicked back tonight, giving him a polished look. In this space and time, he also earned giggles and whispers of admiration from a group of girls in the background. It was no surprise; Ji Hoon was as handsome as ever. Everyone on the street could see that.

"Ji Hoon," Yoori greeted in bewilderment, holding the to-go box close to her chest. She hadn't expected to run into him—or anyone she knew for that matter. She was happy to see a familiar face. In the same degree, she was cautious with this meeting. She hadn't forgotten how awkward they had left things. She hoped this meeting wouldn't be as dramatic.

"Did I scare you?" he delicately asked when he reached her. He stopped in front of her and remained on the curb. The elevated height of the curb made him appear taller than usual, especially with her peering up at him from the pavement of the street.

"No, no!" Yoori said quickly, mustering up a smile.

Albeit things were uncomfortable, she didn't want it to be obvious that she felt awkward. Regardless of all that had transpired, she still had a soft spot for Ji Hoon. The only deterrent to seeing him was that she was instantaneously reminded of Tae Hyun. She was also reminded of the last, painful words she said to Tae Hyun before she ran out on him. Her heart started to clench, and Yoori quickly shoved those thoughts out of her mind. She continued to focus on Ji Hoon, hell-bent on not thinking about Tae Hyun. He was out of her life, and she was going to keep it that way.

"I just didn't expect to run into anyone," she finished quietly. Her eyes strayed to the lavish restaurant behind him. "You just had dinner?"

"Yeah. The company was dismal, but the food was good," he replied with a gentle smile that indicated to Yoori he was walking on eggshells around her. It was evident that he hadn't forgotten how they had left things off either. Yoori was actually surprised that he even cared enough to talk to her. She thought they were done when she chose Tae Hyun over him that night.

His eyes wandered over the to-go box in her grasp. "What are you having for dinner?"

"Just a burger and fries," Yoori said with a shrug. She swallowed past her apprehension and wondered if she should excuse herself or stay and chitchat with him. Persuaded by the genuine happiness that arose in his eyes when she spoke to him, Yoori decided to further the conversation with what she thought would be a nice icebreaker. "So, you're always dressed up in business clothes whenever I see you. Is that your standard uniform?"

Ji Hoon's smile grew wider. He was relieved that she was being conversational. "I have meetings left and right. Someone of my position has to look like he can take on important jobs. Dressing for the part is an everyday occurrence." He shrugged carelessly. "I've been wearing business clothes for as long as I can remember; it's like a second skin to me."

Yoori nodded, not knowing what else to say after that. After a pause, she asked, "How have you been?"

"Pretty shitty since the last time I saw you."

Here comes the awkwardness, Yoori thought morosely.

She should have expected that men like Ji Hoon and Tae Hyun would always get right to the point. Both were similar in that respect.

"It's never too heartwarming when the girl you have your eyes on chooses another guy."

Yoori's heart ached after hearing the comment. It ached for Ji Hoon, but it ached for Tae Hyun even more. She hated that she couldn't stop thinking about him and that she felt guilty for lying to him (even though he was the one who lied to her and hurt her first).

"You just had a meeting then?" Yoori asked, changing the subject to save herself from being thrown into another state of misery.

His features hardened at her obvious ploy to change the topic. Regardless of the reaction, he answered her question nonetheless. "I just had dinner with the Advisors." There was a short pause before he carelessly added, "And Tae Hyun."

Yoori's eyes rounded. "Tae . . . Tae Hyun?"

She was flabbergasted. It didn't take her long to deduce how awful it would be for Tae Hyun to see her with Ji Hoon, especially after the lie she had told him. She wanted to hurt Tae Hyun so he would stay away from her—she didn't want to devastate him by having him see her with Ji Hoon.

But it was too late.

Before she could attempt to excuse herself, she heard someone bid goodbye to a patron. She knew instantly it was the person she wanted to avoid seeing and the one person, as much as she hated to admit it, she missed the most.

"Have a good night, sir."

Yoori saw him when she averted her gaze to the doors leading out of the restaurant. Dressed in light gray pants, a white buttoned up shirt, and a loosened gray tie around his neck, Kwon Tae Hyun emanated nothing but male wonder as he gave a nod of goodbye to the hostess who was clearly smitten with him.

There were men who had faces of innocent angels and then there were men who had the faces of fallen archangels. Tae Hyun was one of those men in life that looked too good to be true. He was beautiful in the most sinful of ways and he made no apologies for it. From his beautiful short black hair to his smooth skin, enticing lips, and perfectly crafted face, he looked like he was born to be adored and worshipped. He was a walking poster of perfection and there were few who would ever combat that statement.

Tae Hyun moved away from the restaurant and turned in the direction she and Ji Hoon were in.

Yoori could hear soft murmuring from the group of girls in the background. Adoration embellished their voices as they whispered about how good-looking and sexy he was. A pang of jealousy spiked within her. When they did that with Ji Hoon, she couldn't care less; when they did that to Tae Hyun, she felt the unbearable need to smack them upside the head. Tae Hyun had always driven her crazy. It irritated her that he drove other girls crazy too, and it irritated her even more that he had his choice of girls to pursue. It only reminded her that she was nothing special to him, and that he would always be someone special to her.

And then, just like that, the three-week time period of not seeing each other diminished when her eyes locked with his. The agony, the betrayal, the sadness, the yearning, the heartache . . . all the emotions that had been numbed since she last saw him surged through her. She swallowed past her pain and tried to keep a cool exterior. The eye contact was only broken when Tae Hyun flickered his gaze from her to Ji Hoon.

Yoori knew it was horrible that she was standing there with Ji Hoon.

She couldn't read Tae Hyun's eyes, but when he quickened his pace toward them, her muscles tensed up. Would he pull her away from Ji Hoon and take her with him? If he did that, what would she do? Yoori wanted to believe that she was strong enough to refuse him. Yet, as she felt her body yearn for him, Yoori was no longer sure how strong she was.

He came closer . . . and closer . . . and closer . . .

His cologne inundated her senses after he walked off the curb. When he was merely a breath away from her, Yoori was certain he would pull her with him. She was thrown off when he simply moved into the tight space between the Mercedes and the Jaguar car ahead of it. He dodged around her as if she were invisible and continued on. Yoori took in a sharp breath when she concluded that he wasn't even walking toward her. His only goal was to get to his car—his brand new Jaguar XF-R.

Yoori was stupefied that he didn't even acknowledge her existence. She watched bewilderingly, unknowingly stepping back onto the sidewalk with Ji Hoon. He had pulled her closer to him just as Tae Hyun pulled his car door open. Tae Hyun still wasn't looking at her. The King of Serpents was primed to get into his car when he noticed the group of girls who were more than eating him up with their eyes.

"Have a good night," he whispered cordially to them, acknowledging their existence and not hers.

A wave of sighs fell from the girls' lips after he got into his car. The engine started and Yoori watched him expectantly, a part of her hoping against hope that he would take one glance at her before he drove off.

Just one look, she pleaded the fates in her mind. *Just look at me once . . .*

Yoori was left stunned when the car took off, merged into traffic, and disappeared into the night.

"Stay out of my life."

That was the last thing she said to him.

As relieved as she was that he was obliging with her wishes, it was also painful to see how easily he could move on. He really didn't give a damn after all. They were done. There was no way around it now. They were officially done.

"He told the Advisors that he was completely done with you—that he would no longer be distracted by you."

She twirled around to face Ji Hoon when his warm breath tickled her ear.

His voice was gentle, but Yoori knew it pissed him off that she was clearly hung up on Tae Hyun. Ji Hoon's words did not surprise her. It made sense that Tae Hyun was quick to announce to the world that he was done with her in order to get his position of power back.

"Did he now?" Yoori asked serenely, the cool exterior returning to her features.

She gazed up at Ji Hoon guardedly. Yoori had always liked Ji Hoon because he was so sweet to her. Nonetheless, she didn't appreciate his propensity to be an instigator when it came to trying to pull her away from Tae Hyun. His end goal was for her to be with him. The lengths he was willing to go to for that to happen perturbed her greatly.

"It pleased the Advisors to hear this," he continued relentlessly. His gaze noted that there was annoyance, but also curiosity, in her eyes. He pulled her to a corner where they could speak privately. "They wanted my confirmation that I was done with you as well."

"And you gave them your confirmation?" Yoori asked coolly, taking a few steps away from him once they reached the corner. She didn't know why she asked this when she already knew his answer. It was evident that he was still interested in making her his.

"I did," he confirmed, bringing a hand up. Almost hesitantly, he ran his hand down her cheek, his fingers reveling in the feel of her skin against his. "But it's clear that I've changed my mind since seeing you again."

No longer able to combat the temptation, Ji Hoon lowered himself, his lips seeking hers. He was quick, but he wasn't quick enough.

"Ji Hoon, we won't work out," Yoori said sternly, tilting her head back just as their lips were about to touch. "Not now. Not ever."

A frown veiled his face. "He doesn't even acknowledge that you're alive and you're still hung up on him?"

There was no hiding the venom and jealousy in his voice. His eyes rippled with rage. Not for her, but for Tae Hyun.

"This isn't about Tae Hyun," Yoori retorted, even though deep down, she knew it was. "We would never work out, Ji Hoon. I told you that night that I cared about you a lot, but that I didn't have feelings for you like that. I didn't then and I doubt I ever will."

Yoori exhaled painstakingly, pressing the to-go box closer to her chest. Soo Jin may have been his girlfriend, but she wasn't. Yoori would be damned if she was with anyone who saw her as another girl—especially someone she didn't want to be. She shook her head, pushing past all the thoughts of An Soo Jin and all that had fucked up in her life since she found out she was the Underworld's infamous Queen. She had to leave and she had to leave now.

"This would never work between us, Ji Hoon. I mean, I can't even entertain the idea of us being friends because I know that you only see me as An Soo Jin. I'm obviously a different girl. I'm *not* her. I never have been and I never will be. Having said this, I think we should just part ways and stay out of each other's lives from now on. It's better for us this way."

Yoori never wanted to be this blunt (or inconsiderate) to Ji Hoon. However, she wanted to get the point across that she wasn't interested in him romantically. She didn't want to lead him on.

Hurt engulfed his eyes. He could barely contain his scoff when he turned away from her for a brief moment. It was obvious that something snapped within him when she mentioned Soo Jin. It was clearer to her that he had enough of her bullshit when she said that they should part ways.

"I don't see you as An Soo Jin," Ji Hoon replied swiftly, his eyes holding hers again. "I *know* you're An Soo Jin."

Her stomach twisted in knots, but she kept her cool. Surely he was just speaking out of anger. He had no idea what he was talking about.

"I beg your pardon?"

"Don't deny it," he snapped at once, his eyes sterner than she had ever seen them. He was at his wit's end. He had no more patience to beat around the bush with her.

"I don't know what you're talking abo—"

"Soo Jin," he stated inflexibly, causing her to cease with her words. He was sick of this charade. "*I* was the one who gave you the formula. I was the one who warned you of all the risks—that if taken under different dosages, then death would not be ensured. I told you that it was likely that other effects, including amnesia, would take place instead." He forged on, his eyes never leaving hers. "I may have allowed you to 'lie' to me in the past about your identity, but don't insult me by continuing with all of this. You may not remember who you are, but I can see in your eyes that you know you're her."

Stunned by this admission, Yoori could only gape at Ji Hoon. She hadn't anticipated any of this to happen.

"You . . . You knew from the beginning when you first saw me?" Yoori stuttered unthinkingly. She recalled all those times when he lied to her, when he told her she didn't resemble Soo Jin. "Why did you pretend to not know?"

"I didn't want to be aggressive and trigger anything," he whispered, his eyes filled with poignancy. He reached out and pulled a dazed Yoori closer to him. "I didn't want to spark any memory from within you."

Her mind was still fogged with mystification. "Why didn't you want me to remember?"

If Ji Hoon had been so pained from seeing her with Tae Hyun, why didn't he try to reawaken her memories so his Soo Jin could return to him?

"My girlfriend came to me three years ago telling me that she wanted to kill herself," he answered tightly. "If you were me, what would you do if you saw her three years later, a completely different, but healthier person?" He sighed, the pain imminent in his voice. "I knew who you were, but I was careful not to trigger anything because I *didn't* want you to remember. I want you as you are now, happier and healthier than you were when you begged me to help you commit suicide."

Yoori was speechless with this disclosure.

Ji Hoon framed his hands over her cheeks. "It has only been you, Soo Jin. For five years, it has only been you. And as far as my heart is concerned, it will only be you. I've missed you . . . so much. I was ready to tell you that I knew you had amnesia when we were on the roof because I couldn't stand that you were so in love with Tae Hyun. I could no longer stand the thought of him touching you when it should be me. I didn't want you to remember anything, but I also wanted you back with me."

His voice was so aggrieved that it agonized Yoori to listen to him.

Desperation hit her like a ton of bricks. "No, no," Yoori begged, her voice utterly broken. "Please stop. I can't do this. I don't want to remember."

She was a coward again.

Yoori was afraid that if she continued to listen, then something would trigger inside her and she would be consumed by Soo Jin. And God help her, she didn't want to risk that chance.

"Please stop this, Ji Hoon. I don't want to be her."

"It was never supposed to be like this," he continued, his hands still framing her cheeks. She could hear the pain magnify in his voice. "Even if you don't have your memories, I had hoped that your feelings for me would awaken regardless. I had hoped that you would choose me over Tae Hyun . . . yet, you never did."

Fury filled his eyes.

The remembrance of her with Tae Hyun broke any shred of control he had left.

"What the fuck is so special about Kwon Tae Hyun, Soo Jin?" he finally snapped. The anguish in his voice dissipated. In its place came an inferno of rage. "What the fuck does he have that I don't have? You hate him and his family for fuck's sake! How can you even stand to be in the same room as him, let alone sleep in his bed?"

"I'm not Soo Jin!" Yoori cried, having enough of this. She violently pulled away from him, nearly bumping into several drunken girls in the process. Yoori went on, knowing that the girls were too inebriated to eavesdrop on them. "You know this! I don't have her memories. I can't help that I fell for him and I didn't fall for you."

"It was never supposed to be like this!" he shouted back. Rage continued to spew out of him. "I'm not supposed to be the other guy in this story." He furiously pointed at himself. "*I* was with you first. *I* met you first. *I* loved you first. *I* gave up everything for you, and yet now you're here . . . moping around for Kwon Tae Hyun instead?"

"I can't control my feelings, Ji Hoon," Yoori told him, breathing past the emotions emitting from her. "If I could, then I would be with you right now because God knows you're healthier for me than Tae Hyun could ever be. If it were that easy, then I would've given my heart to you already because I feel terrible that you're here right now . . . like this because of me. But I can't give you something I don't have. No matter how much I hate him . . . he still has my heart." Her chin wobbled. "And I don't know when I'll get it back, if I'll ever get that part of me back." She gazed at him remorsefully. "But I told you this before . . . I don't have those feelings for you, and I don't want to lead you on. I won't be with you out of pity. I have more respect for you than that. You deserve someone who will appreciate all the things you could give her. I'm not that girl. I doubt I'll ever be."

"Don't do this," Ji Hoon pleaded, not even listening to her. "I can't be without you."

"Soo Jin died, Ji Hoon! She died the moment you gave her that formula and agreed to 'support' her while she ended her life! So, please, just stop this because I don't want to be her!" Yoori shook her head, her heart pounding like thunderous rain. She couldn't do this anymore. "I'm sorry, but I can't be here anymore."

She was ready to run to her car before she felt him encircle his hand around her wrist.

"Never go back to Tae Hyun, Yoori."

"Stop it!" Yoori cried, suddenly fearing Ji Hoon. The way he was behaving disconcerted her.

"I heard about the eleven gang members you killed," he whispered, earning silence from her. He saw her eyes widen and continued to speak. "We both know that only Soo Jin has enough power to do all of that. We both know that, but I don't think you know how much Soo Jin loved her father, how his death made her more vicious. You have no idea what type of person she was. She was loyal to a fault, but she was loyal regardless." His eyes scrutinized hers. "Do you really think she would let you choose your 'love' for Tae Hyun over her loyalty for her father when you fully regain your memory?"

Something stirred inside her when he mentioned her father.

Despite this, Yoori kept her composure.

"Then I guess it's a good thing that Tae Hyun and I are over, right?" she stated with cool conviction. Resolution saturated her eyes. "I'm done with him, I'm done with Soo Jin, I'm done with you, and I'm done with the Underworld."

He smiled at her in pity. "You can be done with Tae Hyun, you can be done with me, but can you really be done with Soo Jin?"

Yoori didn't answer because she knew the truth. Instead, she chose this moment to leave because she knew another emotional breakdown was coming. She was feeling anguish from Tae Hyun, Ji Hoon, and now from Soo Jin. She was afraid of what would happen to her mental state if she didn't leave soon.

"I . . . I have to go."

Yoori knew the truth. She knew as she drove away that she could try all she wanted, but there would be no escaping this world. Whether she wanted it or not, in the end, she would always end up back in the Underworld. No matter how hard she tried to fight against it, the truth was that she had too many ties in this society. If Tae Hyun hadn't brought her into this world, then someone else would've. Someone else would've found her because she was living in the very city where this world reigned; someone else would've found her because this was An Soo Jin's world. The only one meant to survive in this society was An Soo Jin—not the poor, weak Yoori who was so broken that she wondered how much longer she could hold on to her own life.

I was never meant to exist, Yoori brooded as she drove in agonized silence. She was never meant to exist and from the look of things, Yoori had the innate feeling she wouldn't exist for much longer. This was An Soo Jin's world—An Soo Jin's life—and when the time arose and Soo Jin came back to reclaim the life that was rightfully hers, Choi Yoori would be nothing but a mere memory.

This thought pained Yoori because despite all the torment she felt (and despite the difficulty of being associated with this vindictive world), she still wanted to live. She wanted to live because she didn't want to be taken away from the life she had created for herself. She didn't want to forget about the people she loved. Most importantly, she didn't want the monster inside her to come out.

Her conversation with Jung Min flashed in her mind, and Yoori knew that she could no longer avoid the inevitable truth. She hated Tae Hyun, but she would never allow anyone to hurt him. And right now, the biggest threat wasn't Ji Hoon, the Advisors, or the Underworld—the biggest threat was her Underworld counterpart. The Queen of the Underworld may do everything in her power to kill Tae Hyun, but Yoori would do everything in her power to protect him.

Yoori inhaled sharply, finally accepting the reality of her life.

Jung Min was right.

He had been right all along.

A war was coming, but this particular war was not between herself and Tae Hyun; it was between herself and An Soo Jin.

And for the sake of everything she loved in this world, Yoori prayed she'd win this war. She prayed she'd be able to bury Soo Jin, and not allow Soo Jin to bury her.

"And the weak..."

04: Greater Pain

It took Yoori the entire day at the library to recover from the night prior.
Tae Hyun, Chae Young, Ji Hoon, and Soo Jin continued to haunt her. The only
solace she found was in the stories she escaped into. Reading was like a drug.
The instant she took her dosage, she would forget about her pain, forget about
the damning world she lived in, and forget about the dramas of her life. Yoori
knew she couldn't dwell in the world of books forever, but she wanted to stay
in it for a bit longer. Just a bit longer until she found a job, recovered from
everything that happened to her, got on with her life, and continued to keep An
Soo Jin at bay. One could only hope, and all Yoori had was hope.

"Can I join you?" asked a tentative voice.

Yoori lifted her eyes from her book.

She froze when she noted that the person standing before her was Kang
Min's girlfriend, and Kwon Tae Hyun's baby sister, Kwon Hae Jin.

Hae Jin's black hair was tied up in a stylish ponytail that accentuated her
perfect curls. She wore a white turtleneck, black jeans that hugged her tall
body flawlessly, and heels. A black trench coat hung off her arm with
remnants of fresh snow stuck to it. There were two rosy circles on her cheeks,
bringing life to her normally pale face.

Yoori straightened uneasily. She hadn't expected to see anyone at the
library, much less Hae Jin. She glanced to the corner where her unofficial
Serpents bodyguards typically sat. They were nowhere to be seen. Yoori had
the innate feeling that Hae Jin had ordered them to go downstairs so she could
have some alone time with her.

"I know you're upset with Kang Min and Jae Won because they knew
what my brother was doing the entire time," Hae Jin began apprehensively.
She took in a tense breath. "If you think I knew something about it, then I want
you to know that I didn't. I only found out everything after I heard you left. I

really thought you were his girlfriend. I had no idea you were his 'assistant' and that it was his plan to meet you." She smiled uncertainly at Yoori, nervously tapping her fingernails on the oak table where Yoori sat. "With all that said, I hope you're not upset with me as well."

"No, no. Of course I'm not," Yoori assured meekly, edging the stack of books closer to her. It was her silent confirmation that Hae Jin could take a seat.

She had time to mull over things further, and Yoori came to the conclusion that she would've been pulled into the Underworld some other way even if Tae Hyun hadn't been the one to lure her in. Ultimately, she could forgive him for that. However, she couldn't forgive the lies that continued to fester as she grew close to him. She doubted the betrayal of trust was something she could forget.

As though anticipating a more hostile reaction from Yoori, Hae Jin nodded gratefully. "Good. I'm happy to hear that."

Yoori smiled kindly at Hae Jin. It was her unspoken way of assuring Hae Jin that she did not harbor any ill feelings toward her. Hae Jin had always been in the dark about the realities of Yoori's relationship with her brother. Out of everyone in their group, Hae Jin and Chae Young were the only ones who were still in Yoori's good graces.

"Please," Yoori started gently. "Please sit, Hae Jin."

Hae Jin smiled again and nodded.

"I just came from seeing Chae Young," she shared, taking a seat across from Yoori.

Yoori's heart clenched when she was reminded of Chae Young. She had been such a horrible friend. It had been days since she saw her best friend, and she still found no strength to overcome the guilt that continued to plague her. Yoori wondered if such guilt would ever diminish.

Only when I kill Jin Ae, Yoori concluded crossly.

"How is she?" Yoori asked, truly wanting to know.

Moroseness inhabited Hae Jin's brown eyes. "She hasn't been eating much. Jae Won says she's dazed most of the time and has trouble sleeping. She wasn't really receptive to seeing guests when Kang Min and I went to visit, but I managed to slip through with a bowl of soup for her."

Yoori's voice was hopeful when she said, "Did she eat?"

Hae Jin nodded, earning a sigh of relief from Yoori.

"How'd you manage that?" asked Yoori.

They were on the upper level of the library, right in the corner where the encyclopedias sat. Yoori was thankful that it was late at night and that there were no patrons around who could be bothered by their conversation. They could talk as much as they wanted.

"I told her that I understood what she's going through," said Hae Jin. Although her voice remained composed, pain still throbbed in it. "Even though our situations are different, I told her that I still understood."

Yoori nodded forlornly, recalling that Hae Jin was raped by her eldest brother, Kwon Ho Young, before Tae Hyun killed him. Anguish clawed at her. In that moment, Yoori saw how small her problems were compared to Chae Young and Hae Jin's. It was one thing to combat life problems, but it was something else entirely when rape was involved.

"Thank you," Yoori told her gratefully. She was tempted to jump over the table and hug Hae Jin for helping to take care of her friend. She also wanted to embrace Hae Jin as a small form of condolence for everything that she had been through. "I should be the one helping to take care of her—"

"You're going through a lot, Yoori," Hae Jin interjected in understanding. "You can't help someone else unless you help yourself first. It's better that you're here, getting everything in order instead of seeing Chae Young and risking breaking down in front of her. That's the last thing Chae Young needs."

Though Yoori nodded, she didn't feel any less guilty (or shitty).

"We've missed you," Hae Jin added once she saw the ache manifest on Yoori's face. "My brother being at the top of the list."

Yoori froze at the mention of Tae Hyun. She suspected that it would only be a matter of time before they spoke about him. However, that didn't mean she was exempt from the emotions that boiled up whenever he was brought up. The walls that she once had lowered for Hae Jin quickly reassembled. She couldn't allow herself to become vulnerable to the hurt by all of this again.

"Kwon Tae Hyun doesn't miss me," Yoori stated steadily, recalling the previous night in which he didn't even acknowledge her existence. There was conviction in her voice. Yoori may have forgiven him for bringing her into the Underworld—because it was obvious that it would've happened one way or another—but she couldn't forgive him for the rest. She couldn't forgive him for the lies and the humiliation she felt. Perhaps one day, she would truly be over him. For now, she would simply pretend that she was. "Someone as corrupted as him led a great life before he met me. He'll be just as fine without me. After all, he has his precious Underworld and all the girls in the world to take care of him."

Yoori hoped the venom in her words would convince Hae Jin that she was over someone like Tae Hyun.

Hae Jin did not heed the malice in Yoori's voice. Instead, she changed the subject to ease away all the poisonous thoughts Yoori associated with Tae Hyun.

"Did you know that we were really close as a family?" Hae Jin asked instead.

Yoori collapsed into silence at Hae Jin's unexpected question. She knew what was to come. She dreaded hearing it, for it would be information that would probably ruin any hope of her ever getting over Tae Hyun. But because she was curious, she kept quiet. She allowed Hae Jin to go on because as much as her rationale told her that Tae Hyun was a horrible person, she knew that there was more to him than what meets the eye. There was more to Tae Hyun and his Underworld persona, and she wanted to hear it from the only person who knew anything about his past—his baby sister.

Hae Jin continued to speak when it was clear that she had claimed Yoori's attention. "My parents, my brothers, and I were all once very close. Our father was busy, but he made sure the family spent time together. He made sure we went to the lake house every other weekend, he made sure all of our birthdays were celebrated, and he made sure we bonded as a family and loved each other like family members should."

The warm glint in her eyes began to diminish.

"Our lives were great . . . like a fairytale until one event changed everything. When Ji Hoon killed our father, our family began to tear apart. Our father was our glue. He was the one who protected us, guided us, and showered us with nothing but love and affection. When he died, our world fell apart. My mother was the first to go. She started to alienate herself while she mourned the loss of our father. She ignored us and didn't speak to us because she was so depressed. The three of us tried to speak to her—to get through to her—but she was already pushed over the edge. A couple of weeks after his death, she committed suicide and died with him."

Yoori felt the weight of the world push against her chest. She recalled how much Tae Hyun hated it when she ignored him and gave him the silent treatment. She had no idea it was something his mother did to the whole family before she committed suicide.

"It didn't take long for the rest of us to fall apart," Hae Jin continued. "My eldest brother, who was already drinking and taking drugs after my father's death, started to abuse more drugs. Oppa, who took it the hardest because she died a few days before his birthday, escaped by schooling abroad."

Yoori took in a sharp breath. She understood now why Tae Hyun was not eager to celebrate his birthday. Who would want to celebrate their birthday when their mother committed suicide just days before?

"And me," said Hae Jin. "I not only lost my parents, but both of my older brothers too." Her voice started to become shaky. It was expressive in her face that this was a difficult memory for her to revisit. But to give her brother justice, she fought through it. "There was a time where I hated him too, you know? After my father's death, my eldest brother started acting strange toward me. It got so bad that I was afraid to even be alone with him. I told oppa this, and you know what he told me? He said he was too busy—he didn't have time for me and my imagination." She shook her head, exhaling painfully. "He left for college, and I was left alone with Ho Young. Then . . . Ho Young started doing things to me that I knew were wrong. He was touching me, forcing me to do things with him, and just . . ." She took a moment to gather her breath. "And just made my life a living hell. At that instance, I hated Kwon Tae Hyun."

She glanced at Yoori.

"We don't talk about our eldest brother much, but he still haunts us every single day." Her face grew paler. "I'll never forget that night, when my eldest brother came into my room, drunk off his mind, and told me that I wasn't his sister anymore, that he needed me as something else." As though to prevent tears from streaming down her face, she bit her quivering lips. "That night was hard, but it was harder when oppa came home unannounced and found Ho Young on top of me . . . touching me." Hae Jin closed her eyes and tried to steady her breathing.

"The three of us were close growing up, but oppa and our eldest brother were extremely close. Although the Underworld tried to pit them against one another, they never fell for the bait because they loved each other the way brothers should. Regardless, the poison of this world spreads far and wide. My brothers may not have battled each other for power, but they fought nonetheless because this world corrupted my eldest brother. It tainted all of us."

She looked at Yoori. Her eyes teemed with conviction. "What Kwon Ho Young did to me was unforgivable. I'll hate him for the rest of my life for it. But that hatred doesn't quell the guilt of knowing that it resulted in him getting killed by oppa. The hate didn't prevent our souls from deteriorating as we watched our eldest brother take his last breath."

Hae Jin's eyes rippled with tears that she refused to let out.

"My soul was broken after that. It was broken until Kang Min came into my life, until he lifted the demons away and showed me how I could trust another man aside from oppa. I was saved when I was fifteen, when I had Kang Min to lean on. But my brother suffered the most because he never once let out what really happened that night. He didn't want me to suffer any further. He took all the blame and allowed people to think he was a monster, that he would murder his own brother for a throne. The worst part was when he started to believe he was ruthless, heartless, and truly fit for this world. It became his survival technique. His weapon in this society was to be ruthless and heartless because it was the only way to survive as a King in this world. It was the only way he could survive the guilt of murdering his own brother." Hae Jin expelled a weary breath. "If you ask him if he regretted killing our brother, then he'll tell you that he'd kill him again with no hesitation whatsoever. He'll tell you that he has no regrets, that he hated our brother. But what he'll never tell you is how much it hurts him, how it haunts him every day, and how it tears at his very soul. He'll never tell you that he could have all the best cars in the world, but he chose to keep his Mercedes because it was the last gift our eldest brother gave to him. It was a gift that reminded him of the happier, more carefree times in his life. It was a gift that reminded him of how human he used to be before the shadows of this world enveloped him."

Yoori's breathing stilled at this revelation.

His car—the car he loved so much . . .

If it meant so much to him, why would he give it to her?

It didn't make sense.

Yoori struggled through the undercurrent of emotions swaying within her. It was always much more difficult to hate someone when you learned about their broken past. Unfortunately for her, Kwon Tae Hyun was the only human alive who could evoke emotions that she tried so hard to keep controlled.

Hae Jin smiled. She reached over and placed a hand over Yoori's. "If you're wondering why I liked you so much when I first met you, it was because I started to see my brother again. I started to see him come to life once more. I spoke to him on the phone and heard a bit more life to his voice, like when we grew up together . . . before the incident took place. I knew something had changed. *That* was why I went over to his place to see what was up." Hae Jin's smile grew wider at the recollection. "I couldn't stop smiling when I met you. Even then, I knew you were going to save him from the poison of this world. Just like Kang Min did for me, I knew you were going to be the one who changed everything for my brother."

She gazed at Yoori, her eyes rippling with a mixture of hope and apprehension. "How he used you in the beginning was inexcusable, and it's entirely up to you in terms of where you want to go from here. But he misses you, even if he doesn't show it. He doesn't show that he misses our eldest brother, and he won't show that he misses you, but I know that he's hurting because he probably misses you more than he's ever missed anyone. He cares about you a lot—you're not worthless to him. I just came here for him because I wanted you to know that. His feelings for you are genuine. There are few people he lets into his heart, but when you're there, you're there for life. "

Fragmented with nothing but perplexity, Yoori found herself standing abruptly. This was all too much for her; she had to be alone to absorb all of this.

"I really should get going," Yoori announced. She grabbed her black trench coat from the chair where she sat. She hastily pulled it over her white blouse so that the only clothing visible was her coat and remnants of her khaki pants that were tucked into dark, knee-high boots. Tying the belt of her satin coat into a knot and stacking her books together, she distractedly said, "It was good to see you tonight, Hae Jin. Regardless of what happens between your brother and I . . . I hope we'll keep in touch."

"I'd like that," Hae Jin replied, running over to hug Yoori. "Just think about it, okay?" she said before gently pulling away and leaving Yoori's side. Though it appeared like she wanted to hang out with Yoori for a bit longer, Hae Jin knew it was best to leave Yoori alone with her thoughts.

Yoori wasted no time and fled out of the library. She ran into the car that Kwon Ho Young gifted his younger brother, the car Tae Hyun treasured so much. Snow sprinkled all around her as she settled inside the car. A tsunami of emotions thrashed in her already disjointed mind. Yoori took a moment to press her forehead against the steering wheel. The residual snow fell off her hair and melted on the leather seat while she breathed in silence.

The beating of her heart slowed to its normal pace. The world tilted back into place. The silence acted as her companion, and her once inundated mind was cleared of fogginess.

Breathe in . . .

Breathe out . . .

Breathe in . . .

Calmed by the world around her, Yoori's mind ventured on to a recollection that marked itself in her heart. Her mind replayed a memory that pained her soul to relive, but lifted her heart to reminisce . . .

"I know the right thing to do would be to let you go right now because there's no future for us. I wish I could be less selfish and just let you go because you deserve better than me. You deserve better than this life. I wish the little soul I have within me would stop yearning for you so I could just let you walk out of my life . . . so I could just go back to being happy with the life I led. That way, things would be easier and I wouldn't have to stand here . . . never in my life feeling weaker or feeling guiltier for all the things that I've done . . ."

He continued to caress her hair, his eyes holding hers with nothing but desperation.

"I've made mistakes in the past, Yoori," he shared, going back to the first concern she brought up. It seemed that this issue had been plaguing him for quite some time. "Mistakes that I was raised to believe were necessary to get me the ultimate power and keep me alive in this world. Mistakes that are

irreparable . . . mistakes that will probably disgust you to a degree where you won't be able to look at me again . . ."

"Tae Hyun," Yoori started, her voice trembling. She struggled to understand why he was so worried. "What have you done?"

"I would understand if you couldn't look at me afterwards . . . if you hated me after you found out everything."

Yoori had never seen such fear embalm his eyes. It was like he was afraid of losing her.

"Just tell me," Yoori whispered, wanting to cry for him more than for herself.

"But please know that I've fallen for you," he pleaded, still so apprehensive with telling her everything. It broke Yoori's heart to see him so afraid. "I wish I didn't care for you this much . . . that I need you this much, but you have everything of mine. My heart and what's left of my soul. Everything is yours, all yours, and only yours."

Before allowing the pain of that night to trickle back inside her, Yoori started the car. The engine roared to life. She had to go home. She couldn't allow herself to think about Tae Hyun any longer. As soon as her walls went down, they all came flying back up again.

It didn't matter how much her heart softened after seeing Tae Hyun's sister. It didn't matter how much her heart lifted after recalling that life-changing night. None of that mattered to her but getting home safely, showering, and forgetting about Tae Hyun. She didn't want to think about him anymore; she didn't want her trembling heart to miss him anymore.

She was done.

Dear God, she just wanted to be done with him.

■ ■ ■

Kwon Tae Hyun was silent, morose while he sat in his Jaguar, his eyes set on the view ahead. The world around him was peaceful. There was no one else on the street. The only thing that kept him company was the beautiful snow dancing serenely around him. Albeit the city nightlife was breathtaking, it offered no consolation to the storms reveling in his coffee brown eyes. He had just finished a "business negotiation" with one of the most powerful drug dealers in the country, and he was exhausted—not from the meeting, but from something else that had been weighing on his mind.

Wearing a black coat over his white dress shirt and black pants, a weary Tae Hyun closed his eyes and took in a deep breath. He reclined his head against his seat. His windows were open, allowing the fresh winter snow to trickle in. The cascading snowflakes fluttered to one side of his face, kissing the skin of his cheek before crumbling into the interior of his car.

"Quite a fine speech you made at dinner the other night."

Tae Hyun opened his eyes.

Surprise entered his gaze once his eyes landed on his Underworld Advisor, Shin Dong Min.

Dong Min, who was almost the exact replica of his older brother, Jung Min — give or take three to four years younger with no mustache — stood beside the passenger side of the car. He wore a long brown jacket and a black hat. Snow dusted him as he opened the passenger door and helped himself into Tae Hyun's car.

Tae Hyun looked in the rearview mirror. Down the quiet street, he could see a black town car waiting in the distance. It was evident that it was Dong Min's car.

He settled his eyes on his Advisor. Dong Min had just taken off his hat, revealing his dark black hair.

"What are you doing here, uncle?" asked Tae Hyun.

"Considering how far you've strayed, I should make it my mission to arrange surprise visits every day."

"Then that wouldn't be a surprise anymore," Tae Hyun said lightheartedly, though there was no humor in his voice.

Dong Min turned to Tae Hyun with severity. He came with a purpose. He did not have time for games. "You must stop this."

Tae Hyun permitted himself a bitter smile. "I told you what you and Ju Won wanted to hear last night. What more do you want from me?"

"You may have fooled my brother and Ju Won, but you do not fool me. I know when you're lying and when you're not yourself. You haven't been yourself for a very long time." Dong Min exhaled and stared ahead. There was frustration in his eyes when he continued to speak. "How did you stray so far from the path you were on? You were supposed to use her to heighten your power in this world. You were not supposed to fall for her and fall from your throne in the process."

"I am done with her."

"*She* is done with you," Dong Min corrected, and Tae Hyun fell silent. Dong Min forged on, disappointment becoming more noticeable in his voice. "If she so much as calls for you, then you will run to her." He shook his head reprovingly. "If I didn't promise your father that I'd watch over you, then I would rip your head off to end your misery. You are not a God right now; you are barely a King. You are pathetic."

Tae Hyun's silence persevered. He took several seconds to absorb his Advisor's words. When a puff of cold wind carried more snowflakes into the car, he quietly said, "Have you ever fallen, uncle?"

Silence claimed Dong Min's mouth. He continued to stare ahead, his eyes moving over the snowflakes that were still dancing around the car. A few seconds passed before he finally said, "Yes."

Tae Hyun kept his eyes on the road ahead as well. He was not surprised by his Advisor's admission; he had already expected this answer.

"How?" he continued to ask.

"A woman," Dong Min said simply.

"Did Jung Min fall for the same woman?"

Dong Min turned to Tae Hyun in surprise. He did not expect this follow up question.

Tae Hyun's eyes redirected to his Advisor. He gave Dong Min a smile that did not reach his eyes. "There are few things in this world that would make an Underworld King fall from his throne and fewer things that would tear brothers apart. The only thing powerful enough is a woman."

Dong Min gave a taut smile. Like Tae Hyun, his smile did not reach his eyes.

"Yes," he finally confirmed. "We did fall for the same woman."

"How did you and Jung Min rise from your fall?"

"Ju Won killed her. Solved any misunderstandings between us."

Tae Hyun looked at Dong Min in disbelief.

Dong Min's face remained stoic. He averted his eyes from Tae Hyun and returned them to the falling snow. His detached voice betrayed none of his emotions. "He warned us to stay away from her. He told us that she would be no good for us, but we didn't listen. We fought, we made fools of ourselves, and when we lost any credibility in the Underworld, he got rid of her for us."

Tae Hyun scoffed in disgust. Revulsion saturated his next words. "He is a sick bastard, isn't he?"

"He watches over us in a world where the sick and disturbed are put on a pedestal," Dong Min defended calmly. "What he did was a blessing in disguise because there were other crime lords looking to overthrow us . . . simply because we were too distracted to be the Kings we were raised to be."

"Why are you so loyal to him?" Tae Hyun suddenly asked. His tone did not hide his animosity toward Ju Won.

"Why are Jae Won and Kang Min so loyal to An Soo Jin?" Dong Min countered. "Because she saved their lives. Because she is the reason why they are living and breathing. They may fall in love, have wives, and have their own families, but An Soo Jin is their God. In the end, their loyalty to her will supersede everything else." He faced Tae Hyun. "Ju Won is more than my King; he is my savior. I would not be where I am today without him, and for that, he will always have my loyalty."

"But you will always hate him for taking her away from you," Tae Hyun finished for him. "He has your unending loyalty, but he does not have your unconditional love. That is why you and Jung Min are still at odds . . . because your brother is the reason why Ju Won killed the woman you loved. If Jung Min had backed off, then you could've had her. If he'd backed off, there would've been no trouble, and she wouldn't have been viewed as your distraction."

Dong Min smiled brokenly. At long last, he allowed the emotions to penetrate his anguished eyes. "You will never know greater pain than watching the person you love die in front of you, to reach out for them and beg them not to leave you. If you think losing her hurts now, then you will never be prepared for the worst." His poignant eyes urged Tae Hyun to heed his advice. "You will never get to keep her. Just let her go."

"I did."

"Her not wanting anything to do with you does not constitute as you letting her go. Like I said, if she so much as calls for you, you will go running to her." He swallowed tightly before adding, "Ju Won will not let you have her."

"Ju Won is a problem that can easily be remedied," Tae Hyun whispered fearlessly.

"The Underworld will not let you have her," Dong Min amended sternly. "You can fight Ju Won, but do you really think you have a chance against the Underworld itself?"

Tae Hyun stayed quiet and Dong Min went on. His voice was no longer soft and understanding; it was firm and unyielding.

"I fell as a King, not a God. Your fall will not be as merciful as mine. Although you may have fallen, you have not hit rock bottom yet. Get back on your throne, be the King you were raised to be, and become the God you were always meant to become. This world may be unforgiving, but it adores you nonetheless. It wants you as its ruler. All you have to do is play the part and you will have this world in the palm of your hand." He put his hat back on and opened the door. A string of cool air entered the car, bringing with it residual snow. Before he made his exit, Dong Min added, "Stop screwing up and start making the right decisions. I attended the funerals of your parents and your brother, I do not want to attend yours as well."

The door clicked shut, and Dong Min was gone, leaving Tae Hyun by himself. As his Advisor's town car drove past him and disappeared into the night, Tae Hyun continued to sit in silence. Akin to throwing himself into a meditative state, he closed his eyes and sat there, allowing the minutes to pass him by.

Moments later, as if sensing something, his eyes shot open. He narrowed his vigilant eyes onto the top of a ten-story building ahead of him. Even if it was only for a split second, he saw two people crouching there, watching him.

He was out of his car in an instant.

His focus rested on the building in question. It now appeared empty of occupants. He stepped into a narrow alley where snow and trashcans lined the pathway. He stopped when he reached the end of the alley and stood across the empty space where snow was not yet polluted by human footprints.

"Get down right now," he commanded over the billowing wind.

To anyone else, it would appear like he was talking to himself, but Tae Hyun was unfazed. He waited patiently, his eyes firmly solidified on the space before him. It was as though he was expecting company to appear at any moment. Seconds later, as a flurry of snow and wind blew around him, sounds of rattling could be heard. Within the blink of an eye, two figures jumped into view.

They wore dark hoods over their heads. One wore a brown hooded jacket while the other wore a gray hooded jacket. Both had on dark cargo pants with a multitude of pockets for their knives and guns. Shadows obscured their faces as they stood before Tae Hyun. Despite the intimidating aura they radiated, Tae Hyun appeared like he couldn't care less.

To unsuspecting people, they would be no more than ordinary pedestrians wearing hoods to protect themselves from the snow. To the well-educated Underworld leaders, they knew them as a group of highly trained assassins: the Cobras.

They were two of Kwon Tae Hyun's former ten Cobras to be precise.

"Boss," they spoke quietly, their voices suffused with reverence.

They fell to one knee and lowered their heads, greeting him with the respect he always evoked from them.

"You both have some nerve showing up here when I specifically banned you from this city," Tae Hyun said icily. His voice was cold with annoyance.

"We heard about the initiation," started the hooded woman. Her voice was soft with plea. "We wanted to come and be a part of —"

"I got the message from my Underbosses that night, Mina," Tae Hyun interrupted curtly. "You do not have to remind me. As I distinctly recall, I got on to the phone seconds later and ordered all nine of you to stay out of the initiation. In fact, I clearly remember ordering you to stay away from everything that pertains to Serpents business."

"Boss," the man started. His voice was pleading as well. "Please —"

"I kicked you out of my gang," Tae Hyun interjected mercilessly. The annoyance became more prevalent on his stern features. "You have no place calling me that." They were about to say something else when Tae Hyun added, "Your disobedience a year and a half ago has not been forgotten. The only reason you're alive is because of your combined loyalties to me in the past. But right now, I have no patience for you." His eyes sharpened on them with vigilance. "You're here for a reason. I doubt you're here to plead your way back into the gang. The question is, why are the both of you here and where are the other seven?"

Silence emanated from them.

Tae Hyun's lips edged up knowingly. Although he didn't appear surprised that they were being secretive, it still pissed him off.

"Lower your hoods," he ordered tersely.

Without missing a beat, they adhered to his command.

The shadows that once shrouded their faces disappeared.

The male's hood came down first. The light cast by the streetlights revealed a buzz cut and a gold piercing on the center of his lower lip. The woman's—Mina's—hood came down next. The unveiling exposed long brown hair locked tight in a ponytail. The gold piercing on the left side of her nose added to the obstinate mystique she possessed. Both were the type of individuals you'd cross the street to avoid. The one common facial factor between them was an inch long "57" scar that marked their left cheeks.

Tae Hyun exhaled sharply. His eyes scrutinized their scars for a long moment. "When I returned to Seoul three years ago, I found out that one of my assassins died. In addition to that, I also found out that the rest of my highly trained assassins had taken it upon themselves to scar their faces, marking their link to one another. Apparently they chose the number '57' out of respect for their dead sister." Tae Hyun's eyes darkened. "Everyone in the gang believed your story. They believed that you personally scarred yourselves. Yet I knew better because I was the one who trained you. I knew the difference between your shame and your pride. And I knew you held no pride in that scar."

Fury infiltrated his eyes while they kept theirs lowered.

"Do you remember when I gave you that ultimatum?"

They stayed quiet.

"I gave you two options: tell me the truth about how you got your scars or face exile from the gang you grew up in." He sighed. "I've stated this before, but I will state it again. Those scars weren't done on your own merits, were they? Someone else did it for you. Someone else overpowered all ten of you, all ten of my prideful and vengeful assassins. Someone else marked your faces with a scar that you proudly claim as your own in public, yet cover up in shame when you think no one is looking."

His assassins stiffened at the verity of his words.

"I know this scar has something to do with your disobedience a year and a half ago, when you took it upon yourselves to go rogue and burn down houses all over the country." A cold wind came into the alley, and his voice hardened. "Ace . . . Mina. Tell me what happened three years ago. Who gave you that scar?"

Silence was their answer.

That was his last ditch effort, and Tae Hyun had had enough. "Get the fuck out of my face."

"Boss," Ace spoke when an enraged Tae Hyun walked past them and headed out of the alley. "Everything done in the past was to avenge Kimmy and salvage whatever pride we had left, but everything being done now is to protect you and our gang. You're right. There is a reason why we're here. We just wanted you to know that our loyalty is still with you, and we hope you understand that we're truly sorry for everything."

Tae Hyun stopped in his tracks at Ace's last words. When he turned around, they were gone. Gone like they had never kneeled before him and voiced their deepest regret. It was as though they were pleading forgiveness for something they were about to take from him for his own good.

Running over everything in his mind, Tae Hyun took a second to simply stand there, lost in the silence of the snow tumbling around him. Awareness suddenly ignited his eyes. All the cards finally fell into place.

"Yoori . . ."

Tae Hyun sprinted out of the alley like a bull in the night. He pulled out his Blackberry and dialed Kang Min's number. His eyes teemed with panic as he barreled through the snow-infested street.

"Fuck!" he screamed to himself. "Why didn't I put it all together sooner?"

"Boss?" Kang Min answered at the first ring.

"Find Yoori!" Tae Hyun shouted immediately, unlocking his car doors with his remote.

"W-what?"

There was no time to explain.

"Now!" Tae Hyun growled before hurling himself into the car. He floored the gas pedal after his engine revved to life. "Find Yoori, *now*!"

"The distracted..."

05: The Cobras

"Aw man, are you kidding me?" Yoori muttered after flashes of orange lights greeted her.

She blew a breath at the myriad of cones and caution signs ahead. The street she was on was blocked off. There was heavy traffic and cars were being redirected every which way. She groaned, slamming her hand against the steering wheel. All she wanted to do was get home and unwind from her emotional day. Now even that was delayed.

Yoori glimpsed at her rearview mirror. Behind her, thinning traffic veered off to the other available streets. Yoori, who could only go in one direction to head home, moved her car to a stop when it was her turn to speak to the police officer.

She lowered her window to speak to him.

"Where are you headed, miss?" the officer inquired, motioning her to move to a quiet side of the street.

"Is the entire street blocked off?" Yoori asked, her eyes straying toward the horizon. All she continued to see were cones, flashing orange lights, and caution signs.

"We have a situation up there," he answered her. "What street do you need to get on?"

"Jin Street," she replied, wondering to herself how she was going to get home if the entire street was blocked off.

He nodded. He pointed to a dark adjacent street ahead. "Just go ahead and drive straight, make a left at the end of the street, and keep going until you hit a curve. After that, follow that road. You should be able to find the unblocked portion of the street and eventually find your way back on to Jin Street. It's pretty dark up ahead and the signs are small. Be alert while you're driving."

Despite how easy that sounded, Yoori felt edgy. She attributed this to the fact that she always hated taking unfamiliar routes to get home.

"Okay," Yoori said unsurely. It did not matter how much she disliked having to take a new route home. It was either chance a new route or be trapped in this traffic for God knows how long. Yoori wanted to get home soon. She did not want to sit in traffic all night. "Thank you for your help."

"No problem." The police officer stepped aside to allow a hesitant Yoori to drive through. "Drive safely."

Through the veil of snow twirling around them, Yoori could've sworn she saw a scar on his left cheek when the flashing orange light hit his face. Throwing the fleeting observation aside, she carefully drove through the blocked off road. She was careful to not run over any cones or get herself stuck in any big potholes.

Yoori eyed her rearview mirror. The two cars behind her, which were filled with Serpents, were stopped by the police officer.

Nervousness clawed at her.

"Hope they don't have anything illegal in those cars," she whispered.

Cops and gang members were never good combinations.

She mentally wished the other cars well and followed the directions the officer gave her. She initially debated on waiting for the other Serpents, but decided against it. If shit were to go down, she was afraid of getting in trouble with the cops if those Serpents were arrested.

The last thing I need is more trouble, Yoori thought as she disappeared into the night.

Yoori followed the officer's directions without deviation. With every block that she passed, the nervousness within her evolved into full-blown paranoia. The night snow poured furiously onto her car, and Yoori couldn't help but think that something wasn't right.

She surveyed her surroundings. Yoori observed that she was in an unfamiliar, desolate area of town. She kept looking for Jin Street, yet she found no familiar streets signs that would help her off this scary road. Her heart rate quadrupled in speed when it was evident that she wasn't about to find Jin Street, or any familiar street, any time soon.

"Crap," Yoori muttered, already knowing that she was in trouble. Was it possible that the officer gave her wrong directions, or was it something else? Also, where were the Serpents who were supposed to be following her? Did they get arrested? More importantly, where the fuck was she?

Her stomach twisted in dreadful knots.

She had to get out of here.

Yoori instinctively locked her car doors and stepped on the gas pedal. She sped out of the block in hopes of getting to the end of the street. From there, she hoped that she could hop on to the freeway or something. Something about this street scared the hell out of her.

Her fast speed was short-lived when out of nowhere, a loud pop sound exploded in the air.

"Ahhhhhh!"

Yoori's screams accompanied the Mercedes when it suddenly dropped to one side.

Screech!

Two of the tires on the right side had popped out at once. The metal wheels shrieked in the night as Yoori struggled to steady the car. With no other options in sight, she hastily stepped on the brakes. The car squealed to a stop, sliding over the curb and nearly hitting a street sign in the process.

Silence collapsed over Yoori as the car's engine hummed loudly. Once the shock passed, she unbuckled her seatbelt and pushed the car door open. The smell of burnt tires swarmed her nose when she stepped outside.

"Damn it!" Yoori cried after she examined the damage.

She quietly cursed when she discovered that she had not only damaged Tae Hyun's beloved car, but she had also screwed up her chances of getting home. While snow collected on the pavement and piled over her, Yoori raked her fingers through her hair in frustration. Curious as to what she ran over to cause such destruction, she looked around frantically. Her heart stilled when she saw what had destroyed the Mercedes' tires.

"What?" she whispered in disbelief.

Barbwires that were more than sharp enough to puncture holes into the tires sat on the abandoned street.

Yoori crouched beside the barbwires to make sure her eyes weren't playing tricks on her. No matter how much she blinked, the barbwires remained.

This . . . is not good, Yoori thought uneasily.

Who could've placed this here? Was it specifically set up for her or was it just placed here by some hoodlums? Ice dripped into Yoori's bloodstream. Either answer was not a favorable one for her. Shit was hitting the fan in her life, and she needed help.

Yoori withdrew her black flip-phone from her pocket and tried to dial for help. She was flustered when the phone refused to pick up reception. Goosebumps chased after one another on her trembling body. Stranded in an unfamiliar street, Yoori gauged the world around her in fear. Her eyes narrowed onto a club in the distance where music pounded fiercely from its closed doors. She mulled over her options. Stay stranded outside or go into a club filled with people for help?

The choice was easy.

Afraid that she'd be a sitting duck for gang members if she continued to loiter in the quiet street, she sprinted over to the blaring club. She hoped that someone in there could help her. As she ran, Yoori noted that there were several cars on the streets and in the parking lot. She felt more comfortable knowing that she was going into a club that had lots of people partying within it.

What a strange place to party though, Yoori thought in the back of her mind.

She dashed closer to it. The sounds of her trotting boots echoed in the snow-veiled night. She approached the two-story building and reached for the door. A wave of air-conditioned breeze and heavy hip-hop music thrashed upon her once Yoori pulled the door open.

She stopped in her tracks after she entered the club.

Yoori's eyes scanned over the vicinity. With the exception of the flashing blue and red strobe lights dancing off the walls, the club was considerably dark. Yoori was momentarily caught off guard. She hadn't expected the room to be this cold, especially considering the weather outside. Eager to find a phone so she could leave this neighborhood, Yoori raced onto the dance floor with the hopes of borrowing a cell phone from a patron.

Shock assailed her when she found that there was no one else in the club.

Her eyes charted the room, confusion blurring her vision. The darkness and heavy music drowned her senses, nearly driving her crazy. Where was everyone else? Why was this club empty?

A cold chill hit her, and she painstakingly acknowledged that perhaps this club wasn't as empty as she thought.

Silence descended over the room.

Akin to waiting for her grand entrance, the earsplitting music was switched off. Nothing but the multitude of swaying lights filtered into her senses. The sudden hush frightened Yoori. Now that the music was gone, she concluded with certainty that she wasn't alone.

She could hear them.

She could hear *all* of them breathe around her . . .

"Well, if it isn't the Queen herself."

The voice that originated from the upper level of the club scared the hell out of Yoori.

She whipped her head upward, alertness engulfing her.

A dark canvas greeted her eyes. Although she could not make out the silhouette of the owner of the voice, it was clear to her that whoever was in here with her had been waiting a long time for her.

Her senses livened.

Initially, she couldn't hear them over the music. Now that the distracting sound was taken away, she could hear people breathing and moving on the balconies of the club. Every now and then, as the strobe lights lit up the world above, she could see figures standing on the balcony's circular curve. She could literally feel their eyes on her.

Cursing under her breath for the terrifying situation she was in, Yoori made a move to run out. She halted when she noted that there was a tall figure standing in the hallway she had walked through. Like an imposing statue, he blocked her path. Darkness pooled over him until the swaying light hit his face.

"You . . ."

Yoori backtracked when she realized that he was the same "officer" who redirected her and eventually brought her here. She exhaled knowingly, everything becoming clear to her. All along, it had been planned for her to enter this deserted club.

Yoori moved through the darkness, nearly tripping over objects she couldn't see in her quest to find another exit.

Footsteps followed her, causing her fear to amplify.

She wasn't dealing with ordinary gang members. Considering the big production they put on, it was evident she was dealing with a group of highly trained individuals. They were well accustomed to redirecting and inconveniencing an entire city to get to the target they wanted. And tonight, she was that target.

Yoori nearly stumbled over a chair as she continued to navigate through the sea of darkness. From what she could gather from the swaying club lights, the furniture all around her were covered in white cloth. The dust from the cloth collected on her fingertips. The club was abandoned and from the amount of dust that lingered on her fingers, Yoori surmised it had been abandoned for quite some time.

The white cloth slid off the table as she moved by. When the blue and red club lights landed on the surface of the table, it revealed intricate engravings that had bullet holes in it.

Yoori's head started to pound at the sight of the bullet holes.

Screams from a distant past filled her head.

Visions that didn't feel like her own inundated her mind. In those visions, she saw amputated fingers, pools of blood, and corpses piled atop one another. The screams and the vision shook her, nearly causing Yoori to collapse. She struggled to breathe amidst her fear.

She inspected the room, speculating about the significance of this place. Leaving became second priority. The only priority was figuring out why she was lured here in the first place.

"What do you want?" Yoori cried, trembling after several figures jumped from the balconies above.

Eight of them fell onto the dance floor, landing on the pavement like cats. They crouched down, like they'd done this many times before, and with ease, stood up. The man who impersonated a police officer strolled onto the dance floor to join them. Now, there were nine of them in total—five men and four women.

"Aw," a mocking female voice piped up from behind Yoori. "She looks scared."

"She does, doesn't she?" said a male voice to the right side of her.

"You guys have the wrong person," Yoori gritted out. It didn't take a genius to deduce that these people were Soo Jin's enemies. It also didn't take a rocket scientist to figure out that Yoori was going to be executed in this club unless she saved herself. "I have no idea what's going on and—"

"It's a bit poetic isn't it, my Queen?" the same male voice from the balcony drawled. Scorn throbbed in his voice. He didn't deign to listen to her words nor did he relent on his hatred. He edged closer to her, moving with such predatory speed that he was only inches from her now. He went on, circling her like a shark. "It was in this very club where you murdered that poor family, and it was in this club days later where you overpowered all ten of us, killed one of us, and marked our humiliation with scars that would last us a lifetime."

Yoori's world tilted on its axis at the barrel of information that slipped casually from his lips. It rocked her world so hard that she was sure blood stopped pumping in her veins.

"Club?" she breathed out.

She gazed around the room. Her eyes blossomed when the realization hit her. This . . . This was the infamous location of the "Club Massacre." She shook violently, horrified that she was in the very place where she not only murdered an innocent family, but also killed two children in the process. The ghastly visions and screams besieged her again. All the while, the guilt thrashed into her consciousness, nearly suffocating her as she fought to steady her stance.

Yoori attempted to bring herself back on point.

She was about to be attacked by unknown enemies and she was allowing the guilt to handicap her? Yoori wanted to get her priorities straight and gather her strength. Such an endeavor felt impossible when she processed his words again. She not only killed the family in this club, but she came back days later and killed one of them as well?

"Scars?" Yoori asked shakily.

Who were these people? What scars were they talking about?

In lieu of verbally answering her, the rest of the eight individuals took slow steps onto the dance floor. They moved onto the area where the flickering lights were the most prevalent. Their faces were gradually revealed.

Nine intimidating people surrounded her. Two of them, a girl with red hair and the police impersonator, leaned against the white pillars in the club. Three guys leisurely sat against the cloth-covered tables on the side of the dance floor. One had a shaved head, the second had a Mohawk, and the third that completed the trio had an eye-patch. Two women, one blonde and the other with a pixie haircut, were crouched down. The last two, a man and a woman, whom Yoori assumed were the leaders, stood before her, their eyes breeding raw, unadulterated hatred. They all wore dark hooded jackets and cargo pants. Yoori could see the number "57" scar on each of their left cheeks.

The significance of the number was not lost on her.

Branded, Yoori surmised quickly, realizing now why they were here for her.

An Soo Jin had branded them as her victims.

Yoori was absolutely thunderstruck.

What could you say to the people you've victimized in the past? Especially when you couldn't remember victimizing them?

"We thought you died a year and a half ago, An Soo Jin," the female leader whispered. She tilted her head in amusement. Her hair was tied up in a bun. Her features were cold and angry—just like the man who stood beside her. His pierced lower lip glinted in the light when he smirked frostily at her.

Yoori's mind ran amuck. A year and a half ago? She creased her brows in confusion. The math was wrong. Surely they meant three years ago?

Then, the answer came to her.

The math was not wrong.

They truly meant a year and a half ago.

"The fire," she said incredulously, recalling the mysterious fire in her "hometown" that killed her adoptive family. Her adoptive mother had sent her shopping. From what the firefighters told her, she had missed the fire by mere minutes. If she had stayed any longer, she would've perished in that inferno as well.

"Yes, the fires in Taecin," the woman with the pixie haircut replied smugly. She moved to sit on a table next to the Mohawk guy. She played with her silver gun. "Our handiwork."

Yoori was astounded. It wasn't an accident after all. These people set her home on fire and killed her adoptive family—her adoptive parents and her cousin.

"You killed—"

"It's unfortunate the people we killed," the leader started bitterly. "All the houses we burned down in hopes of killing you once and for all. But we should've been more careful and actually checked out who died in those fires.

It was unfortunate that your adoptive parents' *actual* daughter died with them as opposed to you."

Yoori's breathing became shallower.

Finally, the truth.

Her "cousin" was the real daughter all along . . .

The leader continued, his voice becoming more acidic. "We were kicked out of our gang because we went rogue to get rid of you, to kill the last shred of our humiliation and avenge our sister."

Yoori bit her lips, processing all his words. A disturbing truth dawned on her. His voice echoed in her mind: *"All the houses we burned down in hopes of killing you once and for all . . ."*

The homes in Taecin were spread apart. She couldn't have known there were fires all around the city unless she actively sought out the news, which she didn't do because she left almost immediately after the fire. The fog in her mind became denser. Nothing was making sense. Soo Jin humiliated them and got them kicked out of their gang? She killed their sister, drove them over the edge, and caused them to set fires to homes all over Taecin? She ran her eyes over them. Who were these people?

"What gang?" Yoori finally asked, confounded with everything she was learning.

The man leaning against the pillar, the one with spiky hair and a pierced left eyebrow, spoke. Yoori recognized him as the police impersonator. "Because of you, we were kicked out of the very gang we grew up in. Because you humiliated us to such a degree where we couldn't tell our own boss who fucked up our faces, why we went rogue and spread those fucking fires in Taecin." He scoffed resentfully. "We should've been braver and killed you when we saw you walking around that shop in Taecin."

"Yet, you somehow survived the fire," a girl with dyed blonde hair spoke. She was crouched down, staring at Yoori with venomous eyes. "And it appears that you either have an amnesia of sorts or you're faking it. Regardless of the true reason behind your 'I'm so innocent' act, you somehow managed to infiltrate our gang and seduce our King in the process. You are a skilled bitch, I'll give you that much."

In light of all the revelations thrown at her today, Yoori couldn't help but freeze in disbelief.

They were in Tae Hyun's gang.

"Ser . . . Serpents?"

"Former," the male leader corrected spitefully. "Boss kicked us out when he found out about the fires in Taecin. He disowned us when we wouldn't tell him who mutilated our faces; he severed ties with us when we couldn't tell him why we were so intent on killing innocent people in Taecin. All because of you, An Soo Jin."

"I . . . I don't even know what you're talking about."

Remorse gripped her. She had always known that Soo Jin tortured people, but to be standing here with her former victims, it was enough to throw an already emotional Yoori over the edge.

"Your amnesia is very convenient isn't it, An Soo Jin? Or should I call you Choi Yoori? That *is* your supposed name now, right?" The male leader chuckled darkly. "No matter. Boss and the rest of the Underworld may be unsure with you, but we know the person who scarred us. We know the bitch who took great pleasure in mutilating our faces. We've waited so long for this moment and regardless of whether you remember or not, you're paying all the same."

"Tae . . . Tae Hyun knows you're doing this?" she stuttered brokenly.

"Ace. Mina," a male voice spoke from the back, addressing the two leaders. It was the guy with the bald head. "Let's get this over with. We don't have a lot of time, and I don't want her to die a fast death. I want to torture her for what she did to Kimmy, what she did to that poor family three years ago, and most of all, for her trying to endanger our boss."

"He will have our heads once he finds out, but it's for the best," answered Mina, the female leader. She sighed, shaking her head as she produced a knife from her pocket. She narrowed her eyes on Yoori. "We won't allow you to infiltrate our gang, An Soo Jin. You may have stolen our boss's affections with that innocent act of yours, but you're nothing but a monster. You've killed and tortured countless people to entertain yourself, to make yourself notorious in this world. We're going to make you pay for everything. You'll pay for the thirty-five lives you stole in this club . . . the thirty-four family members, and the life of one of our own."

Yoori's heart ripped when she was finally given the number of people she killed in this little club.

Thirty-five.

She killed thirty-four of the family members and one of their own.

The massive amount was an agonizing discovery.

"Innocent people died by your hands in this very club, An Soo Jin," the male leader, Ace, whispered. Behind him, the rest of the assassins stood up high. They watched in anticipation, in hatred. "That sin will not go unanswered."

"We were trained to kill effectively and quickly, but with you, we'll take it slow and easy," the red haired female taunted in the back. "We'll beat you to a pulp and we'll scar that pretty little face of yours as well. Let's see if you have anymore of those An Soo Jin fighting skills left . . ."

Whoosh!

"Augh!"

Before Yoori could take another breath, a powerful kick to the stomach sent her flying backward in midair.

Bam!

She collided against the wooden table behind her. The table broke apart under her weight. She fell with the broken wood, crashing against the cold hard floor with a loud thud. Something sharp pierced into her thigh, and she screamed. Stars fell into her line of vision. Disorientation assaulted her as blistering pain shot up and down her trembling body.

"Augh!" Yoori cried, pulling out a jagged piece of wood from the back of her thigh. A spew of blood erupted from her body. She nearly passed out from the pain.

As this pain consumed her, so did her guilt for what took place here.

Thirty-five, her mind repeated.

So many victims . . . so many innocent people died in this place. So many people died *because of* her. The pain in her body was nothing compared to the mental agony she was experiencing. The realization that hit her was unlike anything else she had experienced in the Underworld. She had been blaming everyone else for her misery, but she realized now that she was a culprit as well. She was one of *those* people, one of those vindictive people who made this Underworld so cruel for others . . .

Yoori was so distracted that she could scarcely move away when another one of her adversaries came for her.

"Augh!"

Air choked at her lungs when a blunt heeled boot kicked the left temple of her head. An explosion of pain erupted in her head. Her skull nearly cracked when it struck the edge of the short flight of stairs that led up to the next platform of the club.

"This one is for Kimmy!"

A large hand wrapped around her throat and lifted her up off the floor. Yoori gasped for air. The pressure on her neck was excruciating, and the feeling of her legs kicking helplessly in midair nearly caused her to black out.

The second bald male, who had a black eye-patch over his left eye, stared at her in rage. In her heart of hearts, she had the sinking feeling that An Soo Jin was the reason why he only had one eye.

He tightened his grip on her neck.

She could've easily hurt him; she felt it in the marrows of her bone. Her killer instincts were waiting to emerge. An Soo Jin was waiting to emerge, but Yoori maintained her control. She didn't want to hurt them. The ones who raped Chae Young deserved to die, but not these people. If anything, *she* was the one who deserved to die for the horrors she inflicted on to them.

With a loud grunt, he slammed her into a glass table.

Crack!

Another torrent of pain sliced through her after the broken glass ate at the exposed area of her skin. Her satin trench coat and boots proved that they were strong enough to protect her back and legs from the impact. Her hands weren't so lucky. Blood began to pool around the small shards of glass that etched themselves into her hands. Although the glass embedded in her skin wasn't enough to make her faint, it was enough to have her gasping for air.

Despite the abuse, Yoori did not fight back.

She was too remorseful to fight back.

"I . . . I'm sorry," she whispered through her anguish.

They didn't hear her apology through their wrath.

The guy with the Mohawk kicked her face. The back of her head slammed against the steps once more. Shortly thereafter, Ace's brown hunting boots pressed heavily on her neck, causing her to violently gasp for air.

"You had this coming, Soo Jin," Ace's voice huffed.

Yoori felt slender hands hold her head still.

Ace produced a knife from his pocket. As Mina angled Yoori's head to the side to reveal her left cheek to Ace, Yoori knew that they were ready to brand her.

"You mutilated us and killed countless others," prompted Ace. "Isn't it time you paid for all those sins with your life?"

Yoori agreed. Regardless of the fear she felt from the mutilation to come, she agreed that it was time she paid for everything her counterpart did. For the first time, Yoori was willing to die to alleviate the guilt spreading through her like cancer. She was willing to die to soothe their anger and to exterminate one more monster from this world. Yoori had feared this decision, but it was the only thing that made sense. If she died, then Soo Jin would never be able to return. She would never be able to wreak havoc over the world, and she would never be able to wage a war against Tae Hyun. Everyone would be safe from her. Everyone Yoori loved would be safe from the monster inside her. For that, at least her death would be worth it.

As she felt the knife press a dent onto her shaking cheek, a commotion burst into the club.

Sounds of heavy footfalls rang across the room.

"Get off of her!"

Ace's foot suddenly lifted from her throat while the knife was pulled away from her cheek. Once free, Yoori was left to instinctively gasp for air.

"You have some fucking nerve touching boss's woman like that." Kang Min's furious voice swam into her psyche.

Moments later, she felt someone lift her and pull her against their chest.

"Hey boss." Jae Won gently shook her, trying to keep her awake. "You're okay, you're okay now. We're here."

The blurs in her eyes were beginning to dissipate when the eye-patch guy appeared out of nowhere and kicked Jae Won across the face, causing him to crash to the side.

"We knew you couldn't be trusted when we told boss that you were one of An Soo Jin's elusive right-hand men," the blonde girl said heatedly, glaring at Kang Min before she ripped out a knife from her back pocket and aimed it for his neck.

Kang Min was not only quick enough to avoid the weapon, but he was also skilled enough to grab on to the handle of the knife. He propelled his hand forward and threw the knife back. The knife pierced into the shoulder of the girl like a bull's eye. The girl screamed, nearly collapsing to the ground when she tended to her wound. Too distracted with the girl, Kang Min did not see it coming when Ace jumped up, used the pillar as a prop, extended his leg in mid-flight, and kicked Kang Min across the head. Kang Min flew across the room and landed on the pile of broken wood that still had remnants of Yoori's blood on it.

Consciousness returned to Yoori at the sound of his pained groans.

Indignation started to breed inside her.

She would let them hurt her, but no one was allowed to hurt Jae Won or Kang Min.

Sounds of skulls being slammed into walls emanated from the background as Jae Won tumbled on the floor with the guy wearing the eye-patch. Fists as hard as iron dented floors, penetrated into walls, and shattered tables. The punches they threw at one another were severe, utterly merciless.

"Enough!" Yoori ordered, feeling the blood seep out of her leg as she finally regained full consciousness.

No one heard her.

The fight grew worse. Gunshots started to fill the room. Chaos broke out. The world around Yoori became a kaleidoscope of confusion as she fought to clear the fog from her vision.

"Enough!" Yoori screamed. She grabbed a Cobra by the back of his neck and threw him to the ground when she saw that he was about to knife Jae Won.

Boom!

The Cobra crashed against several chairs when he fell to the floor.

Yoori did not stop there.

She was no longer in pain; she was seeing red.

She wanted this anarchy to end.

She dodged around the bullets flying through the club when she saw that the blonde Cobra girl was aiming her gun at Kang Min's back.

"Enough!" Yoori cried again. She body-slammed the girl to the ground, elbowed her in the face, twisted her hand back, and ripped the gun from her grasp. Yoori stood up and ejected the bullets from the gun while the girl tried to stop her mouth from bleeding.

"I said, '*ENOUGH!*'" Yoori roared at the top of her lungs, causing everyone in the club to stop fighting.

The bullets ceased, the sounds of destruction stopped, and the fighting came to a standstill. They stared at Yoori, bewildered by the sudden authoritative role she emitted.

Yoori stood still, breathing intently for a few seconds. Unable to withstand the pain mounting in her body, she fell back to the ground. The Serpents in the room were left stunned, paralyzed in silence until they heard the sound of the club doors being kicked down.

The atmosphere in the club morphed from rage . . . to unmatched fear.

Trepidation seized the Cobras' voices when they addressed the one who walked in.

"Boss—"

A bone-crushing punch was heard when one of the assassins fell down, his hands clutching his face in pain. Another sound of scuffling was heard. Yoori could've sworn she felt the entire room shake after a body was thrown against the pillar of the club. Sounds of groaning arose from the violent impact. She heard a few more bone-crushing punches, sounds of people being thrown against walls and chairs broken over them reverberate into the club.

And then, amid the confusion, a whiff of the cologne that she loved so much swam up her nostrils, acting as a defibrillator for her once weakened body. The anarchy Yoori experienced was vanquished instantly. She felt someone lay a palm across her face and next thing she knew, she was gazing up at the one person she had been avoiding for so long and the one person she missed the most.

Tae Hyun.

She was quiet as his captivating brown eyes held hers, his palm framed over her cheek, and his lips locked together in silence. His face glowed like an angel's under the swaying light of the club. Yoori's heart pumped desperately against her chest. It was as though it was fighting to leap out of her in order to be with him. After more than three weeks of trying to forget him, Tae Hyun was in front of her and he was as breathtaking as ever. Then, she recalled the horrible thing she said to him before she left him, the reminder of his betrayal, and the hurt she felt when he ignored her on the street. The reminders were enough to ruin the euphoria she felt from seeing him again.

"Fuck, these bruises are going to last me a couple of days . . ."

Yoori snapped out of her reverie when she heard Kang Min and Jae Won mutter curses to themselves. They had found a seat on the steps of the club.

She sighed. Evidently, the problems between Tae Hyun and Yoori would have to wait until other things were dealt with.

She averted her gaze from the brothers and found Tae Hyun's assassins. Yoori's eyes grew wider. The rest were kneeling. She hadn't even realized they were kneeling until now. All nine, battered assassins knelt in front of Tae Hyun and her, their heads bowed down in shame after their King made his appearance.

"Ahhhh!" A sudden scream issued from Yoori when Tae Hyun moved her closer to inspect all her wounds.

Thrown by her scream, his irate eyes narrowed onto the blood coating around her thigh and the small shards of glass in her skin. There was an inhalation of wrath before he stood up.

"She's bleeding," he told Kang Min and Jae Won. "Wrap her leg up and call Han. Tell him it's an emergency and that I need him to see someone immediately."

Jae Won got on to the phone while Kang Min ripped a white cloth that had been covering a table. He wrapped the cloth around her thigh to prevent the blood from seeping out any further. Tae Hyun directed his attention to his kneeling assassins.

"Do I even have to tell you your fates?" he asked darkly.

He was enraged with Yoori's condition. He was so angry that he didn't give them any warning. Tae Hyun extracted his silver guns from behind his back, cocked his guns, and aimed at them.

"Wait, no!" Yoori cried, pushing past Kang Min.

She staggered over to Tae Hyun, who pulled the trigger. Yoori reached him just in time. She pushed his aim away and the gunshots missed the heads of Ace and Mina, both of whom didn't even attempt to dodge the bullets. As the bullets lodged into the wall behind them, Tae Hyun's assassins remained in kneeling positions, all obediently waiting for Tae Hyun to punish them as he wished.

"Don't kill them!" she shouted, trying to push Tae Hyun's forearms down. She couldn't allow more people to die for her in this club.

His furious eyes were locked on the assassins. "They should've never touched you," Tae Hyun gritted through clenched teeth. "They deserve this."

There was no mercy in his gaze. He gently pushed her away and prepared to aim again.

"Please! For me, for me!" Yoori begged hysterically, nearly tripping over in an effort to take his guns from him. "Please don't kill them."

"Are you fucking serious?" he asked in exasperation. He turned to her in bewilderment. "After all they did to you, you want them to live?"

He wasn't the only one staring at her in disbelief. Kang Min, Jae Won, and the rest of the Cobras were staring at her in astonishment too.

Yoori nodded earnestly. "Please. No more. No more deaths here. Just give me this much."

Tae Hyun let out a frustrated breath. He cursed out loud, acquiesced with her request, and bitterly placed his guns behind his back. He may have spared their lives for Yoori, but he was still intent on punishing them.

His furious eyes stabbed into Ace. "What the fuck were you thinking?"

"Boss," Ace started, his eyes glancing at Yoori. He looked uncertain with how to regard her now. "We wanted to avenge Kimmy, save our gang, and protect you—"

"So you think all of that justifies murdering someone who means the world to me?" Tae Hyun roared, shocking everyone in the room.

Wrath amplified his voice, and his assassins were stupefied by this admission of truth. They hadn't realized how deep his affections for Yoori went. Yoori, herself, was not exempt from the shock that came from this admission. Her only saving grace was that there was no time to mull over his heartfelt words. Business had to be tended to and Tae Hyun was wrapping everything up.

"She's not who you think she is and I'll be damned if any of you get off scot-free. No matter how much she pleads for your welfare, you will pay for your offenses. Now take out your guns."

"What?" Yoori uttered. "Tae Hyun, no!"

He pointed at her leg. "Her thigh is bleeding."

That was all he had to say.

In unison, eighteen gunshots blared through the club.

Yoori's heart almost collapsed at the thundering sounds until she realized that he wasn't ordering them to kill themselves—he was ordering them to shoot themselves in the leg to make up for what they did to her.

They had all shot themselves twice in their left thighs.

Yoori was puzzled. She didn't understand why they didn't just shoot themselves once. Whatever the reason, she had a distinct feeling that this procedure was a significant one for them. It was clearly a punishment that Tae Hyun had given in the past and one with which they were accustomed to.

Groaning voices speared across the room. In spite of their pain, the assassins remained kneeling, trembling while their silver guns shook in their hands.

Tae Hyun, though angry, also looked pained by the fact that he had his own assassins shoot themselves. Nevertheless, he remained cool, collected, and unforgiving.

"If you ever touch her or come near her again, the next bullets will be in your heads. Are we clear on that?"

All nine nodded in understanding.

"Leave the country tonight," Tae Hyun ordered. "I never want to see any of you again."

"Boss, *please*," Ace pleaded. Rivulets of sweat dripped over his forehead from the pain he was experiencing. Despite the direness of his wound, Ace, along with the rest of the Cobras, displayed nothing but reverence and love for Tae Hyun. "We can still be useful to you."

"You're done here, Ace," Tae Hyun dismissed quietly. "You were kicked out. There's no coming back in . . . especially after what happened here tonight." His gaze roamed over them. Disappointment cloaked his eyes. "You've all disappointed me to no end and now you're done for good. Leave the country. If I run into any of you again, I won't be as forgiving."

"But we can help you find Seo Jin Ae!" the blonde girl cried, clutching her hands over her gunshot wound. "You trained us for this. You know we're the only ones who can find her."

Tae Hyun did not budge. "That's not enough to make up for what you did tonight, Sue."

When it looked like he was ready to leave, Mina suddenly shouted, "We know the names of the people An Soo Jin brought here!"

Tae Hyun—along with Yoori, Kang Min, and Jae Won—stilled. It felt like the entire world had stopped spinning to listen to the words coming from Mina's lips.

"Say that again, Mina?" Tae Hyun voiced in astonishment.

Noting the interest searing out of her King's eyes, and with the approval from her fellow assassins, Mina continued. "Before you kicked us out, you had us investigate what took place here during the 'Club Massacre.' We couldn't find much over the course of those years, but after you kicked us out of the gang, we grew relentless. It took a long time, but we were able to find out the name of the family."

"Tell me," Tae Hyun commanded, his interest heightening by the second.

Behind him, Yoori and the brothers listened with undivided attention.

"The Hwang Family," said Ace, clutching on to his wound. "Hwang Hee Jun's family."

Yoori didn't understand who the family was, but judging by the reactions of Tae Hyun and the brothers, this was an enormous revelation.

"You're all sure?" Tae Hyun asked slowly, his breath catching in his throat. He seemed . . . astonished.

They nodded as the one with the eye-patch said, "We wouldn't tell you unless we knew with certainty that it was true."

"Who is your source?" probed Tae Hyun.

"A lost Scorpion," said the one with the Mohawk. "He was one of the few in the nightclub with An Soo Jin when the massacre took place."

"How did you get this information from him?"

"We found him in Tokyo. He had strayed from An Young Jae to start his own gang in Japan. When we found him, we kidnapped him, held him for two weeks and eventually, he cracked."

"He gave you this information under duress. How do you know it's true?"

"We used the interrogation techniques that you taught us," Sue answered carefully. "All he wanted to do was die; he would not have lied to us."

Yoori wondered about the value and reliability of this information. She was still curious when Tae Hyun walked over to her, tucked his arms behind her legs, picked her up, and began to exit the club. When he bequeathed his next orders, she discovered just how reliable and valuable this information was.

"Find me Jin Ae, and you'll all be part of the gang again."

Her eyes expanded.

This revelation was big.

It was so big in fact that it merited an opportunity for redemption for the once exiled members of the Serpents gang.

Settling into the car as Tae Hyun slammed on the gas pedal and rushed her to his private physician, only two questions coursed in Yoori's mind:

Who were the Hwangs and who was Hwang Hee Jun?

"Are punished without mercy..."

06: The Siberian Tigers

"Jae Won, I know you have to go and be with Chae Young. Please feel free to leave. Kang Min, would you stay with her tonight? I've already doubled the security on her," Tae Hyun ordered hours later.

They had arrived at Yoori's apartment after Tae Hyun took Yoori to his private doctor, got her the treatment she needed, and rushed her back home to rest.

Throughout the duration of this, Yoori barely had any alone time with Tae Hyun. Albeit the curiosity about the Hwang family was killing her, the fact that he was behaving so indifferently toward her was killing her more. The guy wouldn't even speak to her. After the torrent of concern he displayed at the club, it seemed that Tae Hyun had time to remind himself that he was indeed over her. His nonchalance and silence were eating her up alive.

"You're not staying?" Yoori finally blurted out, hoping that they would have some time to talk. Granted she hadn't had much time to herself after meeting with Ji Hoon, Hae Jin, and then being attacked by assassins, she still wanted Tae Hyun's company. Regardless of what a headache he was, she was eager to talk to him.

Tae Hyun narrowed his eyes onto her. The words that came out of his mouth stung her. "Why should I when I know that you'd probably prefer to have Ji Hoon here instead of me?"

His harsh question nearly caused her to capsize from her bed. Was that why he was ignoring her? Because he was replaying those words she said?

"I—"

"I'm leaving now," Tae Hyun interrupted, cutting Yoori off. He lifted himself off the bed and was out of the room in a flash. "I'll see you guys later."

Even though she knew it was fucked up of her to tell him that she would choose Ji Hoon over him, Yoori still grew angry and defensive. Tae Hyun had no right to treat her like this. Yoori's immature, feisty personality, which had been bottled up after what transpired three weeks ago, was set loose. Tae Hyun always had the ability, no matter how much he broke her heart, to make her forget about the bigger problems in her life and focus all her attention on him.

"Hey, slow down! I'm injured!" she cried, pushing past the brothers.

She cursed her life as she pathetically limped after him down the stairs. He just saved her life from a bunch of vengeful assassins; he could at least be nice so she could thank him for his kindness. "I'm not done talking to you!"

He wouldn't slow down.

It got so bad that Tae Hyun was actually yards away from her once she stumbled out of her apartment complex.

"Ow, ow, ow!" she cried after she limped out of her apartment.

Yoori was momentarily paralyzed by the chilliness of the night. She looked past the snow raining down on her, her eyes locked on a very fast moving Tae Hyun. She heaved a bitter breath. It would make sense that her overly dramatic life would end with her and Tae Hyun arguing again. Enraged that he was ignoring her screams for him to stop, Yoori bent down, scooped up a handful of snow, and threw a snowball at Tae Hyun's retreating head.

"What the fu—!"

The snowball successfully collided with the back of his head, earning a curse of infuriation from the King of Serpents. He wheeled around in anger.

"Jae Won, Kang Min," Yoori ordered when the brothers ran out. "Leave!"

Alarm entered their massive eyes when they saw that Tae Hyun was glowering at Yoori.

Yoori fumed inwardly. She refused to allow Tae Hyun to keep one of them here to babysit her. She didn't want to be with the brothers; she wanted to be with him.

"Uh . . ."

When Jae Won and Kang Min hesitated, Yoori imparted them with a death glare that had them scurrying off. They gave a bow of goodbye to Tae Hyun, who was too busy glaring at Yoori to even acknowledge them. The engine of the car started soon after and they were off, disappearing into the snowy night.

"What the fuck was that?" Tae Hyun snarled. His feet pressed deep into the snow when he approached her in fury.

"Don't you dare give me attitude about Ji Hoon when you were the one who ignored me on the street like I didn't even exist!" Yoori confronted once he reached her.

They had never been the type of couple who walked on eggshells around one another. Yoori would be damned if they did it now, especially when she was so pissed at him.

"*You* told me to stay out of your life," he snapped back, his eyes just as enflamed as hers. He was infuriated. "You told me if you could do it all over again, you would choose Ji Hoon over me. Then I see you talking to him on the street like you were getting ready to go have dinner together? What do you expect me to do? Grovel at your feet and beg to be back in your life when it's clear that you're ready to move on?"

"I was angry at you!" she barked back, pained by the hurt in his voice. She was also pained by her own frustration. "I didn't mean what I said about Ji Hoon," she finally admitted. "I lied so I could get away from you because I was furious with you!"

Tae Hyun's eyes enlarged at this admission. He appeared simultaneously relieved and pissed that she lied.

Yoori forged on. "It wasn't on purpose that I ran into Ji Hoon. I just came from the library for God's sake! I wanted a burger and fries for dinner. I ran into him. I was only talking to him for a second before your ass strutted out like you owned the world and you walked past me like I didn't even exist."

Tae Hyun shook his head at her last statement. His expression mirrored the exasperation on her face. "You have no idea how much I wanted to pull you along with me. But I remembered your 'order' to stay out of your life. So don't blame me for shit I can't control, Yoori. If I had it my way, you would've never left in the cab that day. However, you made it clear that you no longer wanted me in your life and I'm trying my best to abide by those wishes."

"Do you really have any right to be angry, Tae Hyun?" Yoori asked critically.

Although Yoori knew he had every right to be angry at the horrible lie she fed him, it still didn't come close to the lies that he fed her.

"No, I don't," he acknowledged. His eyes were stricken with storms of guilt. "I deserve this punishment after what I did to you." His jaw clenched. "I may deserve this punishment, but that doesn't mean I'm immune to it. This may come as a surprise to you, Yoori, but I do have emotions and they're pretty responsive whenever it involves you."

He sighed as the snow kissed their skin and the wind billowed around them.

"Why are we here like this, Yoori?" he finally asked in weariness. "I'm trying to stay out of your life, but you decide to chase me down when I try to leave? What are you doing?"

"Do you think this is easy for me, Tae Hyun?" she asked, pointing her white-bandaged fingers over her dust-covered trench coat. "You were my best friend. I trusted and adored you for months. All the shit I said to you may have been said out of anger, but that doesn't mean I'll have an easier time getting over you." The verity of her emotions erupted out of her before she could even think about restraining them. "In case you haven't noticed, it's clear that you still mean something to me, especially when I get pissed off that you didn't even acknowledge me on the fucking street."

He raked his fingers through his hair in aggravation. "What do you want from me right now, Yoori?"

"I don't want you to leave me!" she blurted out, shocking both Tae Hyun and herself. She couldn't stop as the words continued to stampede out of her. "I could forgive you for bringing me into this world because I know that if you hadn't brought me in, someone else would have and I probably would be dead by now. But I can't forgive you for lying to me all those months. I'm so angry and disappointed with you!" Her lips trembled uncontrollably. "I wish I didn't care so much that you followed my request and actually stayed out of my life. I wish I didn't care about you so I could move on. But it's obvious that I can't. I can't stop thinking about you. I'm miserable without you, you addicting bastard! I want you with me so I can stay mad at you." Yoori paused for a moment before brokenly adding, "I don't want you to give up on me."

"Give up on you?" Tae Hyun was floored. "Do you have any idea the things you do to me? If this was any other situation, then I would've said, 'fuck it' to your requests and chased you down already. But since it was you who demanded that I stay out of your life, I respected that because you had every right to be angry and punish me."

He breathed in anguish.

"I don't know how else to apologize to you, Yoori. I fucked up. I know I did. I wish I wasn't as corrupted when I first met you. I wish I wasn't such a manipulative bastard when I brought you into this world." He bit his lips as wind descended upon them. "I wish the corrupted, heartless, and manipulative bastard in me would've been stronger. That way, I wouldn't have fallen for you and be in the shithole that I'm in right now. I'm not the same guy anymore; if I was, then I couldn't care less about who wants to kill you, I couldn't care less about the guys you talk to, and I couldn't care less when you looked me in the eyes and told me that if you could do it over again, you would've chosen Ji Hoon over me. If I was the same guy, then I wouldn't be in a world of hell right now."

Yoori fell quiet for a minute, not knowing how to respond to his words.

"Did you really drive away when you saw me talking to Ji Hoon?" Yoori asked instead, her heart already fighting to jump out of her chest as it yearned for Tae Hyun. The emotions he evoked paralyzed her.

"Of course not."

Relief filled her. "Where the hell did you park?"

"Down the street until he pulled you into a corner and I couldn't see you anymore. I was going crazy until I saw you driving away and saw that you weren't leaving with him."

Yoori smiled to herself.

So, he had been there all along . . .

"I thought you gave up on me," Yoori faintly whispered.

No matter what happened between them, no matter how upset she was at him, no matter what lies she told him, he wasn't supposed to give up on her. They had too many obstacles in their way for him to give up on her so easily. Yoori realized *that* was why she was so depressed when he didn't acknowledge her on the street. She thought he had given up so easily when there were worse things coming their way.

"Our lives would be easier if we gave up on each other, wouldn't they?" Tae Hyun asked, his eyes holding hers.

Yoori nodded. It would be much easier if they could walk away from each other and be fine without each other.

Tae Hyun exhaled, placing his hands into his pockets as if to keep himself from reaching out to her and holding her in his arms. "If you want me to stay out of your life, then I'll do it. If you want me here with you, then I'll do it. Whatever you want, I'll give it to you." He gazed at her. "What do you want, Yoori? What do you need me to do?"

"What do you need me to do?" she parroted stupidly, not knowing what answer to give him. She was conflicted with the need to be angry with him and the need to throw herself in his arms and bask in his warmth.

"I need you by my side," he told her without hesitation. "Plain and simple."

When he said those words, a memory of their first encounter sparked in her head, playing out an image of them discussing the specifics of her job duties in the limo. She recalled Tae Hyun telling her that she could fuck up anyway she wanted to. His only requirement was that she had to be by his side whenever he called for her, whenever he needed her. Yoori smiled at the memory. She doubted Tae Hyun remembered the conversation and the bullshit promise she made him. But to her, a promise was a promise. If she made it, then she would follow it through. Especially when it was a promise to Tae Hyun.

Yoori would've never forgiven anyone else, but this was Tae Hyun. After three weeks of missing him, she knew she couldn't go on without having him beside her. Pride aside, she wasn't sure how much longer she could go on ignoring the aching feeling in her heart. Yoori looked at him with hardened eyes. She refused to be seen as a doormat though. She wasn't forgiving him because she was weak; she was forgiving him because this was his second chance.

"We will not be boyfriend and girlfriend anymore," she stipulated, intent on not making this easy for him. "We will start over. Fresh and on a clean slate."

The smile he gave her was breathtaking. "I'd like that."

Yoori touched his face, using all her might to not allow his charms to distract her. "If you use me or do anything like that to me ever again, I'm going to rip your eyeballs out."

A wider smile took over the curve of his lips.

"Never again," he promised.

"I'm serious," she reiterated.

"So am I," he said without hesitation.

She nodded slowly, and he smiled before saying, "So, are we good? Can I use my charms now?"

Yoori gaped at him strangely. Before she was able to voice her perplexity, Tae Hyun had already filled the space of air between them. He pulled her against him and effortlessly lifted her up. While Yoori instinctively wrapped her legs around his hips, he pressed his lips against hers.

White-hot heat seared through her soul when Yoori kissed him back. The desperation, yearning, passion, and adoration she had for him were all wrapped up in the breathtaking kiss they shared. She could scarcely breathe, but who the hell cared? Hating him aside, Yoori couldn't deny the blazing sex appeal he continued to emanate while he ran his hand down her hair as they kissed like there was no tomorrow. They had more issues to address and more problems to resolve, but for that night, Yoori was content with enjoying Tae Hyun's company. Everything else in the world could wait.

"Never again, baby," he promised, melting her insides just by calling her "baby." "Never again."

"But," she whispered in between their kiss, "we're not boyfriend and girlfriend anymore. You can't kiss me like this . . ."

Despite her protest, Yoori did not attempt to break the kiss. It felt too good to stop.

"We're still friends," he crooned seductively. "Best friends."

He slowly lowered her onto the snowy bench hidden in the corner of her apartment building. She hadn't realized he walked such a long distance while they were making out.

"Wait!" Yoori gasped, staring owl-eyed at him when he was about to lean down and shower her with kisses on her neck. "What are you doing?"

Her bout of horror momentarily lapsed when the sexy God smiled suggestively at her.

Oh no.

She had heard about this, stories about couples getting into big fights and forgiving one another with passionate make-up sex.

"Tae Hyun, we're too young!" Yoori whispered, genuinely panicked about the possibility of them having sex—even though physically, her body was more than ready.

A frown veiled his face. He was affronted. "What the fuck, Yoori? How disturbed do you think I am? We're outside in the snow . . . and in public no less. I'm not going to have sex with you out here. I'll be damned if anyone else sees you naked."

She blinked at him awkwardly. "Then why are we here like this?"

"I just want to be with you outside," he said simply, pulling her up into a standing position. He laid himself across the bench.

Yoori stood beside the bench, scowling down at him. "There's no room for me."

"You can sleep on top of me."

"*What?*"

"You're my girlfriend," he noted with a sinfully seductive voice. He accompanied that beautiful voice with a playful smile. "You can sleep on me. It's not against the rules."

"I'm not your girlfriend anymore," she reminded him.

"You're still my ex."

"Um . . ."

"Stop being such a baby," he provoked impatiently. "We haven't seen each other in three weeks. We should be having steamy hot sex right now instead of hanging outside in the cold. Since we're out here, we should make the most of it."

Now that he mentioned the cold, Yoori realized that she was freezing. Teeth chattering, she said, "We're not staying out here long, are we?"

"No, just for a couple more minutes and then we'll go back inside. Having said that, hurry and get on me. I'm cold and I need body heat."

Yoori grinned bashfully. Even though she wanted to appear demure and shy (since she was no longer his girlfriend and all), she was inwardly excited to be close to him physically. With a blush firmly cloaked on her cheeks, Yoori carefully laid herself across Tae Hyun.

They were no longer a couple, but they were still friends.

It couldn't hurt for friends to do this, right?

She was instantly rolled onto the side of the bench, laying on him slightly while also hanging off the edge. She should've felt uncomfortable, but leaning on Tae Hyun made everything feel safe. His arms were wrapped tight around her, his body heat protecting her from the snow frosting over them. In that moment, everything was perfect in her little world again.

"This is the part where we start over and promise to tell each other everything, right?" Yoori asked, staring at him as snow continued to fall steadily around them.

Tae Hyun nodded, a look of conviction present in his eyes. "Yes. I'm not keeping anything from you. Whatever you want to know, ask. I'll tell you everything."

Yoori nodded at his words. Although their reunion was the highlight of her night, Yoori hadn't forgotten the burning question she had in the club. "Can you tell me who the Hwangs are?"

"If you're really ready to talk about this, then yes." He stared into her eyes. "Are you sure you want to know?"

She understood his hesitancy in telling her. It could trigger something that would break her again. Yoori knew it was probably best to keep herself in the dark. However, she was ready for this, especially now that she had Tae Hyun with her again.

"I have to know who I killed that night." She chewed her lips, fighting past the nervousness. This was the moment of truth. A very scary but much anticipated moment. "Who are they and who is Hwang Hee Jun?"

From there, the road to her enlightenment began.

"Hwang Hee Jun was the King of the Siberian Tigers," Tae Hyun answered. "It was his family in the club that night."

Puzzlement claimed her features. "I've never heard of the Siberian Tigers."

"Yes, you have," he assured her. "You haven't heard their name, but you know of them." As the beginnings of exacerbated confusion morphed over her face, Tae Hyun promptly added, "The Siberian Tigers were the fourth most powerful gang in the Underworld five years ago. I told you about them when I was giving you a history lesson on the Underworld. They were the ones who were—"

"—exterminated by An Young Jae before he took over the Scorpions' throne," Yoori finished for him when she recalled the history lesson he gave her months ago. Something else struck her. "Wait. But you told me that Young Jae killed the *entire* lineage five years ago."

Tae Hyun nodded, encouraging her train of thought.

"But that family was with Soo Jin three years ago . . ."

He nodded again, confirming that she was on the right path.

"The entire lineage wasn't killed," Yoori concluded. She felt something still inside her at her own words. This was becoming unsettling. The wheels in her mind spun faster. "Was this information fabricated by the Scorpions so Young Jae could get his throne?"

"Young Jae only needed to kill Hwang Hee Jun to take over the Scorpions' throne and he did that," said Tae Hyun. "However, it was said that the *entire* lineage was killed when the Scorpions attacked the Siberian Tigers' estate."

Like a new day, knowledge dawned in Yoori's eyes. "Could it be possible that an extended family of the Siberian Tigers went into hiding after the attack and the Scorpions kept quiet about it while they tried to find the rest of the family and finish them off?"

"You would only go after someone like that—especially an entire lineage—if they had information you'd kill to have," Tae Hyun answered, conjecturing what may have happened that night in the club.

Yoori followed his lead as another realization seized her. "Your assassins said that thirty-four people were killed. It wouldn't be possible for Soo Jin to restrain thirty-four people by herself, right?"

Tae Hyun nodded in confirmation.

Uneasiness struck her. "Soo Jin couldn't have been in that club by herself. She had to have been with others. She had to have been with her brother."

Tae Hyun nodded once more before asking her a dead-end question that they both had no answers to.

"The question is . . . what broke Soo Jin to the point where she tried to commit suicide, and what caused An Young Jae to escape from the Korean Underworld and disappear for the years after?"

Hopefulness lit her eyes. "Do you have a hypothesis for that?"

"Not a very good one."

Yoori looked at him eagerly. Tae Hyun was one of the smartest people she knew. She trusted that whatever his reasoning was, it would be a great one. "Share with me anyway."

"Soo Jin was a powerful figure in the Scorpions gang, but she was under Young Jae's rule nonetheless," Tae Hyun provided shrewdly. While he spoke, snow started falling more fiercely around them. "For something of that magnitude, which involved a Royal family that Young Jae supposedly exterminated when he assumed the Scorpions' throne, Soo Jin had to have been under Young Jae's supervision. If I were the King in question, I would only go after an *entire* lineage like that if they had a secret I'd kill to have, or a secret I'd kill to bury with them." He glanced at Yoori intently. "I can't begin to guess what happened that night, but the only thing I know is that An Soo Jin and An Young Jae were very close siblings. Their loyalty to one another was unrivaled. Whatever threat the Siberian Tigers held, it was catastrophic enough to destroy one and break the other. And unfortunately, unless one of them returns to the Underworld and enlightens us about what took place, it is unlikely we'll guess anything concrete."

Yoori paused before asking, "Do you think he's still alive?"

Tae Hyun didn't miss a beat. "Yes."

The certainty in his answer surprised Yoori. "How are you so sure?"

"Because if he's dead, all of the Underworld would know. A dead King cannot command the flow of information that pertains to him; only a breathing King is powerful enough to silence the mouths of those he comes across. Since his disappearance, I have heard little to nothing about him. This only means two things: he is not only very much alive, but he is also still very much powerful."

"Do you think he'll ever make his return to the Korean Underworld?"

"If he has something to come back for, I'm sure he will."

Yoori absentmindedly nodded before leaning in closer to Tae Hyun. She asked her final question of the night. "I'm certain he must've heard about the fires in Taecin. Do you think he knows that I'm still alive?"

"If he does, I don't doubt that he'll make an appearance soon. If he left the Underworld because of you, then he'll return to it because of you."

"May the Kings and Queens who had fallen before you be your examples..."

07: House of Cards

"Do you think I'm too easy?" Yoori asked out of the blue, wincing in pain after Tae Hyun rubbed some ointment around the bruises and cuts on her right leg.

It had been several days since the attack by the Cobras and although many of her wounds remained, many had also faded under Tae Hyun's stringent care. It hadn't occurred to Yoori how "easily" she gave in to Tae Hyun until she mulled over her predicament. There she was, wearing a pink tank top with white short-shorts (Tae Hyun's suggested outfit), being rubbed down by the sexy one himself, and she wondered if she should have waited on forgiving him.

She verbalized this thought to Tae Hyun, who was shirtless and only wearing black lounge pants. "Should I have waited a couple of months before I forgave you? Was three weeks too soon?"

Tae Hyun gave her an unimpressed stare. He then tilted his head to check out the white bandage wrapped around the wound on her thigh. Because the wound was still susceptible to pressure, Yoori had to prop her bent leg up on a wooden chair. Her leg was essentially hovering over Tae Hyun's muscular shoulder while he crouched before her and tended to her wounds.

"Are you asking me if I think you putting me out of my misery 'too soon' was a mistake or are you asking me if I think prolonging my 'punishment' would make me treasure you more as my girlfriend?" He shook his head slightly, keeping his eyes on her thigh. "Your irrationality never ceases to amaze me, Brat."

One would think that after their reconciliation, Tae Hyun would spoil Yoori rotten with sweet talks and compliments. This was far from the case. He was exactly the same with her as when they were "BFF's." He was sweet when he wanted to be, combative when he needed to be, and sexy as hell whenever he chose to be.

Yoori glowered. Although she also treated him no differently, she still didn't appreciate his smart aleck remarks.

Tae Hyun smirked while "accidentally" poking a bruise on her knee, causing her frown to thaw into a wince of pain.

Casually, he added, "For the record, three weeks was long for me. I'm sorry it was too short for you."

"Ow, jerk-face!" Yoori cried, smacking his naked chest with her left hand. "How dare you poke an injured person? You totally did that on purpose!"

"Of course I did," he said guiltlessly. He caressed the area he had poked. "You're the one being a jerk. I can't help but be offended." He chuckled when she mouthed a string of curse words. Sending tingles up her body with soft touches, Tae Hyun gazed up, giving her the most enticing bedroom eyes she had ever seen. "I'm sorry about that. Would you like me to kiss it and make it all better?"

His crooning voice stroked her senses in all the right spots. Yoori not only felt dazed, but also frustratingly enticed. It did not help that he was wearing close to nothing.

How dare you use your sexuality as a weapon? She thought feebly, resisting the urge to nod like a bobble head.

Yoori rubbed her wound, her heart beating dramatically. In lieu of succumbing to another one of his seductions, she forged on with her chain of thoughts.

"I'm not saying it was too short for me—because it wasn't." She held his eyes with hers as she spoke, the bitterness dissolving from her stare. "But I think other girls prolong the punishment so that their boyfriends—or ex-boyfriends—would remember to never hurt them again. I can't help but think that I gave in too easily. I don't know . . . I don't want you to think of me as being . . . you know . . ." She whispered her next words. "*Easy.*"

Tae Hyun's lips stretched into an amused smile. He blew warm air on her thigh. The feel of his breath made her shiver with need. She mentally cursed him for his silent way of seducing her.

"Three weeks may be short to some people, but you forget that we're closer than other couples. Who else do you know have been together for nearly every minute of every single day since they've met?" He leaned in closer to inspect some of the healing cuts on her thigh. He rubbed the last of the ointment onto her awaiting skin. "I don't know about you, but I think we've become one of those stupid couples who are interdependent on each other."

Yoori noted the subtle blush on Tae Hyun's cheeks when he casually stated this. The sight warmed her heart. The all-powerful God in this secret society was blushing as he tended to her wounds. Nothing could beat this adorable moment.

"In essence, three weeks would equate to a three month timeframe for us. And that's too long for me. The time we spent apart was hell—I'm glad it's over." He addressed the last of her concerns with a mischievous glint in his eyes. "And I've been rubbing ointment over your body for a few days now, and I haven't gotten any action. It's safe to say you're not easy."

Butterflies, of both desire and bashfulness, quaked in her bruised tummy.

"Shut up!" Yoori grumbled, blushing immensely.

Though she was flushed, her heart lifted at his admission that he was head over heels for her. She had received these admissions in the past, but they were given under "dramatic" circumstances. It was another thing to have him admit it when they were casually hanging out. She had to take advantage of this rare opportunity.

"What is it about me that you're hooked on?" she inquired, faking coyness.

She was playing a dangerous game since she was his ex-girlfriend. The last thing she should be doing was tease him, but she was curious. She knew without question that he adored her as much as she adored him. What she had never really known was the reason for his interest.

"Is it my wittiness?" she prompted in a sultry voice. She attempted to act sexy when he peered up at her.

Yoori never saw herself as a sexy woman. If anything, she felt dorky compared to most girls. Yet, after being around the walking sex God that was Kwon Tae Hyun, she couldn't help but feel bigheaded that she reeled in the best fish in existence. Any girl would feel cocky, and Yoori was no exception.

"Is it my sarcasm? My fiery personality? My impressive physique?" Feeling oh-so-confident with herself when his amused eyes returned to her thigh, she leaned in closer to give him her best bedroom eyes. "My sex appeal?"

Hushed silence came over the room as she awaited Tae Hyun's reply.

She had already decided that if he said the right thing, then she might actually throw caution to the wind and pounce on him right then and there. They'd never had sex and even though she was a complete prude (and even though he was her "ex-boyfriend"), she couldn't ignore the sexual frustration gnawing within her.

Say the right thing and you might get some, she urged in her yearning mind.

With his attention still on her wounds, he finally parted his tantalizing lips. "Your unrivaled ability to be a really weird flirt. There's something strangely addicting about your social awkwardness."

What?

The rotation of her world came to an earthshattering stop. It only exploded when he added, "Now could you stop leaning in so close? You're blocking the light. I can't see if that big cut of yours is healing or not."

Her once big head deflated in embarrassment. Of course. It made sense that the insensitive Tae Hyun would diss her and inevitably shame her failed attempt to be a super vixen. She growled under her breath. Unable to suppress her bitterness, she pulled her leg off the chair, accidentally kicked him across the shoulder, and pushed him away. Although her efforts weren't physically powerful enough to push him off balance, it was strong enough to seize his unwavering attention.

"Stop touching me," she seethed, standing up with her chin held high. This was what she deserved for going out of her comfort zone and attempting to be sexy—and with an ex-boyfriend no less. "My physical wounds are fine, thank you very much. Now if you'll excuse me, I shall put on my un-sexy pants and ignore you because you're an insensitive jerk."

Yoori bestowed his entertained face with a death glare before limping across the room to retrieve her pajama pants. Her pink pajama pants were an inch away from her grasp when another hand appeared, pulling the pants off the chair they hung from and throwing them across the room.

She was outraged when two arms wrapped around her. "Hey! What are you doin—?"

"I like what you're wearing," he whispered, his voice as sweet as honey.

Tae Hyun whipped her around to face him, held her close to him, and allowed her to drape safely over him as he fell backward. Their welcoming bed echoed with a soft creak as it adjusted to their weight.

Yoori groaned. She didn't want to be tricked into forgiving him again. That charm of his was her kryptonite.

Desperate to stand her ground, she said, "It's winter and I'm wearing a tank top and short-shorts. I'm cold."

She made an attempt to jump out of his hold. He only held on tighter.

"It's winter and you're showing more skin than I've ever seen on you," he continued with a chuckle. His warm body felt like a furnace against hers. "I would be an idiot if I allowed this once-in-a-lifetime sight to be covered by an ugly sweater and grandma looking pajama pants." He grinned at the frown that overtook her face. He allowed his fingers to trace teasing circles on her bare thighs. "You know you love it when I touch and tease you," he murmured, seduction swimming in the gaze he held on her. He lifted his lips close to her ear. "Give in, stubborn one. I promise I won't bite—that hard."

"Your lame attempt to use your sexuality as a weapon, while making it seem like you're a harmless and innocent ex-boyfriend, makes me want to barf out my imaginary red velvet cake."

Tae Hyun blinked, offended that she not only resisted his charms, but that she also insulted him in the process. "Did you really just say that?"

Yoori nodded proudly.

He smirked. He heaved a prolonged sigh that was a telltale sign of his strained patience.

"You're lucky your deliciously plump ass stole my heart or else I would have given you a grand punishment for that insult." His voice held a mixture of bitterness and lightheartedness while he caressed the skin of her leg. "I mean, let's see," he started, counting off with the fingers on his free hand. "You fucked up my precious Mercedes right after I gave it to you . . ."

Yoori pouted at the reminder. Her precious baby was still in the shop.

"You always ruin the moment when I try to get us in the sexy mood . . ."

Yoori smiled like a rebel.

"You kicked an animal that I've adored since I was a kid . . ."

Yoori rolled her eyes at the mention of the dumb ducks she hated.

"And you even chucked a snowball at my head."

He laughed at the last point while Yoori sighed dreamily at the remembrance.

"If anyone else did that, I'd have them wishing for hell, but since it's you, all I require is that you tease me with some skin. Is that so much to ask?" He sighed dramatically. "Maybe I should re-think trying to win you back as my girlfriend. You're pretty prudish, weird, high maintenance, and you only attract trouble."

Yoori laughed at his careless comment. She got up and sat comfortably on his firm stomach. She stared down at him with confidence that only a woman could give to her boyfriend when she knew she had him in the palm of her hand.

"Girlfriend, ex-girlfriend, or BFF, you know you can't live without me and my quirkiness, so you shouldn't even try."

There was no witty retort from Tae Hyun. There was just a smile of agreement as he stared up at her with adoration.

"Plus, it wasn't my fault with the Mercedes," she added. "I didn't know I was about to be attacked."

The words spilled out of her chest and before she could help it, a tense silence devoured them. All jokes and senseless arguing aside, they always knew when to get serious.

"How are you doing today?" he asked, the once playful tone vacating his voice.

Worry marked his face once he was reminded of the attack and every other horrible circumstance that found a home in Yoori's life.

"Better," she said genuinely.

Yoori smiled, recalling her appreciation for him. Since their reconciliation, Yoori had finally been able to release her problems to someone and that someone was Tae Hyun. The weight of guilt from her past sins had yet to disappear (she was nearly certain it would remain forever), but the weight of the world did lift and that meant a lot to her. With Tae Hyun's help and encouragement, she had even been able to visit Chae Young without breaking out into sobs. She actually felt like she was being a good friend again. Although things were far from perfect in Yoori's life, things were definitely looking up and it was looking up because of him.

"Thank you for being there for me," she told him, meaning it with all her heart. "I really appreciate it."

"I wish I could've done more for you," Tae Hyun responded, his fingers caressing the bandage wrapped around her thigh. It was a touch of regret, not seduction. "I wish I could've protected you better."

The feel of his delicate touch on the wound reminded her of his assassins.

"How are they?" she asked, remembering that they shot their thighs twice as their punishment for attacking her. Others may not worry about the well-being of their attackers, but Yoori couldn't help but feel guilt and concern whenever they drifted into her mind. Her past self did a lot of horrible things to them and even after being mercilessly attacked in the club, she found it difficult to begrudge them.

A frown covered Tae Hyun's face. "Healing," he said simply.

Yoori wasn't sure if he was frowning because they were still healing, which meant that they were still in pain, or frowning at the reminder of their attack on her. She suspected it dealt with both reasons.

"They're anxious to find Jin Ae in order to rejoin the gang," he shared, concealing any worry he had for them. "But I have something else for them to do today and already gave them the orders to stay put for a few more days. They are not a hundred-percent yet. I told them I didn't want any fuck ups because of their injuries. There is only one chance for a snatch and it has to be a success."

Jin Ae came to mind and anger lit inside Yoori. Since she couldn't go after Jin Ae, Yoori was anxious for his assassins to go after her instead. In that merciless moment, she didn't care if the Cobras were still healing. They were the ones who could give her the vengeance she wanted; they were the ones who could bring her Jin Ae's head. They should not be resting. They should be out looking for Jin Ae.

"They're your best assassins though," she instigated casually. "I'm sure they can handle it."

Given how they impersonated cops, blocked off roads, and orchestrated the entire attack to lead her to the club, she knew that they were exceptional. Their execution may not have come to fruition because their boss figured out their plan, but their abilities were to be envied nonetheless. If not for Tae Hyun, then they would've achieved what they wanted—her dead. They were the perfect group to capture Jin Ae.

"They may be highly trained, but that doesn't mean they're the best." At the expression of curiosity on her face, Tae Hyun elaborated. "Think about how they were with you. They killed innocent people. They were so consumed with the need for vengeance that they fucked up trying to kill you. My assassins are loyal, but their anger has made me question their rationale. They allowed their emotions to get in the way and that's just as bad as letting an inexperienced group plan an abduction. Hopefully they can capture Jin Ae effectively because they have no emotions toward her. However, I won't allow them to do it unless they're fully healed—both physically and mentally. Jin Ae is not just another girl in the Underworld. She is Ju Won's niece. Her capture will not be easy. If it goes wrong, the casualties will be insurmountable. I'm pissed at them, but I won't let them risk their lives. They will only go when I deem they're ready, when I deem they can come out alive."

She nodded slowly, accepting his reasoning. Regardless of how impatient she was, Yoori agreed that her agenda would only work if everything went according to plan. They only had one chance to do this right. She couldn't foil that chance with her impatience.

Her thoughts ventured on. She recalled the name of the missing Cobra they wanted to avenge—the one Soo Jin killed.

"Who was Kimmy?" she asked quietly.

Poignancy entered Tae Hyun's eyes at the mention of her. "Kimmy was the youngest of the Cobras. They all grew up together and loved each other as if they were blood siblings. This is why they have such loyalty for each other. In the group, if you say that Mina and Ace were the most experienced ones, then Kimmy was definitely one of the most inexperienced ones." He exhaled sharply, visibly upset over the loss of his youngest Cobra. Yoori felt her stomach clench when she noticed the pain hidden in his eyes. "She was no match for An Soo Jin. None of them were."

"I deserved what they did to me," Yoori stated, truly believing her own words. She swallowed past the remorse rising through her. It hurt her to see Tae Hyun in pain, especially over something her past self did. "Just like those gang members in the alley deserved what I did to them, I deserved what your assassins did to me. An Soo Jin's mistake is my mistake. An eye for an eye, right?"

"I don't care what reasons anyone has," Tae Hyun stated inflexibly. "No one can touch you if I'm around."

Yoori smiled guiltily at his prerogative. Her mind wandered before eventually migrating back to Jin Ae.

"I want Jin Ae—*soon*." She did not blink when she said this. "Just like those gang members in the alley, she deserves to be punished."

There was no concealing the remorse Yoori felt for all the despicable things Soo Jin did. There was also no hiding the anger that spread through her whenever she was reminded of what Chae Young went through. Yoori might not be able to capture Jin Ae herself, but she would be damned if anyone else punished Jin Ae.

Tae Hyun nodded. "When the Cobras capture her, you can do what you want to her. But anything dealing with the chase, you're waiting in the back and letting my people take care of it. When it comes to being invisible while abducting someone or gathering information, those nine are the best for the job. I could follow their trails, but I doubt anyone else can."

Yoori bobbed her head absentmindedly, allowing the silence to shroud them. Her mind mulled over a disturbing thought before she voiced it to Tae Hyun.

"Does this side of me scare you?" She stared into his eyes, genuinely curious. "I never had a chance to ask what went through your mind when you came into the alley that morning and saw that I had killed eleven men. And now you're listening to me talk about wanting to punish Jin Ae." Yoori exhaled uncomfortably. She had changed drastically since their first meeting in the diner. It was no secret that a part of Soo Jin was alive inside her, and this acknowledgement scared her. Her heart wrenched at the thought of it scaring Tae Hyun. "Do I scare you?"

His smile was reassuring, unwavering. "There's no other society that's as cruel and heartless as this one." He lifted his hand up and traced it over her cheek. "I've seen things that no human should see and I've done things that no human should do. Killing people has become such a habit that the thought hardly provokes a reaction out of me. But the mere thought of someone touching you makes me want to kill, the thought of you hurting makes me ache, and the thought of you leaving me makes me want to punish the world. You're the only thing that's been right in my life and you're asking if you scare me?" He smirked, his eyes staring at her with adulation. "You scare me more than you'll ever know, just not in the sense that you may think."

Yoori smiled as she held her hand up and rested it above the hand that caressed her cheek. She kissed his caressing fingers and listened as he went on, warming her heart further.

"But to answer the specific content of your question, no, you don't scare me. I could see the pain in your eyes when you speak about those eleven bastards. I could sense the pain as you spoke about wanting to punish Jin Ae. A monster wouldn't feel any of that pain. A monster wouldn't feel pain, remorse, or trepidation. You do not take joy in hurting them; you resent them for *forcing* you to punish them. I've seen atrocious things in this world, and you will never be one of them."

"I wish I forgave you sooner," Yoori lamented, leaning forward again and laying her chin on his chest. She hugged him tightly, wanting nothing more than to feel his body heat. "I wish I never left you because those three weeks were hell. It was a mistake that I won't make again."

"It was a mistake to let you leave, but I'm not letting you leave again," he assured her. "Never again."

"Good," Yoori replied, refusing to tear up because of how sweet he was being.

"I want to open up to you now," he went on, his hand stroking her cheek with care.

Yoori looked at him oddly. "Isn't that what we're doing right now?"

"I want you to see every part of me," he clarified. Tae Hyun sat up and gently laid her across the bed. He supported his head with one arm and leaned over her. His free hand continued to caress her cheek. He stared down at her with conviction. "You've seen the 'human' side of me, but I want you to see the other side. I want you to see the side that's the King of this world."

Yoori looked up at his handsome face in curiosity. "What do you want me to see exactly?"

"I want you to see how the initiation for my world works."

The puzzlement did not leave her face. "I already saw how the initiation works."

"The initiation into *my* gang."

Yoori paused. She sat up abruptly and shot him a wide-eyed look. "I thought outsiders weren't allowed to see that?"

"You are no longer an outsider," Tae Hyun told her, sitting up as well. He cupped his palm over her cheek. "You are part of my world now—a very important part. And I want you to see this."

Yoori was stunned. She was used to Tae Hyun being secretive with her. This concession floored her. "Are you sure?"

He chuckled. "Unless you don't want to see it."

"I do," she whispered, sitting closer to him to express her eagerness. Her heart raced at the thought of finally being welcomed into Tae Hyun's secretive world. "I want to see it."

He smiled softly. A tinge of wariness rippled in his eyes. "Don't judge me too harshly."

Yoori laughed quietly. What a silly thing for him to say. "Why would I?"

The poignancy in his demeanor did not relent. If anything, he looked more serious. It was like he was trying to prepare her for the worst. "I did not get into the position I am in today by being a morally just person. When you see everything . . ." He swallowed tightly. "Don't judge me too harshly."

"I was An Soo Jin in a past life," Yoori told him gently. She held his hands and smiled reassuringly. He was finally opening up to her. The last thing she would do was judge him. If anything, it would only make her adore him more. "I am in no position to judge anyone."

Tae Hyun favored her with a relieved smile and nodded. He laid down on his pillow and pulled her down into bed with him.

"Get some sleep then," he said, tugging the comforter over them. "Because when we leave in a few hours, we will have a long night ahead of us."

"May their demise dictate your choices in life."

08: A King's Memory Lane

Yoori couldn't keep her eyes off the ever-changing foliage.

The beginnings of an infantile sunset had settled over the world as they drove through the hilly road leading up to Tae Hyun's Serpents' estate. Tae Hyun was driving his Jaguar and Yoori was sitting beside him, mesmerized by the view outside.

Trees upon trees surrounded them. Everywhere Yoori looked, she saw plants of different varieties standing parallel to the road, each holding secrets to the different acres of land they sat on. It had been a while since she saw so much greenery, and she had missed it. The vibrant sunset streamed over the land, covering everything with a golden hue. This vision reminded her of the splendor of the lake house community she had visited with Tae Hyun weeks back. Yoori smiled at the reminiscent thought. Anything that could evoke such wonderful nostalgia was a beauty in her book.

"So, this is the infamous Serpents' estate?" she asked wondrously, basking under the sunset's rays. She still couldn't believe she was going to see how the inner workings of the Serpents' initiation worked. It felt like she was about to learn the answer to one of life's greatest mysteries.

"One of them," Tae Hyun stated casually.

"One of them?" Yoori echoed, spinning around to face him.

He nodded, his eyes still on the dirt-paved road. "After I became the King of Serpents, I bought a second estate."

Yoori slanted her head critically. Dressed in a black suit with a green dress shirt and a black tie, Tae Hyun definitely looked like someone who could afford several estates at a time. Regardless, it rubbed her the wrong way that he did own several homes. Even if he had money, it did not mean he should be wasteful with it. "Why would you buy a second one?"

"Because this is not necessarily my favorite one." He grinned at the reproving look on her face and started to explain the reason for his two estates.

"Traditions dictate that all Serpents must be initiated here. I keep this place as a means to uphold my family's traditions. This estate is for their initiation. The second estate is for their training and our gatherings."

Yoori briefly averted her attention to the ever-changing scenery. "Didn't you grow up in this estate?"

He nodded. "Yes." He pointed at a tall tree they were nearing. The tree had a long rope hanging down from it. "That was where I first broke my leg."

Yoori exploded in laughter and faced him in interest. Her long black hair, which was curled today, moved over her white dress. "How?"

"I was eight and my older brother was trying to jumpstart my training into the Underworld. He told me that when he becomes the King of the 3rd layer, he wants to make sure I become the King of the 1st layer as well." He laughed. "He had started his Underworld training already, so he was able to expertly climb that tree. I was jealous and wanted to climb it too. I made it about halfway up before I lost my footing and fell."

Yoori had to smile. Despite what ended up happening with Ho Young, it was still nice to hear this endearing story from Tae Hyun's childhood. "I assume you were out of commission for a while?"

He confirmed with a chuckle. "But when my leg healed, my father brought us back and made me climb the tree. He told me that we are not defined by how far we've fallen, but how far we rise after we fall from grace."

Yoori nodded. She liked that saying. It was fitting for every aspect of life, not just the Underworld. "Did you successfully climb it?"

Pride lit up his face. "Of course."

Yoori laughed before something on the road arrested her attention. Her eyes rounded in vigilance.

"Tae Hyun," she prompted uncertainly. "What is that on the road?"

Yoori squinted her eyes. Under the blinding rays of the sun, this creature looked like a foggy hallucination rather than a true vision. When she determined that her eyes were not playing tricks on her, bitterness began to taint her mood.

"Is that a *duck*?"

Tae Hyun squinted his eyes as well. He, too, was inclined to believe it was simply a hallucination. As they drove closer, it was clear that there was indeed a chubby white duck crossing the road.

"Yeah," he confirmed, worry coating his voice. "I'll slow down."

"Speed up."

Tae Hyun looked like he was about to have an aneurysm. He eyed her in disbelief. "What?"

"Scare it," she stated unfeelingly. Her eyes were still on the duck and, if it was even possible, she was looking more and more serious by the second.

"What the hell?" he uttered, looking at her like she was a wacko. Although he was aware of Yoori's violent history with ducks, he clearly did not anticipate her animosity to go this far.

"Scare it so it poops itself," she repeated, thinking he didn't hear her. Her eyes were still on the duck, which was walking very slowly across the road. Despite how long it had been since a duck fucked her over, Yoori was still feeling resentful. Life had been hard on her. Scaring the shit out of a duck would make her day.

"What the fuck?" he breathed out, utterly outraged. "I bring you on a nice ride down memory lane and you want to fuck it up by having me scare the shit out of an innocent duck?"

Yoori blushed as Tae Hyun carefully maneuvered the car, allowing the duck safe passage on the road. It didn't even flinch when they drove past it.

"Why do you like ducks so much?" she asked, watching sourly as the duck finished waddling across the road without a care in the world. It disappeared into the woods, its poop still intact.

Tae Hyun chuckled disbelievingly. "Apart from the fact that they're cute?"

"Is it just to spite me?" she asked half-jokingly, slowly feeling less agitated now that the duck was gone.

Laughter issued from Tae Hyun. He warmly pointed at the lake they were driving past. It illumed with an array of orange, purple, and pink colors from the setting sun. There were ducks swimming peacefully upon the lake, enjoying life since Yoori was nowhere near them.

"My first pet duck lived there."

Yoori burst out laughing. "No!"

She was amazed with this newfound discovery. *This* was why the King of Serpents was such an advocate of ducks—because he actually raised one.

"I loved it," he went on reminiscently. "When I was nine, I would always come out to this portion of the estate with my father to feed it. My father warned me not to get too attached to it because it would leave me. He said that was the fate of all Underworld Kings: we would outlive everything we loved."

"Your father was an optimistic one, wasn't he?" Yoori remarked carefully. It was astonishing to her the lengths the former King of Serpents would go to in order to educate his youngest son on the rules of life.

"He would teach me all the rules, but he was always the exception to every rule." Reverence teemed in Tae Hyun's voice when speaking about his father. "Growing up, there was no one I wanted to emulate more. He *literally* had everything. He had the throne, he had the woman he loved, and he had a family he cherished. The Underworld gave him everything he wanted in life and no one dared to question his status as a King." He regarded her briefly.

"Everyone tells me that I have the potential to be the greatest King who has ever lived, but every time someone tells me that, all I can think about is my father. *He* is the King who truly had everything. He had everything and was able to keep it all until the day he died." He shrugged, his voice becoming more regretful. "I wish I was smart enough to ask him how he got all of that. I imagine that would've been the last thing he would've taught me before he was taken from us so abruptly."

Tae Hyun smiled to himself. He changed the subject without notice and pointed at the field of green grass they were nearing.

"This was where I tried to run away from home."

"*What?*" Yoori practically shouted. She craned to look at the field. All these stories were making a captive audience out of her. "Why?"

"I was ten. It was hours before I was supposed to start my Underworld training," he explained. "I remember, at the last minute, I became so afraid. I did not want to go. I did not want to leave my family."

"How far did you get?"

"To this field." Tae Hyun shook his head with amusement. "By the time I reached this field, my father had caught up to me and brought me home." He tilted his head bitterly. "I learned then that it's impossible to run away from this world. It will always catch up to you."

He jutted his chin at the stone driveway up ahead. They were still far from it, but Yoori could see from the distance, and from the iron gates, that it was the driveway of the estate.

"That was where my father was killed."

Yoori felt her blood run cold.

Tae Hyun looked at her. "You think my father died somewhere else?"

She could barely find her voice. Yoori had always thought Tae Hyun's father died while traveling somewhere. She never imagined that Ji Hoon would kill him on such sacred ground.

"Ji Hoon . . . Ji Hoon killed him here?"

Tae Hyun nodded. Though his voice was calm, Yoori could feel the fury spew out of him. "Right in front of my mother and sister."

He pointed at a well on the right side of the road. It was the only thing present on that field of grass.

"We have an underground cellar there," he explained while she kept her eyes on the well. It became smaller as they drove past it. "That's where we keep our enemies and do our killings. My first Skulls kill was down there."

"How many did you kill?" she asked, craning her neck to keep the view of the well in sight.

"Thirty."

Yoori regarded Tae Hyun with incredulous eyes. "You killed all thirty by yourself?"

"Yes," he confirmed quietly, returning his solemn eyes to the road.

It was then that she realized why Tae Hyun was sharing so many of his memories with her. He wasn't being nostalgic; he was keeping his promise to her. He wanted to show her every part of him: the good, the bad, and the inhumane side. This was not only a trip down memory lane; it was also a trip down Tae Hyun's journey into becoming a King in the Underworld.

Yoori gazed at his profile in a new light.

She appreciated that he was keeping his word. She could see that it was not easy for him to open up in this manner, especially with her. It would be more beneficial for him to only reveal glimpses of his world to her so there would be a lesser chance of scrutiny on her part. He was doing something out of character—something vulnerable—and she respected that immensely.

Yoori kept quiet and listened as he shared the darkest parts of himself with her.

"My brother and my Cobras wanted to help, but I wouldn't let them. I told them that this was my kill. Before I claimed their heads, I told them that in the future, I would claim Ji Hoon's head as well."

Before giving her a chance to digest his last statement, Tae Hyun pointed at a mausoleum in the far distance. It looked like a small manor rather than a tomb. It was built with white stone and had two imposing pillars flanking either side of it. It couldn't have looked more regal.

"That is where my family is buried."

"Your father and mother?" Yoori asked quietly. She was barely blinking as she stared at it.

"My father, my mother, my brother, uncles, aunts, grandparents, cousins . . . all the Serpents Royals are there." He smiled at her when she whirled back to him. "It is where I will reside when death knocks on my door."

"You will outlive the rest of us," she reminded amiably. The thought of him dying pained her. She would not allow such a thought to ruin their day. Tae Hyun would never die if she could help it. "If you remain a God, you will always outlive your duck."

Tae Hyun chuckled, reaching out to hold her hand. "You're suddenly a duck now?"

Yoori laughed, leaning back in her seat. Intertwining their fingers, she allowed herself to enjoy the feel of his hand on hers. Even though driving down this road brought back good and bad memories, she was thankful she was there to experience it with Tae Hyun. It was a treat to learn about his past, to understand how he became the revered King of Serpents. At this thought, Yoori was suddenly reminded of how Soo Jin became the Queen of the

Underworld. What transpired with Jung Min at Ju Won's estate replayed in her mind.

"Did you know that Jung Min 'kidnapped' me to remind me that I'm meant to be a God?" she asked, shifting uncomfortably whenever she was reminded of Jung Min and the rest of the Advisors. The remembrance of them always brought back the unpleasant memory of the Underworld and all the obstacles that stood in the way of her relationship with Tae Hyun.

"Kang Min told me that Jung Min had kidnapped you," Tae Hyun said tightly. It was clear he was not happy when he heard this. "But I did not know what it was about."

"He sealed me in the coffin that they trained Soo Jin in."

Tae Hyun eyed her incredulously. Even he was stunned by this revelation. "They made her sleep in a coffin every night?"

"On the nights she failed as a God, they would have her sleep in the coffin with the amputated body parts of the ones she killed. They wanted to remind her of her fate. Every night she was successful as a God, she would get to sleep on the throne." Yoori shrugged, still feeling disgusted with their method of training the revered Underworld Queen. "I guess they thought they were being poetic."

"What else did he say to you?" Tae Hyun asked shrewdly. He knew an Advisor would never "kidnap" someone just to throw them into a coffin.

"He shared with me how a God rises back to power from their fall."

Yoori glanced at Tae Hyun. She wondered if he knew the answer to this. She decided to find out.

"How does a God rise from their fall?"

"You step on the corpse of the one who brought you down," he responded like it was the most obvious answer. A smile crossed his lips when she looked at him in surprise that he knew this rule as well. "My grandfather told me," he provided. "It is one of the first things a Royal learns."

Silence claimed Yoori. She breathed tersely, unknowingly tightening her hold on his hand. Almost inaudibly, she said something she knew he wouldn't want her to voice.

"I would," she started slowly, feeling like she was pushing a big rock off her chest, "understand if you've considered it."

He had a lot to lose. It would be foolish of him to have never considered getting rid of her.

Tae Hyun kept his eyes on the road. Nonchalantly, he said, "Have you considered it?"

"I could never beat you," she replied lightheartedly.

"What if you could?" he persisted, his tone still light with curiosity.

"I could never kill you." She smiled to herself. "Who else would entertain me if you're gone?"

Despite her desire to lighten the mood, she still couldn't get over what Jung Min said. She did not fear for herself, but for Tae Hyun. His fall from grace was not a merciful one and she feared his demise would be worse. Yoori did not want that grim future for him. He deserved to live a long and happy life. He should never die before his time.

"Are you a fallen God right now?" she asked quietly.

"Perhaps I am," he murmured, tightening his hold on her hand. "But the rest of this world will never know it. To them, I am a God on the edge of falling, but I will never let them know that I have fallen. I will continue to rule over them and I will continue to initiate new members into my gang because that is what a God in power does. He keeps expanding his reach, his authority over this world." He smirked. "That is a secret that my father taught me. Appearance is everything. If I keep acting like an untouchable God, then perhaps they will believe it."

"I am the only thing that doesn't belong in this lie," Yoori supplied, knowing her place in his life. She was a liability, not an asset.

Tae Hyun kissed her hand, smiling at her with assurance. "If I am a God who will outlive my pet duck, then you will be the God who eats it when it dies." He looked at her with nothing but adoration in his eyes. "We are perfect together as fallen Gods. The only thing the Underworld needs to believe is that we are perfect together as *untouchable* Gods."

Interest filled her at his cryptic words. "How do we show that?"

"Tonight will mark the first night," he said with confidence. "Once you see this initiation, your status will be set."

Yoori still did not follow along. "What status will that be?"

He grinned softly and before he could answer, they arrived at the iron gates of the estate.

Yoori's eyes expanded at the beauty before her. A large mansion that could easily be a replica of the United States' White House came before her eyes. It was pure white with long pillars at the face of the entrance. There was a massive water fountain shooting dancing water into the sky while a vast acre of green grass enclosed its surroundings. It was so large that she was sure they could fit hundreds of people in the estate and still have room to spare.

As they drove up the stone driveway, her eyes enlarged even more when she saw hundreds of Serpents standing there, waiting for Tae Hyun's much anticipated arrival. They were all dressed in black business suits and looked like they could run a nation if they wanted to.

Yoori felt surreal that she was finally at the Serpents' estate. She felt even more surreal at the actions of those around her when Tae Hyun stepped out of the car. One second, the Serpents were all standing. Yet, as soon as Tae

Hyun's feet hit the pavement, they all fell on one knee and kneeled before him with the utmost reverence.

For the first time, Yoori saw the King behind the man she had fallen for.

Not even fazed by this colossal exhibition of respect, Tae Hyun casually came to her side of the car and opened the door. He smiled while he held his hand out to her.

"Choi Yoori," he began, voicing one of the first things he said to her during their first meeting. Only now, it was a completely true statement. After this night, she would truly be initiated into his world.

"Welcome to *my* world."

"You may have been born human..."

09: The Sealed Kingdom

Yoori could scarcely keep the smile solidified on her face when she stepped out of the car. She did her best to ignore the hundreds upon hundreds of Serpents, all of whom were still kneeling before them. She was grateful she chose to wear a nice white dress today. It would have been an awkward sight if she were in her usual jeans and tank top attire.

When Tae Hyun gave her a reassuring smile and interlaced his fingers with hers, Yoori returned the smile. It was comforting to know that although he was a King to everyone else, he was still her Tae Hyun.

She drew in a deep breath and allowed Tae Hyun to lead the way as they strolled past the kneeling Serpents. They climbed the eight steps leading up to the estate and moved through the enormous mansion. Yoori looked around, stunned to find that there were more Serpents here. She felt like a formidable tide when she was with Tae Hyun. Everywhere they neared, Serpents would kneel before him. It was mesmerizing and euphoric. They weren't kneeling for her, but she felt powerful all the same. She could get used to this.

"Yoori," Hae Jin greeted once they walked into the living room that housed a white grand piano and a brightly lit chandelier. Hae Jin stood up from a white leather sofa and approached Yoori and Tae Hyun. She was wearing a black sleeveless turtleneck and a black pencil skirt. Her smile was warm when she opened her arms to Yoori. "So great to see you here. You look beautiful!"

"Thank you, so do you!" Yoori exclaimed, giving Hae Jin a big hug.

"Hey bosses," said two voices from behind Hae Jin.

Kang Min and Jae Won followed Hae Jin off the sofa. They, too, wore black business suits. She had never seen them look so professional.

"Hey guys," Yoori greeted, embracing Kang Min and then Jae Won.

"Always great to see the two of you together," Jae Won said to them when he pulled away from the hug. He imparted a slight bow to Tae Hyun as his greeting.

"You two really look like the King and Queen of the Underworld," remarked Hae Jin as she gifted Tae Hyun with a big hug.

Kang Min leaned closer to Hae Jin when she pulled away from the hug. "I think that's the idea, Hae Jin," he whispered with a grin.

Yoori looked at them strangely. It occurred to her that they were not in the least bit surprised that she was on "hallowed" ground. After all the talk about outsiders being prohibited from witnessing the Serpents' initiation, it baffled her that they were behaving so nonchalantly around her.

"You guys knew I was coming?" Yoori ventured, bewilderment bubbling in her voice. It was the only plausible explanation for their casual behavior.

"Oppa told us a few days ago that he planned on bringing you here for the initiation," Hae Jin confirmed jubilantly. She gave a sly shrug, the warmth mounting in her eyes. "We've known for a while."

Yoori was gobsmacked. She peered at Tae Hyun with inquisitive eyes. She assumed his decision to bring her to the second estate was a spur of the moment thing. It astonished her that he had *planned* to bring her to the initiation all along.

Tae Hyun favored her with a coy smile before freeing his hand from hers. He purposely avoided addressing her surprised expression.

"I have to go prepare for the initiation," he announced. He spared a glance between Hae Jin and the brothers before returning his focus to Yoori. "Will you be okay with these fools for the time being?"

"Hey," all three piped up, pouting in bitterness.

The mischievous girl in Yoori laughed quietly. It was incredibly amusing to watch Tae Hyun pick on other people. She smiled, putting aside the shock of discovering that Tae Hyun had planned to bring her here all along. Whatever sparked his decision, she was glad for it. She playfully pushed him away to reassure him she would be fine. "Go. I'll be fine."

He nodded before turning to the others. "Keep her entertained until I'm done."

All three voiced their confirmation. Satisfied, Tae Hyun bestowed one last parting smile to Yoori before turning on his heels. When he moved away, about ten Serpents followed after him. Yoori's eyes continued to shadow them until Tae Hyun made a turn into another corridor and disappeared into the eastern wing.

She briefly wondered what he had to do to prepare for the initiation.

"Come on, Yoori," called Hae Jin, drawing Yoori out from her reverie. She and the brothers motioned for Yoori to follow them. "Let's get you situated for the initiation."

Yoori stole a final glance at the corridor Tae Hyun had disappeared into before she followed them into another part of the estate. They climbed up a flight of stairs that eventually led to the roof of the mansion.

Yoori folded her arms after she reached the roof. The billowing wind brought forth cold air that made goose bumps materialize on her body. Thankfully, the wind died down the further she walked onto the rooftop.

Her eyes traveled the length of the massive roof. She noticed about fifty people were already on the rooftop. They stood in small crowds, quietly conversing with one another while facing the estate gardens. From above, she could see that there were various people downstairs on the different balconies hanging from the mansion. She went to the edge of the roof in curiosity. She was floored upon finding that there were hundreds more Serpents on this part of the estate. Her eyes wandered over the world below her. Some of the well-dressed Serpents were perched on the balconies' railings, some sat on the Spanish-like stairs that led into the garden, some stood on the landing of the stairs, and many leaned against the estate walls.

Then, at the center of the roof, she noticed a throne that resembled the one she saw at Ju Won's mansion. It was also made out of pure gold and it looked magnificent. The only difference was that on the armrests of this throne, there were engravings of serpents with their heads raised up. The heads of the serpents faced into the gardens, looking like guardians for the initiation to come.

"You can sit here, Yoori," said Hae Jin, tugging Yoori toward the throne.

Yoori smiled nervously, reluctant to obey. She was promptly reminded of what happened when Jung Min kidnapped her and showed her the golden throne at Ju Won's estate. She fell so in love with the throne—so in love with the idea of power—that if she hadn't heard Tae Hyun's name, she would've been lost to the world. She eyed the throne before her warily. She did not want to sit on that throne; she did not want to entice herself with a power she should never seek.

"I'm okay," she said briskly, no longer wanting to look at it.

Hae Jin displayed the "don't-be-shy" look. "This throne was brought out specifically for you," she insisted, completely oblivious to the conflict raging inside Yoori. "You should sit."

"That's Tae Hyun's seat," Yoori desperately uttered. She stared at the throne like a recovering alcoholic would at a bottle of liquor. The last thing she wanted was to fall to temptation; the last thing she wanted was for the monster inside her to come out.

"He's not coming up here," supplied Kang Min, standing behind the throne with Jae Won to the left of him. He beckoned for her to come forward. "Tonight, this is your seat."

"Come again?" Yoori asked, perplexed.

Jae Won lightly rolled his eyes at what he perceived as a naïve question. "Come on, boss," he coaxed with a patient smile. "This is your seat. Just sit."

Yoori's heart hammered while she looked between Hae Jin and the brothers. They were being incredibly insistent, and she did not want to appear problematic. Her experience here would wind up being unpleasant if she had to explain to them *why* she feared the throne so much. It was better to acquiesce and behave normally. When Tae Hyun made his appearance up here, then she would return his throne to him. It was that simple.

Her decision set, she nodded and approached the throne.

When she sat down, Yoori felt all eyes rest on her. It happened very subtly. As she moved her fingers over the serpent armrest, doing her best to not allow the euphoria to overtake her, she could see everyone turning slightly to glance in her direction. They did not say anything and they did not stare for long, but the action caused her to feel timid all the same. She was used to hiding in the shadows of the Underworld to protect her identity. The fact that she was sitting on a throne, on a roof no less, amidst several hundred Serpents made her edgy. It felt strange to be on display like this, like she was a new creature to this secret world.

Yoori took in a lungful of breath and looked ahead to disregard the apprehensiveness she felt.

The jaw dropping sight before her nearly caused her to gasp out loud.

When she initially glimpsed over the garden, she had no idea how big it actually was, and how mythical it looked. She looked past the expanse of the garden and moved her eyes further out into the horizon. There, she could see that a massive maze sat in the center of the enormous green land. It stood approximately eight feet in height, was covered in green ivies, and was large enough to resemble an arena. In the center of this grand labyrinth was a beautiful white stone fountain that had carvings of three serpents with water sprouting out of their mouths. White column-like lampposts surrounded the circular maze, making it appear as if it was a garden fit for the Gods of Olympus.

"This is where he trains them," Hae Jin whispered, following Yoori's mesmerized gaze.

Yoori turned to Hae Jin, wonder having yet to dissipate from her awestruck eyes. "Who?"

"All the new recruits," Hae Jin clarified, standing to the right of her while the brothers stood to the left. "After they are initiated, my brother spends the first month of training here, teaching them the ways of the Underworld and how to survive in it."

"Where is he?" Yoori asked, sobering up at the mention of Tae Hyun.

"Commencing the initiation," answered Kang Min.

She turned to Kang Min as a puff of wind swam across the roof. "Will he come up soon?"

He shook his head, his smile light. "No."

Yoori swallowed awkwardly. The only reason why she agreed to sit on the throne was because she thought it was temporary and that Tae Hyun would appear soon. She was unsettled to learn that this wasn't the case. "Why is this throne here then?" she asked faintly. "I could've sat in a regular chair."

Jae Won chuckled, taking a few steps ahead to sit at the edge of the roof. "Maybe he wants you to get comfortable," he said, sitting down. "It will be a little while before we can begin."

"When are we starting?" she asked, watching as Hae Jin and Kang Min followed suit and moved forward to sit on the edge of the roof beside Jae Won.

All around her, Yoori noticed that the rest of the Serpents moved forward to sit on the edge as well. She knitted her brows together. It felt odd to watch so many well-dressed people sit so casually on the floor. Did this mean the initiation was starting?

"It'll start soon," assured Kang Min. "Until then, just relax."

Yoori expelled a tiny sigh before deciding that enough was enough. The throne may have been brought out for her, but that didn't mean she had to sit on it the entire time. Without warning, she surged off the throne and proceeded to sit on the foundation of the roof with Hae Jin and the brothers.

"You're supposed to sit on the throne, boss," said an amused Jae Won when Yoori moved to sit between him and Kang Min.

"I want to sit down here with you guys," Yoori said petulantly, earning chuckles from them.

With their laughter as consent for her to remain where she was, Yoori took another look around. This time, she felt more comfortable sight-seeing from where she sat. While on the throne, she felt like a Queen overseeing her people. From the ground, she felt like a regular girl appreciating the new world around her.

Most of the other Serpents sat on the roof now, basking under the finalities of the sunset's rays as they continued to have muted conversations with one another. Below, Yoori could see that some Serpents sat on the lawn while many others sat on the mansion's long set of stairs. There was an air of anticipatory energy. It felt like she was waiting at a concert hall for a show to start; like they were all waiting for something incredibly spectacular to happen.

Yoori gazed around again. The scene ahead continued to leave her in awe. It was absolutely gorgeous.

"I can't believe he actually brought me here," Yoori whispered, enjoying the feel of the breeze on the roof. She looked at Hae Jin and the brothers when a curious thought occupied her mind. "Do you guys know how the initiation into other gangs work?"

"Vaguely," shared Kang Min.

Her interest was piqued. "Yeah?"

They nodded before Hae Jin, who was sitting to the right of Kang Min, said, "You want to see a footage of the Skulls' initiation while you wait?"

Yoori was floored by this suggestion. How was it possible that there was a video recording of an initiation when the bylaws of this world prohibited it? "I thought the Underworld is all about confidentiality?"

Hae Jin shrugged her apathy. "No one's identity is revealed. Plus, I think it was Ji Hoon who let this video out. Maybe to show new recruits how lethal his gang is so they would think twice about joining other gangs. Anyway, do you want to see?"

Yoori was too excited to refuse. She was thunderstruck by the proposition, but she wasn't abhorred by it. Anything that would give her more insight into how this secret society operated, she would gladly accept. "I want to see."

Hae Jin got up to retrieve her smart tablet from underneath the throne.

Jae Won leaned forward to bequeath Hae Jin with a scrutinizing look. "Seriously? You hid your tablet under the throne?"

Hae Jin was unapologetic when she returned to the group and handed the tablet to Yoori. "I get bored waiting!"

Yoori grabbed the tablet and turned it on. A video file was already open and ready to be played. As Yoori tapped her finger on the "Play" icon, the four of them moved closer together and leaned in to watch.

"How does the Skulls' initiation work?" Yoori asked when the video showed a reel of approximately fifty men fighting one another in a colossal pit.

"They bring in fifty at a time," said Hae Jin, "but only thirty-six will come out alive."

Yoori watched the men battle one another with knives, stabbing one another without mercy. The very sight of this struck fear inside her. It was so gruesome and barbaric. To her surprise, she suddenly felt grateful to be initiated by the Advisors. If she was in that pit, she doubted she would ever make it out alive.

"What happens if more than thirty-six survive the five-minute initiation?" asked Yoori a few moments later.

"The King of Skulls will join the fight at the last minute and he will kill enough to equate to thirty-six," said Hae Jin. Right on cue, another figure jumped into the screen, going after the rest of the men in the pit. Even though the film was dark and Yoori could not make out his face, she knew it was Ji Hoon.

"Why thirty-six?" Yoori asked, suspecting a symbolic reason for this specific number.

"That was the number of recruits the first King of Skulls initiated when he formed the Skulls. Rumor has it, the Skulls' estate is built upon the bones of the initiates who did not make it past the five-minute initiation, hence the gang's chosen name."

Yoori's insides gave a horrified jolt. The thought of building a home over the corpses of those who didn't make it into the gang disturbed her immensely.

"What is the meaning behind that type of initiation?" Yoori inquired, watching as Ji Hoon's silhouette climbed out of the ditch.

In the pit, thirty-six men started cheering. They were clearly celebrating their successful initiation into the gang now that the other fourteen initiates had been slaughtered.

"The Skulls family heavily values the concept of survival of the fittest and alliances," Hae Jin explained like she was the Underworld's personal historian. "They believe that only a bond formed between people on the brink of death will form a lasting brotherhood. So they simulate a war zone. One where strangers will have to put their trust in one another, one where they will work to betray others, and one where only the most formidable alliances will survive. They believe that only people who rise to power and lose their souls together will show loyalty until the end."

Yoori recalled Ji Hoon's participation in the pit. "What does it mean when the King joins the pit during the last minute?"

"To show them that if they cannot properly obey an order, then their King will choose their fates for them. The King will not discriminate against alliances. He will kill according to his mood, according to his whim. To the Skulls initiates, it is preferable to do your own killing. At least they get to personally decide who dies as opposed to leaving it up to fate."

Even though this was disturbing, it was also highly fascinating to Yoori. She wanted to learn more. She switched off the tablet before looking between the brothers.

"What about the Scorpions?" she asked keenly.

"The Scorpions' initiation is not as straightforward as the Skulls' initiation," answered Jae Won. "It takes place on a more . . . complex level."

"How so?"

"There was a maximum of five people for every initiation," explained Kang Min, attracting Yoori's attention. His eyes became reminiscent when talking about his old gang. "There were five levels, five obstacles. In the first minute, the initiates had to make it out of a locked room with a tiger."

Yoori's eyes enlarged in shock. This was the complete opposite of the video she just saw. "An . . . An actual tiger?" she stuttered.

Kang Min nodded.

107

Yoori was stupefied at the grandeur of this initiation. "Why a tiger?"

"To represent the Siberian Tigers," Jae Won responded before enlightening her further. "Years ago, they were the fourth biggest gang in the Underworld. If the initiates made it out, then in the second level, they were locked in a room with six rival gang members. They had to kill all six and bring their skulls to the next level within one minute. In the third level, they were blindfolded and thrown into a pool filled with serpents. There was always one poisonous snake so they had to be weary of not getting bit by it. If they survived that, they were buried in a coffin with scorpions when they reached the fourth level. In that one minute, they had to ensure that all the scorpions were still alive. In the final round, they had to survive one minute with the Royal family. After that, they would be fully initiated."

Yoori was flabbergasted at the complexity of the Scorpions' initiation. "Why were there so many different levels?"

"The last four levels were to symbolize each gang," Kang Min explained. "The Siberian tiger was there to warm them up for the next four minutes."

"That is a fucked up warm up," Yoori couldn't help but breathe out.

Kang Min smirked in concurrence. "No kidding."

"Could they kill the tiger?"

"They could try, but in that room, there were no weapons."

Yoori blew out an uncomfortable breath. "They basically spent that minute running around?"

"They either ran or died."

"Did a lot die?"

"Oh yeah," confirmed Jae Won. "They didn't even make it to the next level."

Yoori grimaced before moving on with the conversation. "What about the next levels?"

"Essentially the first three levels were to symbolize your cunningness and strength over rival gangs. In life, they will always be the ones standing in the way of your greatness in the Underworld." Jae Won sighed, becoming nostalgic of his past. "The fourth level was where the pace changed. Instead of running or fighting, each of the initiates were locked in a coffin with about twenty scorpions. Even if you got stung or were in pain, the most important thing was to keep all the scorpions alive. It was supposed to represent your loyalty to your gang, that the well-being of the whole gang will supersede yours."

Yoori had to admit that she liked that bit. There was great meaning behind that level.

"And the final level?" she prompted, surprised that she was becoming prideful of the way her—or Soo Jin's—gang worked. It did not feel as barbaric as the Skulls' initiation. If anything, it felt incredibly meaningful.

"If you were still alive, stepping out of the coffin was supposed to symbolize your rebirth and your first sight should only be of your Gods," shared Kang Min. "The Royal family was always at the end. They represented the keys to your new Kingdom, your new family. They did not give access to their Kingdom to just anyone, and this one minute was considered the hardest minute to endure."

Jae Won smiled. Regardless of how difficult this final level was, it was evident he had a lot of pride that he was one of the few who successfully endured it. "When we were initiated, the Royal family consisted of our boss, her brother, and her father."

"'The Holy Trinity' as we called them," provided Kang Min. Warmth infiltrated his voice at the recollection of the Royal Scorpion family.

Jae Won shook his head briefly, clearly recalling his own initiation. "They were vicious, unforgiving."

"You two were initiated at age eight and ten?" Yoori asked to clarify.

They nodded as their confirmation.

She canted her head as a breeze ruffled over the roof. "How did you make it out?"

They smiled as Jae Won said, "Our boss was with us the entire way until the last level."

Yoori furrowed her brows. "What do you mean?"

"The Scorpions family believed in building a family amongst the soldiers. When Kang Min and I were initiated, the 'God' who recruited us had to watch over us."

Yoori's eyes widened at the implication. "An Soo Jin was with you throughout every level?"

Jae Won nodded. "If you were to be initiated during the years where the Scorpions were active, a member of the Royal family had to be with you. It was a symbol of their loyalty to you, their promise to you that if you stayed by their side, they would stay with you until the bitter end. The only time they left you was at the final level. At the final level, the Royal family would initiate you themselves." Jae Won let out a groan as he rubbed the back of his neck. "That was the hardest level because the Royal family did not show pity in that one minute. Most begged for an out in the first thirty seconds."

The thought of an eight and ten-year-old surviving against such revered Royals baffled Yoori. "How did you two survive against An Soo Jin, her brother, and father?"

"Her brother and father beat us for the first twenty seconds, and after that, they gave our boss the reigns. She did not show mercy. It felt like it was an eternity before that level was up."

"From what I've heard," launched Kang Min, "the final stage of the initiation used to be worse. There was a point in time where there was one King and his five sons — the five Princes. We heard a lot of initiates died during that era and few made it through. The gang was going through an extinction when one King finally ruled that the maximum number of any Royals in the final level was three — 'The Holy Trinity.'"

Yoori was utterly captivated. It felt like she was listening to a Greek mythology of sorts. Everything sounded so unbelievable, so mythical. She faced Hae Jin, eager to find out what secrets laid within the Serpents' most sacred day.

"Which initiation does the Serpents' most closely resemble?"

"You will have to see to find out," answered Hae Jin while the colors of the sunset became more vibrant. She looked ahead and smiled. "Sit on the throne, Yoori. It's starting now."

Yoori widened her eyes. She looked around and noticed that everyone around her had grown silent. In a daze, she did as Hae Jin ordered and went back to sit on the throne. Then, she simply watched the initiation unfold before her very eyes. Yoori was fascinated by the inner workings of the Skulls and Scorpions' initiation. She could not wait to witness firsthand how the Serpents' initiation worked.

As if on cue, three white semi-trucks drove onto the massive lawn in a synchronized order. The trucks stopped side by side, sitting there for a few moments while allowing the silence to devour them. Above, the setting sun cast its colorful rays unto the world below, heightening the crowd's anticipation.

Yoori watched unblinkingly, wondering what was in those trucks. Memories of the other initiations played in her mind, churning her already curious thoughts. Were there Siberian tigers in there? Serpents? Skulls? Or perhaps coffins? The answer to her questions came when the doors to the truck lifted open like a veil.

Yoori was stunned when, instead of all the things she imagined, men and women started stepping out of the three trucks. She craned her neck in an attempt to get a better view of the people filing out of the trucks. She endeavored to count how many there were, but stopped when she could no longer make them out from one another. There were so many people. If she could guess, she would say well over a hundred at best. Despite the alarming amount of people, what shocked her most was the uniformity of their unkempt appearances. They were all wearing white and as pure as this color was, their clothes were anything but unsullied. Yoori breathed uneasily, running her eyes over their torn clothes, bloodshot eyes, and bloodied appearances. All looked like they had been to hell and back.

She was flummoxed. Did they already have their initiations in that truck?

Yoori didn't hesitate to voice her thoughts out loud. "Did they already have their five-minute initiation?"

Hae Jin shook her head, her expression unfazed at the world below. "No. They were being prepped for the initiation."

The casualness of Hae Jin's answer did not alleviate the shock Yoori experienced. If anything, it only served to exacerbate it. If this was what they looked like after a 'prep,' what were they in for when the actual initiation commenced?

"How long do the preps last?" Yoori asked thoughtlessly, unable to tear her gaze from the initiates below. She could not believe how fucked up they all looked.

"Five weeks."

Yoori's eyes nearly bulged from her sockets. She finally tore her focus from the world below to stare at Hae Jin. "Five weeks to prepare for a five-minute initiation?"

"Five weeks is not nearly enough to train them for what's coming," Kang Min answered for Hae Jin. His unfazed eyes maintained their focus on the initiates, all of whom were staring at all the active Serpents in trepidation. They were clearly wondering what was in store for them and wondering why they had such a big audience. "They are actually very lucky to even get that much. It is said that the former King of Serpents did not give them any grace period to prepare. Boss was the one who jumpstarted this new tradition — among some other changes to the Serpents' initiation." Kang Min laughed, clearly amused with the apprehensive faces of the initiates. "He said that he did not just want the best — he wanted to *create* the best. He wanted to give them the best chance of survival before they started their initiation."

The Serpents initiates continued to loiter around the area near the trucks, looking around anxiously. Then, several of their eyes landed on Yoori. A sense of awe seized them when they realized that she was sitting on a throne. They elbowed one another, subtly telling one another about her. Soon, nearly all the initiates were staring up at her, curiosity teeming in their eyes.

Yoori did not fault their interest. In a sea of Serpents dressed in black outfits, she was the only one who stood out with her white dress. More importantly, with the rest of the Serpents sitting on the foundation of the roof, the throne elevated her above them. In this picture, she did not look like a simple spectator; she looked like a Queen. As much as she hated to admit it, it felt nice to have them stare up at her like she was a God. The throne made her feel like one, and she enjoyed that feeling very much.

Their marvel of her was interrupted when the three Serpents who drove the trucks started screaming for them to move along. Yoori watched the three active Serpents lead the initiates from the lawn onto the white stone foundation that acted as a pathway to the maze. It was mesmerizing to watch them march in synchronization, approaching the maze like it was a portal into another reality.

She pressed her back against the cushion of the throne and relaxed, for she knew this was going to be an entertaining show.

Two of the active Serpents advanced ahead of the group, one holding a key to a door. They marched toward the only opening of the labyrinth. When they passed the opening, the Serpent stuck his key into the ivy wall and instantly, a hidden door opened for them, granting them entry into the deeper parts of the maze. The active Serpent opened several more ivy-covered doors leading to the epicenter of the maze where the fountain laid.

The initiates followed them in, observing the elaborate maze with marvel in their eyes. Once they were all in, they eventually surrounded the water fountain. The three active Serpents said nothing and journeyed out of the ivy-covered edifice, locking each door on their way out. Once they sealed the last door, the Serpents stood in front of the maze, their hands folded in front of them while they allowed silence to befall the garden.

Yoori became more and more astounded by the grandeur of what was unfolding before her.

"What are they doing now?" Yoori asked in a low voice.

Above, the setting sun disappeared, bringing forth an infantile darkness that began to canvass the world beneath.

"One of them has to get out of that maze," answered Jae Won. Yoori could only see the back of his head, but based on his tone of voice, she could sense his anticipation.

She did not share his excitement. If anything, it felt dull. "Not all of them?" she clarified.

"Only one," confirmed Jae Won, his voice maintaining the same air of anticipation. "After that, they are all initiated."

Yoori laughed, dumbfounded that the initiation was that easy. After seeing them look so downtrodden, she had anticipated a more epic event. Simply having one of them make it out of the labyrinth felt extremely anticlimactic. Perhaps beating them before their initiation into the maze was the Serpents' way of disorienting them? "Really?"

She stopped laughing when the initiates pulled white blindfolds out of their pockets and secured them across their eyes. Her face then blanched when she saw thirty shadows emerge out of the various areas of the lawn. They approached the initiation ground from all different circular points like ghosts in the night. When they neared the massive infrastructure, they used footholds along the wall as props and soared onto the top of the ivy-covered maze.

"How is that not falling apart?" Yoori breathed out.

"The ivy is there for show," answered Hae Jin. "The maze is actually built from bricks. It was created to withstand the weight of hundreds of people."

Yoori watched in wonder as all the shadow figures moved through the entirety of the maze, nearly eclipsing everything but the center, which was still pure with white. They stood on all regions of the maze, watching down on the initiates like guardians. Despite appearances, Yoori knew their primary purpose was not to guard the initiates' safety, but to guard the exit. Leaving the maze in five minutes would not be an easy task, especially when these initiates were not even aware of the Serpents in their midst.

"What are they supposed to be?" asked Yoori, realizing quickly that the initiates resembled trapped mice. They did not know that there were predators ready to feast on them, and they would not expect the ambush when it came.

"In this initiation, they are known as the Reapers," enlightened Hae Jin. Pride undulated her voice. "They were all specifically trained by my brother."

"What will they do?"

"Keep them in that center circle."

Silence presided over the entire estate. Everyone watched in anticipatory stillness. Even Yoori, who was once inquisitive with questions, pressed her back against the throne and sat comfortably, feeling like she had been transported into another reality. She had no more questions; all she wanted to do was sit back and witness the commencement of this new world.

As her heart palpitated in eagerness, a gong suddenly went off in the distance, its echoes resounding onto the garden.

In an instant, the maze went from peaceful . . . to anarchic.

The Reapers jumped off the walls and landed on the ground. They advanced toward the initiates and soon after, sounds of bones cracking penetrated the air. The Reapers showed no mercy as mayhem ensued in that microcosm of a world. They attacked and assaulted the initiates with their bare hands like ferocious beasts. Some of the initiates were able to fight back, even while being blindfolded. Some were able to make it out of the center of the maze, despite having to take on the Reapers. However, the majority was in the circle, blindfolded and struggling to survive against the faceless ghosts.

Suddenly, another gong went off in the distance.

"Take off your blindfolds!" the Reapers started screaming, ripping off the blindfolds of the initiates closest to them.

The Reapers were still assaulting them but this time, at least the initiates had a chance. Once all the initiates removed their blindfolds, the fights that ensued thereafter between the Reapers and the now fully aware initiates were astonishing. Though the initiates were less experienced, they were highly skilled. Yoori could see that the five weeks worth of preparation did them a world of good in this otherworldly arena. They were not only able to combat their assailants, but they were also able to climb onto the maze and give the Reapers a run for their money.

Yoori mentally cheered them on, feeling proud for Tae Hyun that he acquired such a talented group of new recruits. They had a lot to learn, but when they obtained mastery, they would be forces to be reckoned with.

Just when Yoori thought these initiates would have an easier time with the initiation now that some were on top of the walls and close to making it out of the arena, nine silhouettes stepped out of the night and approached the maze. They all had chains wrapped around their hands and were approaching the initiation ground with alacrity. It did not take Yoori long to surmise that it was the Cobras.

Shock rammed into Yoori when she realized that *this* was what Tae Hyun needed the Cobras to do today. He needed them to initiate the new members of the Serpents.

Any sense of relief she felt for the initiates vanquished. Their journey out of this maze was far from over, especially if the Cobras had anything to say about it.

Three of the Cobras filed through the opening and marched through the maze while five others rocketed onto the tip of the maze and walked upon it, approaching the clusters of white initiates standing upon the ivy-covered foundation. As a lone Cobra simply stood in front of the opening, the rest did not waste time. They charged for any initiates in their proximity and started wielding their chains. Yoori cringed when sounds of metal lashing out onto flesh punctured the air. Splatters of blood flew toward the sky, rising over the eight-foot walls, and landing back onto the initiates' white clothes.

The Cobras were a tsunami of force that the initiates could not begin to conquer. All they could do was endure the flood and pray for survival. The Cobras charged into the various parts of the maze with such agility that none of the initiates were able to evade them. Yoori felt like she was witnessing the beginning of a massacre.

The seconds felt like an eternity while she watched the initiates attempt their escape. Some fought on top of the maze, some were on the ground, and some ran to the end of the maze. Five initiates looked like they were about to reach the exit when the lone Cobra, Ace, moved a hidden fence over it and sealed the only available exit. When the initiates arrived, they had stupefied looks on their faces. They did not have time to nurse their shock. Like a waiting lion, Ace made his presence known and wielded his chain like it was a lash from hell. None of the five initiates were spared from his lethal weapon. Within moments, they were on the floor, fighting for breath.

Amidst this chaos, something caught Yoori's eyes.

A breath escaped her when she saw him.

She had been so engrossed in this initiation that she forgot to wonder where he was.

Like the commanding King that he was, Tae Hyun finally appeared, earning the stares of the active Serpents. Yoori could hear all the Serpents murmur in excitement. It was clear to her that as electrifying as this initiation had been so far, it was nothing compared to what Tae Hyun's presence would bring. All along, they had been waiting for him. All along, they had been waiting for their King to make his long-awaited appearance.

Yoori watched him from above, feeling spellbound by his presence. It no longer mattered that there were over a hundred people fighting in the arena. The only thing that mattered was Tae Hyun and his nearness. Her eyes raked over his powerful, muscular body. He was shirtless and wore white pants that were similar to the initiates' white attire. He walked barefoot on the white pavement, stalking toward the maze like he owned the world. Although he made no sound, he commanded the attention of everyone on the estate.

His eyes firmly set on the initiation ground, he did not deign to slow down when he reached to grab a kendo stick from the grass beside the walkway.

"Fifteen more seconds," Hae Jin announced to everyone on the roof, consulting the timer on her phone.

Up ahead, Tae Hyun reached the maze. He extended his arm out, pulled himself up using a foothold on the walls, and easily jumped onto the tip of the ivy-covered maze. With the kendo stick in his grasp, he watched over the inhabitants of the labyrinth like a God who had descended to earth.

"Time," Hae Jin whispered.

Instantly, the Reapers and the Cobras ceased their assaults on the initiates. They stared up at Tae Hyun with reverence and fell on one knee before his presence.

Tae Hyun did not even bat an eyelash. He simply motioned his hand and the active Serpents in the maze stood back up. Tae Hyun leisurely sauntered over to the fire post beside him and lit the torch with a lighter from his pocket. Just as he did this, the torches on the remaining ten posts lit up simultaneously, illuming the initiation field that was once enveloped in darkness.

"Their five minutes is starting," Yoori uttered, realizing how extensive the Serpents' initiation was. They did not follow the same procedures as the other Kingdoms' initiations. This sacred ground was their world and in their world, the "five-minute" timeframe worked differently.

The initiates' fight with the Reapers and the Cobras were their warm-ups. Their initiation with Tae Hyun was the one they had all been preparing for.

"Why are there two parts to this initiation?" Yoori whispered in astonishment.

"One is to welcome them into the Underworld," said Kang Min, never veering his eyes from the initiates. "This one will welcome them into the Serpents."

Yoori could barely catch her breath as she laid her eager eyes on the maze. Another onslaught of silence prevailed over the estate. No one moved an inch. Everyone stared at one entity—one God.

Tae Hyun stood atop the brick wall, staring down at the initiates with firm eyes. It was like he was giving them time to catch their breath before he commenced their initiation.

And finally, when the silence began to become unbearable, Tae Hyun flew off the brick foundation and landed on the ground. As soon as his feet touched the foundation of the earth, he stormed off, jumpstarting the beginning of an initiation that riveted Yoori.

Tae Hyun wielded his kendo stick and attacked every initiate with ease, alternating between being on the ground and jumping onto the walls to throw initiates back onto the garden soil. Every hit he wielded, packs of initiates would fall at once, tripping over one another like dominos. Never once did his kendo stick stray onto the Reapers or the Cobras, all of whom were standing off to the side, looking like ominous statues in the maze. Tae Hyun attacked each initiate with precision, leaving all of them gasping for air.

Yoori observed this scene intently, analyzing his every move and formulating in her mind every countermove she could use to conquer him. Yoori clenched her fists, doing her best to suppress that competitiveness pumping through her. It was the Soo Jin instincts within her, the prideful Queen in her that felt tempted to jump into that labyrinth to battle Tae Hyun. Yoori kept that part of her contained. She was merely a spectator tonight, not a challenger.

When there was only a minute left, Tae Hyun launched himself back onto the top of the maze.

Yoori expelled a breath. She hadn't realized she had been holding her breath the entire time until he stopped his attacks. Below, she could hear the groans of the initiates wheezing for air. They looked like men and women who had been hit by a bomb. They were spent, exhausted, and in excruciating pain.

Curiously, Tae Hyun no longer looked like he was prepared to go in for another ambush. If anything, it looked like he was merely standing there . . . waiting for something else to take place next.

Yoori wondered what it was he was waiting for. She wondered if other Serpents were planning to join this maze with him.

Her unspoken question was answered when one initiate climbed onto the brick foundation to join him.

Hae Jin stopped the timer at one minute, and the entire estate held their breath in anticipation.

"Good boy," Kang Min whispered proudly, watching as the male initiate, who looked to be in his twenties and had dried blood all over his body, stood across from Tae Hyun on the maze.

"Finally," said Jae Won, watching as the male initiate looked at Tae Hyun like a scared puppy.

Yoori did not need to question Hae Jin or the brothers to comprehend what was happening. She understood the meaning behind this segment of the initiation. The initiates were *never* supposed to exit the maze through the opening. They were never supposed to come back the same way they came in. They may have entered the maze as humans, but they must leave as Serpents. They were almost done with their initiation, but not quite yet.

The nervousness within the initiate's eyes became more apparent the longer he stared at Tae Hyun. Although the initiate had never witnessed this before, he too, knew what the final portion of this initiation would entail.

"Stand tall, initiate," Tae Hyun finally said over the wind, his authoritative voice moving the other initiates to a standing position. He was not speaking to them directly, but they listened to his words like they were the gospel all the same. Tae Hyun kept his eyes on the sole initiate standing before him. "Your future brothers and sisters are watching you from above. You do not want to disappoint them, do you?"

The initiate shook his head.

Tae Hyun nodded in approval.

"You have one minute with me," he began to explain, placing his kendo stick aside. "During this timespan, you must not fall from this maze and touch the ground. If you touch the ground, I will start the clock again. None of you will leave until you see this minute through with me. Do you understand?"

While the initiate hesitantly nodded, Yoori asked, "What if he can't do the one minute?"

"My brother will keep beating him until he sees it through, or until he dies," said Hae Jin, her gaze on her brother and the initiate.

When the timer started, Tae Hyun charged at the initiate, elbowed him across the face, kneed him in his stomach, and then tossed him onto the ground like he was a rag doll.

As soon as the initiate hit the earth, the timer was reset to the beginning.

"You see your brothers and sisters up there?" Tae Hyun prompted as the other initiates crowded around the male initiate, helping him stand up. Tae

117

Hyun pointed in the direction of the active Serpents on the estate. His voice thundered with pride as the initiate struggled to regain his breath. "Every second of their five-minute initiation was worth it. Your last four minutes were worth it, but I will see to it that you finish your last minute strong. Now get up!"

With the help of his fellow initiates, the male initiate climbed back onto the brick wall. Although he looked more determined than before to finish this through for his fellow initiates, every time he tried to withstand the one minute, he would get brutally beaten by Tae Hyun before he was tossed back onto the soils of earth.

This occurred so many times that Yoori began to fear for the initiate's survival. Anymore of this, he would never survive the night.

It was evident that this realization was also clear to his fellow initiates.

After the first initiate's tenth fall from grace, another initiate, a female initiate with her long black hair tied back, climbed up onto the maze. She stared at Tae Hyun fearfully. Regardless of her fear, she couldn't let the first initiate go through with this beating any longer.

"Can I take his place?" she asked tentatively.

While the active female Serpents, including Hae Jin, smiled proudly, Tae Hyun nodded and said, "Yes."

Her valor did not help her with Tae Hyun. Like the other initiate, he showed her no mercy. Within seconds, she was thrown to the floor, crashing onto the initiates beneath her. She would try her luck again but every time, she proved to be no match for Tae Hyun. The cycle continued with initiate after initiate climbing onto the maze to take turns for one another, to help save one another. However, none were able to match up to Tae Hyun. They all kept falling, none ever lasting longer than forty seconds.

As the night started to become darker and colder, Yoori's heart began to break for them. They looked like children struggling against a God who could not be defeated. They had heart, but they did not have the strength to withstand his beatings.

Yoori could sense that the active Serpents were also beginning to feel sorry for them; they were beginning to root for the initiates to make it through the initiation. They, too, could see how hard the initiates were trying. When she concluded that this was a hopeless cycle and death was near, a Reaper climbed up and joined Tae Hyun on the top of the maze.

The initiates, including Yoori, gazed at him in disbelief. What was he doing?

The Reaper bowed his respect to Tae Hyun before shocking Yoori by saying, "Can I take their place?"

For the first time that night, Tae Hyun smiled. He nodded at the Reaper, clearly pleased with this turn of events.

"Yes," he said simply.

That was when it all made sense to Yoori. She finally understood what this initiation was leading toward. She understood now why the Serpents loved and revered Tae Hyun so much. The final gatekeeper into the Serpents' Kingdom wasn't their King, but a fellow Serpents member. The initiates had already been initiated into the Underworld, but an active Serpent—one of the Reapers—had to sacrifice themselves to bring the initiates into the Kingdom and welcome them to the family.

The timer started and the Reaper battled Tae Hyun, showing the awestruck initiates below how well Tae Hyun had trained his Serpents. Although the Reaper would never be able to defeat the King of Serpents, he was powerful enough to battle with a God; he was strong enough to stay on the maze during that arduous one minute.

When the final seconds clicked to a close, Tae Hyun ceased with his assaults on the Reaper, who was breathing harshly due to his wounds. He may have survived the one minute with Tae Hyun, but that didn't mean he came out unscathed.

Tae Hyun turned away from the Reaper and walked to the entrance of the maze. By this time, the active Serpents surrounding Yoori all stood up tall, their eyes fastened on their King. Yoori was the only one who remained seated.

After Tae Hyun reached the area beside the opening of the maze, he turned back to the initiates and said, "Climb onto the maze."

They hastened to obey and climbed on top of the colossal brick structure.

The spectacular sight of over a hundred people, all dressed in white, standing atop that maze gave Yoori chills.

"Turn toward the estate," Tae Hyun ordered, his back facing the estate.

In harmony, they all turned toward the estate.

"Kneel before your brothers and sisters."

Without an ounce of hesitation, they all fell on one knee before their predecessors.

"Never forget that you were welcomed into this gang by an existing Serpent," Tae Hyun said over the wind. "He sacrificed his own blood for you because he sees potential in you. Without him, you would have never seen this moment. Your act right now is not of servitude, but of respect. Respect for your elders, the ones who came before you, and the ones who will continue to sacrifice their well-being for you. Now stand tall."

As soon as they stood tall, the rest of the active Serpents beside Yoori fell to one knee. Even Hae Jin and the brothers knelt in the direction of the maze. Yoori was shocked, and so were the initiates. It was startling to witness so many formidable looking Serpents kneel before anyone but their King, especially to a group of newly initiated members who looked like dilapidated rag dolls.

"This is their act of respect for you, for the blood you've shed to join their Kingdom," said Tae Hyun over their astonishment. "You have proven yourselves to them and for that, once you step foot on the ground, you will become part of their family."

He smiled, finally turning around and staring straight at Yoori. Some of the initiates followed his gaze and smiled up at her as well. They knew his acknowledgement of her meant one thing: the initiation was over.

"Now enjoy yourselves," Tae Hyun whispered warmly, his smile growing wider when Yoori smiled back. "You've earned it."

Cheering commenced throughout the estate and from her vantage point, Yoori could see a slew of black and white colors converging as the active Serpents rushed over to welcome the new initiates with opened arms.

Yoori shared in the same excitement as she rushed down from the roof and onto the grass. She excitedly moved through the jovial crowd, thrilled to not only witness such a glorious event, but to be included in this secret world of Tae Hyun's. She sped over to the maze, eager to get to him.

Now that the King of Serpents was done with his duties, she was ready to be with her silly Snob again.

"But you are raised to be a God."

10: The Duel of Gods

Tae Hyun was still atop the maze, waiting for Yoori and watching over his Serpents when she reached him. He glowed under the moonlight, looking positively divine as he rested his attention on her.

Yoori peered up at him, unable to keep the smile off her face. As silly as it sounded, after bearing witness to such an epic initiation, she felt like she was in the presence of a celebrity rather than her BFF. Yoori couldn't stop beaming. She was ecstatic to be in his company again.

"Do you normally initiate with your shirt off?" she cooed, bashfully playing with the foliage of the maze.

Her heart raced when he favored her with a smile.

"No," he said with a laugh. His melodic laughter rolled over the peaceful gardens, triggering her heart rate to accelerate even faster. "I wanted the chance to flex my muscles for you."

Yoori laughed, her cheeks turning scarlet red at his teasing reply. She definitely enjoyed seeing those beautifully sculpted muscles flex. After her laughter died down, she tilted her head, no longer wanting to be so far from him. He looked like a God standing atop that maze, and she wanted to see what it was like to be up there with him.

"Can I join you up there?"

Tae Hyun did not waste time. He swiftly moved over to where she stood and lowered his hand to hers. Yoori shimmied off her heels and took his hand. He easily pulled her up, carefully making sure she was safely balanced on the maze. Once she became acclimated, he pulled out his charms.

"How did you like the show?" he whispered, cradling an already spellbound Yoori close to him. He feathered a kiss over her lips as his way of greeting her.

"It was . . . amazing," she told him breathlessly, overwhelmed by the surge of euphoria that rang through her. She quickly surveyed her surroundings from her new, elevated height.

Yoori felt exhilarated. While on the estate roof, she felt like a Queen overseeing her people. While on this maze with Tae Hyun, she felt like a God who had descended onto Earth. From this vantage point, the mansion resembled a shrine created to honor the Gods. This labyrinth made her feel like the God that was being worshipped. There was an otherworldly quality to this maze that excited her. She felt powerful at this elevated status, untouchable. It was like she was a mountain that towered over everyone else—everyone else except Tae Hyun.

Yoori repressed any competitive feeling that could rouse inside her and focused on answering Tae Hyun's question. She took her eyes off the mansion and faced Tae Hyun. Any thoughts of being a "God" vanquished when she saw his beautiful eyes. How surreal it was to be held by him with such love after witnessing such a spectacular event.

"I couldn't believe how elaborate and how grand it was," she added, the wonder having yet to leave her voice. "In the last minute, I wanted to take the place of those initiates as well."

Tae Hyun nodded as though that was the intended effect. "That's the point. The existing Serpents—primarily one of the Reapers—must want to do the same."

"What if a Reaper doesn't volunteer?"

"Then none of the prospects have proven themselves, and they will not be initiated," Tae Hyun simply stated before he gently pulled her with him. He led her along the maze, sauntering across the ivy-covered labyrinth like they were strolling on the beach.

"Why does it have to be a Reaper who volunteers?" asked Yoori, very much enjoying the view from atop this maze. The gardens had a majestic quality now that it was only the two of them. She especially loved how the moonbeam kissed every square inch of the gardens. It was also exceptionally amazing because she had the King of Serpents holding her hand and guiding her around the maze like he was introducing her to another part of the world. It was tranquil and it felt magical.

"The Reapers will be their guides throughout their entire life cycle as Serpents," Tae Hyun began to enlighten over a delicate breeze. "They will be the ones to show the initiates how cruel this world can be, they will show the initiates the light, and they will be the ones who will keep the initiates strong in the face of human weaknesses. Every aspect of the initiation embodied all these points. The Cobras were there to remind the initiates of the cruelty of the Underworld if they are weak, and I was there to remind them that no one could survive if they choose to go against their King."

"And the Reapers sacrificing themselves to battle you mean that they have given you their assurance that these initiates have what it takes to be a Serpent," Yoori contributed, following along with this symbolism. "They have what it takes to be worthy of entering the Kingdom."

"It's the way it should be," Tae Hyun said proudly. "They may be here to serve me, but they joined for a family. The existing Serpents do not take kindly to newcomers, but when the initiates have proven their worth, they would never turn their backs on them."

Yoori inhaled deeply, loving the meaning behind everything. A curious thought came over her that she had to playfully voice. "Do you think I can last one minute with you?"

Tae Hyun appraised her appreciatively. His sensuous gaze did not conceal his desire for her. "I'm sure you can, but know that I'll give you more than one minute, baby."

Yoori cracked up and lightly smacked his back. "You know what I meant!"

He laughed at her reaction before turning back around. There was a sultry quality to him when he pulled her closer. "Do you want to help me clean up?"

Yoori wrinkled her nose dubiously. "Huh?"

Undeterred, Tae Hyun motioned his hands up and down his body.

Yoori followed his movements and noticed that although his beautiful upper body was free of blemishes, his white pants had dirt and bloodstains from the initiates on it.

It dawned on Yoori what he was asking of her.

The implication behind the act left Yoori feeling shyer than usual. Declining was probably the proper thing to do, especially since she was his ex-girlfriend. However, she did not have the heart to refuse him. Not when he was standing there half-naked, literally asking her to clean him up. She should not be playing with fire, but Kwon Tae Hyun was too mouthwatering to deny. As long as she didn't give in, she would be fine. It was that simple—in theory.

Yoori nodded bashfully at her weak reasoning, eyeing the garden soil while her cheeks turned redder.

Tae Hyun rewarded her with a heart-stopping grin and jumped down from the maze. He reached his arms up and caught her when she followed suit and jumped down. Yoori was thankful that her dress was more form fitting tonight. If not, the wind would've blown the ends of her dress every which way already.

Hand-in-hand, they wandered over to a more secluded part of the estate. It was hidden behind towering trees and was perfectly veiled from the prying eyes of the mansion. Yoori heard the soft trickling sound of water running and craned her neck to look ahead. A man-made pond sat peacefully before her, housing a rock formation that had water pouring from it like a waterfall. There was also a beautiful red bridge that sat suspended over the glowing body of water, pleasing Yoori's already awestruck eyes.

On the grass beside the border of the water, Yoori spotted a white towel and new black pants for Tae Hyun to change into. She surmised that this slew of water must've been fresh if it was used for the Serpents' beloved King to wash up in.

"It's really pretty here," Yoori commented when Tae Hyun unclasped his hand from hers and advanced toward the water.

She stood beside his new change of clothes, surveying the pretty garden with appreciative eyes. The tranquility calmed her and made her feel safe. It eluded her as to why this wasn't Tae Hyun's preferred estate.

"Why don't you like this estate—*OH MY GOD!*" Yoori suddenly screamed when she turned just in time to see him make preparations to pull his pants down.

She closed her eyes, grabbed the towel, and raised it up in the air to block her view of his naked body.

"What are you doing, you pervert?!" she reprimanded, shaking while struggling to keep the towel up. It took all her willpower to not look at him when she heard his naked body move into the waters. "Why didn't you warn me before you decided to get naked?!"

His dark, seductive laughter resounded from the water. "What did you think helping me wash up entailed?"

"I don't know—*a warning*?" she retorted, feeling her hands quiver. The tantalizing sound of the water lapping against his naked physique sent heat coursing over her. She cursed her life. If only he wasn't her ex-boyfriend. If he were her boyfriend, she would take a peek just to satisfy her desire for him. Since he wasn't, she was simply stuck in sexual frustration hell. Fuck. This was her punishment for playing with fire—being teased to death by a naked sex God!

"Aw, I'm sorry," Tae Hyun crooned, his voice moving closer. Despite his words, there was no apology in his voice as the sound of water stirred against his movements. Yoori could hear the water drip from his naked form when his body finally towered over hers on dry land. She felt him tug the towel down slightly to reveal her eyes. Still holding the towel, Yoori looked up. He was peeking down at her with an enticing smile on his face. Water still clung to his hair and face, making him glow under the moonlight. "Luckily we had this towel to give me some privacy, right?"

She nodded shakily, thrusting the towel toward him. "Take your towel and make yourself presentable," she ordered tightly, keeping her eyes downward.

"You're supposed to help me," he combated lightly.

"I am," Yoori retorted. She pushed the towel toward him again. "Here, take it."

What he did next nearly had her fainting from shock. He grabbed her hands, which were still holding the towel, and proceeded to dry himself with her toweled-covered hands as the proxies. He moved her towel-covered hands over his muscular shoulders, skimmed them over his hard chest before shocking her even further when he moved them to his backside. Yoori's heart stuttered to a stop, and she could've sworn her towel-covered hands grazed over his perfectly sculpted butt.

My God, you're so hot . . . Yoori thought in a daze, certain she was going to have an aneurysm from all this teasing. It was as if all her naughty fantasies were coming to life. The only pitfall was that she couldn't enjoy it because this was her reality.

"Tae Hyun!" she squeaked, gaping at him when he showed mercy and guided her hands upward. He enclosed it around his hips like she was helping to hold the towel over his lower body.

He smiled sweetly down at her, causing her breath to further hitch in her chest.

Sweet Jesus, how was she going to survive this?

"What a big help you are," he whispered appreciatively, his lips curving up in amusement. "Now hold that towel up. I'm changing into my pants."

Yoori numbly nodded, holding the towel up. She felt drunk—drunk on Tae Hyun. She could feel her hands clenching while she tried to remember the feel of his beautifully sculpted behind. It was so firm that she could've sworn it was possible to bounce a nickel off that as—

"Done," he announced, dragging her from her perverted thoughts.

Yoori hesitantly lowered the towel. When she peeked out and saw that although he was shirtless, he was wearing his new black pants now, she felt bravery stream through her. A naked Tae Hyun boggled her senses, but a half-naked Tae Hyun was manageable—slightly.

"My upper body is still wet," he complained, smiling at her as he approached her with his glistening upper body. "Want to finish helping me?"

"No," Yoori whispered, gathering what was left of her dignity to sound firm. She handed the towel to him. "Finish it yourself."

Tae Hyun fabricated a groan before putting a fatigued hand over his arm. "Ah, but I'm so sore from the initiation. Those kids did a number on me."

"You kicked their asses," Yoori noted bluntly.

"It still took effort to wave that kendo stick around and beat people to a pulp," he argued. He faked another pained groan. "Come on, Brat. Any longer, I'm going to catch a cold if I'm still wet."

Yoori let out a groan and finally relented. She begrudgingly patted him down with the towel, doing her best to not enjoy it. She failed miserably. As soon as her towel-covered hands made contact with his warm chest, any sense of urgency dissipated. With heat infusing her cheeks, she patted every part of his upper body down with care. Yoori even indulged herself when she got to his abs. She patted his abdomen down slowly, enjoying every rock-hard ridge and the contractions of his muscles while he waited for her to finish. She only stopped when she was an inch away from the lining of his pants.

"There," she announced, moving her hands away.

Tae Hyun caught her hands and urged them back onto his stomach. "You missed a spot," he whispered, holding her eyes. Slowly, he moved her hands down the v-cut muscle that led into his pants. He brushed the towel lower, dragging her towel-covered hands into the spot where the elastic of the pants budged slightly. He stopped it there, his sultry eyes holding hers captive.

"Do you know what I want to do to you right now?" he finally whispered, his eyes looking so mesmerizing that it was a miracle she hadn't self-combusted from wonder yet.

Yoori shook her head dumbly.

His gaze drifted to her lips before he leaned down to rest his mouth against her ear. His hot breath swept over her as he whispered all the naughty things he would do to her after he ripped off her dress and threw her into that pond. It was so scandalous that by the time he told her what they would do while they were on that bridge, she had enough sense to raise her hands in the air and screamed:

"Okay, I forfeit! You win! I totally want you too, but this is too inappropriate, Tae Hyun! We're not even officially boyfriend and girlfriend anymore."

"That's why you should be my girlfriend again," he supplied quickly. Too quickly for Yoori's taste.

Yoori gawked at him when a realization struck her. "Did you bring me to this estate and show me this initiation so you can convince me to become your girlfriend again?"

His shoulders lifted into a shrug as his confirmation. "Two birds with one stone, right? I get to be open with you, and I get to seduce you and convince you to be my girlfriend again."

Yoori sputtered in disbelief and pushed him away.

"This is the story you want me to tell people?" she gritted out, wanting to smack him for using his body as a weapon. "That I only became your girlfriend again because you were acting like a porn star and I wanted to do those fun things you were suggesting in the pond?"

Tae Hyun stared at her like she was crazy. "*Who* are you planning to tell our story to? Our friends don't care how we get back together. They already know it happened since we moved back in together."

"What if I tell this story to other people?" Yoori combated weakly.

"Who?" Tae Hyun questioned critically. "This world is all about confidentiality, remember?" He could barely contain his smile of disbelief. "Plus, who would believe you if you did tell our story to someone outside of the Underworld? No offense, but if you used the terminology of the 'Underworld,' 'King of Serpents,' or the 'Queen of the Underworld' to the outside world, they would probably think you're a lunatic babbling about Greek mythology."

Yoori clamped her mouth shut because he was right. If she shared their story with other people, more than likely, no one would believe her. Her story was too incredible to believe.

Despite the fact that he had a point, she would not give him the satisfaction of feeling like he won.

"Just for that, I'm definitely not agreeing to be your girlfriend tonight."

Tae Hyun let out a defeated groan. "Damn! I almost had it!"

Yoori smirked before pulling his hand and tugging him deeper into the gardens so she could do some exploring. Now that her rationale had returned, she was ready to do some other fun things here. "Now continue to show me around."

At her childish prompt, Tae Hyun laughed, putting all motives of convincing her to be his girlfriend aside to enjoy the walk with her. He held his hand tighter around hers and pulled her toward the bridge, walking over the glistening water that once held a naked God.

"So, this is the thing you needed your Cobras to do?" she launched, staring briefly up at the moon when she remembered the Cobras' roles in the initiation. "Shouldn't they be resting?"

"I told you that they needed to heal physically and mentally. They have been away from the gang for far too long. They should be the ones to help initiate the new members. It's the only good way to re-introduce them to the Serpents. Plus, the initiates were no match for them. To my Cobras, this was the equivalent of taking a brisk walk around the estate."

"I understand now why you were knocked out for so long after your last initiation," said Yoori. "It's still crazy to me how elaborate and big this initiation was." She took a moment to ponder a curious thought. "Do you think I would make it out alive?"

Tae Hyun smiled when they stepped off the balcony and journeyed into the deeper parts of the garden. "You don't need to suffer through it."

"But what if I did have to?" she insisted, curious about his thoughts on this topic. "Do you think I'd make it?"

He did not even think about the answer. "You would."

Yoori laughed, finding it difficult to believe him. "Are you just saying this because you're trying to get on my good side?"

"No," he said genuinely. "I really believe it."

She smiled, briefly casting her gaze at the jewel encrusted canvas above them. The sense of marvel she felt had yet to dissipate. If anything, it only became more potent. "Watching this initiation makes me realize what a rich history the Underworld has. There's so much symbolism to everything. I can't believe this society has been able to keep this a secret from the public. It's so . . . unbelievable."

"The crime lords in the 1st layer do an exceptional job of damage control if and when someone does try to expose the secret." Tae Hyun laughed to himself. "There are few things the Royals in the Underworld agree on, but the one thing we do see eye-to-eye on is that secrecy is everything. Anyone who threatens that will die a very slow, miserable, and agonizing death." He shrugged. "Few are brave enough to anger all the Gods in the Underworld."

Yoori nodded before her stream of thoughts ventured back to the other initiations. "I heard how the initiation for the Skulls and Scorpions worked."

Interest dripped into his voice. "What do you think?"

"I don't think I could survive the Skulls' initiation," she said at once.

"You could survive it," Tae Hyun amended. "The operative word here is 'want.' You do not *want* to go through the initiation. You do not believe in killing your fellow initiates to get into a 'Kingdom' that is supposed to be your extended family."

Yoori inhaled deeply, agreeing with his amendment. Perhaps if she put her heart and soul into it, she would survive the Skulls' initiation. However, she did not want to give up her heart and soul. She did not agree with their value system nor did she want to be a part of that family. Her focus voyaged to the initiation her former self helped administer.

"What do you think of the Scorpions' initiation?"

A warm light illumed Tae Hyun's face when he mulled over the answer. "I like theirs a lot," he shared slowly. "Maybe even a little bit more than my own."

Yoori's brows crept up incredulously. "Really?"

He nodded seriously and elaborated. "I like that a member of the Royal family must be with you throughout the four levels. I think that is a genius concept. The bond created through that initiation is lifelong." He took a deep inhalation. "This is why when Young Jae left Korea, the majority of his gang left with him. This is why he was able to vanish without a trace, because he has the silence and loyalty of so many followers." He smirked before casually dropping a bombshell. "This is why to this day, Kang Min and Jae Won remain loyal to An Soo Jin. Because even in death, she will always be the God who brought them to their new life."

Yoori fidgeted uneasily. This was the first time Tae Hyun ever mentioned anything about Kang Min and Jae Won being Scorpions.

"I knew you were aware that Jae Won was her right-hand man," Yoori started warily, "but I didn't realize you knew that Kang Min was part of the Scorpions gang too."

"I knew who he was the moment he asked to join my gang," Tae Hyun shared, "but since he was so keen on saying that he was from some random gang, I decided to play along."

Yoori regarded Tae Hyun under a whole new light. She wondered what else the King of Serpents was aware of. "What else do you know that you haven't shared?"

"You mean apart from the fact that they are brothers or the fact that Kang Min is my sister's boyfriend?"

Yoori's eyes bulged. She nearly choked when she said her next words. "You know about Kang Min and Hae Jin?"

"That's my baby sister. I know everything." He then glared at her. "Oh, and I appreciate you disclosing all of this to me."

Yoori wasted no time in defending her actions—or lack thereof. "I was afraid you were going to kill him!"

"And I will," he agreed vehemently. "If he ever fucks up with my sister, I will nail him to the wall, cut him up piece by piece, and throw the remains in the ocean for the sharks to devour."

Yoori was mind-boggled. "Why haven't you assassinated him yet?"

Tae Hyun let out a calming breath. "Because he's making her happy."

"I don't get it," Yoori continued, still reeling from this unexpected revelation. "Why didn't you tell them? Why are you acting like you don't know they're a couple?"

He shrugged his indifference. "I think it's more fun to scare the living shit out of them. I enjoy that Kang Min is living in fear. He should get used to that feeling. As long as he is with my sister, I will be his worst nightmare."

"You are evil," Yoori remarked in wonderment.

"And you will keep this between us," he whispered, nuzzling her nose with his as they neared a balding tree in the garden. He stared down at her with tantalizing eyes. "You won't give away my secret, will you?"

"I can't keep this a secret," she provided helplessly.

Tae Hyun feigned disappointment in his gaze. "You kept it a secret from me."

Because you are the psychotic one out of the group! Yoori wanted to exclaim. Instead, she censored herself and played it safe. This was not her business, and she did not want to get in the middle of this. If Tae Hyun wanted to torture Kang Min so he'd live in fear his entire life, then so be it. It would be one of those quirky relationships they would laugh about if the secret ever became revealed.

At the mention of brothers and boyfriends, Yoori was abruptly reminded of the Scorpions' initiation when she saw a statue of three serpents in the garden. She recalled one portion of the Scorpions' initiation having to do with serpents. An odd thought occurred to her that she had to voice.

"While growing up," she began, berating herself for not asking Tae Hyun this question in the past, "did you ever meet my father or brother?"

"I met your brother briefly after I became the King of Serpents," Tae Hyun shared, looking at her in interest. It was clear he was surprised that she was suddenly so curious about his past with her family. Nonetheless, he answered her question without any qualms. "It was at the 'crowning' ceremony. From the brief interaction, he was civil enough with me."

Yoori beamed at the thought of her brother and Tae Hyun getting along, if only momentarily.

"What about my father?" she inquired keenly.

"I met him once," he provided, surprising her with his answer, "when I was very young."

Her curiosity was piqued. "How young?"

"Ten. I was training with my instructor in Japan. Your father knew that instructor, and he stopped by for a visit. He saw me training—or more precisely, he saw me struggling. I hadn't slept properly in days. I was barely able to throw a punch, let alone shoot a gun. He noticed that I was out of it and gave me water. Then, he gave me the same advice that my father always gave me."

"What did he say?"

"He said that this momentary weakness would not last—that the pain I was feeling was weakness leaving my body. He assured me that one day, this would all be worth it." Tae Hyun laughed disbelievingly. "It wasn't until he left that my instructor told me I was in the company of the King of Scorpions."

"What was your reaction?" asked Yoori, engrossed in the story about her brother and father. It made her feel warm inside to hear this from Tae Hyun. Even though she didn't remember her father or her brother, it brought comfort to know that Tae Hyun had met them. Tae Hyun was the person she cared about most in this world and him knowing her family made her feel like she was connected to them. Her family no longer felt like a faceless dream; they felt real due to Tae Hyun's recollection of them.

"Relieved that he didn't kill me on the spot."

Yoori had to stifle a giggle. "Did the Scorpions and the Serpents really hate each other back then?"

He gave her the obvious answer. "All Kings hate each other in every era."

She nodded before her warm thoughts sailed on to what occurred on the estate roof. "Why did you have me sit on that throne while you were initiating your new gang members?"

"So they all know who you are to me," he said without missing a beat.

Yoori sighed. She suspected he was doing it as a means to show her "status" in his life, that she was not only a girl he was seeing, but that she was also a woman who he saw a future with. So much so that he would give her his throne and allow his entire Kingdom to look at her in reverence, just like they would with him if he sat on that throne.

The sweetness behind that gesture aside, Yoori couldn't help but feel unsettled as well. He was putting a lot at risk by doing that. She nervously played with her fingers. "You're not afraid of looking weak?"

"You make me strong," he told her without regret. "Every time I know you're watching, I want to show off."

Yoori blushed, and he leaned in, taking advantage of the moment by catching her off guard again.

"Be with me again, baby," he finally murmured, gently pushing her against a tree in the garden. His carnal eyes peered down at her, weakening her resolve.

"Tae Hyun—" she weakly protested, feeling her control wither away. She was already ready to give in to him when he suggested they come to this estate. She no longer knew how much control she had left. She bit her lips, recalling why she did not want to sit on the throne when Hae Jin suggested it. She wanted to tell Tae Hyun of her concerns, her fears—yet she found it impossible when he stared deep into her eyes.

"Be my girlfriend again," he persevered, cradling her close to his chest while running his fingers through her hair. His beautiful gaze held hers, his eyes teeming with promises of a wonderful future if she accepted his proposal. "I want to be with you," he went on, pressing his forehead against hers while hovering his lips over hers. "I want you to be mine again."

Yoori swallowed with need, feeling downright tempted with his mouth so close to hers. In that brief moment, nothing concerned her but Tae Hyun and his gorgeous lips. She breathed with shallow breaths, her eyes becoming dilated with longing. She did not say anything to refuse, and he took this as his cue.

He leaned forward, nearly grazing his lips with hers when—

"You look so pretty tonight, baby—*oh shit!*"

Tae Hyun and Yoori snapped out of their impending kiss to see two initiates walk into the garden.

The two initiates, the first guy who Tae Hyun beat during the last minute of the initiation and the girl who took his place, stopped in stunned silence upon seeing Tae Hyun.

Rage entered Tae Hyun's eyes when he realized that his initiates had just fucked up his romantic moment with their presence.

"What the hell are you doing here?" he asked them heatedly.

"Uh . . . exploring?" the male initiate said nervously, clearly wishing they had taken another route in the garden.

The female initiate nodded, blushing immensely. She looked like she'd rather be anywhere but there, in the garden with an angry King and his significant other.

Tae Hyun was flabbergasted by their idiocy, namely the male initiate's. "I just got done beating the fuck out of you and you're here 'exploring' with your fellow initiate?"

They laughed fretfully before the male initiate said, "Sorry about that, boss. We'll head back now!"

One second they were there and the next, all Yoori could see was a whoosh of white clothes running off in the direction of the mansion.

Yoori calmly watched them disappear. After a few passing breaths, she said, "They seem like promising initiates."

"How so?" asked Tae Hyun, his voice bitter that they had screwed his "moment" with Yoori.

"They're just like their King. They just overexerted themselves, and they're still horny." She glared, feeling her control return as a result of the distraction. She recalled the powerful feeling she received when she sat on the throne and felt her sanity return. "Way to catch me off guard with your charm, Romeo."

Tae Hyun expelled a breath and tipped his head backward. "How do I convince you to be my girlfriend again?" Weariness was set in his voice. He was so defeated that Yoori was sure any answer she gave him, he would endeavor to do.

"Fight me," she said, taking advantage of this moment to prove a point she had been dying to make.

He looked at her strangely. "I'm sorry," Tae Hyun said dryly, "did you just say something ridiculous?"

"Fight me," Yoori repeated seriously, desperate to show him what a threat Soo Jin could be if she returned. She wanted to show him why he should be careful with her. Her eyes roamed ahead, and she saw that during their walk, they had somehow migrated back to the maze. She pointed at it, determined to make that labyrinth their battleground. "Whoever falls first loses."

Tae Hyun was still looking at her like she was crazy. "You're saying if I kick you off this maze first, you'll be my girlfriend again?"

She nodded.

He scrutinized her, his face becoming inquisitive. "Why do you want to fight me?"

"So you know what you're getting into when you're in a relationship with me." She swallowed tightly, always feeling rattled whenever she brought up her Underworld counterpart. "I may not be a threat, but Soo Jin can be."

"Soo Jin is not here."

"She can be." Yoori sighed at his flippant behavior whenever she brought up the dangers surrounding An Soo Jin. Her evil counterpart was not to be taken lightly, especially by Tae Hyun. If An Soo Jin were to return, he was the one she was going after. "And when she is, she may be a bigger threat than any other rival you've encountered in the Underworld."

He smirked, clearly finding her to be dramatic. Nonetheless, he was prepared to humor her. "So be it. If that's what it'll take to have you be mine again."

Without another rebuttal, he jumped onto the maze with ease.

Yoori looked up at him, never feeling shorter. She cleared her throat. "You're not going to help me up?"

Tae Hyun presented her with his most mischievous smile. "Not right now, Princess."

He started to walk backward, treading on the maze with ease. "What are the rules if my opponent can't even get up on the maze to fight?" he asked with amusement. "Do I win by default?"

"No!" cried Yoori, outraged at his attempt to be a cheater.

"I think that should be the case," he went on airily. Though his voice was playful, she could also tell he was serious. If she didn't get on that maze, she was going to lose by default. "You have thirty seconds to get on before I win."

Panic set into Yoori. She struggled to remember how the Reapers and the Cobras got onto this wall. She moved her hands over the brick infrastructure, attempting to find the footholds they used to climb up this edifice. She blew out a relieved breath when she found the footing underneath the ivies. With a grunt, she used it as her foothold and climbed onto the maze.

The wind picked up when she stood upon the ivy-covered foundation. All around her, trees and plants were rustling while she rested her eyes upon Tae Hyun. He stood approximately ten feet across from her, staring at her quietly. At this moment in time, as he stood before her as an opponent rather than her suitor, Yoori felt the competitive energy surge inside her. She felt like she was staring at a fellow God, not a King.

"Do you realize how much the Underworld would pay to see an event like this?" Tae Hyun asked as though reading her mind. He, too, understood how powerful it felt to be standing here, across from someone else who was also revered in the Underworld. "How many lives they would sacrifice to witness the battle between the King of Serpents and the Queen of the Underworld?"

"A war of the Gods." Yoori smiled as she enjoyed the feel of the breeze running over her. "Ju Won would love this moment."

Tae Hyun's doting eyes observed her under the moonlight. "Are you acclimated yet?"

She distractedly nodded, still marveling at the view from this maze. "Yes."

"Good."

He was in front of her before she could move. He merely brushed past her, and she nearly slipped off the wall. It wasn't until Tae Hyun caught her mid-fall and steadied her on the maze did she realize the "battle" had begun. He didn't even give her any warning!

Tae Hyun grinned at the outrage on her face. "This is the threat you were worried about?"

Anger rose inside her. Yoori knew he didn't mean anything by it, but it infuriated her all the same. She wanted him to know what she was capable of. She wanted him to know that she was not to be taken lightly.

It happened before she could register it. Yoori clenched her fist and with all the force within her, she punched him clear across the face. He stumbled back, nearly losing his footing on the maze while he gaped at her in astonishment.

Yoori smiled in the cunning way that only a powerful Queen could. "Was this the first time the King of Serpents got his ass handed to him in this maze?"

Tae Hyun chuckled. Despite his reticence with battling her on this maze, she could also see that he was intrigued with this challenge. This was truly a monumental moment—even he could not deny that.

"Let's have some fun then," he declared before charging at her and setting the battle into motion.

Yoori smiled. This time, she was ready for him.

He swept the foundation with his leg, and she jumped in time. Unfortunately, she lost her footing when she landed on the ivy-covered brick. Yoori tilted to the right, nearly face planting into the inner portion of the maze when Tae Hyun reached out and caught her. He pulled her tight against him and smirked, stroking her hair with amusement. "You can't beat me, Brat. Let's stop this before you actually get hurt."

Yoori's face flushed red. After all this talk about him watching out for Soo Jin, she couldn't let this night end with him taking the threat any less seriously. More importantly, she could not lose—especially not when he was this smug.

She smiled sweetly at him, throwing him off guard when she propelled her head forward and pounded him right on the forehead.

Bam!

She nearly blacked out from the impact.

Tae Hyun did not fare well from the sudden attack either.

"Fuck!" he cursed, stumbling away from her in disbelief. He was so discombobulated that he nearly toppled off the maze. He was able to steady himself in time to look back at her in complete shock.

Yoori ignored the painful throbbing in her forehead and grinned at him. Something caught her eyes and she looked down. The kendo stick stared up at her, resting on the tip of the maze as if waiting for her to use it. Yoori could not deny its existence. Leaning down, she wrapped her hand around it and stood up tall. What a perfect toy for her to use in this battle.

"Time to play," she stated airily, surprised that she was actually having fun. Her competitive blood heaved in exhilaration, and she wanted to win against the almighty King of Serpents.

She wasted no more time. She charged for him, the kendo stick held tightly in her grasp. She swept the air with the kendo stick, and he jumped out of the way, lunging for the adjacent side of the maze. Yoori chased after him, sprinting throughout the maze while keeping balanced. When she caught up with him, she swung the kendo stick in his direction. Tae Hyun ducked and drew upright, lightly elbowing her away from him.

He still would not use his full strength with her, and this amused her. She would show him.

Yoori lunged for him, and they both fell, landing hard onto the tip of the maze. Tae Hyun was literally lying across the edge of the wall, his body dangerously close to plummeting down. Just one push and he would meet the ground. The only problem was that she was on top of him. If they fell, she would hit the ground first. She would lose first.

Yoori tossed the kendo stick to the ground and pressed her hands on his chest. She began to crawl backward in an attempt to put some distance between them so that she could push him off. She barely moved an inch away before Tae Hyun lifted his body and pushed her off.

"Ahh!"

Yoori screamed when she fell. Luckily, she was able to latch onto the tip of the brick wall, catching herself in midair. With all the strength she had, she pulled herself up and got back onto the maze.

By now, Tae Hyun had just stood up. The smile of disbelief was still plastered on his face. He clearly did not anticipate this "battle" to take this long. Although he appeared to be having fun dueling with her, he looked intent on making sure it ended soon.

"Time for you to be mine again," he declared haughtily.

In a huff, he rocketed toward her like a lion on the attack. Yoori widened her eyes. Realizing that there was no way to avoid him if he rammed into her, she lunged for the opposite side of the maze. She soared in the air and thanked the fates when she found a hard grip on the opposite wall. She grunted out loud and hauled her body back onto the maze. Yoori took a moment to gather her breath as she stood up on the other side of the ivy-covered edifice. Her moment of peace was short-lived.

After re-energizing, she quickly spotted Tae Hyun, who was coming for her at full speed. Prepared for an offense now, she launched back toward him and began to charge as well. Yoori knew she could not beat him by sheer strength alone. She had to use her brain.

And this time, she knew what tactic she had to use.

Let's see how you react to this one, she thought expectantly.

They launched for each other on the maze like speeding trains. Just as they were about to collide, Yoori swooped down and rammed herself into his gut, causing a surprised Tae Hyun to lose his balance because he was too tall to swoop down that low.

"Ugh!"

Tae Hyun fell with a groan, but not before he held on to the tip of the maze and pulled himself back up. Yoori barely had time to run away from him when he held on to her stomach from behind, performed a jujitsu move, and tipped her backward.

"Ah!"

Her back hit the tip of the maze with brutal force, her left leg hanging off the brick. When she saw Tae Hyun stand before her, ready to push her off, she hammered a kick onto the side of his body, nearly causing him to topple off. In the midst of this, she regained her bearings and crouched on the maze, watching with hope that he would tip over.

To her disappointment, he did not lose balance. He stabilized himself and in an instant, was in front of her once more. Tae Hyun caught her arm and tugged her toward his hard chest. She attempted to pull herself free, but he held on to her.

He cracked a smile, clearly impressed with the resilience she was showing. However, that was not enough for him to show mercy. He wanted her as his girlfriend, and if that meant he had to push her off a maze, then so be it.

"I will make sure your fall from grace is a gentle one," he promised before he pushed her off.

Yoori could not have that. In retaliation, she tried to hook an arm around his neck to use him to regain her equilibrium. However, in the process of doing this, she tripped over a loose brick, lost her footing, and fell headfirst toward the ground.

"Yoori!"

In fear of Yoori landing on her head, Tae Hyun jumped after her and caught her before she collided with the ground. He wrapped his arms around her and fell backward, allowing her to fall onto the cushion of his body instead.

A few moments of silence perused between them as they caught their breath. Shortly after, Tae Hyun laughed when he realized he was the one who hit the ground first.

"I think I just lost," he whispered in amusement.

Calmly, he stood up, pulling Yoori with him. He smiled at her and pinned her against the wall inside the maze. He assessed the rustled look in her eyes and saw the fear within them.

"Soo Jin is not a threat to me," he told her with conviction, sensing that she was still bothered by that fact.

Yoori looked at him and then threateningly pressed a loose brick against his neck. Tae Hyun instantly froze.

"She may not be a threat, but I am," she countered, realizing now that it was never Soo Jin that Tae Hyun should be concerned with. After the battle that took place, it was clear that it had always been Yoori who was the true threat.

"Where did you get that?"

"When we laid on the ground a second ago. I saw it and grabbed it before you pulled me up." She exhaled, looking at him with disappointment. "You underestimate what I'm capable of."

Tae Hyun smirked while pulling the brick away from his neck and tossing it to the ground. He continued to stare at her in amusement.

Yoori further explained, knowing he had not fully processed her point. "Now I know why they do not want you to be distracted by me. You are not careful around me."

"Why do you say that?"

"Because you jumped after me when I fell. You could've won, but you gave it all up and jumped after me. You lost because you wanted to save me."

He exhaled patiently. "This is just a game."

"Tonight it is," she whispered. "But what about next time when we actually fight?" She tilted her head. "What if next time, it is no longer a game and it is Soo Jin that you're fighting? Will you purposely lose to her in order to save me again?"

Tae Hyun smiled calmly. "There are five weapons buried in the wall you're standing in front of. When you pressed that loose brick into my neck, I could've reached for any one of those weapons and killed you before you could even blink." He touched her face, his features displaying no fear. "We are both a threat to each other. I am not the only one distracted here." His gentle smile remained. "I know you are a threat to me and my existence, but

137

the difference here is that I *want* you to be my distraction. I do not fear you because I trust that despite whatever power you have, you will never harm me."

He stroked her cheek when he saw hope seep into her once severe gaze. "It is okay for us to be in a relationship where we are a threat to one another. It is not a bad thing; it is called trust." He leaned in, his words breaking through all the fear that held Yoori captive. "I trust you, baby. That is why I brought you here, that is why I put you on that throne for the rest of my Serpents to see, and that is why I'm opening up to you right now. You threaten everything I've worked my entire life for, but you are still here because *I* want you to be. I've had a taste of what it's like to be without you, and I do not want to go back to that life." He moved in closer, his loving eyes holding hers. "Will you be mine now?"

Yoori smiled, feeling her heart warm. Despite her fears of the future whenever she thought about Soo Jin, she couldn't deny how beautiful his words were—how beautiful a future with him could be. Perhaps she was being too paranoid. Perhaps she shouldn't focus so much on the future, especially when she had something so wonderful in the present.

Instead of agreeing, however, she lightheartedly noted something else. "They're watching us," she whispered.

Tae Hyun did not even blink in concern. "No one is watching us."

Yoori hid a smile and tilted her head in the direction of the estate. She had sensed them for a while now, perhaps a little after the two initiates ran from Tae Hyun like two scared puppies. It was only fair that she brought Tae Hyun's attention to them as well.

"Your Serpents are watching us from the mansion."

"No one," he enunciated, turning around and glaring at the Serpents who were all watching from the packed mansion, "is watching us."

As soon as the hundreds of Serpents realized he was glaring at them, they uneasily turned away and pretended they were not engrossed in watching their boss seduce his girlfriend. They awkwardly laughed with one another and looked everywhere else but at them.

Tae Hyun turned back to Yoori and when he did, she did something out of character: she kissed him.

She threw away all her inhibitions and simply kissed the one who stole her heart. What was the point of denying his efforts when she wanted him as well? There was no point. They had been through too much and they deserved this heavenly moment.

And boy was she glad she did.

The moment their lips met, she felt the synapses of her brain explode to life. The world around her jumped in vibrancy, as if coming to life from the kiss she shared with Tae Hyun.

Tae Hyun chuckled into the kiss and wrapped his arms around her, sweeping his lips over hers with a passion that left her weak in the knees. His kiss was hot with intention, intoxicating by nature, and utterly mind-consuming. It was her wildest fantasy brought to life. She cursed herself for denying them this wonderful moment for so long, but she was grateful they could bask in it now.

While continuing to lock his lips with hers, he moved them deeper into the maze.

"Are you mine again?" he whispered in between their kiss, his lips nipping hers.

She nodded and gripped his powerful arms, relishing in their kiss. "Yes, baby."

He chuckled again and lifted her up, allowing her to wrap her legs around his hips as they continued to kiss like there was no tomorrow.

"If they wrote history books about you, they would document this as the moment of your downfall," Yoori whispered as she felt him press her back against the ivy-covered wall.

Tae Hyun grinned, moving his lips from her mouth, and drifting onto the side of her neck. His teeth scraped her skin with decadence, and he started to suckle on the sensitive skin there, earning mewls of approval from her. "I couldn't think of a better reason to fall from the throne."

She nodded distractedly before something else came up in her mind. Despite the immense pleasure she was receiving from Tae Hyun, she had other things to address. She knew the only way to bring it up was to catch Tae Hyun off guard.

Yoori pulled out a folded, silver invitation card from the pocket of her dress. She held it in front of him, interrupting his loving attention on her neck. "Now can you tell me what this is all about?"

She had found the card buried under a stack of mail in their apartment. It was clear that Tae Hyun had seen this invitation card. It bothered her that he didn't mention it to her. She had been waiting for him to bring it up. When it was clear that he wasn't planning to, she knew she had to take the lead.

A frown creased his brows as he closed his eyes in weariness and gently placed her back on the ground. Given his now dampened sexual mood, it was palpable he wasn't happy that she found it.

"That is an invitation to Ju Won's masquerade ball," he said succinctly, the tone in his voice hinting that he didn't want to have this conversation.

"Is it for his birthday?" she asked, disregarding the warning tone in his voice.

Tae Hyun shook his head. "Every year before his birthday, Ju Won throws a charity event to help raise money for his foundation. It goes to help kids with leukemia."

"Does the money really go to that foundation?" Yoori asked skeptically. Judging by Ju Won's morally questionable character, she had a hard time believing he would give any money away.

Tae Hyun's next words surprised her. "Every bit of it."

She blinked. "Really?"

He nodded.

"Why this foundation?"

"Ju Won's only daughter died from leukemia. He throws this event in her name every year."

A swell of sympathy streamed over Yoori when she thought about Ju Won actually loving someone other than himself. She briefly wondered if his daughter was the reason why he chose Soo Jin as his advisee. Perhaps Soo Jin reminded him of his daughter?

"I take it only people from the Underworld are invited?" she asked instead, not wanting to bother herself with thoughts of Soo Jin and Ju Won. There were more pressing matters that needed answers.

"All layers from the Underworld are invited, but it isn't a closed event. Because it's for a cause that has nothing to do with Underworld business, everyone is encouraged to bring dates who are not associated with the Underworld as well. It's one of the rare occasions where enemies converse freely with enemies. Underworld businesses are not dealt with that night." Tae Hyun smirked. "At least not in theory."

"You didn't even tell me about it, and the event is tomorrow. I take it we're not going?"

"We're not going."

Yoori frowned at his haste answer. "Why not?"

"Rumors surrounding you have been scarce. The thing about our world is that it isn't as connected as one might think. Information is important in this society and it isn't shared easily. The only ones in the loop the majority of the time are the 3rd layer Kings and the Advisors because our people spread far and wide. Only a tight circle knows about you and your resemblance to An Soo Jin. An even smaller circle knows that you're actually her and that you have amnesia. Aside from Ji Hoon, the Advisors, and myself, no one else knows the truth about you." He eyed her. "Can you understand now why I'm not about to bring you to a party where all three layers can see you?"

"But you can't miss an event like this," Yoori quickly countered. "The Advisors would use this against you later and say that you're 'distracted' again. You can't be stubborn, Tae Hyun. You have to go."

"I'm not leaving you home alone."

"Isn't it a masquerade ball? I can wear one of those masquerade masks. I can go with you and be invisible."

He was stubborn. "I don't want to chance it. If we go, I'll be pulled away left and right. I don't want to leave you to fend for yourself."

"I don't want you to endanger your position in this world anymore," she replied just as stubbornly. "You're being stupid if you think missing any of these events won't harm you in the end. Plus, I'm not a damn kid. You could leave me alone for a couple of minutes. I promise I won't get beamed up by a UFO, and I won't let terrorists abduct me."

He frowned at her lame attempt at a joke.

"I don't want to go," he stated resolutely, looking away as if that would end the conversation. "I hate masquerade balls, I hate dressing up for themed parties, and I know shit is going to go down. I can feel it."

Acutely aware that she wasn't going to get her way unless she got strategic, Yoori decided to use her sexuality—as limited as it may be—as her weapon of choice.

She hummed melodically and allowed her hands to roam over his chest and pecs. The steel-like muscles rippled pleasingly under her fingers, the tenseness once present in Tae Hyun's body melting under her touch. She leaned forward, her long black hair moving against his chest. The silkiness of her hair grazed his skin, holding his unyielding attention as she moved her lips to his.

"I've never dressed up for a dance," she whispered, feathering her lips over his.

The tactic worked when the resolution that once filled Tae Hyun's eyes became replaced with longing desire. Unable to resist the temptation she was throwing him, a hoarse moan escaped his mouth as he lowered his head to kiss her.

"Will you deny me the opportunity?" she asked briskly, pulling away just as his lips were half an inch from hers.

Knowledge and amusement sparkled in his eyes when he noted what she was doing.

"You're asking for trouble, baby," he whispered huskily.

Yoori had no idea if he meant trouble with her insisting that they attend the ball or trouble with her teasing him and denying him a kiss.

"We're already in trouble." She concealed a smile of satisfaction that this argument was hers to win. "I'm just trying to do what's right for us. The only thing keeping us safe is going to these stupid social events so that no one can claim their King is 'distracted.'"

"You're walking into the lion's den. This event will house the Advisors, Ji Hoon, and the most prominent figures in the Underworld. I don't know about you, but that already sounds like trouble to me."

"Hmm, lucky for me I have the King of Serpents to watch over me." She smiled hopefully. "So is that a 'yes, we're going'?"

He gave a defeated sigh, confirming that they were indeed going. "This is such a bad idea."

"Tomorrow is going to be such an eventful night," Yoori predicted as he started to guide her out of the maze. She insisted that they went for Tae Hyun's protection, however, she knew damn well what type of lion's den she was walking into.

Tae Hyun smirked as he held her hand and maneuvered them around the maze.

"Welcome to the Underworld," he said bitterly. "Every damn second of our life is eventful."

She smiled, her thoughts moving on to something curious.

In a world filled with so many powerful people, yet so few Gods, how could Soo Jin and Tae Hyun not have ran into each other even once?

She didn't miss a beat in verbalizing this question. "How is it possible that you've never met An Soo Jin?"

Tae Hyun gave her a sideway glance. "She and I did not have the same training schedule," he said softly.

"I know," said Yoori. "I know that you were never introduced to each other, but what about annual gatherings like Ju Won's party? You go every year, don't you?"

"I missed a few when I first started my training, but yes, I do make an appearance every so often."

"And she trained with Ju Won. I'm sure she was at most, if not all, of the gatherings. So how come you've never crossed paths then?"

"I told you that I've never met her, but I did not dismiss the possibility of our paths crossing. What you have to understand about Ju Won's gathering is that although it is a time for all the Elders in the Underworld to network and catch up with one another, it is also a time for the younger Royals to let loose from their respective trainings. When you go, you will notice that when the younger Royals meet each other for the first time, they do not introduce themselves to one another. Unless you were introduced to an Elder by your mentor or your parents, it is a rarity for anyone to give each other their true names." He regarded Yoori with a look of ambiguity. "I could've met her at one point, I could've met her several times, or I could've never met her at all. Ju Won's masquerade ball is a time that the majority of us look forward to only because we get to become someone other than a God in training."

Yoori's heart warmed slightly when she realized the underlying motives in Ju Won's party. The charity event was done in his daughter's name, but it wasn't kept alive to only help children with leukemia. It was also a charity for the young people of the Underworld. It was Ju Won's gift to them. A gift of one night where they could hide behind masks, forget about their training, and be the children, teenagers, and college students they were meant to be had they not been born into the Underworld. It was the one night the young Gods could hide behind masks and be human.

"If it's such an anticipated night, why are you such a party pooper?" she teased. "You won't have to introduce yourself to anyone. You can be invisible."

He smiled. "I am a King in the Underworld. I do not need to introduce myself to anyone. When I walk into the room, they will all know who I am." Though his voice was light when they exited the maze, she could feel tenseness in his hold on her. Moments later, he said, "I do not want you to go."

Yoori peered up at his profile. "Why not?"

"The wicked will never rest . . . even at a party like that. I don't want you to be surrounded by all those people." He swallowed tightly. "I can go alone, but I don't want you to go . . . just in case anything happens."

"I have to go with you," she insisted patiently. "They see me as your distraction, remember? I have to at least show up with you to make them think that I have some sort of spine and that I can handle myself at one of their parties." Tae Hyun was about to say something else when Yoori hastened to add, "And I'll be wearing a mask. They will not recognize me as Soo Jin. She's been gone for so many years. I doubt anyone would look for her at the party." She smiled when she finally saw his hesitation. "You're afraid that you won't be able to protect me."

His silence confirmed her suspicions.

"I can handle myself."

"You shouldn't have to."

Yoori laughed softly. "You forget that although I do not have her memories, I still have Soo Jin's fighting instincts. If anything were to go down, I will still have her survival instincts."

"Those instincts only come out when you're a breath away from death. I'd prefer for you to not gamble with such odds."

"This world is nothing but a big game. We have to gamble . . . even if we don't want to."

She expelled an airy breath, doing her best to lighten the mood before they attended a party that housed all the Kings and Queens of this coldblooded society. "Come on, this is a masquerade ball. No one will know my identity. What's the worst that could happen?"

"You are raised to rule over this world..."

11: The Secret of Masquerades

The masquerade ball was held a few hours outside of the city. The night was one of those perfect winter nights. There was little wind, the air was fresh, and the moon was full and blooming. The road to Ju Won's party led up to luscious hills that surrounded the country.

While the limo drove past the overwhelming iron gates, Yoori was blessed with a breathtaking sight of Ju Won's palatial mansion. The infrastructure resembled a white castle that was sprawled over the mountain. It stood on a mountaintop, basking under the kiss of the winter stars. Magnificence couldn't begin to convey the wonder that this mansion emanated. It was larger than life and was definitely more beautiful than life. She would even daresay it was more beautiful than Tae Hyun's Serpents' estate, which was something she once thought was impossible.

"This is so amazing," Yoori commented out loud. Her focus shifted from the mansion to the crowd. Yoori was literally pressing her face against the window to look at everything when they pulled up into the circular driveway. "I can't believe all these people are Underworld crime lords!"

Visions of men and women, dressed respectively in tuxedos and elegant evening gowns, pleased Yoori's awestruck eyes. She readjusted her green, glitter embellished masquerade mask over her eyes for comfort. Her voice couldn't hide her sheer amazement. "I mean, where are all the assassins? Where are the stereotypical bald old men with high-class girls on their arms? Where are all the shady looking people? Everyone looks so . . . normal."

Their limo whirred to a stop in front of the red carpet that led up to the prized mansion.

"They're all shady," Tae Hyun informed her with mild amusement. He watched her gape out of the limo like a child visiting an amusement park for the first time. "They just do a good job of masquerading it under all that glamour."

The melodic sounds of laughter, warmth, and opulence drifted in the air. Many of the attendants, who ranged from their early twenties to early eighties, were already in the mansion. A few were outside, happily conversing with one another on the stairs leading up to the mansion. There were children running up and down the stairs, giggling as they hid behind pillars that ornamented the front half of the mansion. They wore elegant tuxedos and little princess gowns, looking utterly innocent as they accidentally bumped into some of the most powerful people in the country. The warmth of this party was blatant. It felt as though everyone was one big happy family—a big and dangerous family.

"Remember," Tae Hyun reminded her when he stepped out of the limo, "no matter how kind they are to you, do not let your guard down. If necessary, don't talk to them at all. And first and foremost, never—"

"Take off my mask," Yoori finished, rolling her eyes as she allowed Tae Hyun to help her out of the black limo.

He had been reminding her of this for the umpteenth time, and she was getting tired of it. She wasn't a child nor was she some fool who didn't know what type of party she was attending. She wasn't planning on speaking to any of them anyway. She was simply there to help show them that Tae Hyun wasn't distracted with her and that his mind was still on track.

"Anyway," Yoori started. She held a portion of her dress up to bring the hem an inch above ground, making it easier to walk. Her strappy black heels echoed on the driveway as she moved to stand on the red carpet. "I can't believe you refused to wear a mask. Look." She pointed at a group of young men laughing boisterously beside the water fountain. They were raising shot glasses in the air, cheering for a wonderful night with their various silver eye masks on. "Some of the guys got into it and wore masks."

Tae Hyun held an arm around her bare back and closed the limo door behind her. He rolled his own eyes at her remark. Apparently, listening to her chastise him for the umpteenth time about not wearing a mask was wearing him out.

Tae Hyun wore a black tuxedo with a white collared dress shirt and a green silk tie. Though Yoori was used to seeing him in suits, she knew that this tuxedo was one of the best since she couldn't help but drool over his physique. Enthralling, powerful, and eye-catching—the tuxedo not only brought out all the qualities that made up Kwon Tae Hyun, but it also enhanced them with an edge of superiority that only the King of Serpents could radiate.

"I told you already that I hate masquerade balls or any themed parties," he said with resignation. "The masquerade theme used to be for confidentiality, but times have changed. Now, it is only meant to entertain the women and children we bring to the party. It is very much optional for guys." When he caught her scowl of disapproval, he charmingly added, "Plus, it's better this way. People need to see that the King of Serpents is alive and well, right? Wasn't that part of our plan and the only reason why we're here?"

Yoori was certain that allowing people to see his face was merely an added benefit of not wearing the mask. It was not the primary reason. He didn't wear it simply because he didn't want to.

"Good thinking," she humored, accepting that she wasn't going to win this argument. It was futile. Tae Hyun was a stubborn and prideful individual. If he didn't want to do something, there was no forcing him.

"Are you sure you're ready for this?" he prompted ominously. "It's not too late to get back in the limo and go home before we have to deal with this mess. Because knowing you, you'd probably attract trouble as soon as we walk in."

Tae Hyun wrapped an arm around her again and held her close to him. They walked up the stairs, looking like the King and Queen of the night. The emerald green silk dress that Yoori chose to wear as her gown for the event was a v-cut, halter dress that hugged her body in all the right places. It was backless, giving an allure of sexiness when she turned around. The silk fabric flowed like water down her body and swam into the small train of the dress. She looked classy, elegant and as Tae Hyun jokingly told her, she looked very much like "trouble wrapped in a present."

"You attract trouble as much as I do," she countered, shivering when the cool air grazed her bare back.

He smirked at her comment before laying his fingers on her back. As if feeling her shudder seconds prior, he allowed his warm hand to thaw the chills that once coursed up her spine. The casualness of his touch sent a hot, electric current up her body and warmed her up like a furnace.

"I may attract trouble," he crooned, pulling her closer with affection, "but I'm not a fish in this ocean of sharks."

Yoori muttered a curse and decided to pinch him before they entered the mansion. She disliked his constant references that she not only attracted trouble, but that she always went looking for it as well.

"Are you implying that I'm Nemo?" she sassed back, glaring up at him after he flinched from her pinch. Her reference to "Nemo" was strange, but it was the first thing that popped into her mind when he mentioned sharks, the ocean, and fishes.

Half moon marks appeared on his forearm from the pinch of her nails.

Tae Hyun frowned at Yoori. "If you pinch me like that again, I swear I'm going to handcuff you to the bed when we get home and spank you to death."

As Yoori rolled her eyes at Tae Hyun's warning, he added, "And what the fuck is a 'Nemo'? Does it sparkle in the sunlight too?"

Yoori blinked slowly, floored by his limited knowledge pertaining to pop culture.

"It's a famous trouble-finding fish, Tae Hyun!" she whispered incredulously, eyes darting around to make sure no one heard that comment. "Seriously, what the eff is wrong with you? You didn't know what a 'BFF' was and now you don't know what a 'Nemo' is?"

Tae Hyun hardened his face in defense. "Stop assuming that everyone is up to date about all the teeny-bopper crap that you always reference stuff to. I don't know what a 'Nemo' is, but I'll be sure to address you as such from now on since you're so in love with it."

Her jaw slackened. "Don't you dare call me Nemo—*Crap!* This is amazing!"

Yoori was about to embark on an all out bickering war with Tae Hyun when waves of splendor fell upon her after they entered the lavish mansion. Screw bickering at a lost cause. She had a mansion with soaring ceilings and Swarovski chandeliers to gawk at.

Wow!

Much like Ju Won's other mansion that housed her initiation, this mansion had also been stripped of furniture. It was like it was specifically furnished to be a ballroom. Waltz music ambled in the air, moving over the waves of people who were dancing in the ballroom. Yoori had never seen so many extravagantly dressed people in one place. The room wasn't pitch black, but it was dim enough to give the illusion of an otherworldly dance floor. Magnificent views of city skyscrapers and majestic gardens glowed in the backdrop, further fostering the fantasy-like ambiance of the mansion. It truly felt like they were in a castle high up in the sky.

Despite the wonders of such a scene, what claimed Yoori's undivided attention wasn't the fact that the mansion was more lavish than anything she had seen in her life. It was the fact that although people continued to dance and converse freely, there was an obvious change in the air once Tae Hyun entered the ballroom.

When he strolled in, all gazes fell on him with unrivaled, unshaken interest; *that* was how powerful his aura was. If Yoori was "Nemo" and the rest of the Underworld were sharks, then Tae Hyun was the equivalent to the ocean in which they all swam in. He didn't just take up space in a room he walked into; he saturated the entire vicinity with his presence just by breathing the same air as them. She now understood what he meant when Tae Hyun spoke of becoming a "God" in this world. In a world filled with Kings and Queens, the only thing left to be was a God—or the "Lord." It was a position that was highly prized and it was a position that was more than prevalent in

Tae Hyun's near future. Having witnessed all of this, she suddenly felt silly for pinching him and chastising him for not being up to date on pop culture references. What a tough slap back to reality it was to realize how intimidating your boyfriend truly was. He didn't have time to watch cartoons; he had an entire world to preside over.

It didn't take long for Yoori to freeze up when the gazes unanimously shifted to her. The attention was unexpected, and she felt like a deer caught in headlights. No doubt they were either wondering who the hell she was or wondering if she was the girl who was distracting their beloved King. In that moment, she was extremely thankful that she had her mask on. Who knew what type of reaction she'd get if people saw her face and discovered that the "Queen of the Underworld" was back—and was with the King of Serpents, no less.

"You still think you're ready to play with the sharks?" Tae Hyun whispered, interlacing his fingers with hers. Despite his playful question, Yoori suspected he was only saying it to ease her anxiety. There was no doubt that he could sense how uncomfortable she felt.

Comforted by Tae Hyun's gesture, Yoori bobbed her head. She may have been the smallest fish in this sea, but she was with the biggest shark of all. For tonight, she was untouchable in this ocean.

"I was born ready," she replied, surprised at the ironic truth of this statement.

And with that, they descended into the ocean and began the uncomfortable process of sifting through the crowd to start their "meet and greet."

During their meet and greet, Yoori spotted Jung Min on top of one of the balconies. He wore a black suit and was conversing and laughing with his Underworld associates. Jung Min made eye contact with Yoori when he noticed her stare on him. He looked down at her and then at Tae Hyun, who was still busy speaking to his mentors. Jung Min shook his head like he was too disgusted to look at her now that she was back with Tae Hyun and turned away from her. Yoori smirked when this occurred. At least she knew with certainty that he was not going to be bothering her tonight.

When they moved around the ballroom, Yoori also caught sight of Ji Hoon. He, too, was not wearing a mask. His arm was wrapped around his beautiful date as he spoke to a group of mid-level Advisors and some of his mentors from the 1st layer. Apparently both Kings commanded the attention of all the "sharks" in the room. Yoori wasn't sure, but she could've sworn she saw Ji Hoon look her way several times. She hadn't forgotten their last meeting and was hoping that any contact with Ji Hoon would be minimal tonight. As Tae Hyun aptly put it, she didn't want to attract trouble. She cared about Ji Hoon, but not more than Tae Hyun. At this point, Tae Hyun was her one and only priority.

The duration of the socializing was both a boring and fearful experience for Yoori. She could literally feel the power and danger that surged from the people she met. This was by no means a party filled with harmless elites. All of the Underworld power figures convening in one estate only served to remind everyone else that they were in the presence of Gods—not humans. It was an odd thing for her because she could've sworn some people were looking at her curiously. It was as though they were trying to make out her face behind the mask. As if they were trying to figure out if they had met her in the past . . .

Yoori felt so nervous around all these people that she even asked Tae Hyun if his best friends were in attendance. She really wanted to meet them, for she knew they were two of the few people whom Tae Hyun genuinely trusted in the Underworld.

A grin crossed his lips at the reminder of his friends. "Those bastards are always late at arriving to any party. I think they're partying somewhere else before they'll deign to make an appearance here. Perhaps, if we stay out of trouble tonight, we'll see them." He gazed at her doubtfully. "But knowing you, *Nemo*, I'm praying that we'll hold out long enough so we can actually see my friends . . ."

Yoori laughed at the strange new pet name. It was a peculiar endearment, but when it was Kwon Tae Hyun who purred that name to you, it sounded so damn sexy nonetheless.

When they journeyed to one corner of the ballroom, she was pleasantly surprised when she saw the brothers. Both deviated from the tuxedo dress code and simply wore black slacks and nice dress shirts. Kang Min's collared shirt was maroon while Jae Won's shirt was a dark gray tone. They were in the corner, socializing with several other gang members. Like Tae Hyun, they also didn't wear masks.

"I told you only the women get dressed up for this party," Tae Hyun said next to her ear, earning a bitter smile from Yoori.

"You're all such party poopers," she commented lightly, laughing as they continued with their meet and greet.

"Damn, this is so boring," Tae Hyun shared moments later. His voice was unusually louder than before. It was as if he wanted others to hear him.

"Yeah," Yoori replied, distractedly looking through the crowd and searching for someone in particular.

They finally pulled away from the masses and went into a quiet area of the ballroom. Tae Hyun moved behind her, led her back into a dark corner, and pressed his lips against her shoulder. At first Yoori thought it was a flirting tactic, but when he parted his lips, she discovered it was something else.

"Don't react," he warned quietly. "But up above the ceilings, there are ten snipers and they're all watching you right now. Some even have their guns aimed at you."

The memories of her initiation came rushing back, causing her to stiffen in trepidation. Ju Won's snipers had become more skilled at being invisible. She didn't even hear them over the peaceful ballroom music.

Sensing her fear, Tae Hyun embraced her from behind as his means of comforting her. "I'm telling you because I don't want you to overreact if you see Jin Ae or any of her men. I know that you're looking for her right now and I want you to remember what you promised me."

Yoori clenched her jaw. She was trying to be subtle while looking for Jin Ae. It was apparent she didn't do a good job if Tae Hyun caught her. "I—"

"You promised me that you'll leave it up to my Cobras to do what they need to do," he interrupted firmly.

She looked at him. This was why Tae Hyun announced out loud that he was bored. He wanted to make it appear as if he was feeling her up in the corner as opposed to having a private conversation with her about Jin Ae.

Yoori couldn't contain her desire to find Jin Ae.

"Have you seen her—?"

The words drowned in Yoori's throat when she caught sight of them. Not Jin Ae, but Jin Ae's men—Woo and the other two guys whose names she couldn't remember. They were standing in a small circle with dates of their own. They were laughing heartily, enjoying their nights. Pain stabbed Yoori's conscience. She had no doubt that Woo and the other two guys were involved in what happened to Chae Young. Her furious eyes wandered around. Where the hell was Jin Ae?

"*Don't* do anything," Tae Hyun cautioned again, resting his lips close to her ear. "The snipers will shoot without hesitation if you give them a reason. Everyone in the Underworld has made an unspoken pact to leave their animosity for one another at the door when they entered this party. Don't be the one to disrupt this ambiance. Trust me . . . as easily as you've gotten on their good side, they could flip on you just as quickly. You don't want to be on anyone's bad side in this world, especially not with this crowd. If you cause a scene, then the snipers will take it as their freedom to eliminate you as a disruption. You know I won't have that. I'll kill them before they get a chance to do anything to you, but—"

"—that would defeat the purpose of us coming here," Yoori finished, understanding what was at stake. For tonight, she couldn't let her killer instincts come out if she ran into Jin Ae. She couldn't cause any commotion because she was certain that Ju Won's snipers were very much like him; they were all looking for a reason to kill her.

"I get it," Yoori confirmed, placing their momentary safety over her quest for vengeance.

Jin Ae would get what was coming to her. It may not be tonight, but she would reap what she sowed. Yoori would make sure of that.

"It's great to see both of you tonight," a voice slithered from the side.

Tae Hyun and Yoori lifted their heads. When they emerged from the dark corner, they found Seo Ju Won and Shin Dong Min in front of them.

Ju Won was dressed in a dark gray suit, a white dress shirt, and a dark gray tie. Although he was about to celebrate his 65th birthday soon, he looked utterly fit for a man of his age. He had no hair on his head, and the only feature on him that betrayed his actual age was his gray mustache and the subtle wrinkles on his face. Dong Min, who stood beside him, wore a light gray suit and a white dress shirt that was topped off with a matching gray tie. They smiled cordially at Yoori and Tae Hyun. Much like Tae Hyun, they were not wearing masquerade masks.

Ju Won continued to speak, his eyes moving from Yoori to Tae Hyun. "We were under the impression that you weren't going to be here tonight, Tae Hyun."

His voice was warm—too warm.

"Impressions were wrong," Tae Hyun answered with a warm voice of his own. "I wouldn't miss this for the world."

"No," Dong Min said pleasantly, "you have something else that may be more important to you than the world, right, my boy?" The muscles in Tae Hyun's body tensed when Dong Min averted his stern gaze to Yoori. "I see that everything has worked out well for our young lovebirds."

"And it's going to stay that way," Tae Hyun said with a nod, earning a disapproving glare from his Advisor.

"Young lover's quarrels," Ju Won noted with hearty amusement. He turned to Dong Min with a chuckle. "Didn't I tell you and Jung Min that I knew they would get back together soon? I knew our boy couldn't stay away from the one who stole his heart."

Yoori could detect the sheer anger in Ju Won's gleeful voice. Outward appearances aside, he was extremely pissed off that Tae Hyun was still with her. It went against all their warnings.

There was forced amusement in Dong Min's smile, and this alone scared Yoori. He was, if not more, pissed.

"I'm glad it all worked out and I'm glad you came," Dong Min said to Tae Hyun, still trying to maintain his cool. "I just spoke to some of your mentors from the 1st layer. They brought some of their colleagues from the 1st layer in China and Japan to meet you. We should go and see them. They're anxious to meet you."

Tae Hyun nodded. He protectively intertwined his fingers with Yoori's. "Of course, I would love to introduce them to Yoori."

"Actually, would you mind if I spoke to her for a moment?" Ju Won interjected gently. "We haven't had a chance to converse. I would love the opportunity to get to know her. From the looks of how things are going, she may be the new Queen of Serpents, right?"

"That won't be necessary," Tae Hyun declined swiftly. He made no effort to hide his warning glare. There was no way he was going to leave Yoori alone with Ju Won.

"Tae Hyun," Dong Min chimed in warningly. "There are certain topics that Yoori shouldn't be privy to when we're having important discussions with your mentors." His eyes grew gentler when they roamed from Yoori and then back to Tae Hyun. "This is a great night for a great cause. There will be no troubles brewing; Ju Won just wants to get to know Yoori."

Tae Hyun was prepared to decline the offer again when Yoori said, "Tae Hyun, just go. I want to get to know Ju Won."

She received a less than pleasant stare from Tae Hyun when she unclasped her hand from his. He wasn't happy that she was looking for trouble with one of the biggest sharks of all.

"Yoori—"

Yoori cut Tae Hyun off with a big smile to Ju Won. "I would love to keep you company." She would be damned if she allowed Ju Won to intimidate her any further. This old bastard had been a nuisance in her life. She was ready to give him a piece of her mind. "I've heard so much about you. It would be an honor to have some quality time with you."

She smiled wider, giving a pissed off Tae Hyun a stare that told him she would be fine. She turned back to Ju Won while Tae Hyun closed his eyes in defeat.

Dong Min chuckled approvingly while Ju Won smiled in victory.

"Well, that settles it then!" Ju Won exclaimed, grinning at Tae Hyun, whose expression was guarded with worry. "I won't go far. I'll speak to her on one of the patios. When you're ready, you can come and find us there."

"Uncle," Tae Hyun voiced politely, brushing past Ju Won. He stopped when he was arm-to-arm with him. "I trust that Yoori won't be upset when I come back for her. It would definitely dampen my evening if she was anything but comfortable."

The contents of his words were respectful, but the deliverance dripped with warning.

"Spoken by a true King," said Ju Won, unperturbed. He took a step to the side to allow Tae Hyun to pass. He faced Yoori and extended his arm to her. His expression radiated warmth when he said, "Now if you'll excuse us, we'll be outside if you need anything."

With a nod of goodbye and a brief expression of worry from Tae Hyun, they soon parted ways. Although she was with one of the top sharks in the Underworld, Yoori felt no fear. Yoori knew Ju Won wasn't looking to harm her tonight. As long as she didn't cause too much trouble, Nemo was safe from all the sharks for the time being.

She apprehensively took his arm and walked with him. Yoori felt sick to her stomach while she walked arm-in-arm with Ju Won. Being this close to someone so evil made her nauseous, to the extent where she wanted to run away. Albeit she was revolted, Yoori kept a pleasant expression on her face. Appearances were everything in this world and there was no one better to practice this with than the master himself.

There were three sets of patios that adorned Ju Won's mansion. The one in the west overlooked the vastness of the hills they were on. The one in the east held the view of the city in all its glory and the gargantuan one in the center led into Ju Won's majestic garden. For their meeting together, Yoori and Ju Won headed in the direction of the west patio, the one furthest away from the life of the party and the one secluded enough for muted conversations.

"Is Jin Ae here, sir?" Yoori blurted while they swept across the dim ballroom. She didn't know why she asked, but she had to get the question out. She had been at the party for a while now and she hadn't even caught a glimpse of Jin Ae. She was beginning to wonder if the girl was even here.

A smile broadened his lips. "After what happened during your initiation, I didn't feel it was necessary for her to make an appearance when you're in attendance. I do hate it when my guests feel uncomfortable."

"That was very considerate of you," Yoori voiced when they approached the patio doors.

They stepped onto the marble foundation of the patio. She detached her arm from his. She briefly wondered if Ju Won knew the things Jin Ae did to Chae Young. Yoori concluded that Ju Won must've known what Jin Ae did. This was why Jin Ae wasn't present tonight. The thought made her blood boil. Her hatred for Ju Won grew exponentially. It was no surprise that a bitch like Jin Ae would have an uncle like Ju Won.

The cool air greeted their walk toward the railing of the patio. Since it was considerably cold, everyone was mingling inside, leaving Yoori and Ju Won with the patio to themselves. The only breath of warmth came from the heating lamps that were scattered on various parts of the patio.

As the world inside the mansion continued without them, a sudden curiosity hit Yoori.

"You said that you didn't feel it was necessary for Jin Ae to be present while I was in attendance." She eyed Ju Won while they walked side by side. "How did you know I was coming?"

"I knew that you wouldn't miss this party for the world." He smiled to himself. "Masquerade balls have always been your favorite events."

Yoori broke eye contact and looked at the world outside the mansion. Her eyes roamed over the panoramic view. Ju Won's infinity pool spilled into the dark horizon that was bejeweled with distant skyscrapers and twinkling lights. Even though she didn't enjoy her company, she had to admit this patio offered the most spectacular views.

"You mean masquerade balls were Soo Jin's favorite events," she corrected silently, almost defensively.

"I know about your meeting with Jung Min," Ju Won said coolly. His eyes wandered over the panoramic view. "There is no need to beat around the bush. It's just us. No one else is here. You don't have to hide your curiosity about her. It is okay to hate her and be fascinated with her. There is a reason why this world hasn't forgotten about her."

Yoori tightened her jaw. She did not say anything to refute his words because that was exactly what she felt: hatred and fascination with An Soo Jin. Albeit he was correct with his words, she would not give him the satisfaction of her verbally confirming it.

He smiled at her silence. "Do you not wonder about her past? About the Queen behind all the legends?"

Yoori swallowed tightly again. She allowed the silence to sweep past her. Curiosity gnawed at her, but she kept it contained. She knew why Ju Won was doing this. He wasn't intent on reminiscing about Soo Jin; he was intent on trying to trigger her memories. Yoori was determined to not walk into this trap. She had to keep Soo Jin at bay.

"Tae Hyun told me that you throw a charity event every year in your daughter's name," she launched, changing the subject and breaking the small silence that perused between them. "That's very admirable."

Yoori wanted to vomit at her own words as she stared out into the distance. "*Admirable my ass*," she thought, sickening clouds storming her mind.

Ju Won chuckled bitterly. He did not look deterred with her blatant disregard for Soo Jin's past, but he did look perturbed by her words. As if reading her thoughts, he said, "I am one of the longest living crime lords this world has ever known. There's nothing admirable about throwing a charity event once every year for my daughter."

Ju Won, like most of the crime lords she had met, wasn't in the mood for her bullshit. Evidently, the art of beating around the bush was not a valuable virtue for any of the crime lords in the Underworld.

He went on, his voice growing icier. "I do my part because I love children and I love my only daughter even more. There's no need for admiration. I think you know that I, of all people, don't deserve any admiration." He cast a sideways glance in her direction. "I know you have a lot of animosity for me. Let's address it, shall we?"

Yoori smirked, relieved that she was able to lose it with the geniality. She would give him credit for being charitable every year for his deceased daughter's sake, but she would give him no more than that.

"Fine, we'll cut the bullshit then," she began severely. Her ice-cold eyes pulsed with warning. "I'm sick and tired of you trying to pull me and Tae Hyun apart. You may have a hold over Soo Jin, but you have no hold over me. I know you requested that both Tae Hyun and Ji Hoon stay away from me because I'm a distraction, but I'm not with Ji Hoon, and I would appreciate it if you stayed out of my relationship with Tae Hyun. Just because he wants to be with me doesn't mean he'll lose sight of the power he seeks in this world."

Ju Won kept his tranquil eyes on the view ahead. His arms behind his back, he continued to look unfazed by her hardened words.

"Behind us is the gathering of some of the most powerful people the world will ever know. The majority of the people in there are so high up that they could strike fear in government officials and silence the world as they please. At the top of that magnificent pyramid are Tae Hyun and Ji Hoon." He turned to her, unreadable poignancy teeming in his eyes. "Do you not see it, my child? Even crime lords from other countries are flocking here to meet them — both of them. They want to meet them because they want to know who the next potential Lords are." He held his father-like gaze on her, his voice growing gentler. "You may not understand it, but everything that is being done right now is done for your own good — for all three of you. Love gets in the way of everything and the three of you shouldn't fall victim to it, especially not with all the talent you have. You're better than that."

"So planting seeds of doubt in us, instigating, and pitting us against one another is for our own good?" She exhaled patiently, wondering if it was possible for Ju Won to see the steam coming out of her ears. She was so angry. His words were pure bullshit. "You're not helping any of us, Ju Won," she confronted fearlessly, a foreign part of her giving her the strength she needed to talk back to Ju Won. "All you're doing right now is entertaining yourself because you know your death is near and your glory days are over."

Her insult snapped the last shred of his patience.

"*You ungrateful fool!*" Ju Won gritted through his teeth. For the first time since Yoori had met him, Ju Won finally displayed anger. "How dare you speak to me that way? You think just because you have the young Kings in the palms of your hands that I'd be afraid to do anything to you? Think again," he spat, his eyes burning with rage that scared the living hell out of Yoori.

Ju Won noted the fear in her gaze and instantly subdued the fire in his eyes. It was only then did Yoori experience a déjà vu of sorts. Ju Won scared her when he was composed, but he scared her—and the Soo Jin buried deep within her—even more when he lost his temper.

He took in a deep inhalation and averted his gaze unto the horizon. The coolness in his voice returned. "You have so much to learn. Power is fleeting in this world. All those people in there may adore and admire Tae Hyun, but this is a cruel world. Behind their smiles, they are waiting to find out what the great King's Achilles' heel would be." He sharpened his eyes onto her. "Soo Jin was the Achilles' heel for Ji Hoon and he was knocked down a notch from power because these people saw his weakness. Do you think you won't be the same downfall for Tae Hyun?"

Tenseness occupied his wrinkled face. "I've faced two disappointments already. Ji Hoon had his moment to shine after your death, after his power was at its highest and just before Tae Hyun came into power. But he fucked that up because he allowed his affections for you to cloud his judgment. And *you* . . . I told you that night when I initiated you that I had always favored you. I favored you because you were the one I trained directly, because your father was like a brother to me, and because you were the one who reminded me of my daughter. But in the end, you became the biggest disappointment of all. Now, it is no secret that Tae Hyun is the pride and joy of this world. As the top Advisor in the 2nd layer, it is my duty to mold the first true Lord and make him the best this country has ever seen." His voice vibrated with raw, unfettered determination. "Tae Hyun will be that mold, and I'll be damned if you stand in the way of that."

Overwhelmed with all that he was telling her, something snapped in Yoori.

"Why was Soo Jin such a disappointment?" she bit back, unable to ignore the elephant rampaging in the room. There was no point. No matter how hard she tried to keep Soo Jin at bay, it was inevitable that Yoori would drown in her. Now that the forbidden floodgate was opened, she might as well lead this conversation on to the topic she wanted to address. "Because she didn't complete the 'task' you assigned her?"

Ju Won studied Yoori's face. Mockery began to surface in his gaze. "I have no idea what you're talking about."

"Give me the answers I want, Ju Won," she snarled, her right hand gripping on the railing so hard that if it were someone's neck, that person would've suffocated instantly.

"You're not asking for answers," he told her, taking inventory of the wrath she was exuding on to the railing. "To truly want answers, you'll ask for the equations in which the answers derive from."

Yoori scoffed. "You're speaking in riddles."

"Because you don't even understand the question you're asking."

"You wanted her to do something before she committed suicide," Yoori went on loudly. "Whatever it was you had her do, it messed her up to a degree where she tried to kill herself. What did you need from that family, Ju Won? What did you need from the Hwangs?"

A spark of astonishment lit his eyes. He faced her. "You know about the Hwangs?"

Yoori could not decipher the emotions spreading through his face. Was he surprised or pleased that she knew this? She could not tell. She only knew that she had claimed his undivided interest.

"I know who they are and I know you had something to do with that massacre," she told him confidently. She squared her shoulders in hopes of intimidating him into giving her an answer. "I just don't know what power you held over her and her brother. What was so important, Ju Won? Why did you have them murder that family?"

Just as she poured it all out, a professional looking man in his forties appeared at the door. He wore a black suit and had white gloves on. He bowed at Ju Won. "Sir, it's time for your speech. Are you ready?"

A lingering silence moved between them as Ju Won stared thoughtfully at Yoori. He peered inside the ballroom and then to the man at the door.

"Yes, go set it up. I'm ready."

He nodded as a gesture for the man to proceed ahead and that he would follow soon. He returned his cold gaze to Yoori. He gave a slow smile, his expression unwilling to divulge in any secrets that he may or may not know.

"I gave you back your gun as a reminder for you to finish what you started that night," he told her instead. "Dong Min has lost hope in you, Jung Min is on the fence, but I still have some hope. Though I must admit, I've been more than disappointed with your shortcomings in the last three years. Perhaps you can figure out this conundrum and prove yourself."

Yoori shook her head. "Whatever it was you wanted me to do, I won't do it now."

"Then, Choi Yoori, you'll die and you'll have no one to blame but yourself. Now, if you'll excuse me, I have an entire Underworld waiting for me."

With that, he left just as the MC announced that Seo Ju Won was about to give a "thank you" speech for everyone in attendance. Yoori watched him disappear into the ballroom, a round of applause commencing.

"Then, Choi Yoori, you'll die and you'll have no one to blame but yourself."

Ju Won's words ricocheted in her mind when Yoori rested her elbows on the patio railing. She buried her face into her hands. What a waste of time. She risked coming outside with him and came out learning little to nothing about what he wanted from Soo Jin. All she got were more questions. This was no doubt an epic failure on her part. She couldn't be more disheartened.

"I was counting down the minutes for him to leave so I could have a few moments alone with you," a familiar voice whispered just as Ju Won's amplified voice saturated the ballroom.

He was thanking everyone for coming and for their generous donations.

"Ji Hoon," said Yoori, releasing her face from her hands once she saw him step foot onto the marble patio. He was dressed in a black tuxedo with a white dress shirt underneath a red tie. Much like Tae Hyun, the tuxedo did him a world of good and made him look more handsome than ever.

"You're the belle of the ball, Yoori," he noted favorably, approaching her with a kind smile on his face. He looked extremely happy to see her. "Even when you're only wearing a mask, all eyes of the men ate you up as you walked into the ballroom. It was like this entire event was made for you."

Yoori smiled bashfully at his compliment. She had just got done with one intense conversation; she was definitely not looking for another one this evening. Tae Hyun was right. She did attract trouble.

"I was with Tae Hyun," she said, bringing up Tae Hyun right away to dissuade any impressions he may have that she was available. "I'm sure I received the runoff of the attention because everyone was wondering who this new girl hanging around one of their Kings was."

"If only they knew it was the Queen herself they were looking at," he replied, his face hardening faintly at the mention of Tae Hyun. "I must admit, I'm very surprised that you and Tae Hyun are back together already. But I guess regardless of what happens, it's difficult to stay away from the one you love."

Dread overwhelmed Yoori when he said those words. She knew it not only applied to her and Tae Hyun, but it also applied to herself and Ji Hoon. Or, perhaps not her, but it did apply to Ji Hoon and Soo Jin. He was in love with Soo Jin, and she wasn't Soo Jin. That was all the reason she needed to know that she should not be around him a second longer.

"I imagine you didn't come to this event alone. You should go keep your date company."

She hoped he would take the hint and let her be.

Ji Hoon was not the type to give up easily. "You're above any date I bring tonight," he replied, getting so close to her that Yoori had to back away from him in cautiousness.

Hurt drenched his gaze at her actions. He sighed at her overt show of displeasure with merely being around him. "I just want to speak to you for a few minutes, Yoori." Concern teemed in his eyes. "It's not safe for you to be here alone. Let me watch you until Tae Hyun comes back for you. I just want to make sure you're alright."

Yoori's heart ached at the distress spilling out of Ji Hoon. She knew he was worried about her. His only intention was for her to be safe. She appreciated his genuine care for her. Nevertheless, she couldn't heed his pleas. There was too much at risk.

"If Tae Hyun sees you with me, he'll toss you into the pool without hesitation," she said flatly. "I know the two of you. I know you'll get into a fight the first chance you get." Resolve palpitated in her voice. "I can't have that happen. People are already looking at me as a distraction for both of you. I'll be damned if the two of you get into a fight here. Thank you for wanting to keep me safe, but I'll find Tae Hyun by myself."

Yoori dodged past him and flew back into the ballroom before Ji Hoon could reach out to her.

"Yoori!" he whispered, running after her. He tried as hard as possible to seem casual and not bring attention to them.

The clacking of her heels quickened while she skirted past various crime lords and their dates. She drew deeper into the sea of people gliding on the ballroom floor. Since her absence from the mansion, it seemed that everyone had taken the opportunity to move onto the dance floor to prepare for a slow dance. The room was more packed, acting as an asset for her to lose Ji Hoon in the crowd. Her gut quaked guiltily. Yoori hated that she was running away from Ji Hoon when he only wanted to take care of her. She took in a painful inhalation. But this was for the best. It was the best for all three of them in the long run.

She could hear Ji Hoon's whispers for her name. He was trying to find her in the crowd. The looming darkness distilled over them, setting the mood for the melodic music that overtook the room. Yoori frantically looked around. She had to find Tae Hyun before she got lost in the crowd. Right when she was about to step away from the ballroom, someone grabbed her hand and dragged her to the side.

"Lil sis, where have you been? I've been looking for you," the male voice said softly.

He gently pulled her to the area of the dance floor that was closest to the doors leading into the gardens. People around them were already slow dancing to the music; everyone was in their own world as Yoori fought the stranger's firm grasp.

He was wearing a tuxedo with a white dress shirt and silk blue tie. Unlike the majority of the men in attendance, he was wearing a silver mask over his eyes. She couldn't really make out his face, but judging by his profile, she could tell he was also a handsome man.

"Excuse me," Yoori cordially said to the masked man. She was careful not to raise her voice. She didn't want to draw attention to herself. She tugged at the grasp he held on her. "You have the wrong person. I'm not your sister."

The man turned around. He stopped in his tracks and assessed her. Moments later, his eyes swelled in mortification. He instantly released his hold on her hand.

"Oh damn," he groaned, smiling embarrassingly at her. Dimples appeared on either side of his cheeks. "I'm so sorry. I saw you from the corner and I thought you resembled my sister. I've been looking for her for a while, but this damn ballroom is so big. I wanted to surprise her and force her to do what she hates most—dance with her older brother." He laughed disbelievingly to himself, earning a laugh from Yoori too. "Now I feel like an idiot. I can't believe I grabbed the wrong girl. I'm really sorry."

"No, no. It's okay!" Yoori laughed, for some reason already feeling comfortable with this man. There was something endearing about his adoration for his younger sister. "You've been treading around, looking for your sister so you can punish her with a dance? Gosh, how evil are you?"

His shoulders lifted with laughter. "Yeah, she hates it. I haven't seen her in a while. I figured it'd be a good way to catch up." He groaned, running his fingers through the black hair that fell to the nape of his neck. "I can't believe I thought you were my sister. This is so embarrassing." He squared his shoulders awkwardly. "Well, since we're here, will you dance with me? I don't want to be some idiot who caught the wrong girl and wasted her time."

Yoori looked around nervously. "I really shouldn't. I think my boyfriend is looking for me. Plus, the only time I've danced was when I was barefoot. I'm known to be accident-prone and I'm wearing stilettos now. I would hate to be the one who stabs holes into your feet."

He chuckled, waving away her excuse. "I'm sure your boyfriend will be fine for a few minutes." Yoori was about to politely decline until he cleverly added, "It also helps that I'm wearing one of the sturdiest leather shoes there are. Come on," he urged, grabbing a hold of her waist. "Help me warm up before I find my baby sister."

There was something in the way he spoke to her that made it impossible for her to refuse him. He didn't appear to be one of those sleazebags who were looking to bed her. And for reasons unknown to her, a part of her also wanted to dance with him, especially whenever he mentioned his younger sister.

Reluctantly, she said, "Okay."

"Good," he approved, smiling wider after Yoori placed her hands on his shoulders. They began to move to the rhythm of the music, following the sway of the crowd surrounding them.

Yoori's heart began to warm. Thoughts of being angry with Ju Won and escaping from Ji Hoon eased from her mind. The presence of this person made her feel so comfortable.

"I'm sorry," the masked man started kindly. "I didn't catch your name."

"Yoo—" Yoori cut herself off before making the executive decision to not give him her actual name. "—na. It's Yoona," she lied with a nervous smile. "Yours?"

"AJ," he answered, his smile growing warmer as they moved cohesively. "My name is AJ."

"Not succumb to its weaknesses."

12: The King of Scorpions

"Yoona, you lied to me," AJ remarked moments later, dancing to their third song of the night. "You said you weren't a great dancer. Look at you! You're not tripping or stepping on my feet at all."

Yoori smiled widely at his compliment. "I don't actually dance much so I assume I am. I danced one other time with my boyfriend, but it was because he's a good dancer and he pretty much swept me off my feet. I figured I became good for him. I didn't think I'd be this good with anyone else though!"

Yoori was elated. She and AJ had been talking about what type of food they enjoyed and how boring they thought this charity event was. They were getting along incredibly well. He was such a cool guy, and she was excited to introduce him to Tae Hyun. Perhaps AJ was one of Tae Hyun's friends from the 1st layer?

"I'm okay when it comes to dancing," AJ told her, his voice matching her optimism and energy. "I'm only exceptional with my wife, and I suck on purpose to embarrass my sister."

Yoori laughed at the latter portion of his reply. "Oh no, where's your sister? Won't she be looking for you?"

He chuckled, his face contorting in bitterness. "Nah. She's probably busy breaking hearts somewhere. She'll find me soon enough."

Something else clicked in Yoori's mind. She shifted uneasily, starting to feel perturbed. "Wait, where's your wife? Is she here?"

Crap. She didn't think he was a sleazebag, but what considerate married man would dance with another woman? Yoori felt disappointment bubble within her. To think she thought he was cool!

"No, she's not here," he replied casually. "She's at home resting."

"She won't mind that you're dancing with another woman?" Yoori asked awkwardly. She contemplated kicking him in the balls for subtly cheating on his wife while dancing with her. She held in the temptation. She did not want to cause a scene.

"Another woman, yes. But she won't mind you," he clarified with a genuine smile. As though reading her mind, he went on. "Trust me, I'm not cheating on her. I love my wife, and though you're wearing a mask right now, I know I'm not attracted to you. You don't have to worry about being a home wrecker."

Yoori smiled in relief. She assessed the tone in his voice and concluded he was telling the truth. He truly adored his wife. Curiosity got the best of her. She wanted to know more about them. "How long have the two of you been married?"

"Three years."

"Congratulations!" Yoori chirped excitedly. She continued to probe, hoping he wouldn't find her too intrusive. It was exciting for her to meet someone, other than Tae Hyun, Ji Hoon, and the brothers, that she actually got along with in the Underworld. It was also remarkable that he was married. He could give her pointers on how to make it last with Tae Hyun. "How did you guys meet?"

"She was working for my sister, but we've pretty much known each other our whole lives. It was inevitable that if I were to settle down with anyone, it would be her."

Yoori nodded dreamily. Apparently, it was one of those "I've-loved-you-since-forever" type of loves.

"How long have you been with your boyfriend?" he asked, pulling her out of her dreamy sigh.

"A couple of months," Yoori said, unable to keep the sheepish smile off her face when she was reminded of Tae Hyun.

It felt like a lifetime ago that we met, Yoori wanted to add, but held back. She knew that the timeframe for her and Tae Hyun was a short one in comparison to other couples, but she didn't care. Time was irrelevant. When she took into consideration all that they had been through together, their relationship was the equivalent of a three-year relationship anyway.

"You're blushing," AJ observed, his kind eyes staring down at her from his silver mask. "Is this your first relationship?"

Yoori blushed some more. She nodded at his question. "This is my first."

That I remember, she supplied in her mind.

Ji Hoon was another story, but then again, he would always be another story.

"So, I saw you walking in with the King of Serpents," AJ noted offhandedly. "I take it he's the boyfriend you're talking about?"

The blush that once heated her cheeks froze under icy caution. The dark tone in his voice unsettled her. Yoori nodded hesitantly, feeling vigilant. Was it her or did he tense up when he asked about Tae Hyun? It was instinct on her part, but she had a hunch that he was against her being with Tae Hyun.

Her suspicions were fully confirmed when he said, "This may be too forward of me, but I don't think it's a good idea that you're with him."

"Why is that?" she asked cagily, looking around to find that Kang Min and Jae Won had parted from the group they were having a conversation with.

They stood in the center of the ballroom, their eyes wide as they observed her and AJ. They looked worried. They were clearly wondering who the masked man dancing with her was.

Yoori shook internally when she took stock of the vigilance in their eyes. No longer feeling comfortable, Yoori continued to dance with AJ, unknowingly moving closer to the exit that led into Ju Won's majestic gardens.

"It's never a good thing to be labeled as someone's distraction, but it's worse to be labeled as Kwon Tae Hyun's distraction," he forged on, unaffected by the discomfort that riddled her face. His eyes were still gentle on her. "I'm sure you know that in this world, he's at the very top of the pyramid. There are countless people who are invested in his future of being the first official Lord of the Korean Underworld. Any woman who means anything to him will be the weakness this world looks for when they want to make him fall from his throne."

Not another one, Yoori thought indignantly.

That was when she knew it was a bad idea to dance with anyone from the Underworld. No matter how nice they appeared, they always had ulterior motives. She *was* Nemo, Yoori admitted grudgingly. She either attracted trouble or went looking for trouble. In this case, both things happened. Why was she reeling in all the unpleasant people?

"I take it you're a supporter of Tae Hyun who doesn't want him to be distracted?" Yoori asked blithely, feeling comfortable enough with this AJ guy that she wasn't afraid to at least talk back to him. At the moment, it didn't appear as if he would hurt her. "Are you here to tell me to stop seeing him?"

"I'm actually one of the people going against him," he corrected simply. "I'm telling you to stop seeing him, but the reason doesn't pertain to him being a contender to become the Lord of the Underworld."

Yoori's stomach gave a horrid lurch after he basically told her that he was Tae Hyun's enemy. A wave of cold chills rippled over her skin when his grip on her tightened. He was anticipating her to run away from him, and he made damn sure that wasn't going to happen. Yoori looked around frightfully. Would he hurt her at a charity event where there was an unspoken promise to keep all the external drama out? Was he an assassin or something? Was he here to kidnap or execute her? Yoori's eyes roamed the ballroom for help. She wanted to kick him in the balls and make a run for it. She vetoed that idea as she still didn't want to make a scene. Yoori desperately considered her options. Would a short-term gain make up for the long-term consequences if she brought enough attention to herself? What if people started to realize that she was An Soo Jin? If that occurred, she wouldn't have to just worry about Tae Hyun's enemies coming after them—she'd have to worry about Soo Jin's as well. It was a catch-22 for her—she was screwed either way.

Tae Hyun! Read my mind and find me, Yoori prayed in her mind, hoping her non-existent telepathic ability would help her in her time of need.

As if hearing her plea, in the sea of dancing silhouettes, her frantic eyes locked on Tae Hyun. He had just emerged from a crowd from the west side of the ballroom. When she sensed someone else, she looked over and saw that Ji Hoon had emerged from the east side of the ballroom. They caught her eyes before flickering their gazes to each other, and then back to Yoori and her masked dancing partner.

From the point she and AJ were standing in, a triangle was formed between the crime lords and herself. Both Kings steadily strode toward the center of the ballroom, merely a couple of feet away from her. Both, just like Kang Min and Jae Won, had curious expressions marked on their faces. They, too, were wondering who she was dancing with.

"What right do you have to tell me what to do?" Yoori asked, shifting her attention back to AJ.

She was hoping that she could stall him from hurting her. Tae Hyun was now subtly veering through the crowd to get to her. He, much like Yoori, did not want to make a scene that would transfer all the attention to her. Ji Hoon was also sifting through the crowd, but his pace was slower. There was a glint of awareness in Ji Hoon's eyes; it was as if he was trying to make out AJ's face. It was evident AJ looked familiar to him.

"My blood gives me that right."

Yoori's own blood froze when she heard those words.

All the fibers in her body seemed to have awakened as the contents of his statement streamed over her, leaving her with nothing but mystification. Her eyes expanded as she stared up at his. She tried to make out his face behind the mask.

"What did you just say?"

Shock electrocuted her.

He couldn't be.

He couldn't be who she thought he was.

There was no way. There was just no way.

"You don't recognize me right now, but I know that you know who I am, lil sis."

Yoori blinked quietly.

It was then that she couldn't deny it anymore.

A sense of familiarity gushed through her after he called her "lil sis." She could see in his eyes that he was the one who haunted her dreams. He was the one who hid her from this world and the one who set everything in motion. Her older brother—the King of Scorpions—had finally made his long-awaited appearance.

He did not give her time to react to their unexpected reunion.

Next thing Yoori knew, he was jerking her closer to him, and in an instant, she was cradled against his chest as he ran out onto the patio. They descended down the stairs, hurtling through the perfectly manicured lawn at record pace. The last image she saw before Young Jae ran like the wind was Tae Hyun and Ji Hoon's eyes enlarging before they ran after her through the crowd. They may have been fast, but An Young Jae was faster—much faster.

"What are you doing?" Yoori cried, fighting against his grasp. "Where are you taking me?"

Finally meeting her long-lost brother aside, she knew it was a bad idea that the guy was now kidnapping her. Yoori fought to keep her heels buried in the damp grass. Her efforts were in vain. His strength and speed overpowered hers. It didn't take long for Yoori to deduce that one of Young Jae's "special skills" was running. He was damn fast.

"They said you died in that fire," he breathed out, flinging his silver mask across the lawn before staring down at her.

Yoori gasped inwardly. A strong facial structure, prominent nose, and thin lips made up his face. His black hair was grown to his nape, giving him a regal appearance befitting of a King in this world. Finally, there was a face to put on the brother who always appeared in her dreams. A multitude of emotions teemed in his eyes as he stared down at her. Remorse and guilt were the most prevalent emotions.

"If I had known that you didn't die, then I would've searched for you sooner. I should've never left you alone in Taecin." He shook his head, increasing his pace and keeping his grip on her. "I'm sorry that you came this far and got sucked into this world again. But there's still time to make things right. Only a select few knows about your existence and we'll keep it that way. I'm taking you somewhere safe. Somewhere far away from here, where the Underworld can't find you."

"*What?*" she cried, forgoing all emotional bondage that came when being reunited with your long-lost sibling. Her brother just came back into her life, and now he was taking her away from Tae Hyun?

"No! No, please!" she pleaded, fighting to disentangle her wrist. She wasn't going to leave Tae Hyun. She had been through too much to be with him. There was no way in hell she was leaving Tae Hyun again. "I don't want to go!"

It would've been an endearing sight: an older brother dragging his baby sister away from a party for her own good, but Yoori thought it was anything but endearing. At this point, she was just pissed at her brother.

"Damn it!" she snapped. "Let go of me! I have a life here now. I can't just leave!"

"You don't even know how much danger you're in right now," he shouted, easily holding on to her despite her fighting him. "Of all people, how the hell did you wind up with Kwon Tae Hyun?"

And then in that instant, they had company.

"Young Jae!" Ji Hoon screamed from behind them. "Let her go!"

Then—

"Get the hell off her!"

It was Tae Hyun who sped out from the darkness like a wolf and pulled Yoori out of Young Jae's grasp. Yoori tripped to the side, her mask drooping off her face while her brother tilted to the opposite side. He nearly toppled over at the force of Tae Hyun's sudden attack.

Oh God, oh God, Tae Hyun! Thank God, you're a cheetah, she thought happily.

Yoori wanted to raise her hands in joy and praise Tae Hyun. In reality, she was too busy huffing and puffing for air. Tae Hyun shielded his body in front of her, blocking her from her brother. While doing so, he helped her up.

His worried and angry eyes roamed over her. "I leave you alone for a few minutes, and all this shit goes down. You thought I was being paranoid, but do you see why I didn't want to come now?"

Yoori took her drooping mask off and rolled her eyes. No matter the situation, leave it to Tae Hyun to always pull the "I-told-you-so" card. She wanted to scream out her own fighting words, but resisted the urge. The predicament they were in really didn't call for useless bickering.

"Well, well. If it isn't the chosen King himself," Young Jae mocked, rising to his full height. He straightened his back. His nose was flaring while his eyes brimmed with hatred. "Kwon Tae Hyun, this world may spoil you with its adoration, but I don't give a fuck about their favoritism. Let go of my sister right now. I won't allow her to be with you any longer."

"You're not taking her away from me, Young Jae," Tae Hyun told him, pushing a panting Yoori closer behind him.

At this moment, Ji Hoon finally appeared out of the darkness. His eyes flickered to Tae Hyun, Yoori, and finally landed on Young Jae.

Tae Hyun went on, conviction present in his voice. "I don't want to fight you, but I won't let you take her either."

"You don't want to fight me?" Young Jae burst out in derisive laughter. The King in him awakened at the challenge. He did not show even the slightest sign of fear. "Are you insinuating that you'll win?"

"No," Tae Hyun answered, allotting Yoori time to breathe a sigh of relief. She was thankful that he placed his pride on the backburner. She was pleased with the consideration he was showing until he added, "I'm telling you that you'll lose."

"Damn it, Tae Hyun!" Yoori cast him a stern look, gripping her fingernails around his forearms in warning. "That's my brother. Don't provoke him!"

She may have just met Young Jae today, but she had enough sense to know how much her brother meant to her. No matter the lack of memories, he was her brother, and this alone demanded her loyalty. It just sucked that he and Tae Hyun were already on bad terms. She didn't appreciate Tae Hyun allowing his prideful testosterone to worsen matters. Big brother hating boyfriend? It was every girl's worst nightmare—amnesia or not.

"He shouldn't have pissed me off then," Tae Hyun snapped back, unwilling to back down.

"Arrogant fuck," Young Jae growled, having enough.

He was about to charge at Tae Hyun, who was more than ready to fight him, before Ji Hoon ran in. He maneuvered himself around Young Jae and pulled him back.

"Young Jae, that's enough!" Ji Hoon yelled, dragging Young Jae away from Tae Hyun. "This is the first time your sister is seeing you and you act like this?"

"You piece of shit!" Young Jae cursed, suddenly whipping around to punch Ji Hoon across the face.

Yoori was at an absolute loss for words.

Did Young Jae hate all the boyfriends that Soo Jin had as well?

"You let the woman you claim to love be with Kwon Tae Hyun of all people?" He was disgusted with Ji Hoon. His eyes were icier than the winter night. "Your enemy? *My* enemy?"

Ji Hoon spat blood from his mouth. With fire burning in his eyes, he furiously grabbed Young Jae by the collar. Young Jae wasn't the only one pissed off.

"Three fucking years!" Ji Hoon hollered. "You lied to me for three fucking years! You told me that you fulfilled her wishes and that you killed her. I didn't even know what happened until I saw her a couple of months ago! You fucking hid her, gave her amnesia, and you didn't even tell me where you hid her. You should've given her to me! I would've taken care of her!"

By now, it wasn't even about Yoori or Tae Hyun. It was about Ji Hoon, Young Jae, and the one at the center of all this drama—Soo Jin.

"She has amnesia," Young Jae countered, pushing Ji Hoon off of him. Fury radiated from him. "From the formula that *you* gave her. Why would I give her to you? Why would I let you keep her in this world when she wanted to kill herself because of it?"

"Why are you back, Young Jae?" Ji Hoon snarled. "She's not Soo Jin—she doesn't remember anything."

"She can't be with Kwon Tae Hyun," he told Ji Hoon decisively. He whipped back to face Tae Hyun. He lifted a warning finger at him. "You're not keeping my baby sister. If you want to be with her, you'll have to kill me first."

"That can easily be arranged," Tae Hyun said coolly.

"Tae Hyun," Yoori warned rigidly, unable to talk to anyone but Tae Hyun.

At her call, the primitive violence exuding out of Tae Hyun subsided. He backed down, curbing the temptation to beat the fuck out of her brother. Yoori knew Tae Hyun wasn't the type to take people's shit. He was maintaining his composure for her. For that, she was grateful.

When he calmed, Yoori took an unsteady look at the scene around her.

It was a strange experience for her to stand there. She had nothing to say to her former boyfriend and her long-lost brother. She should have stepped in and said something, but she had no idea what to say. All she wanted to do was be invisible.

"She won't listen to you," Ji Hoon voiced firmly. "She thinks she's in love with him. Why do you think she's with him and not with me?"

"I'll make her remember then," Young Jae uttered unthinkingly.

Even Yoori didn't believe Young Jae meant that.

"You hid her for years so that she wouldn't remember anything," Ji Hoon commented, verbalizing Yoori's thoughts.

"That was before I found out she fell into bed with my biggest enemy!"

Tae Hyun grew tense again. He took in a long, distended inhalation. He was clearly annoyed and was tired of listening to all of this.

"Young Jae," Ji Hoon called, inching closer to Young Jae. "Three years ago, she came to us saying that she wanted to kill herself and that the only way she could do it was if you injected her with the poison. That was the only way for her to expunge the oath she gave to you and the only way she knew you'd kill her."

Yoori stiffened when Ji Hoon turned to her.

For the first time, she felt nothing but shame while gazing at Ji Hoon. She had always known that he loved Soo Jin, but to hear him convey it in this degree amazed Yoori. Though she didn't love him, she did feel guilty towards him. He lost someone he loved, and now this someone was in love with another man. Almost anyone could understand his pain, and Yoori was the one who was affected by it the most.

"Look at her," Ji Hoon pressed on. "She's healthy right now. That's all that matters, and I won't let you revive her memories. You'll have to go through me if you want to do that."

The speech not only touched Yoori, but it also touched her brother. Moved by Ji Hoon's statement, Young Jae's anger dispersed. As though Ji Hoon's words were the water he needed to douse the inferno raging through him, Young Jae nodded understandably before narrowing his hardened eyes on Tae Hyun.

"Who are *you* to come between them?" he incited, his voice as cold as the arctic ice.

"Young Jae, *stop*," Yoori gritted out, walking out from behind Tae Hyun.

Albeit it was unfortunate that Ji Hoon was left without the one he loved, she refused to stand there as her own brother chastised Tae Hyun. It was her decision who she wanted to be with. Tae Hyun would not be blamed for her choice.

Tae Hyun raised his hand for her to not get involved. He remained quiet, allowing Young Jae to continue. Like a brewing storm, he paid close attention to whatever argument Young Jae wanted to present before he deigned it was necessary to unleash his own wrath.

"Do you know what they've been through?" Young Jae went on venomously. He disregarded the expression of warning on Yoori's face. All that mattered to him was the relationship he approved of. "He was there for her when she wanted to kill herself and he's still taking care of her now. Do you really think you have any right to hold her like that, like you're above everything he is to her?"

"I can't control time, Young Jae," Tae Hyun finally responded. His expression was composed as he stared into the eyes of the one who despised his existence. "I can't help that she met Ji Hoon first. I can't help that they were together before me. I can't help that they were 'in love' before me and that fate made me come later in her life when I would've given anything to be there for her first."

Tae Hyun's words tugged at Yoori's heartstrings. She despondently gazed up at him. She hated that he had to explain himself to them, and she hated it more that Young Jae and Ji Hoon weren't remotely swayed by the sincerity of his words.

"You really think all of this is genuine on your part?" Ji Hoon asked doubtfully. His face matched the same distaste that adorned Young Jae's visage. "I know you, Tae Hyun. I know how competitive you are. The only reason why she means anything to you is because she means everything to me."

"I hate you more than I've ever hated another human being," Tae Hyun responded, animosity prominent in his voice. "But you're mistaken when you say that she means something to me because of how you feel about her. Your feelings for her have no effect on mine. As far as I'm concerned, you were never the reason for anything, Ji Hoon. It just happened to be that you're the guy I'm competing with when it comes to her. It could have easily been any other guy, and my feelings for her would remain. I would fight for her all the same." His eyes grew firmer. "But make no mistake about it. If I was there for her in the beginning, then she wouldn't be here right now." He then narrowed his eyes on both Young Jae and Ji Hoon. "I would've never helped her kill herself when she begged for my help. I would've never given up on her. I would've never made the mistakes both of you made and allowed her to leave me. I would *never* let her die."

He faced Ji Hoon, who was staring at him with fire blazing in his eyes.

"It was your mistake that you let her go. It was your mistake that you lost her. And it's your mistake that you feel the 'first-come, first-serve' basis applies when emotions are involved. You play the brokenhearted prince charming well in this story, but in the end, it has always been your fault. I don't give a fuck if you look at me as the other guy or if you feel that I stole someone who was yours. I will never apologize for the circumstances of how we met, and I will never apologize for being the one who came after your mistakes. *I'm* the one she chose; *I'm* the one she wants to be with. You may have come first, but in the end, it will always be me."

Done with an angry Ji Hoon, Tae Hyun reverted his focus back to Yoori's brother.

"Young Jae, listen up. I said all that I needed to say in the matters pertaining to the 'she-belongs-with-Ji Hoon' crap, but know that I'm holding more patience with you than you'll ever know. There's a big difference between protecting her and taking her away from me. It will be her choice if she decides to leave me, but if you even dare to forcefully take her from me, I'll put you in a body bag. Do you understand me?"

Young Jae gave a mocking snort. "Your threats may work on the minions at your feet, but they don't work with me." He dodged past Ji Hoon and went straight for Tae Hyun. His fists were clenched and he was ready for a battle. "You may be the favorite to rule over the Underworld, but you're not the Lord yet, and as far as I'm concerned, our ranks are still the same in this world."

"Young Jae! Stop coming at him like this!" Yoori interjected, pushing Tae Hyun to the side when she saw Tae Hyun's jaw tighten. He was pissed, and he really might put Young Jae in a body bag if he continued to push his limits.

"Stay out of this, lil sis!" Young Jae snarled. He made a move to lunge for Tae Hyun, but was stopped when Ji Hoon popped in front of him once more.

"Young Jae, she's not going anywhere with you," Ji Hoon chimed in, pushing Young Jae back. "We'll figure out the rest later. But for now, stop overwhelming her. She doesn't need the stress of being with you to trigger anything."

"This is Tae Hyun we're talking about, Ji Hoon," Young Jae argued heatedly. "I don't give a damn about the things he says right now. Power is everything to him, and in the end, if given the opportunity, he'll return to his old ways and my sister will be the casualty of his betrayal."

"Don't provoke me, Young Jae," Tae Hyun growled back, the muscles in his jaw tightening even more. "You don't know me, so don't act like you do. I can respect the fact that you're her older brother and that you're looking to protect your baby sister. I can empathize with that. But you're not protecting her if you pull her away from me. She won't be safe anywhere else, and I can't have that. I went through too much to be careless with her now."

Young Jae smirked. There was nothing but revulsion in his eyes. "You have as much respect for me as you did for your brother?"

Yoori saw Tae Hyun tense up at the mention of his brother.

Young Jae noted the same tension and fed on that. He barreled on with his verbal attacks. "I hated Kwon Ho Young with a passion. He killed my father, and even though it wasn't you, you know that in this world, we share in our family's mistakes. The blood that pumps in your veins will never excuse you from the hate I feel for your family. You may have been the one to kill him, but you disgust me even more because in my family, there's a thing called family loyalty. You have none of that so I can't trust that you'll have any loyalty for her when the end comes. I'd be a fool to think you would protect her when you murdered your own brother. You're a disgraceful monster—even by the standards of our world."

"Young Jae, that's enough!" Yoori commanded. She was pissed beyond words with how he was speaking to Tae Hyun. Tae Hyun was now quiet as the remembrance of his brother drained the blood from his face. The very sight of him in such a state infuriated her. "Tae Hyun doesn't deserve to be spoken to like this. You will stop this right now!"

"He doesn't deserve you," Young Jae replied. His voice softened when speaking to her. "You deserve better than him."

"That's for me to decide," she retorted stubbornly.

"You're not making decisions off valid memories or rationale."

"I'm not a brainless twit!" Yoori screamed, incensed with his hardheadedness. "I know who I want to be with! You don't know better than me. Just stop it."

Young Jae was unyielding. "In the future, you would never forgive me if I didn't try to pull you away from him now. I'm doing this for your own good."

"I would never forgive you if you pull me away from him now." She released a deep exhalation. "Now stop it." Before he could say anything else, she unthinkingly said, "Please, oppa. Just stop it."

The ice on Young Jae's visage thawed after hearing her refer to him as "oppa." Warmth pulsed in his eyes. It was clear that he hadn't been called "oppa" in a long time, and it was clearer that it was an endearment exclusively given to his baby sister. In spite of his own reservations, he finally gave in to her request.

"You don't even need your memories to be stubborn," he bitterly whispered, abandoning all desires to fight Tae Hyun.

The comment Young Jae made was a careless one, but it was one that merited disgruntled smiles of agreement from Tae Hyun and Ji Hoon. Just before another word could be spoken, the Kings and Queen were interrupted by two familiar voices.

"Boss!" Jae Won and Kang Min called, racing toward them from the mansion.

It was evident to Yoori that Tae Hyun ordered the brothers to guard the entrance to the garden from any other visitors. The brothers' eyes grew wide when they made out Young Jae's face under the moonlight. They meant to call Tae Hyun "boss," but when their eyes averted from Yoori and then to Young Jae, it was obvious they were thrown off guard with the scene before them.

"What is it?" Yoori, Tae Hyun, and Young Jae unknowingly asked at the same time.

"An Advisor?" Ji Hoon asked, looking into the far distance as if seeing a figure emerge from the mansion.

The brothers nodded.

"Shin Jung Min," said Kang Min, glaring at Ji Hoon. "He's looking for you. He's heading here right now."

"My Advisor can't see Young Jae right now," Ji Hoon said to everyone. "It won't be a good idea. Whatever he sees, the other Advisors will be informed of as well."

"I don't care if he sees me," Young Jae declared. "I may have left this world for three years, but I still have more than enough power to regroup my Scorpions if I choose to. Those old bastards are of no threat to me—"

"The Advisors despise you, Young Jae," Tae Hyun interrupted, for the first time agreeing with Ji Hoon. "Your disappearance pissed them off like no other—them and the rest of the Underworld. We keep this quiet for now, for Yoori's safety. She doesn't need to deal with a dead older brother who just appeared in her life. She has other shit to deal with."

Tae Hyun looked sideways at Ji Hoon.

"He's your Advisor," he prompted, pretty much telling Ji Hoon that it was him who should go and deter Jung Min from his tracks.

Though there was hostility in his voice, his eyes were less hostile as they regarded Ji Hoon. There was no hate in them nor was there the disgust that normally inhabited his gaze. For a split second, Yoori could've sworn she felt Tae Hyun's silent respect for Ji Hoon. Respect that he still cared about Soo Jin (and ultimately Yoori). Ji Hoon shared in that same silent respect as he gazed back. It was as if at that moment, they realized that they didn't love the same woman. They loved two different women who were now one person. Such a precious moment was fleeting. Within seconds, annoyance reveled in their eyes once more.

"Just take her home safely," Ji Hoon bit out to Tae Hyun before drawing away to diverge his Advisor's attention.

As Ji Hoon melted into the distant darkness, Tae Hyun turned to Yoori. His eyes softened upon holding hers. "We have to go now. I think we've gotten into enough trouble tonight."

Yoori flickered her gaze to her brother. The overwhelming urge to simply speak to him took over.

"I . . . I actually want to talk to him," she began, returning her gaze to Tae Hyun. "Can you give us a moment?"

Tae Hyun deliberated her request. If he wanted to object, then he showed no sign of it. He nodded before turning to Young Jae. Tae Hyun stalked to him, and when he was close, he stood before Young Jae. He was a bit taller than Young Jae, but their respective presences were equally intimidating.

Staring at Young Jae dead in the eyes, he said, "At the end of the garden, as I think you already know, there's a path that leads into the driveway. When you're done speaking to her, head in that direction. I'll be in the limo waiting for her." His voice became more inflexible. "I trust with how we settled things, you won't take her away. Because you know I'll tear this city apart to find you. And when I do, I will rip you apart and bury you all over this country when I'm done with you."

Young Jae heaved a bored sigh and blinked as his silent confirmation. "Keep her safe, Tae Hyun. For tonight, she'll stay with you, but I'm not done with this argument. Not by a long shot."

"Fair enough," Tae Hyun replied just as tightly.

He moved away from Young Jae, took off his jacket, and wrapped it over Yoori's shoulders. She didn't even realize she was cold until the warmth of his jacket thawed her freezing skin. After draping the jacket over her, Tae Hyun allowed his fingers to trace her cheek before saying, "Take all the time you need."

Butterflies quaked in her tummy. She stared up at his handsome face and nodded.

Smiling at her briefly, Tae Hyun turned to the brothers.

They were as quiet as mice. They stared around the gardens, looking at anything and anyone but Young Jae. Yoori could see that they were still shocked that their old King had returned from his three-year disappearance.

"Do any necessary greetings and give them their time alone," Tae Hyun told the brothers. "I'll be in the limo."

The brothers and Yoori's eyes expanded at the unexpected order from Tae Hyun. He understood the complexity of loyalties when it came to switching gangs, and he essentially gave them permission to greet Young Jae as their "King" if they wished. Tae Hyun revealed to Yoori that he already knew that Kang Min and Jae Won were former Scorpions. He also shared that he knew they were brothers. It was one thing to have him reveal this to her, but it was completely different when he subtly revealed this to the brothers, who still looked stupefied beyond words. It was obvious to them now that there weren't many secrets one could keep from Tae Hyun, especially when he had people like his assassins watching out for him and letting him know the ins and outs of the people surrounding him.

Without another word, Tae Hyun imparted one last rigid stare in Young Jae's direction, one last reassuring glance at Yoori, and then disappeared into the darkness with his Blackberry held to his ear. Once he did this, movement began in the brothers' corner. They were about to get down on one knee when Young Jae extended his hand out and motioned for them to stop. Concern plastered on their faces, they did as they were commanded.

"Your loyalty was never to me," Young Jae said severely. There was no forgiveness in his voice. "You were given the option of leaving with the rest to Japan, yet you chose to stay here. As far as I'm concerned, you are no longer Scorpions. Don't bother greeting me by kneeling. There's no point. I don't deal well with ingrates."

"They've been watching over me," Yoori interrupted, refusing to allow anyone to label Kang Min or Jae Won as ingrates when they, along with Tae Hyun, had been taking care of her since the beginning.

"I know they have," Young Jae replied, his voice always gentler when speaking to her. "That is why they still have their heads."

Young Jae exhaled breathily, noting the expressions on their faces once the brothers turned their attention back to Yoori. They not only looked shocked, but they also looked stunned with happiness.

It didn't take Yoori long to understand what they were thinking: their boss, An Soo Jin, had been with them all along.

"Let me guess," Young Jae hypothesized. "By the looks on their faces, you still haven't told them that even though you have amnesia, you already know that you're An Soo Jin?"

She fretfully shuffled her feet, nodding in confirmation.

Yoori guiltily turned to the brothers and approached them. They were staring down at her like she was a living angel.

"I'm sorry for lying," she began hesitantly, holding Tae Hyun's jacket to her shoulders to keep it from falling. She hadn't prepared herself to have this conversation with the brothers. She was feeling extremely nervous. However, now that it was all out in the open, she had to address it. "It was a lot for me to handle—the only person I told was Tae Hyun. I was too afraid to tell anyone else. I hope you guys aren't too upset with me for lying. If I were brave enough to tell you, then I would've told you. I just didn't want to believe it myself . . . 'cause you know . . . you guys know how I feel about her."

"You even told us stories of what you were like as a kid when you grew up in Taecin," Kang Min mumbled quietly, staring at her with glistening eyes.

Yoori smiled awkwardly at the emotions spilling out of Kang Min. It was always Jae Won who was adamant that she was Soo Jin in the beginning. She was sure that over time, Kang Min convinced Jae Won that he was wrong, that Yoori wasn't Soo Jin. She could only imagine what was going through his mind right now as he stared at the girl he was once so sure wasn't his boss.

"I told you so," Jae Won whispered to his brother, his eyes still on Yoori. "I told you she was our boss." He smiled in disbelief and shook his head. "I can't believe you had me doubting it too."

There was a companionable silence that fell between the three before the brothers fell to the ground on one knee. They respectfully lowered their heads.

"Please don't," Yoori quipped feebly, taken aback by their display of respect. "This is completely unnecessary, you losers."

"Boss," Kang Min started, calling her that for the first time (and truly meaning it). Beside him, Jae Won stared at her with admiration in his eyes. They continued to kneel before her as if making up for all the years she went missing. "Even if you don't remember, it's great to be in your presence again."

Yoori swallowed convulsively, bowing her head slightly. This was all too emotional for her and she had other emotional things to deal with. She had to make them leave before she started to tear up.

"Now hurry and get up," she urged. "Go to Tae Hyun, please. I need to speak to my brother alone."

Unable to wipe the smiles off their faces, they nodded. They gave her another respectful bow before they stood up, walked past Young Jae, and bowed their heads in the same manner of reverence for him. They departed the garden, finally leaving Yoori alone with Young Jae.

"When we were kids and found them in the alley, an inch away from death, I remember telling you that you'd regret recruiting them because they were fated to be cowards." Young Jae smirked self-mockingly. "It seems that I have to eat half my words tonight. They weren't loyal to me, but they're still nothing but loyal to you."

Yoori smiled uncomfortably at her older brother. It felt strange that she was more relaxed around him when she first "met" him and danced with him. Now that she was alone with him again, and after realizing that he was actually her brother, she didn't know what to say. What could you say when you had amnesia and you just met the brother you had never seen? Yoori didn't know how to react, but it didn't matter. Young Jae knew how to react. As the wind rustled the leaves in the garden, he pulled her to him and held her in a tight embrace. It was an embrace that only an older brother could give to his younger sister.

"I've missed you, little one," he murmured, resting his chin on her head. When he did this, Yoori felt her heart ache at his breaking voice. "I know that you don't remember anything right now, but the only thing you should know is that I love you." He inhaled sharply, his eyes glistening with tears. "I thought you died in that fire. I thought I lost you . . ." He held her tighter against him, painfully closing his eyes. "I've missed you so much."

"I've missed you too," Yoori uttered, truly meaning it. She returned the embrace with the same intensity. She wasn't certain if it was her own emotions or if it was Soo Jin's emotions fighting through, but she could feel the adoration she had for her brother. Though she couldn't remember, she could also feel the lifetime of memories they had while growing up together.

Anticipation submerged her while they hugged. She was finally in the presence of the one who could enlighten her. She was finally in the company of the one who could shine a light on all the mysteries that shrouded her past.

Yoori couldn't resist the temptation to finally uncover the secrets of her life.

"Why did you leave for three years?" she asked, slowly pulling out of the embrace. She peered up at him with curious eyes. A string of other questions escaped her lips. "Why did Soo Jin want to commit suicide? What happened in that club? I knew you were there with her. What happened?"

Despite his sigh, she saw in his gaze that he anticipated these questions from her. The unshed tears from his eyes started to dry under the cool night. "Wasn't it just moments ago that you were determined to not remember anything?"

"I don't want to remember, but that doesn't mean I'm not curious."

Yoori chewed on her lips, staring at him pleadingly. She shouldn't tempt herself with the forbidden fruit, yet it was so enticing. She fought between keeping herself in the dark and stepping into the light. Her curiosity soon won out. She knew that out of all the people who could shed some light on this (and protect her at the same time), it was Young Jae.

"That formula that Ji Hoon gave me, the one I gave you to 'kill' me with," she prompted. "It gives me dreams . . . dreams that I don't know are memories, scrambled memories, or just figments of my imagination. I'm alive, yet in the dark. I'm stuck between wanting to freeze my life as it is and wanting to know what happened to me." She bit her lips harder. "What happened in that club is the key to everything, and I need to know what brought me to this moment in time. That's all I want to know. I don't want to remember anything else."

"You wanted to end your life because of what happened that night. I know I was angry earlier and spoke about wanting to help you remember so that you would leave Tae Hyun, but I can't risk you going back to the way that you were. I can't risk you wanting to kill yourself again. What happened that night will be your trigger to remember." He shook his head. "I don't want you to relive any of that pain. You came from hell and back—literally. I won't be your trigger. I won't."

"Will you do what you can then?" she bartered desperately. "Without recounting anything that you feel may be a trigger? I just need to know why that family was chosen, why I killed those people, and if possible, why we were there in the first place."

"You're playing with fire right now, lil sis."

"Hwang Hee Jun," Yoori launched, knowing that the names would be the pendulum that would sway her brother in the direction she wanted him to go in. "It was Hwang Hee Jun's family that was there. All thirty-four of them. I have to know why."

A flash of emotion elicited from his eyes.

"No one but Soo Jin, myself, and a couple of Scorpions would know that information. How did you know?"

"Please tell me something, and I'll tell you how I know." She could see in his eyes that knowing who told her wasn't as important as keeping her in the dark. Anticipating his hesitation, she hastened to add, "I need to know who I killed . . . and why I killed them. They haunt me every single day. They make me hate myself even if I can't remember what Soo Jin did to them. They make me hate Soo Jin. Despite all the remorse she felt at the end, I still can't help but hate her because I can still *feel* her guilt." Yoori took in a deep, preparatory breath. The hardest person to forgive is always yourself. "I want to close a chapter in my life so I can move on." She bit her quivering lips, her eyes pleading. "Please oppa . . . give me something."

Young Jae considered her request for a few seconds. When Yoori saw the surrender in his eyes, she knew he had given in. She was elated, for she knew from this moment forth, there would be no more hearsay, no more assumptions.

For the first time, she was going to get a first-hand account on what really took place at the infamous "Club Massacre."

"If you are weak, then you are not fit to be a Royal."

13: Blood Secrets of the Siberian Tigers

"We were interrogating them to find Hwang Tony," Young Jae disclosed after a long moment of silence.

"Hwang Tony?" Yoori confirmed, grateful that her brother finally heeded her request. Her heart rate gathered speed at this information.

"The last remaining heir to the Siberian Tigers' gang," Young Jae explained solemnly. "Hwang Hee Jun's younger brother."

Yoori canted her head with intrigue. "Wasn't he killed when you exterminated the gang five years ago?"

The trees in the garden rustled when a cold breeze flew through them. He shook his head.

"We thought he was killed, but he survived. I was told that he spent two years recuperating after the attack. It wasn't until an informant of mine caught sight of him in Seoul was I made aware of his existence. I didn't like that he was alive. Word had already gotten out that I had exterminated an entire lineage. His existence threatened that belief. I didn't care if the gang was already broken. I knew I had to kill the last remaining heir."

A muscle worked in his jaw when he recalled what transpired three years ago.

"Word got around to Tony that I was looking for him, and he fled. While we were searching for him, we found out that there was an extended family that existed and had been in hiding. Determined to find Tony, I had several Scorpions kidnap them and bring them over to the club I had just purchased. The area was completely secluded and perfect for what we needed to do."

Yoori did not need to ask who the main Scorpion that led the abduction was. She did her best to swallow past the remorse and dread that boiled in her stomach.

180

Slowly, she said, "The plan all along was to kill the entire family after we found out the information?"

Young Jae nodded, watching her warily. He was careful with making sure she could handle what was being told. "The only ones I was willing to even entertain sparing were the mother and her twins. Out of the extended family members, they were the only ones purely unrelated by blood, and they were the only ones I cared to take pity on."

"But An Soo Jin was the one who handled them?"

Young Jae looked up at the moon as his confirmation. "In the nature of interrogations, I handed things over to Soo Jin because as my right hand, she was known as the enforcer and the interrogator. Soo Jin's reputation in the Underworld had always been a vicious one, which was for good reason because it had always helped her in procuring the information we needed. Her favorite form of interrogation, and one of the most effective ones, was to cut off fingers each time they refused to give her the answers she wanted. Apart from the twins and their mother, all thirty-one people were tortured as we pried for information on Tony's whereabouts." He stared at her worriedly. He assessed the fear that bubbled in her eyes. "Is this too much for you to hear?"

Yes, she answered in her mind.

"No," Yoori lied, fighting back the rising nausea she felt. She was finally given a flashlight for the darkness she lived in. She refused to let this opportunity pass her by. She would deal with the guilt later. Now was the time for enlightenment.

"So, the family was killed," she prompted as her way of telling Young Jae to continue with the story, "just to find out where Hwang Tony was?"

Young Jae nodded, finally confirming Yoori's suspicions that Young Jae knew about Ju Won's request. "That night, we had two things we were interrogating them for. We found out Tony's whereabouts after Soo Jin shot and killed sixteen of the family members. After that, we were trying to find out something else . . . something else for Ju Won."

An uneasy feeling twisted inside Yoori. She knew it was the Soo Jin in her recalling the familiarity of these words and the scene Young Jae was about to paint for her.

"Why were you guys helping him?"

Young Jae had a faraway look in his eyes as he recounted memories from a distant past. He continued to speak, finally shedding light on to a mystery that had eluded Yoori for so long. He finally told her what happened during the fateful "Club Massacre."

■ ■ ■

Three years ago . . .

"I don't trust him," Young Jae whispered as they stood on the balcony.

His eyes roamed over the dimly lit floor that was covered with writhing bodies. The people below had been beaten so viciously that their faces were barely recognizable. The floor was littered with blood, amputated fingers, torn flesh, and the stench of death. They had just killed sixteen of the stubborn family members and had found Tony's whereabouts. In spite of this success, they had no luck in procuring the information Ju Won requested from them.

The remaining family members groaning on the dance floor were either good at keeping secrets or they simply didn't know what the hell Young Jae and Soo Jin were talking about. Young Jae was betting on the latter as he lowered his gaze to his sister.

"What could it hurt if we continued to torture them?" his baby sister suggested beside him.

Splatters of blood tarnished the black jacket and jeans she wore. With her black hair tied up in a ponytail, her hand holding a bloodied knife, and her face void of remorse, Soo Jin was the epitome of the Underworld's best interrogator. She had the face of an angel and the moral flexibility of the Devil. Those who didn't know her would come to fear her, and those who feared her would never forget her. She was the very best right-hand soldier and the best person to force out information from these people—that was if they knew the information to begin with.

"Nothing matters anymore," she went on, her voice as cold as her emotionless face. "The moment they stepped foot in here, they were going to die anyway. Why not try to find out something for Ju Won while we're at it?"

"You trust him too much, lil sis," Young Jae said severely. "Ju Won is a snake and the worst possible kind. Nothing he offers you should be taken lightly."

"He's offering our family his empire, oppa," Soo Jin argued, still sounding respectful despite her raised voice. "You know the pendulum of power that comes with that exchange."

Soo Jin looked down at the scene below her.

Resolve overcame her.

"The Serpents are becoming stronger. Kwon Ho Young not only has the support of China's Underworld, but he also has a trump card—his younger brother. His brother is on his way to ruling over the 1st layer. You know how influential that layer is when the Corporate Crime Lords are united. If we don't move Ju Won over to our side, then all the power will shift to the Serpents. Is that what you want? For this world to kneel under the rule of the Serpents? The fuckers who murdered our father?"

There was judgment in her eyes that she gave away for a split second. It was a look that insinuated Young Jae did not care about their father's death as much as she did.

"Don't speak to me as if our father's death affected you more than it affected me," Young Jae warned, reading her mind. "You have no idea what I'm going through."

Soo Jin bowed her head in apology. "I'm sorry. You know how much I hate them whenever I think about our father." She softened her gaze, her eyes imploring him to see her logic. "Our world is changing, oppa. The three gangs are growing stronger and stronger everyday, but there's a shifting of power now. Pretty soon, once things are in order, there will only be one Lord of the Underworld to rule over this entire layer and the two layers above it. I can't stand here and allow the Serpents to have that power, especially when all we have to do is find out whatever it is Ju Won wants from the family below."

Her eyes narrowed on to the floor where the unharmed mother and twins sat huddled in the corner, their faces paled from horror. The mother wore a yellow sundress, and the twins wore yellow t-shirts and khaki shorts; they looked utterly out of place in such a monstrous scene.

"You're not touching them, Soo Jin," Young Jae commanded, following her gaze.

"Look at how they shake," Soo Jin observed, callous amusement sparking in her eyes as they rested on them. "That woman was Hwang Hee Jun's girlfriend, and although the children aren't his, I'm sure he loved them like his own. From the fear in their eyes, how they shudder, and how they looked at me when I tortured and shot those sixteen people, I know that they are the ones who have the answers we're looking for."

"You're entertaining the idea of torturing a mother and her two children?"

"In every war, there are casualties," said Soo Jin, the emotions in her eyes now completely unreadable. "I plan on interrogating them, and I'll do what's necessary if they refuse to tell me the truth." She turned to him, already resolved on what she had to do for her gang. "Have the others leave, oppa. It should only be the two of us who hear any of this."

"You're not invincible, baby sister. Murdering gang members is very different from hurting innocent people."

"She should've known better than to get involved with the King of Siberian Tigers then," Soo Jin voiced with a shrug. There was no remorse or apprehension in her tone. She held his gaze with hers. "What happens tonight will be placed under my name and my name alone. I killed those sixteen people, and I'll finish the rest. What I do to the mother and her children will have no effect on you. I don't want to do this either, but if it's for the good of our gang, then I'll torture them all night if I have to."

Young Jae took a long, thoughtful moment to deliberate everything. Finally, he acquiesced. "Don't hurt them too badly."

183

A smirk came over her face. "You were always the kindest of the two of us."

A breath later, she jumped over the balcony. Her boots landed easily on the floor, crushing two amputated fingers beneath her. Soo Jin wasted no time. She sped over to the mother and children at once.

And then . . . it began.

"Get the fuck over here," Soo Jin growled, grabbing the mother by the curls of her black hair. She dragged her over to the corner of the club where there were stairs and a white pillar.

Screaming in agony as her children chased after her and Soo Jin, the mother tried to fight, but found it was futile as both her hands and legs were bound with sturdy ropes.

Soo Jin kicked her face, and the mother was left wailing. Her children crawled beside her and tried to tend to her. They didn't get too far before Soo Jin kicked them both out of the way and bestowed the mother with another kick to the face. A loud crack whipped in the air, indicating that her nose was broken.

"You bitch!" the other family members bellowed over their pain. They continued to shudder in shock as they screamed out to Soo Jin. "Leave them alone! They don't know anything!"

"Go outside," Young Jae ordered the four Scorpions watching the scene from the nearby balcony. "My sister and I will take care of this."

"Yes, sir," all four said before walking out of the club and slamming the door shut.

Young Jae looked back on the scene. Soo Jin was still beating up the mother while the children kneeled beside her, crying and begging for Soo Jin to stop.

"Just tell me where it is! I know that you know it!" Soo Jin screamed, opening the woman's mouth. She stuck in the blade of her knife and held it there, the pointed edge of the blade promising to rip her cheek apart. "I know that Hee Jun trusted you," Soo Jin snarled. "He couldn't be sure that he would survive, and I know that of all people, he told you."

"I really don't know!" the mother cried, blood spurting out from her mouth.

Soo Jin smirked and pulled the knife out. She was careful with not cutting any skin. She veered her attention to the children. They were kneeling before her, still crying loudly as they begged her to stop torturing their mother.

"Would your sons know?" Soo Jin evilly prompted, already grabbing them both by the collars and throwing them toward their mother like they were rag dolls. "Did Hee Jun tell them instead?"

"No! No! Please, don't touch them," the mother begged, tears gleaming her eyes. "Don't hurt my babies!"

Echoes of the children crying invaded the club. Soo Jin's breathing became more intense after she closed her eyes in frustration. Their incessant crying was driving her crazy.

"Please!" one of the boys screamed, choking on his tears. "Please don't kill us or our mommy!"

"Shut up! Shut up! Shut up!" Soo Jin spat out, her face paling at the sight of them crying. Her patience obliterated, she raced over to the woman and pulled her by the collar of her dress. "Tell me now because I have no more fucking patience. I'll start cutting off their fingers if you don't start talking."

"Soo Jin, that's enough," Young Jae ordered from above. The sounds of the kids crying drove him mad with guilt. He couldn't stand watching it any longer.

He commanded her to stop, but Soo Jin did not heed his command.

The boys continued to cry along with their mother, and Soo Jin continued to scream at them to shut up so she could hear their mother speak. But they wouldn't listen to her.

"57!" the boys started crying out. "57!"

"I told you to fucking stop crying!" Soo Jin snapped.

Her furious screams only made the kids cry harder.

Infuriated, she slapped them across the face to shut them up, but they still wouldn't listen. They continued to cry and continued to shout out the number. Soo Jin was rubbing her face in irritation. She began to crack under the emotions spilling out of her. Their cries grew louder and louder. They became so desperate that they were even ready to rush over to Young Jae for his help.

Two heart-stopping gunshots were suddenly fired.

Boom! Boom!

The whole place shook as the gunshots reverberated on to the walls.

The crying stopped as two small, lifeless bodies fell on to the floor.

The club erupted into bloodcurdling screams.

"Noooooo!" the mother sobbed. "Oh God! Nooooooooo!"

Young Jae felt the air leave his lungs. He nearly keeled over at the appalling scene before him. His sister—his baby sister—just shot two children.

"Noooooooo!" the mother continued to cry out. "Nooooooooo!"

Soo Jin shook uncontrollably, her eyes enlarged from what she just did. An exhale of relief emitted from her before she calmed herself down. Tucking her loose bangs behind her ears, Soo Jin pointed her gold gun at the mother. There were tears forming in Soo Jin's eyes.

"Now!" she demanded through her tears, her gun trembling. "Tell me now. Tell me something, and I'll let you go with them. If not, I won't even let you die. I'll keep you alive and have you stare at them until they begin to rot away!"

The mother's tears mixed with the blood on her face. As though apologizing to her dead boyfriend, she closed her tearful eyes and finally told Soo Jin what she needed to know.

"On the left side of the Siberian Tigers' estate . . ." she whispered through her tears, staring at Soo Jin dead in the eyes as she took her final, fading breath, "buried deep in the ground under the red roses. What you're looking for, you'll find it there."

■ ■ ■

"What happened after that?" Yoori asked, shivering not from the cold, but from the nausea devouring her body.

She could feel the bloodstains on her. She could hear the screams. She could feel the guilt constricting her breath. An Soo Jin . . . that monster . . . that heartless monster. Yoori couldn't believe it. She couldn't believe that Soo Jin was the one who tortured them—the one who killed them. Yoori wanted to sink down to the ground and cry as the remorse stabbed at her heart. Yet, with mighty effort, she took in a deep, shuddering breath and continued to persevere to gather more information. As long as she wasn't feeling faint, as long as she wasn't blacking out, she had to fight it out to learn more.

"Soo Jin shot her," finished Young Jae, "and we killed the rest of the family members."

"Did we find Tony and that . . . that thing for Ju Won?"

"Yes," he confirmed. "We found both."

Yoori nodded, pressing her clenched fists against her stomach to ease the pit of despair within it. She didn't know how she was still breathing when there was so much guilt pumping through her.

"When did Soo Jin become consumed with guilt for killing those kids and their mother?"

"Right after we found it," said Young Jae. His expression became pained at the reminder. "She took one look at it, fell apart, and disappeared afterward. I had no idea where she went until I heard rumors about someone spotting her and Ji Hoon at the club. I hadn't realized that she returned to the club."

"Can you tell me what that thing was?"

"It wasn't worth it," he said plainly.

"Wasn't . . . Wasn't worth it?" she stuttered.

He nodded.

Yoori waited for him to actually tell her what it was. When he refused to elaborate, she pressed on. "Can you please tell me what—?"

Young Jae shook his head, effectively interrupting her. "This is where it ends, little one. I can see how all of this has taken a toll on you. I've already told you too much. I'm not telling you anymore."

"But—"

"No more," he dismissed with a wave. "You've heard enough." He squared his shoulders. It was clear that recounting this story also took a big toll on him. He ventured back on to the topic that convinced him to reveal all of this in the first place. "Now tell me how you found out it was the Hwangs."

"Tae Hyun's assassins," Yoori answered, unsatisfied that he wouldn't disclose what it was that Ju Won wanted, what was worth killing thirty-four people for.

"The Cobras," Young Jae said knowingly. "I should've known they would be the ones who would find out that information for their boss." He sharpened his eyes on to her. "The fires in Taecin were made to look like it was an accident, but I knew it was too much of a coincidence. I wasn't sure before, but I'm pretty damn sure now that it was them who set the fires."

Yoori remained silent at her brother's accurate assessment. She did not want to confirm that he was right because it would give him more leeway to hate Tae Hyun.

Young Jae caught her reaction nonetheless. It did not take him long to figure out the truth. "His assassins tried to kill you a year and a half ago."

And a couple of days ago, Yoori supplied in her mind.

"And you're walking around hand-in-hand with their boss? Do you not comprehend what a dangerous position you're in right now?"

"I'm safe with Tae Hyun," she assured him. There was no fear in her when it came to Tae Hyun. "He cares about me. His feelings for me are genuine. I know it."

"The Cobras are well-known in this world, lil sis. They possess the same qualities that Tae Hyun possesses. They are vengeful and prideful. They may heed his orders to not kill you now because he wants you by his side, but they will protect him at all costs. Rest assured that they are not done. They will find out something about you and tell him. And in turn, Tae Hyun will throw you out and feed you to the wolves."

Yoori remained unfazed by her brother's ominous words.

"I know that Soo Jin hated the Serpents family. That information isn't new to Tae Hyun or me. And he knows that Soo Jin killed that entire family, so that isn't new either. I'm not worried about them finding out anything from my past. Tae Hyun wouldn't care."

"There's another one, lil sis," Young Jae said forebodingly. "One more secret that would be strong enough to rip apart anything you have with him. It would be destructive, and I'm afraid if the Cobras dig enough, they will find out what it is and tell him."

A cold wind breezed through her hair as goose bumps chased after goose bumps on her body. She was feeling unusually cold, and if the pit that worsened in her stomach was any indication, then she had the feeling that this was a terrible secret.

"What is the other secret?" Yoori asked with caution, fearing with all her heart what the answer could be.

"Ask him," he whispered, gauging her reaction, "how his mother died."

Her heart gave a horrible jolt.

"She committed suicide," Yoori said flatly, suddenly shaking in her wits as the wind around her grew colder and less forgiving.

Young Jae gazed at her, his solemn eyes rippling with pity. "Nothing is what it seems in this world. Masquerades don't just extend to the theme of tonight. It extends to all other realms of this world as well."

He sighed, noting the trepidation that enveloped her eyes.

"Just ask him, lil sis. Just ask him how his mother died, and you'll understand."

"And if you are not fit to be a Royal..."

14: Serpent's Instinct

"Damn it, Choi Yoori," Tae Hyun complained from across the little coffee table they were sitting at. "I just bought you a big slice of red velvet cake. You can't eat something this good and pout like you're at a funeral."

Yoori, dressed in a black velour ensemble to fight against the winter cold, scowled at Tae Hyun's incredibly blunt statement. She grudgingly watched him eat his beloved cake.

After parting ways with her brother the night before, Yoori went back to Tae Hyun ashamed, traumatized, and not in the talking mood. After opening the door of the limo, where Tae Hyun and the brothers awaited her, she threw herself in. Yoori announced that she was tired and sought refuge on Tae Hyun's lap by sleeping on it. Of course, she didn't really sleep, but spent the time mulling over everything her brother had told her.

If it were any other situation where it was just herself and Tae Hyun, Yoori would have already divulged in what happened with her brother. But due to the brothers' presence and her adoration for them, Yoori was afraid to share the contents of what transpired that night in fear of the brothers changing their respectable opinions about her. Yoori was ashamed. She was ashamed of the heinous crime Soo Jin imparted to that poor mother and her two kids. She knew that the brothers grew up with Soo Jin, but she doubted they were ever present for something as immoral as killing two children. She didn't want to wreck any respect they may harbor for her. In addition to her worry, she couldn't forget the question her brother implanted into her mind.

"Just ask him, lil sis. Just ask him how his mother died, and you'll understand."

Yoori didn't have the courage to question Tae Hyun on how his mother died because she was afraid of what she would find out. She didn't want to understand. She was happy with Tae Hyun. She didn't want to risk anything breaking them apart. If denial and avoidance were going to keep her with Tae

Hyun longer, then she didn't want to know the answer. In this case, ignorance was truly bliss for her.

It wasn't until the next day, when they woke up and decided to go for a winter afternoon jog, did Yoori share everything with Tae Hyun (except for that one ominous question). After she told him everything, Yoori found herself stuck in another wave of nausea and guilt. It was something that appeared to be a habitual routine for her as of late.

Sensing her journey into the land of misery, Tae Hyun casually suggested that they quit jogging and stop by the local bakery to treat themselves with dessert instead. Yoori agreed and languidly sat at one of the bakery's coffee tables while Tae Hyun ordered them two big slices of his favorite cake.

Yoori had just finished telling him how Soo Jin tortured the mother and killed the two children when he placed her cake in front of her. She was sick to her stomach with guilt. She couldn't even eat her cake, hence the reason why Tae Hyun was scolding her.

"Don't tell me what to do," Yoori retorted.

She was thankful that the bakery was intimate. The tables were small, there was an aroma of warm pastries, and an abundance of shuffles of patrons' feet. Her voice was drowned in the upbeat music and the constant buzzing of the people around her. No one, other than Tae Hyun, could hear her.

With her legs crossed together over the wooden chair, she added, "You buying me a cake doesn't mean anything. I will frown as I wish."

"Yeah well, it would be great if you could turn that frown upside down because we're out in public right now and . . ." He looked around bashfully, shifting restlessly in his seat. He was dressed in a brown zip-up hoodie and black windbreaker pants. His hood was up, making him sinfully mysterious and handsome as he ate his cake. The deterrent to this enigmatic façade was the sight of him blushing from the condemning stares he received from the people around them. "And I think people think I'm abusing you or dumping you right now because you look so damn miserable. The Underworld already sees me as a heartless jackass; I don't need the outside world to see me as a jerk as well."

"Oh Jesus . . ." Yoori laughed at Tae Hyun's unintentional cuteness as he drank from his cup of milk. He metamorphosed from looking like a sexy wolf to an adorable puppy. She was positive that this was one of those moments where Tae Hyun's tactic of endeavoring to "make-Choi-Yoori-feel-better" was to piss her off. No doubt he was trying to coax out her fiery wits so she would scream at him and forget that she was miserable. If any other guy tried that method with her, they would be looking at an early grave. However, Tae Hyun's oozing charm allowed him to be the only one who could get away from such a grim fate.

Regardless of his efforts, she couldn't help but release another sigh. Her thoughts journeyed back to the mother and children. She was silent for several more moments before she started to finally eat her cake. A massive pit materialized in her stomach while she chewed. Yoori hesitantly peered at Tae Hyun. She wondered what his thoughts were on the conveyed information.

"So," Yoori drawled. "What do you think about everything I told you? You're not the least bit disgusted with me?"

He finished the last of his cake and stared at her with nonchalance. "Why should I be?"

"Because . . ." She surveyed her surroundings and leaned in closely. "Well, you know why."

She killed children for goodness' sake.

The thought was sickening to her. It disturbed her every time she thought about it. She could only imagine how Tae Hyun must feel to be sitting across the monster who performed such an immoral act.

"You're not the same person," he assured her with conviction. She could see the contemplation in his eyes as he thought about the woman and her children. At the same time, she saw the confidence on his face. "You and Soo Jin are completely different. I understand how guilty you must feel right now, but you also have to remember that it wasn't you who did all those things. It was her and her alone."

"You really see us as being different?" Yoori tentatively inquired. Although she had asked Tae Hyun this particular question numerous times in the past, she had never wanted his reassurance more than now. "That what she did has no reflection on me?"

Will you really forgive me for all the sins she committed? She wanted to add.

"Yes, Nemo," he confirmed, lifting Yoori's heart up with hope. He then pushed the cake closer to her. "Now hurry up and finish eating. I'm done with my cake. I don't want to sit around and wait all day for you."

Yoori furrowed her brows at her new pet name. He had called her that during the ball, but she thought it was an isolated incident. It was so strange to hear him call her that when he didn't even know what a "Nemo" was the night before.

"Are you seriously calling me 'Nemo' from now on as my pet name?" she asked offhandedly, throwing her plastic fork onto the empty plate. She grabbed her plate and gave him a quick glare before standing up and tossing it into a nearby trashcan.

Tae Hyun shrugged with a hidden smile. He collected his trash and threw it away.

"If I feel like it," he drawled out with his sultry and smooth voice.

"It's not a sexy name though," Yoori childishly complained as she stepped out of the bakery and onto the crowded sidewalk.

She felt the icy, winter breeze lash against her skin. Just as quickly as the breeze picked up, warm, electric currents coursed through her body when Tae Hyun wrapped his arms around her hips. He gravitated towards Yoori and bestowed her neck with a quick kiss. Yoori smiled uncontrollably at this display of affection.

"Nicknames rarely are," he purred into her ear. He playfully bit and nibbled the tip of her earlobe, triggering an involuntary whimper from Yoori's lips as they immersed into the crowd.

"Tae Hyun!" Yoori mumbled halfheartedly, pulling away from his grasp. "We're outside!"

Although being teased to death by Tae Hyun was certainly one of Yoori's favorite pastimes, she was still a prude at heart. How could he make her whimper like that when a kid could have heard her on the street?

Unaffected by her reprimand, Tae Hyun merely chuckled at the rosy blush forming on her cheeks. Releasing a breathy sigh, he pulled up her velour hood to protect her against the cold and entwined the gaps between her fingers with his. Hand-in-hand, they sauntered down the street together.

"What do you think they're looking for?" she questioned as the frosty wind gusted past them. They instinctively moved closer together to avoid bumping into other pedestrians on the crowded sidewalk. Though her guilt had subsided after talking to Tae Hyun, she still had other things she wanted to address with him, especially matters pertaining to the mysterious item. "I know that by the time you took the reign, the Siberian Tigers were already exterminated, but have you heard anything about them? Things that they may have owned? Things that might be of importance to someone like Ju Won?"

Tae Hyun stopped abruptly in the middle of the sidewalk to deliberate for a moment. "Before I took over the Serpents' throne, Dong Min gave me some information about the Siberian Tigers. Apparently, in addition to the Scorpions family, the Siberian Tigers family was a family that Ju Won was close to as well. There's not much more I can tell you apart from that. You already know that it was your brother who exterminated them, and we both know what happened to the extended family that night."

Yoori shook her head with resentment, recalling that her brother wouldn't disclose more information last night.

"He just won't tell me more than that," she groaned, reclining her head towards the overcast sky.

They reached another dead-end in the conversation, and she felt unsettled with her emotions. Yoori understood that her brother hid this information away from her because he didn't want to risk her remembering the past. Yet, she also couldn't deny how enticing the secret was. She felt allured to its enigmatic secret and desired to uncover the truth. Although she wanted to closet her memories, she still had this innate desire to know what the mentally deranged Soo Jin was up to.

"In about three days, I'm leaving to go back to the second Serpents' estate," Tae Hyun announced casually, stirring her from her thoughts. "I have business I need to take care of there."

"What do you need to do there?" Yoori asked, momentarily distracted with this new announcement.

"Ju Won's 65th birthday is near," he explained as they continued to walk hand-in-hand. His voice was weary and spent. "You've only been introduced to a diplomatic Underworld so far. Like it's been previously mentioned, we're all holding back on the bloodshed until his birthday. But once his birthday comes, this world will revert back to its old ways. I need to prepare my Serpents for the things to come."

"Oh . . . Oh okay," Yoori faintly responded, disturbed that the current Underworld was considered peaceful. She couldn't and didn't want to envision what a "regular" Underworld would be like with the amplified bloodshed and internal warfare. The thought of the Underworld and Tae Hyun becoming more violent petrified her.

She gazed at him, her thoughts migrating back to what he said about returning to the Serpents' estate. She wondered if this meant he was leaving her for a while. It would suck to be alone in the apartment without him. "Should I stay at a hotel or something while you're away?"

"I actually want you to come with me," he said instead, catching her by surprise.

Yoori gawked at him. She was still floored that he would even share his first Serpents' estate with her. She did not expect to be invited to the second estate. Being present for the secret initiation was one thing, but being privy to the second estate where the Serpents were trained was something else entirely. "But I thought I'm not allowed. Hae Jin told me I had to be initiated into the gang before I could go to the second estate—"

"You're allowed entry if a King grants it to you," he informed her, his brown eyes softening on her. "And I want you to come with me."

"Why would you still do that?" she asked stupidly. "You already did that with the first estate."

He laughed, eliciting the careless charm that he radiated so brilliantly. "I told you before, I brought you to the first estate because I wanted you to know everything about me. I want every part of my life—all my secrets—to be open to you. This is not a store, Brat. I'm not picking and choosing when to be open with you. I want it to be consistent, and I want to share my second estate with you as well."

Uneasiness inundated her thoughts. His prerogative to be candid only reminded her of her cowardice attempt to keep the secret behind his mother's death from him. Her brother's damning words echoed in her mind, reminding her to ask Tae Hyun the dreaded question. She waved the question off in her mind. She could not deal with this right now.

"You don't have to, Tae Hyun," she appeased feebly. "I understand that there are secrets I shouldn't know about your gang. You don't have to let me in on everything. I'm satisfied with being privy on how the initiation works. You don't need to show me more than that."

"You don't want to see if we can find something at the Siberian Tigers' estate?"

Yoori stopped in her tracks.

She gaped up at him in confusion.

"But—" Realization dawned in her eyes. Adrenaline gushed through her veins when she realized what was being insinuated. "Are you saying that the second Serpents' estate was originally—?"

"The Siberian Tigers' estate," he finished for her. "When I came into power, I wanted to move away from the old estate that my brother housed. The Siberian Tigers' estate was abandoned, so it didn't take me long to stake claim over the property and establish that estate as the main Serpents' estate. It's been a while; there might not be anything left there." He shrugged again, readjusting his hood to keep it firmly above his head. "You don't have to go if you don't want to. I'm just putting it out there for you."

Yoori's eyes were beaming. She would go anywhere if she had the chance to discover something new.

"Of course I'll go," Yoori coolly replied, smiling as something else came to her mind. Since they were already on the topic of being honest and open to each other, she couldn't let this opportunity pass by. "I know we already discussed this, but can you come with me and have dinner with my brother the day after tomorrow?"

The mood suddenly dampened. She had already invited Tae Hyun once and he had already declined her offer. They got into a heated argument about it earlier in the day. Yoori was upset that Tae Hyun wouldn't give her brother a chance and Tae Hyun was upset that Yoori would demand him to, especially considering how Young Jae treated him the night before. The dispute was eventually settled before their jog, but as it appeared, the fight was ready to rear its ugly head again.

A frown darkened Tae Hyun's visage. He swayed his head agitatedly, unclasping his hand from hers.

"You always know how to ruin the mood, don't you?" he reprimanded, striding ahead of her.

Yoori stared after him in bewilderment.

"What a freaking jerk," she muttered to herself when she realized he had just ditched her. All because she invited him to have dinner with her big brother? Well, she couldn't accept his childish antics!

Yoori picked up her pace and caught up with him. She was vexed, but she knew patience was a virtue that should be employed with an incredibly stubborn Tae Hyun.

"Stop it. Just come have dinner," she urged, nearly crashing into a little toddler as she struggled to keep up with Tae Hyun. He was walking inhumanly fast. She cursed under her breath at his stubbornness. "What's the big deal?"

"Why should I? Weren't you there last night?" he snapped, quickening his pace. He was beside himself. "Your brother's fucking insane."

"He's just overprotective," Yoori amended weakly.

She understood the hostility on Tae Hyun's part. After what took place, it wouldn't have surprised Yoori if Tae Hyun completely wrote her brother off as a lost cause. Despite his qualms about her brother, Yoori hoped that Tae Hyun would still make the effort to get on Young Jae's good side. After all, he was her boyfriend, and the universal rule for all boyfriends was that they should do everything in their power to get on their girlfriend's older brother's good side.

"No," Tae Hyun corrected swiftly. He finally stopped to face her. He wasn't going to allow her amended categorization to go by without his input. "Overprotective is me telling Kang Min that if he hurts my baby sister, I'm killing him and making sure he dies a slow and painful death. *That's* overprotective."

He shook his head disbelievingly.

"But your brother is insane because it appeared that overnight, I became his most hated enemy. I mean, I met him briefly when I was crowned the King of Serpents, and at that time, he was actually civil with me. He didn't seem to hate me at all. Hell, I'd even go as far as saying that your brother was *nice* to me when we met. But apparently last night, I became his biggest enemy because I'm seeing his sister? Do you not see how insane that is? I can handle it if the guy acted like he hated me from the start, but it's like he flipped a switch and only decided to hate me so he could pull you away from me. There's something about that guy that I just can't—"

When he glanced over and saw the disappointment in Yoori's eyes, he relinquished his verbal thoughts and went silent. He had his own opinions, but he wasn't keen on hurting her with them.

Yoori closed her eyes at his nonsensical babbling. Normally she would let him have his way because she realized how stubborn Tae Hyun could be, but this was different. This was her *brother*, her only family member. She also couldn't ignore the insinuating tone from the last part of his speech.

"Where is this all coming from?"

The muscles in his jaw bunched. He looked away. "I don't want to say it."

"Damn it," she commanded, grabbing his arm to have him face her. "Just tell me."

"I don't trust him," he finally shared, "or Ji Hoon."

Yoori expelled a tired breath. She should have known they were going to voyage on to this topic.

She gazed up at him doubtfully. "Wasn't it just last night that you and Ji Hoon showed each other an ounce of respect? What changed?"

"That was before I had time to think about it in the limo," he told her. "I can't pinpoint what it is, but there's something off about them and how they behaved last night."

When Yoori sighed, Tae Hyun became defensive.

"I heard shouting," he explained, sensing that she was ready to mentally block whatever he was trying to tell her, "in one of Ju Won's rooms when I was speaking to some of the crime lords. Then I heard more shouting and a big commotion. Moments later, Ji Hoon came out and he was heading towards the west wing. From what you told me about what happened last night, I think he went straight to you afterward."

She folded her arms across her chest and feigned interest. "Did you see who else came out?"

"No. I was too distracted with Ji Hoon. I think the other person slipped out while I wasn't looking."

"So, Ji Hoon and my brother had an argument," Yoori deduced logically. "Probably the same one about Ji Hoon trying to make sure I don't regain my memories."

"But he was *pretending* he didn't know it was Young Jae when we found you dancing with him."

"Tae Hyun . . ." Yoori wearily responded before Tae Hyun interrupted her.

"I knew you were going to react this way," he told her, his eyes emitting disappointment that she was categorizing his suspicions as trivial.

"Look, I know you're thinking that there's something else to it, but stop being like this. My brother and Ji Hoon really care about me. They'll never hurt me." She exhaled before unthinkingly saying, "You're just being paranoid."

"Paranoid?" He gaped at her incredulously. "This isn't paranoid. In this world, there is no such thing as paranoid. I'm being careful right now." His steel-eyes scrutinized her. "You've been introduced to another level in this world, Yoori. All the people we've met, they are masters of deception. Some of them are so good that even *I* get fooled. Last night, for example, I was momentarily fooled by Ji Hoon. But the thing I've learned—the thing that has gotten me to where I am—is my ability to find anomalies in their behaviors because even the best liar slips up. It's up to the one being lied to, to catch those slips."

"You're telling me that my brother, the one who hid me from this world for my own safety, and Ji Hoon, the one who's so in love with Soo Jin that he gave up power in this world for her, are trying to hurt me?"

"I don't know," he said with exasperation. "I'm just telling you that nothing is always as it seems. You have this thing about you, Yoori, where you try to see the good in everyone when there's no good for you to see. You've only seen the side that Ji Hoon wants you to see, but I know Ji Hoon. He can't be trusted. Period."

Yoori inhaled sharply, not even absorbing the substance of his words. "Are you going to tell me you think my brother can't be trusted either?"

Suddenly, a hostile conversation about her brother and Ji Hoon was quickly transitioning into a venomous conversation between Yoori and Tae Hyun. She felt horrible for conceiving such idea, but she couldn't help but think about the moment where she found out that *he* had been deceiving her. He shouldn't be so quick to venture on to the topic of "trust" when it was only recently where she found out that he betrayed her trust. She had forgiven him, but sins like that were rarely forgotten.

"Look," Tae Hyun began, reading her mind. "I know that I've fucked up in the past, but I'm really trying to make things right here, Yoori. Trust me when I say that I wouldn't be treading on this topic unless my gut is telling me that something is wrong. My gut tells me that something is off about your brother, and it's not because he hates my guts. And something is definitely off about Ji Hoon—"

Yoori unfolded her arms in defeat. She really wanted to end this conversation. They were getting nowhere.

"I don't doubt that you want what's good for me. I just think your rationale is understandably biased when it comes to Ji—"

"You don't believe that I'm looking out for you when I warn you about Ji Hoon?" Tae Hyun interrupted, his voice throbbing with hurt and insult.

Yoori was now at her wit's end. "What more do you want me to say? I trust Ji Hoon, too, Tae Hyun!"

How could she not?

After all Ji Hoon had given up for Soo Jin, how could she not trust him?

"He can't be trusted!" Tae Hyun snapped. His face was evident of repugnance once he saw how emotional she was getting about Ji Hoon. "All the façade that he's giving off right now, it's not real!" He scrutinized her in distaste. "I didn't even realize how affected you were by the façade until I saw the sympathy in your eyes when you looked at him last night. But now . . . now I see that you've been pushed into the deep end of this. To think I thought you were one of the few who saw through him."

"Kwon Tae Hyun, stop it!" she bellowed, unable to contain her anger. "You're just being like this because you're jealous and you're afraid I'll leave you for Ji Hoon!

Tae Hyun fell silent at her words.

Yoori, herself, went quiet. She bit her lips in frustration, already regretting what she said. She was such a dumbass to say such things. She didn't mean it. She wanted to apologize, but it was too late. Tae Hyun would have none of it.

"So, you really think jealousy is all that's driving me right now?" Insult marked his face.

"Choi Yoori," he chided sternly. "I was just trying to watch out for you. People think I'm the most ruthless person in this world, yet I know better. It had always been Ji Hoon, and if you can't see it now, you'll see it soon when he shows his true colors and screws you over." He took one last hard glance at her before saying, "You know what? Fuck this." He walked past her. "I don't need to deal with this. Go be with your Prince Charming, but don't come crying to me when he fucks you over. *I'm done.*"

Are you kidding me? Yoori thought as she watched Tae Hyun storm off into the growing crowd.

Guilt gone, she started to feel infuriated as well.

"Kwon Tae Hyun!" she shouted irritably, hoping that he would return to her after hearing her call.

Within moments, he was gone, leaving her blindsided with shock. She was absolutely beside herself. How on earth did an innocent day end up like this?

"Then you are no longer a God."

15: 57

"I can't believe what an ass he's being right now!" Yoori complained when she stepped into the hotel lobby.

"He was watching out for you and you called him paranoid and jealous. What reaction did you expect from him, boss?" Kang Min questioned, walking alongside Yoori. Four other Serpents treaded behind them. They were all dressed in black with the exception of Yoori.

Since their altercation on the street, Yoori and Tae Hyun had been ignoring each other. Because Tae Hyun was too pissed off at her to accompany her, and because Jae Won was preoccupied with Chae Young, Yoori was left in the company of Kang Min and four other Serpents who served as her bodyguards. Initially, she didn't mind the company because she thought Kang Min, who was always the more sensitive one, was going to side with her. Unfortunately for Yoori, she found that he was on the enemy's side.

Yoori scoffed. Her ivory halter dress bounced in the air as she huffed and puffed to herself. Holding a red velvet cake box close to her chest, Yoori said, "You and Jae Won . . . you guys are always siding with him."

"I'm not siding with anyone," Kang Min told her quietly, his eyes roaming around the hall with vigilance. Even while speaking to her, he was still keeping his eye out for danger. "I told you before that I didn't trust Ji Hoon, remember? Well, that fact holds true to this day and it's not because of anything Boss Kwon says."

"You know what?" Yoori started when they approached the suite her brother was staying in with his wife. "I really don't want to talk about this right now. I have to eat dinner with my brother, and I'd like to be in a good mood while doing so. I just want to forget about Tae Hyun's nonsense." She eyed him begrudgingly. "And yours as well."

Yoori turned away from him when they neared her brother's suite. There were four Scorpions dressed in black suits at the doorway, gazing at her expectantly. All four bowed their heads down to her before moving away from the door to give her the opportunity to knock.

Yoori gave them a polite smile before sighing to herself.

She was still feeling exasperated. She was tired of everyone bad mouthing Ji Hoon when it was clear he had done nothing but sacrificed himself for Soo Jin. No one deserved this type of crucifixion, least of all Ji Hoon. With that thought in mind, Yoori decided to put everything on the backburner and focus on her night with her brother. She knocked on the door, unaware that Kang Min was frowning at her dismissal of his warnings about Ji Hoon.

"Do you want to join us?" she asked Kang Min belatedly. No matter how angry he made her, she still adored Kang Min and would love for him to join them for dinner.

"No," he told her after he caught the glare the four Scorpions were giving him.

Yoori swallowed uncomfortably when she noticed those glares. Evidently Young Jae wasn't the only one pissed at Jae Won and Kang Min for joining another gang. The four Scorpions out here begrudged Kang Min as well.

"Are you sure?" she whispered, wanting to help take Kang Min out of that uncomfortable situation. The last thing he needed was to wait outside with a group of people who clearly despised him. He should at least go inside with her. Albeit her brother was not a fan of Kang Min either, at least it was just one person as opposed to four people who disliked him.

"Yes," Kang Min said succinctly, taking his place with the other Serpents against the wall from across the door. They all stood parallel from her brother's Scorpions. All the bodyguards stared straight ahead, avoiding eye contact with one another.

"Have fun," said Kang Min, clearly preferring to be amongst four Scorpions who disliked him as opposed to being in her brother's company. "We'll be out here."

Before Yoori could say anything, the door clicked open.

"Little sis," her older brother greeted, distracting her from Kang Min. He held the door open with a smile. Dressed in a black turtleneck and khaki pants, he radiated nothing but warmth.

Yoori smiled, feeling better now that she was in her brother's presence. At that moment, nothing else mattered but hanging out with him. If Kang Min wanted to be in the hall, then so be it. It was time for her to forget about everything else and enjoy dinner.

"I brought you some dessert," she told her brother, holding up the cake box.

"Wonderful! Come in," Young Jae told her warmly, easing the box from her hands and ushering her in.

Yoori stepped into the luxurious penthouse suite. As her eyes perused the room, she was floored by how big it was. With a living room, dining room, and kitchen of its own, she would say that the hotel suite was as big as Tae Hyun's apartment. She craned her neck and noticed that it even had its own pool outside. She gasped in her head, thoroughly impressed. This place was a dream. She wouldn't mind staying here either.

"I heard this type of cake is good," her brother commented when he peeked inside the box. "I'm excited to taste it."

It's Tae Hyun's favorite, Yoori wanted to casually share with him.

In lieu of that, she said, "Yeah, it's delicious! My favorite."

She casually surveyed the apartment while she walked beside her brother. She was still distracted with thoughts of Tae Hyun (and how she really wanted him to be here with her only family member), but kept a pleasant expression on for her older brother. "This is a beautiful suite, by the way."

"This will do for the next week or so," Young Jae told her.

He politely herded her into the living room where a tall Korean man with blonde hair greeted her with a bow. He was wearing the typical black suit attire that all the gang members appeared to be donning tonight.

"This is PC," Young Jae introduced. "You probably don't remember him, but he's my right-hand man. Back in the day, the two of you were the ones I depended on while I dealt with Scorpions business."

Yoori smiled cordially at him, not really knowing what to say. It was odd that she probably worked closely with the guy, but didn't remember him at all.

"Nice to meet you, PC," Yoori said meekly, nodding her head at him while he straightened his back.

"It's been a while. I can't believe you're here with us again," he said respectfully, giving them another bow before he stood off to the side. "Welcome back, Ms. An."

"Thank you, PC," Yoori replied, unable to contain her smile. It was a rare occasion for anyone to feel at home with people they just met. In Yoori's case, as she started to spend more time with her brother and his Scorpions, she couldn't help but feel safe—like she was at home.

"It'll just be my sister, my wife, and myself tonight," Young Jae told PC kindly. "Tell the other Scorpions that they can rest for the night. I'll see you tomorrow. Thank you again for all your help."

PC nodded at his King's orders. "I'll let everyone know. Good night, boss."

With another bow to both Yoori and her brother, PC left without another word. Soon, it was just the two of them.

"I hope you're hungry, little one," Young Jae uttered, hugging Yoori from the side as he walked into the dining room with her. He placed her cake on the table. "My wife was ecstatic to hear that you were coming over and went crazy with the food."

Yoori's eyes wandered across the wide array of food that embellished the rectangular dining table.

"No kidding," she murmured appreciatively. "Wow, everything looks so delicious!"

"And here we have the woman of the hour," Young Jae announced, his eyes elsewhere while Yoori admired the assortment of food in front of her.

She followed his gaze. Her eyes landed on a beautiful woman who just walked into the room. Thin and graceful, Young Jae's wife appeared to be in her late twenties. She wore a yellow blouse and a white skirt that accentuated her tall figure. She had her black hair tied up to one side and was smiling uncontrollably at Yoori.

"Yoori . . ." Young Jae said, pulling her alongside him towards the woman. "This is my wife, Anna."

If Yoori knew what a family reunion felt like, then she could've sworn this was what was occurring as her brother introduced her to everyone. She could detect the adoration in his voice when he introduced his wife. It was the same tone of voice that Tae Hyun had when he introduced her to other people. Afraid that she'd get sucked into another crestfallen state at the reminder of Tae Hyun not being here for her, Yoori pushed back the thoughts of him aside. Instead, she smiled genuinely at her brother's wife.

"Nice to meet you, Anna."

"Boss," Anna greeted, suddenly falling to one knee with her head bowed down in respect. "It's been a while. Welcome back."

Yoori's eyes enlarged. She turned to her brother in shock. "Why is she kneeling before me? She's your wife."

"Her oath and loyalty to you supersedes what she has with me," Young Jae explained to her. "If you hadn't recruited her, then she wouldn't be alive today. She's just showing you the respect she has for you."

But still! Yoori thought appallingly. This was her brother's wife! She couldn't have the poor girl kneel before her, especially when she felt that Soo Jin didn't deserve such respect.

"Please, Anna," Yoori voiced, bending forward to help Anna up. "Please, no kneeling or anything like that. You're my brother's wife. You never have to do that again."

Anna beamed appreciatively at Yoori. Tears began to glisten in her eyes. "It's so good to see you again, boss." She sighed, wiping her fingers underneath her eyes to prevent any tears from streaming down. "Young Jae and I have missed you so much."

"Anna gets emotional easily," Young Jae whispered into Yoori's ear as Anna playfully smacked him.

"Let's eat, let's eat," Anna ushered with a laugh. She grabbed Yoori's hand and pulled her to the dining table where she took a seat beside her.

Young Jae took a seat at the end of the table, beaming at his younger sister and his wife.

"We have so much to catch up on!" Anna exclaimed.

And they did.

As dinner progressed, Yoori was elated to be in the presence of her family. She only wished that Tae Hyun were there with her too. As they ate, she casually asked her brother and Anna what they had been doing in Japan. As expected, they told her that they had been hiding from the Korean Underworld. A few loyal Scorpions followed them to Japan to help make their stay there safe. Young Jae had been traveling to meet with old business associates in Japan who still adored him. Evidently, his new job as a business consultant paid quite well. He was no longer involved in Underworld business and his Scorpions were also sometimes contracted as bodyguards. It was a peaceful life and one that they were enjoying.

The conversation eventually shifted to her brother and Anna asking her what happened to her after her home was set on fire in Taecin. Yoori told them that she had been living by herself and that she was a waitress at a local diner for a while. She concluded the story by sharing how she met Tae Hyun and how she came to live with him. Even while telling this story, she couldn't help but be amazed at how crazy her life had gotten. It was amazing how fast things could change within a blink of an eye.

Dinner continued on really well after that. Yoori loved Anna just as much as she loved being around her brother. She thought it would continue to be pleasant until her brother decided to journey on to the topic of Tae Hyun.

"So, I take it you didn't ask him?" Although his voice was gentle, Yoori did not miss the sternness behind it. The disapproval in his eyes made Yoori slightly uncomfortable.

"No," Yoori admitted, feeling like an adolescent who was about to be scolded by her father. "And I'm not planning to."

The sound of Young Jae's fork clinking against his plate reverberated through the room. He shook his head at her.

"Lil sis," he began wearily. Before he could say more, his wife interrupted him.

"Young Jae, that's enough," Anna said in Yoori's defense. "She's no longer your baby sister. She's a grown woman, and she'll do what's right for herself."

Young Jae frowned at his wife. "She can be ninety and she'll still be my baby sister."

"How unfortunate for her," Anna joked blithely.

Yoori giggled with Anna. She thanked the fates that she had Anna by her side. It was nice to have someone back her up.

"Unbelievable," Young Jae murmured, bitter that his wife and his sister were colluding with one another and uniting against him.

"I've been curious about this," Yoori began, looking between them. "How did you guys know that I was still alive?" Surely it wasn't a telepathic thing that led them back to her.

"We heard about what happened in the alley," Anna answered. "Your signature move had always been broken beer bottles, and you had very specific methods in how you used them. Once we heard how one of those guys were killed, we knew it had to be you."

Yoori felt chills form at the reminder of what she did to those gang members in the alley. It didn't take long for her mind to travel back to the incident at the nightclub. She had been tempted to ask him this entire time, and she didn't think she could avoid it any longer.

"Oppa," she started hesitantly. She knew she shouldn't tread on to this topic, but she couldn't fight the urge. "You really can't tell me what it was that Ju Won wanted?"

"That's enough," Young Jae dismissed sternly. Any warmth from his demeanor depreciated. "I told you the other night that this is where it ends. I'm not telling you anymore."

Yoori turned to Anna. Hope surged in her eyes. "Do you know?"

Young Jae's jaw tightened dangerously. He did not give his wife the opportunity to reply. "Lil sis, *stop it*."

Yoori sulked in her seat. Defeated, she said, "Fine. But if you said it was worthless, then why would Soo Jin try to kill herself? Why would you leave Korea?"

He scoffed. "You think I left the country because of what I found?"

Yoori nodded expectantly.

Young Jae leaned forward and rested his arms on the table. He kept his eyes glued on Yoori's. "I left because my sister was so traumatized by this world that she kneeled before me and asked me to kill her so she could cut ties with it. I left because I was in love with Anna. I left because I wanted to marry her and give her a safe and healthy life. I left because I knew that I could never have the life I wanted if I were stuck in the Underworld." He leaned back, took a sip of water, and continued. "The only reason why I'm back is because I want to take you back home with me—to Japan. I brought back all the Scorpions to escort you home, lil sis. I brought my wife, and we came back to a society that despises us for leaving it. Do you really want us to come all the way here for nothing so you could play house with Tae Hyun?"

It was Yoori's turn to scoff rudely. The last thing she needed to listen to was her brother mocking her relationship with Tae Hyun.

"Don't insult me by minimizing my feelings for Tae Hyun," said Yoori, articulating every angry thought in her mind.

She was offended that everyone and their mother were seemingly convinced that she was only infatuated with Tae Hyun as opposed to actually caring about him. She wasn't playing house with him; she wanted to build a life with him.

"I told you the other night and I'll tell you this again: I'm not some brainless twit who can't make decisions for herself. I'm sick and tired of everyone telling me what to do. I'm not playing house with Tae Hyun; I genuinely care about him and I really believe I have something special with him. With that said, you have to stop with these understated insults. I'm not leaving him—I won't. Nothing you say or do will make me leave him."

She saw that her stern words had worked when her brother's face softened.

"Okay, okay," Young Jae pacified, not wanting to piss her off. "We won't talk about you leaving Tae Hyun anymore."

Yoori nodded shakily. She appeared inflexible while speaking to him, but truthfully, she felt horrible that she spoke so sternly to her older brother. It was just that she had to make her point about Tae Hyun. She refused to allow anyone to dictate her decisions in life. She gathered her breath to compose herself and nervously glanced at the silver watch on her wrist. It read: 8:57 P.M. When the number flashed in front of her eyes, something occurred to Yoori.

She returned her gaze to her brother, realizing something important. "Oppa . . ."

"Hmm?"

She concealed the eagerness in her voice. "Do you by any chance know what '57' means?"

"I don't know." He tilted his head at her, intrigued by her query. "Why do you ask?"

Yoori shook her head and stood upright. She manufactured a playful smile.

"'57' means it's 8:57, oppa," Yoori replied lightheartedly, "which means that it's getting late and I should get going now. I don't want Tae Hyun to worry."

"But we haven't eaten dessert," said Anna, gently grabbing Yoori's hand as she stood up with her.

205

Yoori unknowingly flinched when Anna touched her. After a breath, Yoori struggled to maintain her smile. She felt awful that she had to leave so abruptly. She gave Anna and her brother, who was clearly unhappy at the mention of Tae Hyun, an apologetic pout and a wordless apology.

"Thank you for having me over for dinner."

She embraced Anna tightly before returning to her brother. He did not give her just any old hug—he actually picked her up off the floor and spun her around as he embraced her. They laughed together, and if Yoori weren't in such a hurry, she would've hung out with her brother longer. Despite wanting to bond with her family, the epiphany she had was an enormous one. She had to get home as quickly as possible to share it with someone else.

Yoori reached for Kang Min's hand when she stepped out of her brother's hotel suite.

"Let's go! Let's go!" she whispered impatiently.

"What?" Kang Min cried, nearly tripping and falling on his face as she hauled him with her.

The other four Serpents were running down the hall as well. They were all giving each other "what-the-hell-has-she-been-smoking?" looks.

"Boss!" cried Kang Min. "What's going on?"

"Take me home," Yoori ordered, running into an already opened elevator. "As quickly as possible. I need to talk to Tae Hyun now!"

■ ■ ■

"Kwon Tae Hyun!" Yoori cried long moments later, barging into the apartment. The door flew open and nearly slammed back into her when she skidded into the living room.

She was immediately blessed with the sight of a bare-chested Tae Hyun. He stood in the hall, wearing nothing but white lounge pants. He was drying his wet hair with a white towel, his muscles rippling teasingly in front of her. It was clear that he had just gotten out of the shower. He would've looked like a glorious fallen angel to Yoori if he weren't wearing a scowl on his face when he spotted her. It scared Yoori because even with the scowl, she still found him utterly sexy.

However, determined to not allow momentary awe (on her part) to overshadow her pride, Yoori frowned at the scowl. She would typically be more inclined to keep her part of the "cold shoulder" going, but desperate times called for desperate measures. She had discovered something important and needed to share it with her partner-in-crime.

Still livid with her, Tae Hyun was in the process of turning around when a bitter Yoori caught his arm and twisted him around to face her. Okay, she didn't exactly have enough strength to twist him around, but she was strong enough to stop him in his tracks.

He was the one who wheeled around in impatience.

Yoori growled as soon as their eyes locked. "What are you doing, Snob?" she confronted indignantly. "I just called out to you, and you still ignore me?"

"Oh, I'm sorry, Princess," he started sarcastically. Contrary to his words, he was unapologetic. "I didn't realize you'd stoop so low as to talk to someone who's paranoid and jealous."

There was such venom in his voice that Yoori was surprised she didn't keel over from the toxin. Yoori growled internally. Man, she was tempted to choke him with his own words.

Nevertheless, she kept cool, folded her arms, and looked at him critically. "We're still on this?"

"Yes, we are, because I'm still pissed," Tae Hyun answered blithely. Though, judging by how his eyes were softening on her, and how he was unknowingly approving the outfit she wore with his gaze, Yoori knew she was already melting his attempt at giving her the cold shoulder.

"Just because I trust Ji Hoon too and because I think you're overdoing it when you tell me that you think he's not the person I *know* he is?"

Her mistake was allowing that question out of her lips. As quickly as his eyes softened on her, they were quick to harden once again.

"You know what? I don't have time for this," Tae Hyun snapped back, beside himself that she still couldn't see past reason. He turned and made his way back into the bedroom.

He only stopped when Yoori shouted her next words to him.

"He doesn't know what '57' means!"

He turned to face her and looked at her quizzically. "What are you talking about?"

"My brother," said Yoori, feeding on the light of interest in his eyes. "From the story I told you . . . those kids were screaming '57.'" She swallowed slowly. "My brother doesn't know what it means."

"And?" he probed, his interest piqued.

"This doesn't change anything, by the way," Yoori warned before she went on. Despite being distracted with a big discovery, Yoori couldn't misplace her pride. "Just because I'm initiating the conversation doesn't mean that I forgive you. I'm still pissed at you."

"Touché," Tae Hyun replied just as stubbornly. He rolled his eyes at Yoori's need to save her pride. He made an impatient gesture with his hand for her to keep talking. "Now go on before I choke to death on your stubbornness."

Yoori's eyes momentarily morphed into poisonous slits. She quickly absolved Tae Hyun of his offense, for she had other pressing matters to tend to. She was more content that both Tae Hyun and herself understood the prideful boundaries that went with this conversation. Eager to share the golden nuggets of her epiphany, Yoori got back to the business at hand.

"When my brother told me those kids were screaming out '57,' at first I thought they were going crazy with fear. However, it just occurred to me that when Soo Jin was asking the mother for the answer, I think those kids were trying to help their mother by *giving* Soo Jin the answer. But Soo Jin didn't know it was the answer. She only thought they were going crazy, so she went crazy as well and shot them. I think that the number 57 is crucial and Soo Jin must've realized this. She must've been trying to figure it out when she ran into your Cobras at the club." Yoori shifted uneasily, her next thoughts disconcerting her. "The only thing I don't understand is why she chose to scar the Cobras with that number. It could easily be that she lost her mind or something like that . . ."

"But whatever the reason," Tae Hyun finished for her, already knowing where she was headed with her train of thought, "if Young Jae doesn't know what the number 57 means, then that probably means they never found what they were looking for that night . . ." He gazed at her. "Have you told your brother this?"

"No," Yoori answered without delay. "He's living a blissful life right now. I don't want to get him involved. Plus, he would never let me try to find it if he knew. It's better that you know so you can help me find it. If it's still there, that is."

"Right," Tae Hyun said caustically. "Give your brother another reason to despise me, right?"

Yoori purposely ignored his acidic remark. "What do you think? Do you think that woman gave Soo Jin the right answer, but an incomplete one on purpose?"

Tae Hyun pondered her question. "An Soo Jin was known as the enforcer and the interrogator of the Scorpions gang. It wouldn't be easy to lie to her and have her believe you, but—"

"—if you give her an incomplete answer, then you're still telling the truth and it'll show in your eyes." Yoori stared at Tae Hyun wide-eyed. "Do you think whatever it is they were looking for is still somewhere at the estate?"

"The only way to find out is if we go," Tae Hyun told her. Resolution saturated his eyes. "Tonight. We'll go tonight. There's no one at the Serpents' estate right now, and we'll have it all to ourselves. Whatever we need to find, we'll have the place to ourselves to find it there."

"There's a storm coming tonight though," Yoori noted. Her heart was thumping, both ecstatically and fearfully, at the little treasure hunt they were about to embark on.

"Storm or not, you know we both won't be able to sleep a wink tonight if we don't figure this out soon. I don't know about you, but all this secrecy is getting to me. I want to know what the fuss is all about."

Yoori felt the exact same way.

She was swimming in a dangerous territory as far as her memories were concerned. However, at that very moment, she didn't care. The only thing pumping through her was adrenaline and excitement. Finding out more about her past had always been a drug. It wasn't a healthy drug, but it was a drug — an addiction — nonetheless.

Yoori gazed at Tae Hyun with resolve in her own eyes. "What are we waiting for then?"

"We have no room for humans in our society."

16: Master of Deception

Tae Hyun's second Serpents' estate was the thing that dreams were made of.

The secluded road led up to gold gates that allowed entry into the well-protected estate. A few hours outside of the city, the palatial mansion rested on acres upon acres of land that stood beside its very own lake. Five-story windows stretched across the massive infrastructure, showing off the brightly lit chandeliers from within. Shimmering rays from the chandelier cascaded over the double staircase that rose from the foundation and led to the next quarter. The terrain of Tae Hyun's second estate was colossal. Yoori could only imagine how many Serpents occupied this estate during occasions that called for mandatory meetings. It eclipsed the first Serpents' estate and it no doubt made Ju Won's mansion at the masquerade ball look tiny and, quite frankly, insignificant.

Although she was overcome with awe, the one overpowering awareness that consumed Yoori while she treaded across the estate with Tae Hyun was that there was a familiarity to this place. It felt like she had been here before.

You came here with your brother when you were Soo Jin, she assured herself when they stepped onto the manicured lawn and jumpstarted their exploration.

"On the left side of the Siberian Tigers' estate, buried deep in the ground under the red roses. What you're looking for, you'll find it there . . ." Yoori repeated long moments later as she and Tae Hyun continued to stalk across the enormous lawn.

There were still sparks of tension surrounding them—as they were still "pissed off" at each other—but there was also camaraderie for the situation they found themselves in. Yoori was upset with Tae Hyun, but in the end, she knew she couldn't count on anyone else (or trust anyone else) to know how to protect her should the threat of a triggered memory occur. Out of everyone, the only one who could keep her from being consumed by Soo Jin was Tae Hyun.

The dim light from Tae Hyun's mansion embraced the space they were in. A second later, a blast of thunder clapped overhead. Yoori had since changed from her ivory halter dress into a white zip-up hoodie. Her black jeans were tucked into her long black leather boots. Tae Hyun, on the other hand, wore black jeans, white sneakers, and a dark gray zip-up hoodie. They wore their hoods up to protect themselves from the rain.

"Crap, I don't even know where to begin," Tae Hyun miserably declared. A grimace of disappointment darkened his face. He crouched down and touched the damp grass. It was as though he was hoping for a blast of inspiration from the mere touch.

Yoori nodded in the same dejected manner. Sprinkles of rain continued to pour over them. Her eyes roamed the massive lawn they were on. All that surrounded them were well-cut grass, beautifully manicured bushes, and trees. There were no roses, no flowers, nor any sign of disturbance in the soil— ultimately no hints as to where they should even begin to look. Frankly speaking, Yoori (and she was sure Tae Hyun) realized that they may have been a bit too ambitious and optimistic when they drove over to the estate. They expected answers right away. Clearly, this mystery would not be an easy one to solve.

Tae Hyun's eyes wandered all across his spacious lawn. Yoori could see that the prideful one was pissed that he didn't know if there was anything hidden on his estate. He glanced to her direction, and she felt self-conscious. She could tell, by how he looked at her, that he was hoping for one of those miracles where she would suddenly sprout antennas and tell him that she not only remembered what her and her brother did here, but she would also tell him where to look.

Yoori shot him the "you-wish-it-was-that-easy" look. It was a look that Tae Hyun sighed at. With only roadblocks in front of him, he went back to using his brain.

His eyes charted the dark estate. "Repeat it to me again."

Yoori didn't miss a beat. Her voice carried over the steadily falling rain. "On the left side of the Siberian Tigers' estate, buried deep in the ground under the red roses. What you're looking for, you'll find it there."

Lingering silence suspended between them. The quote, which soon became the mantra of the night, ricocheted in their minds. With her heart hammering and her body freezing, Yoori was ready to give up on their little quest. She was on the verge of voicing her surrender when she saw a flash of realization stir in Tae Hyun's eyes.

He gazed up at her, his expression awash with knowledge. "When you spoke to Ju Won, was there ever a point during the conversation where he looked into the ballroom?"

She knitted her brows. "What?"

"Humor me," he told her, yet there was no hilarity in his voice.

Yoori eyed him suspiciously and rummaged through her memory to recall her meeting with Ju Won. She slowly nodded. "Yes, when one of his men came in and asked if he was ready for his speech. Ju Won looked at me for a bit and then he gazed into the ballroom. After that, he told the man to go ahead and that he was ready." Yoori fastened her eyes onto Tae Hyun. He was still crouched down and staring up at her. "What does this have to do with anything?"

A lopsided grin tugged at Tae Hyun's lips. Her answer was exactly what he wanted to hear. "The thing you should know about Ju Won is that he is a vigilant old bastard. When you spoke to him, there was a point in the conversation where you told me you pressed him for answers of what he wanted Soo Jin to do. We have to presume that he didn't give you the obvious answer because he was afraid that someone might be eavesdropping from inside the ballroom. Now tell me about your conversation with Ju Won again, the part where you demanded that he give you answers."

Though Yoori wasn't sure where he was headed with it, she obliged because out of everyone, she trusted that Tae Hyun would be the one to help her figure all of this out.

"He said to me, 'You're not asking for answers. To truly want answers, you'll ask for the equations in which the answers derive from.'"

A full smile lit Tae Hyun's face. He propelled to his feet. He towered above her, arrogance beaming from his strong stature. He heard the words he wanted to hear from her. He was finally ready to enlighten her.

"He was hinting the answer to you the entire time." Tae Hyun laughed in awe. "Damn, the old bastard is smart."

"What . . . What are you talking about?" Yoori asked, wondering if Tae Hyun was in the right state of mind with all the rain that was deluging upon them.

Tae Hyun elaborated on his current train of thoughts. "In the Underworld, sometimes a red rose symbolizes someone's body. For instance, if you were to receive a red rose on your doorstep, it would mean that harm is about to come your way or your death is near."

By now, Yoori was not only freezing her ass off, but she was also confused. "What does that have to do with anything?"

Tae Hyun peeled every layer of his reasoning for her. "When you're burying something, you have to stab the shovel into the red roses—or the bodies—in order to get to the ground. And 'estate' in the Underworld would also signify someone's wealth or their pride."

"To truly want answers, you'll ask for the equations in which the answers derive from."

Ju Won's words replayed in her mind, and Yoori finally understood what Tae Hyun was doing. He was solving the conundrum given to them by using the clue that Ju Won secretly gave her. In order to uncover the real answer, they needed to decipher what the prominent words in the riddle symbolized.

"Yoori," Tae Hyun called out when the puzzle pieces started to fall into place for him. "The acronym for Siberian Tigers would be 'S.T.' When you *physically* look at that acronym, doesn't it resemble something else?"

Yoori's eyes swelled up at this simple, yet eye-opening revelation. Tae Hyun's knowledge was contagious. It didn't take long for Yoori to get swept up in the enlightenment. She bestowed him with her own pearls of wisdom.

"The number 57 . . . 'S.T.' resembles 57." Her heart thumped in exhilaration. "The number '57' represents 'S.T.,' the acronym of the Siberian Tigers."

For so long, the significance of the number "57" eluded her. She couldn't believe she didn't put it all together sooner. Thank goodness for the pathway Tae Hyun paved for her.

Tae Hyunnie, you fucking gorgeous genius.

Yoori was in a state of thrill. The urges to jump on him, hug him, and compliment him with all that she had surged through Yoori. But she held back the impulse. Distracting him from his momentum of revelations would not help them in the end. Perhaps when all of this was good and over, she'd shower him with the enamoring kisses he so rightfully deserved. Right now, they were here for business and anything else would have to wait.

Yoori's bout of distraction did not deter Tae Hyun from his thoughts. He was still on track; he was still on his way to unearthing the secret that had them spellbound.

The weather around them became unforgiving. The dark sky rumbled and growled while the rain splashed viciously at their faces. There was no warmth left on their bodies. In spite of how merciless the storm was becoming, Yoori and Tae Hyun were so lost in their own little world that being drenched from head to toe was the least of their worries.

"On the left side of the Siberian Tigers' estate, buried deep in the ground under the red roses. What you're looking for, you'll find it there," Tae Hyun repeated again. It was clear something crucial had flickered in his mind. Silence embalmed him for a brief second before his glittering brown eyes met Yoori's. His gaze was one filled with exhilaration, disbelief, and utter confusion. "I don't think the woman was telling Soo Jin *where* any item was hidden. I think she was telling Soo Jin *how* to perform a procedure."

Chills seeped through Yoori.

"A procedure?" she breathed out, unable to figure out why she was abruptly afraid. A paranoid part of her envisioned a cult-like process that involved cloaks, knives, red roses, burials, and sacrifices. She speedily eradicated those ridiculous thoughts from her head. A cult-like procedure would've been too easy of an explanation for the secret they were sitting on. Whatever it was that they were trying to uncover, it was more than an "item" that Ju Won wanted.

Still mystified, Tae Hyun reflected further. He repeated the riddle to himself again. A realization lit up on his face. He suddenly turned to Yoori with widened eyes when it all became crystal clear to him.

"I think for the procedure, the woman was telling Soo Jin to scar the Siberian Tigers' pride—the number '57'—onto the left side of the body *on* someone else's pride." His voice heightened with knowledge. "My Cobras were the pride of the Serpents three years ago. I think *that* was why An Soo Jin chose to scar the left side of their cheeks . . . because of this procedure."

"But why?" Her brain struggled to put the puzzle pieces together. She couldn't understand any of it. "Why the hell would she tell Soo Jin to scar your Cobras?"

"I think it's universal, Yoori. I think my Cobras stumbled across Soo Jin that night and they were perfect for what she needed."

"I don't understand." Yoori blinked the rain off her eyelashes. "Ju Won was trying to find out a procedure?"

Frustration marked Tae Hyun's visage. He pulled his hood off and raked his fingers through his now damp hair. Rivulets of rain poured down his face. He shrugged irritably. "I'm at a dead-end too."

Anxiety besieged her. The exhilaration that once livened her soul vanished. Yoori's mind ran in circles. Did the "item" even exist? Did Ju Won give her a hint the other night because he knew she'd decipher what the woman said? Or was it just a coincidence? Why did Soo Jin scar the Cobras? Why would the woman tell Soo Jin to scar anyone when Soo Jin was specifically asking for the *location* of an item? Nothing . . . Nothing was making sense to her.

"This is so frustrating!" Yoori groaned, lowering her hood. She ran her fingers through her hair in aggravation. A migraine began to ensue in her overwhelmed mind. "It's like once we figure something out, the puzzle becomes bigger and bigger!"

Sharing in the same confused state as Tae Hyun, Yoori's eyes aimlessly wandered all throughout the estate. The world surrounding her was now submerged with water. Completely drenched from the rain, it was only when a streak of lightning lit the world up did an awareness dawn on her.

214

"I've been here before," she said mindlessly, casting her gaze at the mansion without blinking.

Intrigue came over Tae Hyun. "With your brother?"

"No." Her eyes did not waver from the grand infrastructure. It seemingly glowed in contrast to the dark world around them. It acted as her haven, a magnetic haven. An unfamiliar sensation gripped her. Thunder boomed in the near distance, and she broke into a run for the mansion.

"What are you doing?" Tae Hyun asked, running and keeping pace with her.

"I've been here before." Her boots dug into the muddy grass as she accelerated her pace. "In my dreams. I've been here before in my dreams."

It was a dream she had right before she woke up and found Chae Young in the diner. It was a dream that felt so alive to her, but she categorized as immaterial. It did not matter that she couldn't remember much from the dream because her body remembered plenty. It continued to steer her toward the mansion.

Just like in the dream, Yoori kicked down the door to the estate and looked from left to right. Over the years, the mansion had evolved from the memories within her dreams. Luckily, some aspects of it remained the same. Yoori followed her instincts and ran down the corridor. She kicked another door down, nearly knocking it off its hinges. She sped down the stairs with Tae Hyun fast on her heels. They were in the basement where the Serpents stored their weapons and other miscellaneous items. The entire room was cloaked in darkness before Tae Hyun switched on the lights.

Yoori's eyes zeroed in on a particular spot when the basement illumed with color.

Recalling her dream, Yoori threw herself on the ground. She proceeded to move several brown boxes out of her way, revealing a brick wall parallel to her. Her hands shook from the remembrance of what occurred in the dream. Her lungs hyperventilated for air as she reached for the brick. She carefully pulled it out, unearthing a hollow space.

Yoori's breath hitched.

Something sat inside that hollow space . . .

The world seemingly stopped in its rotation and stood with breathless anticipation as Yoori gazed at what was inside the hollow area.

Oh God, Yoori thought when she realized that she had just ran across an enormous estate and found the same exact thing that the Soo Jin in her dreams hid. Her eyes swelled incredulously. She assessed the item that saturated the confined space with its small presence. Yoori was almost afraid to touch it. She felt Tae Hyun stand beside her, his eyes locked on the same thing.

A gold handkerchief rested in the hollow area.

Even under the dim lighting of the basement, it was evident that there was a bloody handprint on it. Yoori also noticed that an object was wrapped within it. She took in a deep inhalation to calm her nerves and to prepare herself for the revelation to come. Her quivering fingers reached in and wrapped itself around the handkerchief. With bated breath, she pulled it out and unfolded the handkerchief. A gasp fell from her lips when the item was finally revealed.

Lying above the gold fabric was a small jade knife that had the face of a tiger carved in the center. There was a small hole punctured at the tip of the knife where two red strings ran through it, clasping together at the end to form a necklace. There were remnants of dried blood on the surface of the knife.

"The jade knife of the Siberian Tigers," whispered Tae Hyun, observing it from where he stood. Amazement came over him. He regarded it like it was a missing treasure. "It was rumored that the Siberian Tigers possessed a valuable jade knife as their treasured heirloom. It is only passed down to the succeeding Kings or Queens who will take over the gang. No one outside the members of the gang has seen the knife." Genuine wonder inhabited Tae Hyun's voice. "I was under the impression that it was all a rumor and that the knife never existed."

"*This* was what Ju Won wanted?" Yoori breathed out, holding the knife like it was an item immersed with the plague.

Disgust boiled within her.

Countless people died . . . for *this*?

The longer she cast her gaze upon it, the worse the throbbing in her mind became. The surface of the jade knife burned through her skin like scalding lava.

"Yoori," Tae Hyun called out from behind her. "In the hollow space, there's something else in there."

He crouched on the floor beside her and pulled the item out.

A silver chain dangled from the tip of Tae Hyun's index finger. On the chain hung a thick, silver heart pendant. Tae Hyun inspected the innocuous object. He turned the necklace around and found that there was a tiny engraving behind it that read: "To my daughter, the best are never distracted."

Yoori's heart leapt at the words. She knew instantly that the necklace had nothing to do with the jade pendant. It was merely hidden there by Soo Jin because it was a gift from her father—from Yoori's father.

Tae Hyun continued to examine it. "Why is this locket here?" he asked, unbeknownst to himself that his girlfriend had already formulated the answer.

"To remind herself that she had to be ruthless and that she had to avenge him," Yoori replied intuitively.

The heart pendant acted like a small trigger, unleashing something so massive that she was not prepared for it. Yoori was promptly reminded of the dream she had about Soo Jin and Ji Hoon . . .

"If you're not going to support me, then that's fine," she uttered, stopping abruptly. She gazed at him unblinkingly, her determination never faltering on what she had to do. "But do not think for one second that you can change my mind!"

She breathed heavily, gazing at his frozen countenance. "Tonight is the night where he helps me make things right," she continued, her voice breaking. She held back the tears that were ready to stream out of her eyes. "Tonight is the night where I make things right. If you love me, then you'll help me make things right as well."

Another gasp escaped Yoori's lips. It suddenly occurred to her that Soo Jin didn't mean killing herself would "make things right." Yoori had always assumed that the Soo Jin in her dream meant killing herself would "make things right," but she realized now that it wasn't what Soo Jin meant.

Yoori's rapid stream of thoughts ventured on to the incident at the club.

"Is that what you want? For this world to kneel under the rule of the Serpents? The fuckers who murdered our father?"

There was judgment in her eyes that she gave away for a split second. It was a look that insinuated Young Jae didn't care about their father's death as much as she did.

Soo Jin loved her father immensely. Yoori could feel the love in the marrows of her bones. Was it possible that Soo Jin believed Young Jae was incapable of leading the Scorpions because he couldn't exact vengeance for her father? Was it possible she felt she would be the best candidate for it because her brother was too "distracted"?

Positively unsettled, Yoori went on to recall her brother's meeting with the brothers on the lawn . . .

"Your loyalty was never to me," Young Jae said severely. There was no forgiveness in his voice. "You were given the option of leaving with the rest to Japan, yet you chose to stay here. As far as I'm concerned, you are no longer Scorpions. Don't bother greeting me by kneeling. There's no point. I don't deal well with ingrates."

Yoori didn't think about this too in-depth before, but it was boggling her mind now. Why didn't Kang Min and Jae Won follow Young Jae to Japan? They had always been so trustworthy. She knew they would not be the type to be disloyal. Still, the whole situation didn't make sense to her. Shaking, Yoori then recollected the memory of when she was in her room with Kang Min, after the brothers had saved her from Jin Ae and while he was helping pack her things for Tae Hyun's apartment.

The brothers appeared close enough to each other, but there was one thing that didn't make sense. Why would two brothers split off and joined different gangs? Why didn't they stay with their boss if they were so loyal to her? Why would they leave?

"Why did you two part ways and joined different gangs?" she asked, finding it hard to keep this question to herself.

Before Kang Min could even think to answer, he was punctually interrupted by a familiar voice.

The truth became clearer when another bombshell hit.

"57!" the boys started crying out. "57!"

"I told you to fucking stop crying!" Soo Jin snapped.

Her furious screams only made the kids cry harder.

Infuriated, she slapped them across the face to shut them up, but they still wouldn't listen. They continued to cry and continued to shout out the number. Soo Jin was rubbing her face in irritation. She began to crack under the emotions spilling out of her. Their cries grew louder and louder. They became so desperate that they were even ready to rush over to Young Jae for his help.

Two heart-stopping gunshots were suddenly fired.

Boom! Boom!

Then, it all returned to the dream she had about Ji Hoon and Soo Jin.

"He's not going to help you kill yourself."

"If he's the person I know he is . . . he will."

"Baby, don't do this," he pleaded, grabbing her arms to prevent her from retreating. "We'll figure out another way to make things right. You can't risk your life like this."

And finally, as her heart raced beyond limit, as the air around her became insufficient, and as the blood drained from her face, the puzzle pieces came together for her in the most horrific way.

"Tae Hyun" Yoori began brokenly, finally holding his eyes with hers.

He watched her part her shaking lips, his eyes filled with nothing but worry.

"It . . ." Yoori continued shakily. "It was never in her plan. It was *never* in Soo Jin's plan to die."

Tae Hyun looked at her like he had seen a ghost.

He questioned her again to be sure he heard right. "What did you just say?"

Despite the pain coursing through her, Yoori struggled with great difficulty to explain. "What happened in the club, all the guilt she felt . . . it was all just a smokescreen to hide the bigger part of her plan." She held Tae Hyun's hand in feverish fear. Her eyes grew wider from shock. "Before she went into that club, Ju Won must have already told her that the answer was

218

going to be given to her in riddles." She covered her mouth in anguish and trembled even more. "When the kids started screaming out the answer, she shot them because she didn't want Young Jae to hear it. She didn't want him to hear the true answer to the riddle."

Yoori ignored the constriction in her chest and continued to speak. Tae Hyun held on to her, his warmth giving her comfort in face of the dark abyss she was swirling into.

"Ji Hoon knew she wasn't trying to kill herself. That's why in my dreams—*my memories*—he said to her, 'you can't *risk* your life like this.' He was in on it the entire time. Her guilt, the tears she shed for that family, and the guilt she felt for betraying her brother may have been real, but the guilt didn't derail her from her original plan." Yoori shook her head while a worried Tae Hyun eased the bangs from her pale face. "I think that part of the plan was for her to fake her death and for Ji Hoon to come back for her in the alley. There was also a plan for the brothers, and whoever was under her jurisdiction, to split off and infiltrate other gangs. The formula she gave Young Jae was given to her by Ji Hoon. Soo Jin must've known how much she would need to fake her death but—"

"But she couldn't anticipate Young Jae giving her amnesia and hiding her in a secluded city to protect her from trying to 'kill herself,'" Tae Hyun finished for her.

The expression on his face said it all: he was astounded by this revelation.

He exhaled disbelievingly. "But why would Soo Jin disclose to Young Jae what Ju Won wanted her to do?"

"Because she still needed the information, and she knew that Young Jae would take the answer as a literal meaning, not a riddled one," explained Yoori. "Ju Won must've had Soo Jin ask the woman a specific question to get a specific answer. I think the woman, or one of her children . . . one of them had the jade knife on them."

"Which was why Soo Jin returned to the nightclub the second time that night. She went back to retrieve the jade knife," Tae Hyun thoughtlessly finished for her before something else illuminated in his eyes. "Yoori," he launched. "To scar my Serpents, that must mean that Soo Jin was sending a message to the Siberian Tigers out there who know of the procedure. Similar to Ji Hoon when he carved a drawing of skulls on the faces of the ones who died in the business district, Soo Jin was using the same tactic for publicity. Only in this case, this specific 'procedure' was one only recognized by the active members of the Siberian Tigers. She was sending out the message to them that a new Royal had been crowned, and that they were supposed to wait for the one who had the jade knife."

219

"An Soo Jin annihilated an entire family to assume the throne of the Siberian Tigers," Yoori concluded painfully.

"But why would she need Young Jae to help 'kill' her?" Tae Hyun asked moments later.

Thunder boomed in the distance.

"She needed to be excused from the oath she took for him, and she needed him to believe that she was dead so that she could have time to resurrect the Siberian Tigers. She also needed time for her loyal supporters to infiltrate or form other gangs of their own." Yoori bit her lower lip. "I think she kept everyone in the dark, only telling certain people what they needed to know."

And then, Yoori felt her heart crack.

It became clear to her why Soo Jin needed her own brother to believe she was dead.

The memory of her conversation with Tae Hyun, when she found out he murdered his own brother, hurled into her mind. She remembered the words she said to him when she thought he killed his own brother to assume the Serpents' throne. Although those words evaded her understanding before, it made complete sense to her now.

"Why did you kill your brother?" she asked, growing infinitely more curious.

"Why are you so angry with me?" he fired back, dissatisfaction prominent in his voice. "Did you talk to Ji Hoon to punish me?"

"What? No. I ran into—" She paused to regain her composure. This wasn't about her. She was not the one on trial here. "No, it doesn't matter. What's your reason?"

"You answer my question first."

"I asked you first."

"I care about your answer more. Just tell me—"

"I empathize with your guilt," she proclaimed thoughtlessly. Her gaze rounded when she realized what she said.

Frustration dissipated out of Tae Hyun's eyes. Stupefaction took its place. "What?"

Yoori bit her lip, berating herself for answering without thought. The answer also didn't make sense to her. What was she thinking giving him that nonsensical answer?

"Forget it," she voiced irritably, aggravation mounting over her flushed face. "I really don't care enough to delve deeper into this. Whatever your reason, I hope it was good enough to kill your own brother."

Blood drained from Tae Hyun's face. The ticking clock of the bomb in their minds ran to a close. He, too, understood the sickening truth.

"Ju Won never wanted anything from the Siberian Tigers." His eyes noted the excess of shame and remorse resonating from Yoori's trembling stance. "All along, he wanted—"

"Young Jae." Tears embroidered her reddened eyes when she finished Tae Hyun's sentence.

They gazed at one another, the storm becoming more and more ruthless outside. Her world tilted on its axis. The bomb she had been sitting on had finally detonated, and Yoori was left in shambles. All this time, Yoori and Tae Hyun had been talking about people in the Underworld being masters of deceptions when in truth, the biggest master of deception had been Soo Jin all along.

Just when I thought you couldn't be more of a heartless monster, Yoori thought disgustedly.

Revulsion inundated her now frail body. If Tae Hyun weren't holding on to her with such care, then she would've allowed herself to fall over and slam her head against that loose brick.

"*That* was the unfinished business that Soo Jin owed Ju Won," Yoori said with difficulty.

She fought past the tears that were rising up through her throat.

"To be officially crowned as the Queen of the Siberian Tigers, and to be a potential candidate to become the Lord of the Underworld, she had to betray Young Jae and give Ju Won her older brother's head. All along, she had planned to murder her own brother."

"For we are plagued with the never-ending pursuit of power."

17: The Dissolution of Blood

For the following days, Tae Hyun became occupied with Serpents' activities, the contents of which he wouldn't divulge to Yoori. Yoori, on the other hand, had locked herself in his apartment while avoiding calls from her brother. The more Young Jae tried to call, the guiltier Yoori felt. She was continuously reminded of the plans she—or more specifically, Soo Jin—had for him.

Yoori couldn't eradicate the guilt that seemed to increase every time she took a breath. She could not believe Soo Jin conspired with Ju Won to betray her own flesh and blood. Yoori's insides churned at the mere thought. How could someone be so evil? How could someone be so heartless?

Yoori was so revolted with Soo Jin, and ultimately herself, that she didn't know what to do.

She despised herself for being curious about An Soo Jin. Nothing good ever came out of learning more about her heartless alter ego. Yet Yoori, always weak when it came to wanting to learn about her past, gave in. Now the repercussion of giving into this despicable addiction was rearing its ugly head.

The only solace Yoori took in being Soo Jin was that the monster (and Yoori used this word very kindly) felt guilty enough to try and kill herself to make things right. However, after discovering that Soo Jin never planned to die, and that she had an intricate plan to betray her brother, Yoori was at her last straw. How much longer could she attempt to separate herself from the very monster who owned the body she was in right now?

Yoori was on the edge and she knew it. She had never felt more broken and weak in her own skin. In addition to all of this, she had never felt more alone. She still felt terrible and didn't want to burden Chae Young with her problems. She wasn't ready to confront the brothers about their involvement in Soo Jin's plans. She didn't want to involve Hae Jin since she, along with Chae Young, were the only two in the group who saw Yoori for Yoori—and not as an alter ego of Soo Jin. She sure as hell wasn't planning on going to Ji Hoon for consolation. The fact that he was more than willing to help Soo Jin carry out her plan drastically changed Yoori's opinion of him. Though his love for Soo Jin was partially admirable, it wasn't enough to subdue the suspicious nerves within Yoori. There was too much about Ji Hoon that she didn't know, and frankly, she didn't want to deal with him. She was afraid that Tae Hyun's warning about him may be right, and that in the end, she would probably end up hurt by Ji Hoon.

The only person she needed, and the only person who was capable of comforting her, was Tae Hyun. Sadly, he was nowhere in sight. The distress piling in Yoori's gut worsened at the remembrance of Tae Hyun. His behavior toward her was disconcerting her. She had no idea if he was out of sight because he was revolted with Soo Jin or if he was avoiding her because he finally realized that she was the enemy. Yoori didn't know what to think. He wouldn't talk to her and that was enough to amplify the weight of despair in her already heavy heart.

"Tae Hyun, are you still upset with me?" she finally asked him over the phone. "Is that why you're ignoring me right now?"

She had avoided calling him for days now, hoping against hope that he would come home and talk to her. After days of not hearing from him, she couldn't dispel the desire to simply hear his voice. Giving into another weakness of hers, which was Tae Hyun, she disposed of her pride and made the pitiable call.

His dark, yet soothing, voice permeated the phone, calming her nerves, but leaving her to yearn for his presence.

She pressed the Blackberry closer to her ear.

"No, that's not it at all," Tae Hyun replied swiftly, alleviating the paranoia she was feeling. The alleviation was only diminutive in its effects. She could hear the strain in his voice. It sounded like he was keeping something from her and this made her uneasy. He went on, the strain becoming more apparent to her. "I've just been really busy, that's all. Just stay home and rest. Once I get some things settled here, I'll be with you soon. But for now, I've sent Kang Min over to keep you company."

Yoori digested his words. Although bothered that he was keeping something from her, she took solace in knowing that she didn't revolt him.

Her mind went elsewhere when she thought about Kang Min. "You're not upset that he merely joined the Serpents under Soo Jin's orders?"

"His loyalty to you makes up for any disloyalty to me," he assured her without hesitation. "I'm not angry with Kang Min or Jae Won." The tension that once held his voice was replaced with firm conviction. Yet, as he continued to speak, she could still hear an underlying distance attached to it. "I knew what I was getting into when I allowed Kang Min into the gang. I knew I was never going to have his full loyalty, but I wanted him anyway for his skills. So far, he has been nothing but an asset to the gang. And Jae Won joined the gang because of a forced merge. I already knew I wasn't going to get much loyalty from him. However, both have been nothing but loyal and vigilant with helping to watch over you. I'm not faulting them for anything."

Unable to help herself, Yoori allowed something that crossed her mind to sift out as she sensed the distance from Tae Hyun's voice. "Are you thinking about all the stuff Soo Jin did? Are you disgusted with her? Is that the real reason why you're avoiding me right now?"

The pitifulness in her own voice no longer mattered to her. She yearned for Tae Hyun to appear by her side so he could take away her pain, even if it would only be momentarily. If there was one thing she feared might push Tae Hyun away, it would be if he found out what a heartless bitch Soo Jin truly was. After what they discovered the other night, Yoori could understand why Tae Hyun might be keeping his distance from her. Understanding, however, didn't help mend the pain. The selfish part of her still prayed that he would accept her regardless. Wasn't their relationship stronger than that?

"No," he answered quickly, clearly sensing the desolation that had cloaked over her.

Yoori knew that Tae Hyun had probably straightened in his seat if he was sitting. She could envision his face contorting in worry at the accusation. She could still detect his intense feelings for her even if he still wouldn't tell her what was going on.

"I'm not avoiding you, Yoori," he told her in a hushed voice. "What I'm doing right now, I can't tell you yet. But know that it's important. I wouldn't leave you for it unless it's something that is really pressing."

The silence to come told her that she was getting no more out of this conversation. Her heart dropped at his passive dismissal. Defeated that her own boyfriend was keeping secrets from her, she decided it was best to end the call before she became any more paranoid. The old, combative Yoori would've called him names and demanded that he give her an answer. However, Yoori wasn't feeling like herself. She simply felt . . . crippled.

"I guess," she started, her chin wobbling slightly, "I'll see you when I see you then."

Yoori vaguely heard Tae Hyun bid his swift goodbye before ending the call.

She attempted to disregard the heaviness in her chest.

The doorbell rang right after Yoori hung up the phone.

Knowing that it was Kang Min, though surprised that he had arrived to her apartment so fast, Yoori prepared herself with an artificial smile on her face. She didn't plan on confronting him or Jae Won about Soo Jin's plan; she didn't plan on making herself more miserable.

Get it together. Just deal with Tae Hyun and the Soo Jin crap later, she told herself.

Yoori stood and straightened the white cowl neck sweater and the blue jeans she was wearing. Eager to forget about everything and hang out with Kang Min, she drew in a preparatory breath and opened the door without looking through the peephole.

Her smile was wide and filled with warmth. "Hey Kang—"

Yoori's greeting dissolved in her throat once she saw that the person standing before her wasn't Kang Min.

It was her older brother.

"Hey little one," Young Jae greeted delicately, smiling at her. He was wearing a black trench coat and black pants. His face was as warm as ever.

"Oppa," Yoori croaked bewilderingly, feeling the guilt and worry bubble within her like volcanic lava. "What . . . What are you doing here?"

She had just gotten off the phone and was already stressing over her relationship with her boyfriend. She wasn't mentally prepared to deal with her older brother.

Crap! Shit like this only happens to me, she thought glumly, attempting to do away with the "deer-caught-in-headlights" expression on her face.

Yoori continued to panic internally. What was she going to do? She wasn't ready to face her brother of all people!

Her worried eyes kept their gaze up on her older brother. His smile was warm, yet despondent, as he stared down at her.

Was it normal for her to feel such love for him when she had only "met" him several days prior? She didn't remember anything about him, but she could feel the adoration, familiarity, and warmth that came from merely being in her brother's presence. That was the thing that Yoori came to realize about her amnesia. Despite not remembering specific memories, the instinctive nerves of her body—her heart—remembered clearly the sense of comfort that only siblings could share with one another. She loved Young Jae. She loved and cared about her brother with all her heart. This alone made it all the more difficult to stand before him.

"You haven't been returning my calls, and I'm leaving soon," Young Jae confronted, confirming her suspicions as to why he had finally made an appearance on Tae Hyun's doorstep. Disappointment was pressed in his deep voice.

Yoori didn't know how exactly he had gotten passed Tae Hyun's guards. She thought about it further and concluded that it was probably the luxury that came along with being a King of the Underworld. If Tae Hyun wanted something, doors would open for him. She imagined this was the case for her brother and Ji Hoon as well. When a King of the Underworld was near, no doors were strong enough to keep them away.

"I don't know . . . I've been worried," he trailed before shrugging involuntarily. "I thought Tae Hyun was keeping you from seeing me, so I decided to come over to find you myself—just to make sure that you're okay."

"He would *never* try to keep me from seeing you," Yoori reassured. The unworthiness that ignited inside her in response to her brother's care and concern tormented her. "I've just been busy. That's all."

His eyes measured the empty apartment behind her. "Where is he?"

"Meeting with his Serpents," Yoori lied, unsure herself of where Tae Hyun was. She didn't need to disclose to her brother that Tae Hyun was acting strange and avoiding her.

Young Jae nodded again before casting his focus to her. There was a pregnant pause before he said, "So, can I take you out to lunch?"

Yoori's heart leapt into her throat. It was a simple request that required nothing but a simple confirmation on her part. She truly wanted to have lunch with him. She wanted nothing more than to hang out with her brother. Nevertheless, she couldn't place aside the troubling reality of what Soo Jin had planned to do to him.

Desolation drained any ounce of hope left within her. She deserved none of his care. For his safety, she needed to stay away from him.

"I really shouldn't—" she started with a heavy heart.

"Please?" he pleaded before she could refuse him. Yoori could surmise by his awkward expression that pleading wasn't something Young Jae did on a daily basis. "Today is our last day in Seoul. Anna and I are leaving tonight with the rest of the Scorpions. I want to spend time with you again before I go back to Japan."

She was blindsided. Go back to Japan? Already?

Her lips quivered at the unexpected news. "You . . . You're leaving tonight?"

He nodded.

"But you just got here . . ."

"We can't stay long," he replied. Young Jae sighed at her stubbornness. He continued to speak, his voice smaller than before. "Are you angry at me for disapproving of Tae Hyun? Is that why you're avoiding me?"

Yoori shifted guiltily. How horrible was it that her own brother thought she was behaving this way because she was punishing him?

He's leaving tonight, thought her inner self. *Are you going to let your only brother—your only family member—leave without hanging out with him one last time?*

Yoori peered up at him, nervously fidgeting with her fingers.

She couldn't. She couldn't let him leave like this. Despite all the shit that hounded her, Yoori knew her selfishness would prevail. She had to see her brother one final time before she cut all ties to protect him against herself.

"I'm not angry with you, oppa," she told him with a comforting smile. "I just had plans to eat with Tae Hyun," she easily fibbed. "But I'll ditch him for you."

Young Jae laughed at her attempt to break the ice.

All negativity aside, Yoori would never forgive herself if she allowed the last moment with her brother to be spent in awkwardness. This could very well be the last, happy occasion she spent with him and she wanted it to be as positively memorable as possible.

"Is everything okay between you and Tae Hyun?" he asked when she grabbed her card key to leave with him. "You seem a bit more . . . miserable since the last time I saw you."

The overwhelming bluntness (and accuracy) in her brother's question surprised her. She flashed him a bright smile and did her best to maintain her mask of composure.

"I'm fine," she lied, slipping her black Ugg boots on. She wrapped herself with a black zip-up jacket with a fur-trimmed hood. "If I look miserable, then it's only because it's winter and I'm suffering from all the snow that has been falling as of late."

Young Jae shook his head and chuckled at her reply.

Yoori grabbed her long white cashmere scarf that hung from the dining room chair. She sped back toward her brother, grabbing the doorknob to pull it closed on her way out.

"Where are we going for lunch?" she asked eagerly, relieved that for a few moments, she would be able to spend time with her family and forget about all the evil in her life. She slung her arm around her brother's. Yoori grinned uncontrollably as they moved to the elevator.

"To a new sushi place that just opened," Young Jae shared just as they stepped into the elevator.

His reply earned a cheer of approval from Yoori. She had been craving sushi for a few days now. Perhaps some good food would help chase away the crappiness that was in her life.

"Yes! Sounds good. I've been craving sushi!"

Young Jae laughed happily, playfully pulling Yoori closer to him after the elevator descended down.

"Good. I'll call Anna and have her meet us there. It'll be a good place to have our family lunch before we part ways."

■ ■ ■

Moments Prior . . .

"Why didn't you tell her what you've been doing for her?" Ace inquired after Tae Hyun hung up the phone with Yoori.

Sporting a forest green jacket and black cargo pants, Ace had been standing in Tae Hyun's office—one that rested in one of Tae Hyun's many nightclubs—and overheard the conversation between his boss and Yoori. Curiosity marked his scarred face.

Tae Hyun glanced up from his desk. He was dressed in a light blue, pinstriped dress shirt and dark gray pants. His fingers still held his Blackberry as he rested it on his brown mahogany desk. Conviction was etched on his face when his eyes latched on to Ace. Though there was resolution in his gaze, it was also evident that the conversation he had with a depressed Yoori had taken a toll on Tae Hyun.

"She doesn't need to know that I'm having my Cobras investigate her brother because I think there's something off about him," he informed Ace, weariness seeping out of his voice. "Especially when I don't have all the details on him yet."

"You've been at this for days, boss. Perhaps if you just went home and got some rest—"

"Her safety supersedes my fatigue," Tae Hyun said stubbornly. "It also supersedes the frustration of being away from her and having her think that I'm avoiding her. At the moment, I have a bad feeling about her brother. I need to make sure I know enough about him so that Yoori will be safe." He sighed, looking at Ace with sternness in his eyes. "You and the rest swore to me that you'd eradicate all vengeance towards her if I allowed you back into the gang. Right now, she is my priority. Is she yours as well?"

Tenseness filled the room before Ace answered. "What happened with Kimmy will be something that haunts us, but you should know that we owe our lives to you. I'm sorry about what happened before. We didn't know how much Ms. Choi meant to you. We're not ingrates. We all know that the only reason why we're here right now is because she begged for our lives, even when we tried to take hers. Despite anything that happened in the past, we were raised to know better. Obeying your orders aside, I still owe her my life, and I haven't forgotten about that."

228

A small smile appeared on Tae Hyun's lips. He nodded in approval at Ace's answer.

Ace noted the warmth that ran over Tae Hyun's face. "You've really fallen for her, haven't you, boss?"

Tae Hyun chuckled sullenly at Ace's question.

"She will be the death of me," he murmured, staring distractedly at his Blackberry.

Footfalls emanated from the hall. Seconds later, Mina stepped into Tae Hyun's office. She wore a black bomber jacket and dark pants. The only thing that stood out from her dark attire was the manila folder she held in her hand. She respectfully greeted Tae Hyun with a bow when he turned to look at her. Mina then took her place beside Ace.

The mood instantly shifted from a companionable one to a tense, anticipation-filled silence. There was knowledge in that folder. It was knowledge that Tae Hyun knew dealt with Yoori's safety. His stern eyes went from the folder and then to Mina.

"Yoori told me that Young Jae was doing some legitimate business in Japan," Tae Hyun launched, getting right into business. "Did you find any evidence that corroborates this?"

Mina shook her head. She stepped forward to place the manila folder on Tae Hyun's desk. She slid it beside his hands.

"The Cobras and I had to do a lot of digging, but we finally happened upon a good informant from the Japanese Underworld. Apparently, over the course of the last three years, Young Jae has been working as the new shadow gang leader for the 3rd layer of Japan's Underworld. He goes by 'AJ' in that world. From whispers, it is said that he's now at the top of the food chain. He hasn't gone public with it, but from all the recruits he garnered, including all the airborne Scorpions who continue to linger in Korea, if Young Jae wanted, he could resurrect everyone and have as much power as you and the King of Skulls."

"Fuck," Tae Hyun muttered, thunderstruck by the weight of this new information. "I knew there was something off about him, but I didn't think it went this deep."

Mystification twisted Ace's face. "Why didn't we know about any of this?"

Although his question was directed to Mina, it was Tae Hyun who replied.

"Because Young Jae is an opportunist," Tae Hyun answered, his firm eyes running from one Cobra to the other. It all finally made sense to him. "Because of what happened with An Soo Jin, and because it was spread throughout the Underworld that he became 'broken' after her death, the crime lords of this world didn't press for his whereabouts. We all assumed that he lost his mind and was hiding out because he no longer wanted to be involved in this world. The only reason why he was able to disappear safely was because Ji Hoon and I were in the process of taking over this layer. Everyone was distracted with the prospect of a new Lord deriving from one of us. No one thought twice about the fallen King who decimated his gang because he was 'too depressed' over the loss of his baby sister."

Tae Hyun smirked to himself.

Everything became clearer to him.

"He used his sister's 'death' as an excuse to leave one Underworld so he could infiltrate another . . ."

Suspicion then sparked in his eyes. He glanced up at Ace, the spark igniting with more fire. He had, at long last, realized something crucial.

"A year and a half ago, I sent the nine of you to Taecin because there was evidence that suggested my brother had business there. When you went to the areas suggested, you ran into Yoori. How did you wind up stumbling into the store she was at?"

Ace and Mina eyed one another before Ace replied to Tae Hyun. "There were records of your brother paying a substantial amount of money to a storage place in Taecin. We couldn't find the address of the storage area, but we knew the radius in which the money was transferred to. We inspected the area, found nothing, and instead, stumbled upon Ms. Choi. She was walking around in a local store and everything went to hell right then and there. We lost track of her and became enraged. Our need for vengeance got the best of us and we decided to set fire to the homes surrounding that area because we wanted to kill her."

Prickly silence blanketed the office as Ace and Mina stood uncomfortably.

Though the reminder of what the Cobras did to Yoori hardened his face, Tae Hyun did not allow it to override the more important matters at hand. Tae Hyun turned to Mina, his mind paving a road for something that no one thought to venture on.

"Bring up my brother's account. I want to see all records of his money transfers. You couldn't find anything a year and a half ago. We'll see if I can find anything now."

Mina knotted her brows. She clearly didn't understand the significance of Kwon Ho Young when they were speaking about Young Jae and the possible danger he presented to Yoori.

"Boss, I don't understand—"

"Just do it," Tae Hyun commanded, resolution and urgency fixed in his eyes. "Now."

"Morals cease to exist here."

18: The War of Scorpions

"Hi Anna!" Yoori happily greeted after she and Young Jae hurried into the quiet restaurant.

The heavy snow outside was deluging like rain, and she was grateful to be out of the storm. Her teeth chattered as she made her way into the restaurant. She could feel the residual coldness from the weather outside linger on her sensitive skin. Her only solace was that being in the restaurant meant that she would be able to eat soon. Yoori was also elated to be in the company of her family. Though her guilt was still present, it did not overshadow the joy she received from being with Young Jae and Anna.

"Yoori!" Anna greeted, rising from the table she was sitting at. She straightened her black blouse and pants before raising her arms up in a welcoming hug. "Where have you been? Young Jae and I have missed you. We came here for you and couldn't believe how hard it's been just to get a hold of you." Anna embraced Yoori tightly. "You're not pissed at Young Jae for blabbering on about Tae Hyun, are you? He can get annoying."

"Thanks, baby," Young Jae remarked bitterly.

Yoori cracked up at Anna's blatant insult.

"But he means well," Anna added with adoration. She gave her husband a playful wink. "He's always been overprotective when it comes to you."

"No, no. It had nothing to do with Tae Hyun!" Yoori assured, pulling out of the embrace. "I've just been really busy, but I've missed you guys too."

A wave of apprehension swept through her, causing Yoori to smile halfheartedly. Why was she feeling so . . . uneasy all of a sudden?

The restaurant, which was named Bada, was a lot bigger than Yoori had anticipated for a sushi place. She assumed that since it was such a new restaurant, it would be hip and swarming with patrons. It was surprising to her that the place was pretty empty. As far as she could see, it only housed herself, Young Jae, Anna, PC, and two of her brother's bodyguards. The guards, who were all dressed in suits, were standing near the bar, smiling at her when she walked in. She didn't see any workers, but she imagined they were in the back or on break.

"Good," Anna approved, pulling out a chair for Yoori, and dragging Yoori from her thoughts. "Let's enjoy ourselves and eat then. I'm starving."

"Yes!" Yoori concurred, quietly chastising herself for her unwarranted paranoia. She was with her brother and his wife for goodness' sake. What was she getting nervous for?

"I'm so excited for sushi," she shared, taking her place beside Anna at the big round table.

Young Jae gave Anna a quick peck on the lips before he took a seat on the other side of Yoori.

"God, I'm starving," Young Jae breathed out. "Anna sucks at trying to make sushi so I always have the worst cravings for it."

"Me too," Yoori chimed.

She was scooting her chair closer to the table when the melodic sound of her Blackberry sang into the restaurant. She pulled it out from the pocket of her jacket and glanced at the screen. The glowing caller ID revealed that it was Tae Hyun calling. Her heart leapt in joy while a gush of happy thoughts entered her mind. Perhaps he was finished with his Underworld duties and could finally hang out with her. She would normally ignore any calls if she was with her brother, but given all the avoidance from Tae Hyun as of late, she couldn't bring herself to disregard his call. She wanted to hear his voice again.

"Excuse me for a second," she told her brother and Anna.

They nodded and smiled at her when she left the table to privately speak to Tae Hyun.

"Tae Hyun? Yoori answered happily, meandering to a private corner. She pressed the phone close to her ear. She was ecstatic to be speaking to him.

The anxious voice that came over the other line squashed the euphoria inside her. "Yoori, where are you? Kang Min just got to the apartment and he said that you're not there."

His voice pulsed with worry and it scared her. It did not help that the uneasiness, which twisted her insides, was worsening while speaking to him.

"With my brother," she answered, pressing one hand against her tummy in an attempt to diffuse the restlessness barreling out of it.

"Fuck!" she heard him curse, tripling the panic she felt.

"What?" Yoori asked, unknowingly trembling where she stood. What the hell was going on? "What is it?"

"Where are you right now?" he asked, not yet divulging in why there was worry in his voice.

"At a sushi place."

"What's the name?"

"Bada. It's new. It's on Jade Street. Why? Are you coming?"

"Yes, I'm coming for you. But Yoori, what I'm about to say, you can't react to this message."

A paralyzing fear took hostage of her.

This definitely wasn't good.

"What . . . What is it?"

"When Kang Min called and said that you weren't at the apartment, I called the Serpents I had shadowing you to see where you were. They didn't answer, and I had Kang Min look for them. It turned out that they had been murdered—their necks were snapped apart."

Yoori's heart started to pound feverishly while he went on.

"I'm sorry to tell you this, but Young Jae's been lying to you. He hasn't been doing any legit business in Japan. He's actually a shadow Underworld King in Japan. He's garnered so much power over the past three years that he's at the top of the Japanese Underworld now."

The blood drained from Yoori's face while the eerie dread she felt skyrocketed.

"I think he's up to something. You're not safe with him, Yoori. But don't act like you're afraid. Just act normal with him. I'm coming right now. I'll be there soon—"

The phone was snatched from Yoori's hand. Soon after, a loud crack permeated the air. The phone was thrown against the restaurant tiles and shattered into several unrecoverable pieces.

Flustered, Yoori whirled around.

Shock stamped her face.

It was Anna who snatched the phone out of her hand.

Yoori took an unsteady step back. She was thunderstruck by the vicious look on Anna's face. It was a complete opposite to the kind visage Yoori was used to seeing. There was a dangerous glint in Anna's eyes. Her stare on Yoori was cold, unforgiving.

The doors to the restaurant suddenly slammed close, and the nerves in her body went cold. From the corner of her eyes, she saw PC and the two bodyguards move from where they were. They went over and stood behind her brother. Young Jae was still sitting at the table, his face void of emotions as he gazed at her.

Yoori knew instantly that she had walked into a trap.

All eyes were on her and they were all shrouded with rage.

After a long oppressing silence, her brother finally imparted words that had her blood freezing in her veins.

"Your betrayal has been disappointing," he stated solemnly, staring at her with daggers forming in his eyes.

There was no more love, comfort, or protectiveness that radiated from him.

All that existed was wrath and the yearning for vengeance.

Yoori shook and continued to back away from Anna.

She helplessly looked over to her brother. Her eyes pleaded for him to help her. "Oppa, I—"

"Anna," Young Jae prompted, interrupting Yoori by looking over to his wife. He was clearly uninterested in what she had to say. He had business to take care of. He was ready to get to it.

Yoori's eyes averted to Anna.

Fear encased her when she saw Anna nod after her brother's prompt.

She knew what Anna was about to do.

"I've always wanted to do this," Anna said with satisfaction.

Before Yoori could back away or avoid the attack, a powerful kick was delivered across her face.

Pain exploded inside Yoori as she fell to the floor.

The last thing she remembered was the feeling of someone grabbing her ankles and dragging her across the tiles before she lost all consciousness.

■ ■ ■

Yoori jolted to consciousness when icy water splashed across her face.

The pain of the stinging kick from Anna continued to throb on the left side of her face, causing Yoori to take several long seconds to lift her eyelids. It also took her several long seconds to remember the grave situation she was in.

Young Jae knows about Soo Jin's betrayal, she reminded herself.

She took in a sharp, painful breath and lifted her gaze from the ground she was sitting on.

In the far corner of the room, her eyes landed on the two male Scorpions. Both held a bowl that she knew was once filled with cold water in their hands. Their icy eyes teemed with hatred. It was the polar opposite to the warm smiles they gave her when she walked into the restaurant. Her eyes roamed the restaurant. She quickly discovered that the hatred for her wasn't confined to the two Scorpions in the corner of the room; it also spread across to all the other inhabitants. PC was standing beside Young Jae and Anna, both of whom were sitting at the table she was once at. All three wore the same icy look on their faces.

A nasty chill crawled throughout Yoori's quivering body when she recalled Tae Hyun's cautionary words. He was right. It was indeed her own brother who was now the biggest threat to her. The guilt she felt was now coupled with despair. Young Jae knew about Soo Jin's betrayal. He planned on making Yoori pay for what Soo Jin did.

"How does the old Underworld saying go, Soo Jin?" Young Jae mused short moments later, sitting comfortably beside his wife. He sipped from his champagne glass. His mouth curved into a light and dangerous smile. "Oh, yes, 'you can never forgive the ones who betrayed you. You have to make an example of them by reminding them what you're capable of.'"

He narrowed his eyes onto her, feeding on the fear that emitted from her body.

"You are a smart one, little sister," he complimented in a careless tone. "I almost fell for it . . . your little 'I'm human again' act."

Yoori paused. "You knew about Soo Jin's plans?"

It was a mindless question that she already knew the answer to. Regardless, she couldn't stop herself from voicing it. She did not know how to interact with him now. Yoori knew she wasn't just speaking to her older brother; she was also speaking to a renowned Underworld King. And just like any other Underworld King, he was an asset to have on your side and a force to be reckoned with if you were against him. It was obvious now that he wasn't on her side, and it was excruciatingly obvious that he was looking to remind her of who she was dealing with. He was a King in this world and Kings punish people by beheading them.

"Of course he knew," Anna voiced with distaste, scaring an already terrified Yoori with her overt loathing. "Do you think he became the King of Scorpions by merely blood right?"

Yoori clamped her mouth shut. The venom in Anna's voice disconcerted her. She was so different from before. What did Soo Jin do to her to have Anna hate Yoori so much?

"Anna," Young Jae whispered firmly, his eyes gentle on her.

At his stern whisper, Anna, very bitterly, pressed her lips together and glared at Yoori. Silence claimed her lips. Though it was evident she had more to say, she kept quiet for her husband.

Yoori swallowed past the tears that were rising through her. She cursed the misery that was her life. She was so excited to eat lunch with her only family and now, she was being stared upon like she was the incarnation of the Devil. Even then, Yoori knew that her blood was going to be shed for Soo Jin's sins.

Young Jae went on, taking stock of Yoori's quivering state. "I would've never anticipated your betrayal if Anna hadn't told me of the secret orders you gave to your gang members, for them to separate and infiltrate other gangs." His dangerous smile darkened. "And you even had the audacity to lie to them and tell them that it was all done under my covert plans?" He shook his head at her, unimpressed with the flaw in Soo Jin's plan. "It didn't take me long to piece everything together."

"You knew Ji Hoon was helping Soo Jin," Yoori stated unknowingly, realizing Soo Jin's error in judgment. Though Soo Jin kept crucial information to herself, there were still enough holes in her plan that if someone were to have even one piece of the missing puzzle, they would be able to decipher what she was up to. The puzzle piece that Young Jae had was Anna. It was clear to Yoori that if Soo Jin had known about Anna's relationship with her brother, then she would not have involved the girl in her plans to take over the Underworld and kill her own brother. Now, Young Jae not only knew that Soo Jin had faked her suicide attempt, he also knew of Ji Hoon's involvement in giving her the formula.

"He isn't aware that I know," Young Jae provided. He took another sip of his champagne. There was revulsion in his voice that he didn't try to conceal. "The thing with Ji Hoon is that his love for Soo Jin blinds him in so many ways. He put on a wonderful show about not wanting you to remember anything because of your 'suicidal' tendencies, but I imagine he was only against you getting your memories back because he didn't want to deal with you fighting him for the throne. You see, the original plan was for Ji Hoon to come for you after I injected you with the 'poison.'" Young Jae chuckled, smiling proudly to his ingenious plan. "Of course, he couldn't have anticipated me throwing in a disfigured corpse and playing it off as you. The bastard really thought you had died."

His dark eyes bore into hers. It was a look that reminded Yoori of a lion's predatory gaze before it was ready to annihilate its prey.

"You've always had a God-complex. You've always believed that you're the one pulling all the strings when in truth, your biggest weakness has always been your underestimation of people." His face hardened in animosity. "I suppose it was my fault. I spoiled you too much as my right-hand soldier. All Ju Won had to do was whisper a couple of things into your ear and you were all in, ready to betray me of all people."

"You didn't come back to take me home with you," Yoori said brokenly, knowing very well where the conversation was headed. All along, the comfort she took in her relationship with her brother was that he loved her and wanted to protect her at all costs. Yoori knew now that all of that was merely a ploy to gain her trust. It was a lie used to lead her into this trap. "That night, when you grabbed me from Ju Won's mansion, when you tried to pry me from Tae Hyun, you were trying to get me away from the estate so that you could kill me."

It dawned on her that Young Jae never hated Tae Hyun or preferred Ji Hoon over Tae Hyun. He only hated Tae Hyun because Yoori was under Tae

236

Hyun's protection. That was why Young Jae expressed so much hatred toward Tae Hyun, because he was trying to break them apart so he could have Yoori at his mercy.

"I should've snapped your neck when you kneeled before me, staring up at me while devising a way to kill me so that you could inherit the Siberian Tigers' throne," he snarled, confirming her suspicions that he knew what Soo Jin was up to. "I didn't kill you then because I was still weakened by the fact that you're my sister. I was weakened by the fact that you're my own flesh and blood." His eyes grew sterner, ice penetrating them. "But I won't make the same mistake. I won't let you get away this time, little one."

It occurred so fast that Yoori didn't see them coming.

In a second, two of the Scorpions were standing quietly beside her and in the next, they were inches closer to her, raising the bowls they were still holding.

Bang!

One slammed the bowl against her head, the jagged edges of the bowl eating away at her skin. The other stabbed his foot into her gut, causing her to gasp out for air. Before giving her a chance to catch her breath, the one who slammed the bowl across her head kneed her against the nose. Blood spurted from her nose as the back of her head collided against the wall behind her. Excruciating pain clawed at the nerves in her body. Yoori struggled to apply pressure against her head while hunching over and pressing her shaking hand over her bloody nose.

It was happening.

Young Jae was punishing her for Soo Jin's sins.

The Cobras punished her previously, but she knew just by the strength imparted from her brother's Scorpions that she was dealing with another level of assault. Her body was in for a world of pain and the instinctive part of her— the survival part of her—was begging her to get up and fight back.

Despite her desperation, Yoori did not allow Soo Jin's instincts to take over. Everything that was happening . . . she deserved it all.

Yoori stared up at her brother in anguish. The breathing of the bodyguards became nothing but background noise when she locked eyes with Young Jae.

A fear unlike any other consumed her: the fear of death.

Yoori knew that she deserved all of this. She wanted to take it all in stride because she felt that it was something she owed her brother. However, the more the pain became apparent on her body, the more desperate she became.

The image of Tae Hyun's handsome face, the warmth of his love, and the happiness that ran through her whenever she was around him overtook Yoori's thoughts. She didn't want to die. Although she hated her life, the one thing she loved more than anything was Tae Hyun. She couldn't bear the thought of leaving him. She had no idea where he was or if he was near. With the rate of how things were going, she was afraid she would be dead before he arrived to save her.

"Please," Yoori implored. The pleading word escaped from her lips before she could catch it. For the first time, she found herself begging for her life. Desperation shackled her. "Please . . ." Her voice broke. "Please, just leave me alone. I wasn't the one who did all those things to you."

As if slapped across the face, the inescapable reality of the situation he was in caused Young Jae's eyes to soften slightly. He stared down at her and, to her surprise, he acknowledged her plea.

"I wanted to save you, Yoori," he told her, the tone in his voice worsening her fears. He wasn't going to yield on the punishment he planned to give her. Anguish etched his voice while he spoke to her. "When I danced with you at Ju Won's mansion, I saw my baby sister. I saw the person she was destined to be if she hadn't been corrupted by Ju Won."

He smiled resentfully to himself. He knew well that although he was punishing Soo Jin's body, it was someone else who was paying for her sins.

"Soo Jin was a backstabbing ingrate, but the irony of this entire situation is you, Yoori. Soo Jin made her bed, but I'm sorry that you have to lie in it. I'm sorry that you have to pay for all her wrongdoings. I'm sorry that it's you I have to punish."

"I'll stay away from you," she pledged desperately. Tears bubbled in her widened eyes. "I won't come near you." Her terrified heart raced while trying to take its last breath. "Please don't kill me."

There was no courage in her voice. She wasn't afraid to die with the Cobras because with them, she took a life and it was more than fair that they took hers as well. With Young Jae, though the guilt of Soo Jin attempting to murder him haunted her, Yoori didn't feel the same fairness existed in the situation she was in. She may have deserved the punishment, but that didn't mean she was ready for death. It didn't mean that she was ready to leave Tae Hyun. Her heart ached at the prospect of never seeing him again. She didn't even get to say a proper goodbye to him . . .

"I saw you flinch when Anna touched you the other night," Young Jae whispered, the regretful tone in his voice wishing that Yoori hadn't done so. Perhaps if she hadn't reacted in that manner, all of this may have turned out differently. "You may not remember anything, but your instincts are more than alive and well. It's only a matter of time before you regain your memories; it's only a matter of time before you come after Anna for her betrayal. I know how Soo Jin is. I know how ruthless she is when she wants someone dead. I can't let you live and risk you coming after the woman I love. I can't risk you picking up where you left off and coming after me."

He sighed, pushing the empty champagne glass away from him. It was a silent prelude of the things to come.

"You provoked all of this, little sister. I would've had your back until the end if you hadn't betrayed me first. I would've protected you with my life if you hadn't conspired with Ju Won. But now that it's all said and done, the only thing left to do is for me to return the favor and punish you as I would any other Scorpion who dared to betray me. I can't allow you to live when your death will set the precedence to anyone else who would ever think of betraying me."

"Why did you go through the trouble of hiding me in Taecin if you wanted me dead this much?" Yoori inquired, feeling the blood seep from her nose and head.

The blood dripped onto the wet tiles beneath her as her mind churned with questions. It didn't make sense to her. Wasn't this the life Young Jae wanted for her? Wasn't this the life he gave her?

Oppressive silence hung over the room.

Young Jae stared quietly at her. It was as if he was debating about whether or not he should answer that question. After a long pause, he finally parted his lips and said words that Yoori couldn't have anticipated hearing.

". . . I wasn't the one who hid you."

The breath lodged in Yoori's lungs. "What?"

Before her thought process could lengthen, a loud sound emerged from the doors of the restaurant. Seconds later, the roaring of gunshots blasted through the room.

Yoori's ears nearly blasted apart from the sudden breakage in silence.

Like wild tigers, Mina and Ace sprung into the restaurant, each holding silver guns. Their vigilant, predatory eyes charted the restaurant. When they spotted Yoori and saw the ones around her, they started firing at everyone but Yoori.

Two loud grunts sang into the air, causing Yoori to jump in her seat. Warm blood splatters spilled upon her face and body.

The two male Scorpions were shot, the bullets burying into their foreheads and exiting through the back of their heads. Dying with their eyes wide open, the two Scorpions collapsed to the floor. One nearly landed on a horrified Yoori. She would've been buried under his weight if she hadn't scrambled away in time.

"PC!" Young Jae shouted in the background, whipping up from his seat. He withdrew two black guns from behind his back and fired at Ace and Mina. The two Cobras jumped away before the bullets pierced through their heads.

Using the moment of peace to his advantage, Young Jae turned to his right-hand man. "Take Anna back with you. I'll deal with the Serpents."

"Young Jae, I'm not leaving you!" Anna fought, standing up with him.

"Anna," Young Jae spoke urgently. "Our agreement for you to come back to Seoul was for you to leave whenever I tell you to leave. You're leaving with PC and you're going now."

"But—"

"I'll be fine," Young Jae interrupted. He placed his guns on the table and cupped her worried face in his hands. "Just go first. I still need to take care of Soo Jin."

Anna did not get to say anything else before PC pulled her away. While they ran out through the back exit, Young Jae grabbed his guns and jumped over the bar of the restaurant. With the bar as his shield, he leaned over and started firing at Mina and Ace.

The two Cobras used the doorway they entered as shields and were firing back at Young Jae. They were careful not to hit Yoori.

Still reeling from what she discovered from her brother—and finally processing that she was now covered in the blood of others—Yoori did her best to hold on to the last shred of her sanity. Momentarily flustered, Yoori was on guard when she locked eyes with her brother. He had just fired four more shots toward the Cobras before making his way to her in their distracted state.

The look on his face said it all: he was ready to finish her off once and for all.

Panic struck her like a lightning bolt.

She scrambled to her feet and tried to make a run for it. To her horror, her legs were still weakened from the assault. She didn't get far before falling back down, nearly crushing the dead body that rested beneath her. The panic exacerbated inside her. She quickly looked over her shoulder. Young Jae was aiming a black gun at her while still firing the other one at the Cobras.

Her eyes expanded, and she speedily leapt to the side just as the gun fired.

Boom!

"Ahh!"

The bullet skimmed past her upper shoulder, ripping through her jacket and taking with it a thin layer of her skin. Warm blood oozed from her body. The pain ricocheted crazily through her. Holding her quivering hand to the surface wound on her shoulder, she peered up again.

Her world froze in horror when she saw that Young Jae was standing close to her, aiming the gun in the direction of her head.

Boom!

A gunshot was fired, and Yoori thought her brother had shot at another part of her body. Her eyes enlarged even further when she heard a scream and saw her older brother clutching on to his right arm. It was now bleeding from a gunshot wound.

Someone sped past her, jumped toward Young Jae, and performed a roundhouse kick that left Young Jae spurting blood from his mouth. The assault didn't end there. He followed that move by delivering a spinning air kick that left Young Jae to fly across the room like a speeding bullet.

Kwon Tae Hyun.

Just like all the previous moments of her life, her dark knight had arrived for her and he looked livid. Her heart raced when she gauged how furious he looked. She knew what Tae Hyun was planning to do to her brother.

"Tae Hyun, don't!" Yoori cried when Tae Hyun sped over to her brother with his silver gun in hand. Despite all that he had done to her, Yoori still loved her brother. She would be damned if she allowed her own boyfriend to kill him off. "Please don't. He's my brother!"

At the plea in her frantic voice, an enraged Tae Hyun stopped midway. The posture of his body told her that he was itching to beat the hell out of Young Jae before killing him. He was only holding back for her.

Tae Hyun stood with unforgiving rage, his silver gun pointed in the direction of Young Jae. Her brother was still groaning on the floor. His hand was clutching on to the bullet wound on his opposite arm. Young Jae struggled to stand after the assault Tae Hyun bequeathed unto him.

"How could you do this to your own sister?" Tae Hyun asked in disgust.

Young Jae laughed bitterly, staggering to stand up. There was no fear in his eyes. There was just hostility and the thirst for blood.

"Stay out of this, Tae Hyun. My fight has never been with you."

"Anything that involves her involves me," Tae Hyun replied without hesitation. Anger was prominent in his dark voice.

More laughter erupted from Young Jae. He continued to clutch on to his wounded arm, looking at Tae Hyun with the utmost pity.

"Oh, the irony," he drawled out in a patronizing tone. "The chosen King . . . the very pride of the Underworld . . . falling victim to the very thing that's known to be the downfall of all great Kings in this world." Young Jae smirked, the irony being too much for him to handle. His eyes slid from Yoori and then back to Tae Hyun. "And of all people, it just had to be you two who fell for each other."

His dark eyes pierced into Tae Hyun. "You have no idea what you're getting yourself involved in, Tae Hyun. An Soo Jin is a ruthless bitch in every sense of the word. She was willing to betray me—her own flesh and blood—for a shot at power. What do you think she'll do to you once she regains her memories? The one person who's the leader of the gang she despises the most? Do you think you'll have a happily ever after with your Yoori? Think again. Soo Jin will take over and your precious girlfriend will cease to exist in this world." Determination marked his voice. "Help me now, Tae Hyun. Choi Yoori is a useless cause. Save your throne, and I won't bring forth a war that will be your downfall."

"I don't fear you, Young Jae," Tae Hyun said darkly. "Your bullshit threats mean nothing to me."

"Bullshit?" Young Jae asked disbelievingly. Another derisive chuckle issued from his lips. "For the past three years, I've spent my time under the wings of Japan's most notorious crime lords. I've been rising through the ranks as a shadow King and have formed a powerful gang that no one had anticipated. All it takes is the snap of my fingers and my loyal Scorpions throughout Korea will resurrect. All it takes is a simple phone call and my soldiers from Japan will come running. Is this the war you want, King of Serpents? All for the Queen of the Underworld who will not hesitate to battle you for your throne once she regains her memory?"

A suspended moment of silence spread over the room while Tae Hyun absorbed Young Jae's words.

Yoori, who was now frozen with apprehension, was quiet as well because she knew what Young Jae said was true. Yoori was on the brink and everyone knew it. It was only a matter of time before she regained her memories; it was only a matter of time before Soo Jin reclaimed the life that was stolen from her. More importantly, it was only a matter of time before Yoori ceased to exist. Thoughts like this had invaded her mind in the past, but its effects had never been this strong for Yoori, who was now so broken that she couldn't help but wonder what was happening in Tae Hyun's mind.

Tae Hyun, whose voice teemed with resolution and determination, breached the silence. "I've told you once before that I can't control time, Young Jae. I can't control the fact that she used to be Soo Jin and that she would've been my enemy if we'd met under different circumstances. I can't control the fact that Ji Hoon was there for her first, that he came before me. But it's my time now. As far as I'm concerned, you will not touch a hair on her head if I'm around. If you want to get to her, you'll have to do it over my dead body."

Relief entered Yoori's body at the heartfelt words expressed by Tae Hyun. She had always known that he would protect her. To hear him proclaim it under such circumstances touched her heart even more. Her heart's moment of reprieve was fleeting before her brother broke it further.

Young Jae scoffed mockingly. "Then you're a better man for her than Ji Hoon could ever hope to be."

Before giving them time to truly soak up his words, Young Jae's severe eyes zeroed in onto Yoori.

He wasn't staring at her like she was his sister; he was staring at her like she was his most hated enemy.

"Soo Jin," he began. "From this moment forth, there will be no more hesitation or mercy on my part. For the next days to follow, I'll give you the time to enjoy what's left of your life. It will be my final gift to you. But rest assured that after today, I'm severing all ties with you. The next time I see you, I *will* bring war upon you." He glanced at Tae Hyun. "And anyone who stands in my way." He returned his focus to her, a dark shadow crossing his face. "I came back to Seoul for your head and I won't leave until I show you hell." He smiled cruelly, his eyes running from Tae Hyun and then to her once more. "Good luck with the King of Serpents before he sees you for who you really are."

Horror laced Yoori's pale face at the last of her brother's words. She knew he was referring to the issue pertaining to Tae Hyun's mother and how she died. She had hoped that it was a bullshit thing Young Jae concocted to break her from Tae Hyun. Yet, deep in her heart, she knew she couldn't escape the truth.

It was unmistakable.

Soo Jin had something to do with the death of Tae Hyun's mother.

With that, Young Jae disappeared out of the nearest exit, leaving Yoori and Tae Hyun alone. Behind Tae Hyun, Mina and Ace stood at the doorway, gazing at their boss for further instructions. Tae Hyun clutched on to his gun, his body more than ready to chase after Young Jae.

It was Yoori's voice that caused Tae Hyun to finally turn around, his regretful eyes boring into her.

"Just let him go . . . *please*," she begged.

Blood dripped all around her while tears clouded her doe-like eyes. She owed her brother that much. She owed the one who took care of her, the one who once loved her, and the one she betrayed that much.

"We're going to regret letting him go," Tae Hyun told her softly, throwing his gun to the floor before finally running to her.

He wrapped her closer to him after Yoori jumped into his embrace, shaking while holding him and finally crying into his arms. She wasn't sure if she replied with anything. All that she could feel was her soul shattering as she sobbed into his arms. All that she could remember was crying over the loss of her only family member. All that she could remember was crying because she knew that Tae Hyun was right.

One day, they would both regret letting Young Jae go.

"When you become human..."

19: Before Hell Takes Over

Yoori wasn't sure how long she sat in the bathtub, shaking with self-loathing. She was aware she looked pathetic, but she no longer cared. What was there to care about when her world had fallen apart? Along with the world, her identity and her sense of purpose crumbled.

After the revelation that shook her to her core, Yoori excused herself from Tae Hyun's hold when they returned to the apartment. She proceeded to barricade herself in the bathroom, not even bothering to turn on the lights before she crawled into the empty bathtub. She did not want to feel the presence of light; she merely sat there in total darkness and allowed the misery to consume her.

I'm a monster . . . I caused all of this . . . this is all my fault, she told herself, rocking in the darkness.

Yoori could feel her memories thrash against the wall she meticulously built. There was a monster inhabiting her body, breathing in silence as it awaited freedom. The monster plagued her with its existence and there was nothing Yoori could do but try to fend it off. It was fast becoming a futile battle because she was losing horribly. The end was near, and she was close to snapping. All she could do was cry to herself, wallow in her own despair, and abhor herself for breathing.

I should've died three years ago . . .

Yoori recalled the hatred her brother and his wife had for her, the hatred the Cobras had for her, and the hatred she had for herself. How could she blame them? Even *she* detested her own existence. She wanted to save herself from death before, but now, Yoori wasn't so sure how much she wanted to live. She could no longer catalog her thoughts and sense of purpose in her life. She wanted to die one moment and live the other. Now, she wanted to die because she was a mess. Was she losing her mind? Was this what it was like to lose one's sanity?

She was so consumed in her thoughts that she hadn't realized the door had cracked open until a single beam of light from a lighter penetrated the darkness.

Yoori gazed up with lifeless eyes. In her periphery, she saw that Tae Hyun was walking through the door. He had changed out of his clothes and was now shirtless and wearing a white, lounge drawstring pant. With a lighter in hand, he reached over the marble sink and lit a single white candle before diffusing the lighter. He tossed the lighter onto the counter, closed the door, and approached her in the candle-lit darkness.

"You've been in here for a while, Brat," he noted gently.

He casually stepped into the dry bathtub and sat across from her. His face glowed gorgeously under the kiss of the single candle illuminating the bathroom.

"Why are you here?" Yoori asked bluntly.

She hugged her knees to her chest. Looking down, Yoori noticed she was still wearing the clothes she wore earlier. There were splotches of dried blood staining her once pure clothes. The dried blood reminded her of the Scorpions her brother ordered to attack her. The sudden horrid flashes of Anna kicking her, the Scorpions abusing her, and her brother pointing a gun at her, ready to kill her, haunted Yoori. She made sure to keep her tears to herself when she gazed at Tae Hyun. Though she broke down when she saw him at the restaurant, she was determined to keep composure now. She was sick of crying in front of him.

"Why wouldn't I be here?" he asked. His tone was marginally offended that she would ask him such a question.

"You've been avoiding me for the past couple of days." She didn't attempt to hide the resentment in her voice. "I don't see why it's important that you come see me now."

When Yoori and Tae Hyun went to Dr. Han to tend to their wounds and give Yoori the stitches she needed, Tae Hyun confessed that he had been busy for the last couple of days because he was digging up information on her brother. Yoori should have been relieved when she learned this. On the contrary, relief was the last thing she felt. She understood that everything Tae Hyun did, he did to protect her. Nevertheless, she resented that he kept something that important, especially regarding her brother, away from her.

"I didn't feel it was necessary to share that I was busy digging up information on your brother, especially with the state you were in," he explained.

His hands reached out to hold hers, but Yoori quickly withdrew her hands from his reach. She wasn't ready for him to touch her, to care for her. If he touched her, then her control would disintegrate. She would simply crumble apart and cry into his embrace again. And God help her, Yoori wanted to maintain some dignity, some strength in her life—at least for a little while before she broke down again.

Sadness painted the canvas of his face when she denied his efforts to hold her, to love her. His hands should have been caressing the locks of her hair, but instead they were touching frigid, still air. He unwillingly pulled his hands back, but maintained his caring gaze on her.

Though Yoori was still resentful that he hadn't divulged any of this information when she called him, she also understood that she wasn't in the best state of mind. Quite frankly, if she were in Tae Hyun's position, she would not have told herself anything either.

A few passing breaths of silence spread over them while Yoori and Tae Hyun sat still in the darkness. The wheels of her mind spun, replaying the event at the sushi restaurant. A recollection of something Young Jae disclosed illumed in her memory like neon lights; it had haunted her since the restaurant and it continued to haunt her now.

Yoori took in a deep breath before rupturing the silence that was beginning to suffocate them. "He wasn't the one who hid me in Taecin." The verbalization of this thought tortured her. It acted as a reminder of her brother's true intentions with her, that he was not the person she thought he was. Young Jae was not the one who hid her and granted her a new life to protect her. If anything, his intentions were the polar opposite. He wanted to punish her, destroy her. Yoori closed her eyes in misery. She felt her insides rip at every damning thought. The caring, warm older brother in her dream did not truly exist. He was simply that—a dream.

"I know," Tae Hyun quietly replied.

Yoori snapped her head up, struck by his answer. Thoughts and memories were frantically pacing around in her mind. She wondered how he knew this, when he knew, and who had told him. She then recalled that he had been digging up information on her brother. If he knew that Young Jae did not hide her, then he must know who did.

"Do you know who hid me in Taecin?"

He nodded.

"Who?"

Tae Hyun kept his lips pressed together. It was clear he was concerned with telling her too much and risking her falling apart—more so than she already was.

"Who?" Yoori urgently pressed again, her big eyes scrutinizing his under the candle's light. When his hesitation persisted, she started to get angry. He was treating her like a fragile china doll and she was sick of it. As his silence reigned, Yoori angrily said, "Stop keeping secrets from me. Whatever it is, I can handle it."

Tae Hyun looked away from her scrutiny. Despite his own reservations, even he knew that he couldn't keep this from her.

"It was my brother," he finally shared, causing Yoori's eyes to dilate in shock. "It was my brother who hid you, Yoori. It was my brother who wired money to that family and it was my brother who took care of all the bills at the hospital you stayed in."

This new piece of information stunned her so hard that Yoori had to fight to breathe.

"*How?*" she uttered incredulously. "How is it possible that it was your brother who hid me?"

Of all people who could have hidden An Soo Jin, it was Kwon Ho Young?

The puzzlement on Tae Hyun's face mirrored that of Yoori's. "I don't know."

By now, Yoori was left tunneling into a quicksand of confusion. The Pandora's box had been opened and hundreds of questions paced through her mind. Was Soo Jin involved with Ho Young? Was she working with Ho Young? Why would she collude with the enemy? What the hell was wrong with Soo Jin? What was she up to during the last few days of her life?

Yoori buried her face in her hands, frustration brewing within her like acid. "The puzzle gets bigger and bigger when it comes to Soo Jin, doesn't it?" she asked, wondering how it was possible that one human being could retain so many secrets.

There was no need to learn more about Soo Jin to know that she was a dangerous person. Yoori felt ghastly when she considered the possibility that if she regained her memories, it was impossible to prevent Soo Jin from destroying everything she loved, including herself. She was no longer left with any options. The realization caused Yoori's face to be void of any color or life. She had to protect everything she loved while she still had a chance.

"I . . . I have to leave you, Tae Hyun," Yoori announced long moments later, knowing that she couldn't ignore her unforgiving reality any longer.

Her distraught heart broke at the thought of no longer having Tae Hyun by her side.

It's for the best, she assured herself, biting her lips to keep from crying in front of him.

"Why do you have to leave me, Yoori?" Tae Hyun questioned, his voice low and gentle.

The way he looked at her made her want to crawl into his arms and forget about the world around her. It took all her control to resist this urge. She no longer had the luxury of doing that. She no longer had the luxury of escaping from her reality and seeking solace from Tae Hyun. If she wanted any chance of preserving her sanity, she had to face her problems head on.

"I begged him to not kill me," she whispered, drawing her knees closer against her chest. She resembled a broken child. "I looked up at my own brother and begged him not to kill me because it was An Soo Jin who betrayed him. I begged him . . . just like those kids begged her before she shot them."

She closed her eyes momentarily, agonized by the memory of Soo Jin's crimes. She heard the children begging, screams of chaos, and saw flashes of splattered blood everywhere. This was karma in its most sadistic and sinful form. This was karma, and she was paying dearly for everything.

Yoori pressed on, ignoring how her heart was throbbing in agony. "Young Jae will bring war upon you to get to me. He will bring in reinforcements from Japan and he will punish you for protecting me." She inhaled painfully. "I shouldn't be around you, especially when we both know how ruthless and heartless Soo Jin could be."

There was no way around it. As long as she was with him, then Tae Hyun was in constant danger. There were already so many others who were after him; she did not want to add her brother to that list. Most importantly, she did not want to add Soo Jin to that list. It wasn't feasible for Tae Hyun to watch over her forever. What was going to happen? Was he going to come to her rescue every time? She could no longer put him through that burden. In order to guarantee his safety, she had to leave him.

"I'm not afraid of Soo Jin," he assured her.

Tired of the distance between them, he reached out and pulled her closer to him.

"I'll deal with anything that comes my way if it means that I get to be with you."

"I'm losing this battle with her, Tae Hyun," Yoori hoarsely voiced, doing her best to release herself from Tae Hyun's hold. She did not want him to weaken her resolve on what she had to do. "Everyday, I'm being pushed further and further over the edge. I'm no longer the same girl you brought into this world, and I'm afraid that pretty soon, I'll cease to exist when Soo Jin finally takes over." She regarded him with fresh tears in her eyes. "Perhaps it's better to just let me go. Let me leave this place and let me fend for myself. Maybe it's best if I let Young Jae take me out so I could save all of us from Soo Jin."

"You think I'm just going to sit by, watch you leave, and allow you to die?"

"You've reached the point where that's all you can do," she informed him dejectedly. She herself wished that this wasn't true. "I'm beyond saving."

"Yoori, look at me," Tae Hyun ordered, readjusting her so that she was lying atop his body.

As she faced him, his strong arms pressed against her back while he held her to his bare chest.

Yoori looked into his eyes and wished she hadn't. Nothing but promises teemed inside his eyes—promises of a happily ever after and promises that she no longer believed in. Yoori was no longer a fool. She no longer believed in fairytale fantasies. Her fate was too intertwined with Soo Jin's. Someone like Soo Jin didn't deserve a happily ever after, and as a result, it meant that Yoori would never get her happily ever after as well.

Despite this belief, she found herself falling deeper into the realm of promises as Tae Hyun smoothed a hand over her arm and cupped her cheek with love and devotion with the other. He held her full attention when he spoke. His voice was tender, yet filled with strength. His enticing brown eyes gazed down at her and for a heavenly moment, he erased all painful memories of anything else that occurred in her world. All that mattered at that moment was the two of them; all that mattered was Kwon Tae Hyun and Choi Yoori.

"When I stood out there with you on the balcony and told you that none of this was going to be easy, I knew what I was getting into." Still holding her tightly, he leaned in and feathered his beautiful lips over hers. "I'm not afraid of Young Jae, I'm not afraid of the crime lords in this world, and I'm not afraid of what Soo Jin is capable of."

A single teardrop escaped Yoori's eye. The blank canvas that once inhabited her face started to release all her restrained emotions. She could no longer suppress her feelings. All she wanted to do was kiss him back. All she wanted to do was kiss the man who stole her heart.

He continued to speak while his lips kissed hers, comforted hers, and simply loved hers. "All that matters to me is keeping you safe, keeping you alive, and keeping you with me. The only reason why I'm fighting so hard for this throne is because the power I get from it will allow me to protect you."

"You're making this so much harder," Yoori whispered. Her hands pressed flat against his chest. She felt his warm heart throbbing, triggering her own to race. Despite what she was saying, she leaned in and kissed his lips because he was her walking paradox. She simply couldn't resist doing so. "You're making it so much harder to leave you."

"Do you want to leave me?" Tae Hyun inquired as he lowered his lips to the nook of her neck. He continued to adorn her with his affections, kissing her while more tears rippled in her eyes.

"No," she replied honestly, feeling both blessed and cursed with the life that was given to her.

She was cursed with An Soo Jin, but blessed with Kwon Tae Hyun. The conflicting emotions inundated her sanity. She hated that she couldn't let him go. She was too selfish. The love she felt for him went beyond infatuation or puppy love. It was love in its rawest form. Although it was painful to love him, the pain was nothing compared to the euphoria she felt whenever she was with him.

"I need you," she admitted without a drop of shame in her voice. Yoori no longer cared about sounding pathetic or weak. She loved him, and just as he was ready to give up everything for her, she was more than ready to give up everything for him.

"Don't push me away," he painfully pleaded. He coaxed her by feathering his sensuous kisses over the skin of her neck, heightening the pleasure overtaking her. "Let me be here for you."

Yoori mindlessly nodded, choking on the onslaught of emotions scorching inside her. While running her slender fingers up and down the contours of his arm, she bit back a curse and allowed herself to get lost in the realm of pleasure.

While his face was buried in her neck, she felt him whisper, "I'm sorry for everything." The blatant melancholy in his voice caused her heart to clench. He forged on, and for the first time, Yoori realized that Tae Hyun's pain was synonymous to hers. Remorse dripped from his guilt-stricken voice. "I'm sorry for bringing you into this world. I can't change the past, but please know that you mean the world to me. I know everyone has been telling you that I'm ruthless . . . but know that to me, you're worth more than this throne. And if it's between you and ruling this world, in the end, I'll give up everything and choose you."

Yoori wanted to cry. The sincere promise in his words touched her heart profoundly. Even though his beautiful promises made her heart surge, she couldn't discard the ominous, lingering shadow that had been plaguing her for months.

"If I remember everything, I'll be your enemy."

His tender hand found her hair and he stroked over it, his confident eyes holding hers. "You will never be my enemy," he easily assured her. "If Soo Jin wants the throne, then she can have it. I'm not going to fight her for it."

"What if she tries to kill you?"

Without allowing a full second to pass by, he stated, "Then I'll let her."

Tae Hyun said this without hesitation, and Yoori knew he meant his words. It troubled her because she did not want him to mean it.

She looked deeply into his eyes as resolve ripped through her chest. "If there is ever a time in the future where I try to kill you, then I want you to know that I forgive you if you kill me."

Never in her life did Yoori imagine that she would be having the conversation she was having with Tae Hyun. Yet, she knew this was a topic they couldn't escape from. She wanted to mentally prepare for everything that could transpire in the future. She wanted him to have his options, especially with someone like Soo Jin.

"Do you think I could ever be capable of killing you?" Tae Hyun questioned, lovingly lowering her and laying her onto the cool surface of the tub. While doing so, he positioned his body over hers, his lips hovering over hers as well. "Do you think I could ever give up on you?"

Hope swelled in her dwindling heart. Yoori gave Tae Hyun an appreciative smile. It wasn't a response she anticipated from him, but it was a response that more than extinguished the fears that coursed through her. Unable to resist, Yoori wrapped her arms around him and lightly danced her fingers over his shoulder blades.

Yes, please don't give up on me, she whispered in her mind, arching herself up and kissing him along his jaw, loving the feel of him breathing in approval.

"Tae Hyun?" she whispered, wanting to address one last issue before she allowed the warmth of being with him, kissing him, and loving him to shroud over her.

"How did your mother die?"

She wanted to ask this, but found no courage to.

Instead, she sadly said, "In the future, please don't fault me for the things Soo Jin did."

"Never," he promised her. "Never, Nemo."

Her heart hummed rapidly against her chest at her pet name. She loved it when he called her that.

Closing her eyes tightly, Yoori swallowed past the tears she refused to shed and kissed him. Every breath Yoori took acted as a knife that stabbed her. Yet, every kiss and caress from Tae Hyun acted as the ointment to mend her wounds. She had never felt more protected and loved in her life. On the flip side, she had never felt more helpless and desperate in her life.

Yoori fought back the sobs when an image came in her mind: the moment Tae Hyun finds out that somehow, some way, An Soo Jin was involved in his mother's death. She suppressed the tears as she thought about the disgust and hatred forming in the brown eyes she loved so much. She had always known that her past would overshadow her future, but it couldn't be more apparent now.

She hated Soo Jin, but she hated herself more.

She kissed him and moved her fingers over his back, reveling in the feeling of being loved because she knew that once they were separated again, it would not be as short as three weeks. It would probably be longer, so long that it would most likely kill her.

Please let me keep him, she prayed to the fates as she desperately held on to him. *Just a little while longer,* she compromised, knowing in her heart that it was too much to ask for them to be together forever.

All she wanted was a little while longer.

Just a little bit longer so I can remember what heaven feels like . . . before hell takes over.

"Then you have become a parasite."

20: One Last Heaven

Sometimes in life, there are no ways to explain where we gather the strength from our deepest cores when it feels like the end is near.

For Yoori, this definitive moment in her life occurred as she stared at her reflection in the mirror. She wore a pink sweater and pink pajama pants that exuded the vibrancy of life. It was a shame that the colors failed to exude the same effect on her paling, sickening face.

It had been six days since her brother's attack on her life, and this was the first time she realized how pathetic, miserable, and suicidal she looked. Her face was chalk white, there were shadows under her fatigued eyes, and she looked frailer than ever. Misery had befriended her, and it was all too clear in how pathetic she looked. She looked ugly, inside and out.

She sighed, her mind drifting away while she recalled the night prior, when she hung out with Chae Young and Hae Jin.

Worried about her sensitive state of being, Tae Hyun insisted on inviting his baby sister and her best friend over to their apartment. He wanted her to have some sense of normalcy instead of being cooped up in the apartment with him. It was an assertion that a tired Yoori was grateful for. She missed her two only girlfriends.

While Tae Hyun, Kang Min, and Jae Won hung out on the balcony, the girls were snuggled up on the big leather couch in the living room. They were watching "Finding Nemo" on the 50-inch flat screen TV. Beside them, the fireplace breathed melodiously, spreading warmth.

"You look ugly when you're miserable," Chae Young softly spoke to Yoori. She pulled the white comforter they shared closer over her body. Her pale face was marred with strains of worry for Yoori. Even through her own pain, it was apparent that she was still trying to take care of Yoori.

"Do I?" Yoori asked quietly, looking sideways at Hae Jin.

Hae Jin was the only one out of the three who had the blush of vitality on her face. She was a ball of energy and strength, and Yoori was envious of her for that.

"You look prettier when you smile," Hae Jin amended diplomatically, smiling at Yoori. She eyed Chae Young's own withering exterior. "Both of you."

For the first half hour since the movie started, Yoori found herself immersed in a conversation with her girlfriends instead of paying attention to what Nemo was up to. Although she wasn't too smiley, she felt tremendously better. You could never go wrong when in the company of your friends.

Chae Young had gotten better since the last time Yoori saw her. Yoori credited this progression to Jae Won, Chae Young's father, Kang Min, and most importantly Hae Jin, who had been through a similar experience and was the only one in the group who knew what Chae Young was going through. With her family and friends' insistence, Chae Young had given in to seeing a therapist to help her get through this ordeal. It was a decision that Yoori could already see progress for. She was thankful that Chae Young appeared to be getting better. Yoori could only imagine the pain that still haunted Chae Young. She had high admiration for her best friend for being able to hold her chin high while taking it all in one slow but progressive step at a time.

In the same token, she was also grateful to see that Jae Won was doing better too. The boys sat on the balcony's glass railing, warm breath floating from their lips, and the city's views underneath their feet while they spoke to one another. Since Chae Young's attack, Tae Hyun had given Jae Won the necessary time off to be there for Chae Young as they both tried to move on with their lives. It had been difficult for them, but despite what they were going through, they continued to stick together through thick and thin.

And of course, the backbone of this support was primarily Hae Jin and Kang Min, both of whom were there with Chae Young and Jae Won every step of the way. It amazed Yoori that the two babies of the group were the ones taking care of everyone. Age had no impact on inner strength, and Yoori saw this in them. They were lucky. They were all very lucky to have Kang Min and Hae Jin by their sides.

Yoori wished with all her weakened heart that she could be the one strong enough to be by Chae Young's side. She wished she was strong enough to live up to the title of "best friend"—just like Chae Young did for her when she was raped and refused to lure Yoori out for Jin Ae. She wished for all of this, but she also couldn't forgo the overwhelming guilt that handicapped her every time she even considered visiting Chae Young.

It did not help that the Cobras were having trouble finding Jin Ae. Punishing Jin Ae was the only way to assuage the guilt Yoori felt for Chae

Young being raped because of her. All she had to do was punish the one who orchestrated it. Once that was over, she would be able to face her friend again.

"I don't blame you, Yoori," said Chae Young, holding her hand under the blanket as if she could read Yoori's thoughts. Her gentle eyes held Yoori's. "I know that you've been avoiding me because you feel guilty, but I just wanted you to know that I don't blame you. I've never blamed you."

Her heart swelled at her friend's words. The weight of the world seemed to have lifted off Yoori's constricted chest.

"I'm sorry for everything," Yoori finally blurted out. A wave of distress flooded her mind as she spoke to her friend.

Chae Young, Hae Jin, and the brothers had no idea about Jin Ae's involvement in Chae Young's rape. Chae Young had forgotten about the little detail she informed Yoori—about a woman being there during her attack—and fell unconscious after the doctors came in to see her again. Yoori and Tae Hyun decided that it was best to keep this information to themselves to prevent the brothers or Hae Jin from acting out on impulse and endangering themselves in an attempt to sever Jin Ae's head. They wanted to put them out of harm's way as far as Ju Won was concerned.

"I can't change the past, but I promise you no one will ever touch you again. I'm going to make things right, Chae Young. I'll make everything right if it's the last thing I do. No one is going to ever hurt you again."

Yoori was miserable and hated her life, but she still held on to the anger that continued to sear in her blood whenever she thought about how she found Chae Young. She was going to sever Jin Ae's head if it was the last thing she did.

"You can make things right by telling us what's been going on with you," Chae Young amended, concern for Yoori brimming in her eyes. "I know it has nothing to do with any arguments you may have with Tae Hyun, so what's been going on? Why are you so sad?"

"I tried to ask oppa, Kang Min, and Jae Won, but no one would say anything. What's going on, Yoori?" Hae Jin asked as well, worry saturating her soft voice. She hooked an arm around Yoori's as the three of them snuggled closer together.

Yoori wanted desperately to tell them that so much had happened. They had no idea how much she was dying to tell them about the hell she had been through. Her desperation to share everything took a backseat to their safety. It was best to keep them in the dark. In the Underworld, being in the dark was sometimes the safest place one could be.

"How are the two of you so strong?" Yoori asked instead, forgoing answering the question while moving them safely along into another territory. The offhand question was one that she really wanted to know the answer to. Yoori was aware that her despair was nothing compared to the miseries that

Chae Young and Hae Jin had to endure. How Chae Young was coming back from her horrific experience left Yoori in awe, and how Hae Jin was so bubbly after all the horrors she had to endure with Ho Young raping her left Yoori amazed. "How do you do it?"

"Tell her what you told me," Chae Young said to Hae Jin, her voice hopeful that it was a piece of wisdom Yoori would take to heart.

Yoori glanced at Hae Jin, who said words that Yoori went to sleep reciting.

Hae Jin gave one of her most buoyant smiles that could light up anyone's dark world. "I tell myself that I don't deserve any of this misery. I didn't do anything to deserve it and I deserve to be happy."

These simple words spoken by the one she had always viewed as her baby sister and concurred by her best friend, replayed in her mind as Yoori stared at herself in the mirror.

Akin to a light switch going off, the simplicity of her situation finally became crystal clear to her.

She didn't deserve *any* of this misery.

It was as though a fire had been lit in her world of darkness when these thoughts emanated from her mind.

I deserve to be happy, she told herself, feeling a bit of her old, spunky personality returning.

Yoori further assessed herself in the mirror. After days of punishing herself and consequently punishing the loved ones who surrounded her, Yoori realized something so simple that it eluded her nearly her entire life. She was a good person. She did nothing to deserve the pain she was experiencing.

Things became clearer while her world lit up like a football stadium.

A sense of empowerment gushed through her like a flood.

If the end was near, then it would only make sense to make the most of her life before it all ended. If she was going to cease to exist once the evil devoured her, then she was at least going to attempt to be happy, live life with a bit of a smile, and enjoy the blessing she was given before it all diminished into oblivion.

An Young Jae, An Soo Jin, and whoever else in this Underworld may be intent on bringing war upon her, but today and for however long she could keep it, Yoori was determined to bring bliss unto herself. She was determined to enjoy her life with the people she loved most—those prominent ones being Chae Young, Hae Jin, the brothers, and most of all, Tae Hyun.

In all truth, Yoori wasn't positive what love was. However, if what she was feeling for Tae Hyun wasn't love, then love must be a pretty damn powerful feeling because she didn't know how it could ever go beyond the adoration, admiration, appreciation, and desperation she had for her boyfriend.

If Soo Jin was her black hole, the one person capable of ceasing her entire existence, then Tae Hyun was her anchor, the one person capable of keeping her locked onto the soil of life. Throughout this ordeal, Tae Hyun had been her solid rock. Not only was he the one who was constantly there to mend her pain, but he was also the catalyst for her to hang on for so long.

Yoori recalled her night in the bathtub with him and remembered the desperation she felt while she held him and kissed him. She remembered her pain. She had begged the fates for more time with him. She begged and begged for a little bit more time with him, and she was given this time. And what did she do with it? She wasted it crying to herself and leaving him miserable in the process. She saw things clearer now. Yoori would be damned if she didn't start making the most of her time with him.

"Kwon Tae Hyun . . ."

Stirring under the feel of her lips feathering past his ear, Tae Hyun bunched his muscles for a brief moment before slipping back into his peaceful sleep.

After walking back into their bedroom, Yoori decided to get started on their day by waking up her partner-in-crime.

He was sleeping soundly on his stomach. The comforter was draped slightly over his legs, revealing his bare, muscled back. She considered giving him time to sleep in longer. Yoori quickly vetoed that thought. She felt like an impatient kid on Christmas. She simply wanted to open her present—basically him—*now*. It had been a while since they hung out in a carefree manner. They might as well start early in the morning. A new life had burst through her, and she wanted to share this moment with him. Who knew how long she would be happy like this again?

Feeling quite impatient, Yoori playfully jumped onto the soft bed, crawled on the mattress, and comfortably sat on his lower back, reveling in the feel of Tae Hyun sleeping beneath her.

"Kwon Tae Hyun," she prompted quietly, leaning across his back. She purposely brushed her lips against his ear, loving the scent of his cologne enrapturing her senses.

Unable to resist the tempting proximity of his skin, Yoori began to bestow doting kisses along the line of his strong jaw. He stirred underneath her, clearly enjoying the feel of her spoiling him with affection. Yet, he still wouldn't open his eyes.

By now, Yoori had a good hunch that he was already awake and was just messing with her.

"Hey you duck-loving Snob," she whispered in a low, sexy voice. "Hurry and wake up before I give you the same treatment I gave that duck in the park."

At first, she wasn't certain if Tae Hyun would find this tone of voice to be sexy. Once she felt him exhale a breath in bliss, she knew he was very much a fan of the teasing voice. Though a smile lined his lips, his eyes were still shut tight.

Okay, this was getting ridiculous, Yoori thought impatiently, hating that he was ignoring her when she was making such an effort to wake him up so they could enjoy their day.

"Hey! Boss Kwon!" she griped loudly, playfully biting his earlobe. "If you don't wake up soon, I'm going to kick you so hard, I'll have you wishing you woke up faster—*Ah!*"

Next thing she knew, her back was thrown against the cushion of the bed. Tae Hyun was suddenly on top of her, his eyes still closed yet his lips very busy as he dove straight for her neck and nuzzled himself there.

"Tae Hyun, stop! Ahhh, it tickles!" Yoori cried once his tongue peeked out.

Without mercy, his mouth began to suckle on the sensitive skin there. There was lazy sensuality to the affection Tae Hyun's talented mouth showed her. It made her burn, both in bliss and laughter. Because in adjunction to seducing her, he was also purposely nuzzling himself in the ticklish area that he knew would have her squirming around in laughter. It had been a while since she laughed like that and it was a euphoric feeling.

"Bad girl," he purred seconds later. He easily controlled her squirming by pinning his body onto hers. He did not put all his weight on her, but he did put enough to allow Yoori to feel each and every part of him. And boy did she like feeling all those parts.

Eyes still closed, his tongue traced the column of her neck before moving to her mouth. He began to nip her bottom lip. He kissed her leisurely and passionately, acting like he had the rest of the lazy eternities to do this. It left her breathless when he alternated between filling her lips with paradise and speaking to her.

"You know I don't respond well to threats, and you actually threaten me?"

"You were awake and ignoring me," Yoori argued, holding back her stupid, girlish whimpers from all the joy she was getting from the sexy beast himself.

"And you called me 'Boss' too," he added with amusement. "Do you know what that does to a guy when he's in bed with his girlfriend?"

"What does it do to a guy?" she humored, liking very much how their morning was starting out.

His lids lifted, and Yoori was graced with the translucent eyes that held promises of sinful pleasures and divine paradise. Yoori had to gasp for breath. He was already melting her like butter on toast.

"Breaks him."

"Breaks him?"

Tae Hyun nodded, languidly pulling his lips away. He stared down at her, ardor flicking in his captive gaze. "It makes Kings fall from their thrones; it causes them to dismiss the realities of life when all they want to do is lay naked above their woman, revel in the feel of her nails clawing their skin as she screams in the most climatic of ecstasies."

Whoa, Yoori thought candidly, her big brown eyes widening as said images popped into her mind.

"What a dangerous power for a man to give to any woman, right, my little prude?" Tae Hyun asked, his eyes sparkling at the sight of her eyes widening. He could see she was playing out the images he placed in her head. He was well aware of the power he had over her, and being as considerate as he was, he relinquished that power by bringing them on to a more serious topic. Concern materialized in his eyes. "You're different today," he noted with a tentative voice. "Are you actually feeling better or am I dreaming all of this up because I want you to be better?"

Still reeling from the naughty images that played like a movie in her mind, Yoori nodded.

"I decided that I deserve to be happy," she told him honestly. "I've been a loser-face for cooping us up in misery when we don't deserve any of it. I don't want to be unhappy any longer, especially for things I have no control over."

Tae Hyun nodded, his expression relieved that she finally understood this.

Elated and reminded of all that he had done for her, she teasingly pecked her nose with his.

"Thank you for being by my side, Kwon," she told him affectionately. She meant every word. "It would've sucked to go through this alone. I couldn't have done it without you."

A smile of profound contentment glowed on his angelic face.

"Anytime, Choi," he told her simply, yet she knew his emotions were more complex than those simple words. She could feel the happiness exude out of him, radiate into her, and she knew he was dying from happiness that she was finally smiling and becoming her old self again.

"Damn, I've missed your spunkiness," he told her, steering the topic along to more carefree things. His full body weight fell on top of her in some sort of relief. He exhaled dramatically. "We have been getting along so well that I was wondering if the immature couple in us had left already."

Yoori laughed inwardly. Outwardly, she feigned a menacing glare.

"You love ducks, and I hate ducks. I think it's safe to say that we'd never truly get along," she uttered, thoroughly enjoying the feel of his body draped over hers like a mouthwatering blanket.

Sadly, the supply of air was becoming an issue. Yoori was conflicted on what she should do. Should she tell him to get off or keep the sensual heat going by being aggressive? It would make sense for Yoori to gather some common sense to pull down the obtrusive blue pajama pants he wore and further enjoy the feel of his body draped over hers. She really wanted to do that since she would like nothing more than to run her fingers over his entire body. Alas, enjoying the sight of his nakedness would be a bit useless if she died from suffocation. Though it wasn't a popular decision, she made the rational choice.

"Now get off me, piggy!" she cried, smacking his back. She wiggled her legs beneath him. "You're so heavy! I can't breathe!"

The name-calling was irony at its best. There wasn't an ounce of fat on Tae Hyun's toned and muscular body. Everything was rock hard and immersed with tempting heat. Any other girl would probably kill to die under Tae Hyun's half naked body, but being seduced by sex gods aside, Yoori couldn't be distracted because she still had to let him know about the itinerary she planned for them. More importantly, she needed to breathe.

Thinking she was just being a tease, Tae Hyun proceeded to steal her breath some more by brushing his lips with hers, kissing her with deliberate and sensuous passion. Though she was fighting for air, Yoori fell victim to those irresistible lips and kissed him while she squirmed beneath him. She kissed until she couldn't take it anymore. She pulled away from the kiss and panted for air.

"Hurry!" she shouted dramatically, knowing exactly what to say to get him off of her. "You're squishing my boobs!"

"Oh fuck! Fuck!" he shouted, horrified with himself that he could forget for a moment how small she was under him.

Like a launching rocket, he freed her from beneath him and jumped off the bed. There was an expression of worry on his handsome face that she might have gotten hurt in his bout of teasing. He stood up and gaped at her. She could literally hear Tae Hyun berate himself for losing control and allowing the majority of his weight to fall upon her.

Yoori sat up with the biggest grin. The adorable concern on his face melted her heart. Here was a renowned King, who was feared all throughout the Underworld, and he was worried about possibly squishing her boobs? The irony was too much for her. Yoori burst out laughing. She pointed at Tae Hyun, who now had a disgruntled expression on his face.

"Look at your face!" she said in between laughs. "You really thought you squished my boobs!"

It was definitely immature of her to laugh, and Tae Hyun was the first one to put her in her place.

"The lack of air must've gone to your head because you look like a perky fool right now."

Yoori instantly stopped laughing and gave bitter slits to Tae Hyun.

Yes, all was well in their world if the former boss and assistant were bickering about nonsensical crap again.

Yoori cleared her throat, getting back on to more important topics. It was time to let him know about her plan.

"We're going to be a normal couple today, Tae Hyun."

His face gleamed with curiosity. "What do you mean?"

She smiled, lifting her chin up with pride while the contents of her "dream day" played out in her mind.

"Today, you're going to take me out . . . maybe to a park or something, and you're going to buy me my favorite ice cream. We're going to sit on that park bench, amongst the sea of all the normal people in this city, and we'll simply enjoy ourselves. Maybe even kiss if you don't make me mad. We can probably even nap on the grass for most of the day because the weather is really nice today and I want to take a nap on your stomach."

His lips tilted in smug amusement, and Yoori could've sworn she saw his abs tighten in pride. Folding his arms across his chest, he gave her a look that said, *Stop gawking and finish what you're saying.*

Blushing with her chin held high, she resumed with reciting her list. "Then after that, we're going to go to a really fancy restaurant. You'll pull my chair out for me, and we'll eat, laugh, and probably argue about stupid things that are never worth arguing about to begin with. But we'll have a great time regardless because we're tight like that. After which, you'll buy me ice cream again, and we'll take a walk around the city at night, enjoy the cool air, and just hold hands because we're cute like that."

He held back a smile at this.

"Then, we'll hang out with Chae Young, Hae Jin, and the brothers because I miss hanging out with everyone as a group. After that, you and I can come home and maybe have more fun by ourselves."

Yoori hoped that Tae Hyun would be clever enough to pick up the subtlety of her last sentence. While deciding in the bathroom that she deserved to be happy, Yoori also decided that she was ready to "get more intimate" with Tae Hyun. The sexual tension between them was becoming unbearable, and Yoori could no longer deal with being a prude. It was becoming more difficult to resist when sex pretty much radiated from Tae Hyun.

261

They would "do it" after their normal day—that was if the guy would make this prospect easier by catching her hint!

Instead of catching her insinuation, there was actually a bored expression on his face that told her he wasn't really interested in doing those silly things with her.

"Hanging out with my sister, Chae Young, and the brothers is fine. But what makes you think I'd be cooperative and do anything else with you?"

Though the content of his words were dismissive, the tone he delivered already told her that he was more than willing to do whatever she wanted to do. He just wanted to present a challenge for her so she didn't think she had so much power over him.

Yoori grinned inwardly, humoring him.

"Fine, you don't have to," she replied with a bored sigh. She shrugged her indifference. "I'm sure I could find another guy to fill in for you. He could hang out with me, eat ice cream with me, hold hands with me, and cuddle with me."

Outrage fluttered like flames in his eyes.

"Who the hell are you going to find?" he asked, enraged at the thought of Yoori walking around the city with another guy.

Yoori concealed a sneaky grin as she continued to speak in a careless tone. "Oh, you know . . . I have so many options. When I was working at the diner, I had so many guys hit on me it was crazy. All I have to do is snap my fingers and I'm sure a line of them will appear, ready and willing to woo me—"

"I'd kill any bastard who dares to touch you," Tae Hyun snapped, the muscles in his body rippling with tenseness. The sight of this caused the breath to stall in her lungs. How the hell was it possible that she hadn't slept with the guy yet? He was built to give women pleasure.

"Possessive much?" she teased, swallowing tightly to regulate her breathing. Damn. She was tempted to abort the whole "be a normal couple and make normal memories" plan and bond with him in bed instead.

"Just jealous," Tae Hyun corrected tightly, throwing Yoori off with his candidness.

Yoori gaped at him like she had just heard the Pope curse. Kwon Tae Hyun admitting that he was jealous was something that Yoori never thought she'd hear. And goddamn, she loved hearing it.

He forged on, unaffected by the surprised look on her face. He was strong as ever, even as he admitted his weakness. "It is a rarity for any other guys to evoke any jealousy from me, but it took me a little over an eternity to convince you to be my girlfriend. I'll be damned if I let some other bastard hold hands with you or cuddle with you."

Yoori grinned teasingly, her heart elated at her boyfriend's admittance to a weakness and how prideful he continued to look even after admitting it. "Does that mean you'll be my date today then?"

There was more to what she was leading on in terms of what she wanted to do with him. She thought it was best to only tell him after she made him jealous about her non-existent suitors.

Knowing her too well, Tae Hyun arched a suspicious brow. "What are you up to, Nemo?"

Yoori beamed, reaching underneath her pillow and whipping out silver handcuffs that were once in the drawer. She shook it suggestively, naughtiness contrasting the innocence in her doe-like eyes.

"Let's have some fun."

Any other alpha male would have been thrilled at the sight of handcuffs. In Tae Hyun's case, his latest experience with them prohibited any arousal that would've worked its way through his body. Unenthused and actually somewhat cautious, Tae Hyun's eyes morphed into hard slits. He knew her too well to fall for any tricks.

"You suck at life so I know I can't get my hopes up. Whatever it is we're doing, I'm sure it doesn't involve me handcuffing you to the bed while ripping all your clothes off. So tell me, my little prude, why are you smiling like that, and what are we doing with the handcuffs?"

■ ■ ■

"Is all of this still necessary?" Tae Hyun sullenly asked later that night.

They were walking on the busy winter street, and he was freezing under his long black trench coat. Tae Hyun shivered while one hand held his cookies and cream ice cream cone and the other held Yoori's hand. Their wrists winked with silver under the city light. They were handcuffed to one another while they dawdled down the sidewalk.

Dressed in a long white coat with white furry earmuffs to shield her from the cold, Yoori smiled sheepishly at Tae Hyun. She squeezed his hand for encouragement while licking her own ice cream cone. In the background, cars, people, and bicyclists whizzed past them in the hectic night.

For the majority of the day, much to Yoori's delight, the itinerary she mapped out had gone exactly as planned. Though Tae Hyun was a relatively good sport all day, he was becoming quite unruly as the night lingered on. He didn't complain much while they were eating ice cream in the afternoon, but now that dinner was over, he was becoming bitter that he still had to eat ice cream in the cold. He was also seemingly bitter that they were still handcuffed together while they shook under the mercy of the winter cold.

It surprised Yoori that he hated the cuffs so much. She brought out the cuffs because she wanted to reminisce with him about the good old days, which ironically didn't appear like good old days to her when she was living through it. Who would've thought their boss and assistant days were some of her most favorite memories? The reminder of the "innocence" of those days brought a genuine smile to her face.

Such a happy moment was polluted when someone said:

"Give me your watch and no one gets hurt."

What the fuck?

Yoori came out of her reverie in disbelief. She stared at the young teenager before her, shock hitting her at full force.

He looked like he was about seventeen. He wore a red beanie and had a baby-like face that reminded her of Kang Min. He was standing in front of them, wearing a big black coat with a gun pointed at them—or more specifically Tae Hyun, who was still holding his ice cream in indignation.

It took her a few moments to realize that they were being held up at gunpoint.

It took Tae Hyun a few moments longer to realize the same.

"Are you deaf?" the guy said irritably. His chapped lips shuddered in the cold. He gestured his black gun at the expensive Rolex blinging off Tae Hyun's wrist. It glimmered under the city lights, letting everyone know just how spectacular it was. "Give me your watch or I'll shoot!"

Tae Hyun looked dumbfounded and then seconds later, annoyed.

He looked at Yoori, his eyes outraged that he had been reduced to this state in life. She could only imagine how insulting it was for the King of the Underworld to be held at gunpoint by some teenage street thug.

"Is this really fucking happening?" he breathed out to Yoori, clearly unable to grasp his embarrassing reality.

Yoori merely blinked at him in shock.

She couldn't believe this crazy shit either.

"Is this fucker really doing this to me?" he went on manically. "In my own city? While I'm holding a *fucking* ice cream?!"

"Don't hurt him," Yoori said a second later, afraid that Tae Hyun's wrath would be the kid's demise. Her chin wobbled under the flurry of snow. "He's just a kid."

"I won't hurt him if he gives me his damn watch!" screamed the kid, thinking that Yoori was talking to him.

He had no idea how wrong he was.

Beside her, the King that had thousands of soldiers at his disposal was getting angrier and angrier by the second.

"He's a little asshole that's trying to mug me," Tae Hyun growled back to Yoori, his eyes glaring at the kid like a shark in the night.

"We're supposed to be normal," said Yoori through clenched teeth.

Across from her, the kid was still pointing the gun at them, looking around edgily to make sure there were no witnesses. He clearly didn't anticipate this mugging to take so long. He also didn't anticipate Tae Hyun to be so scary.

Yoori glared at Tae Hyun sternly, ignoring the kid. "You promised me a normal day."

"Normal people don't get mugged on a normal day," gritted Tae Hyun, his eyes never straying from the attempted mugger. "I should teach the little fucker a lesson."

Yoori could see that the guy was beginning to regret holding them up. He obviously did not expect to be threatening some psycho who looked like he could rip his head off at any moment.

"Look," the attempted mugger said, trying to not appear fearful of Tae Hyun. "I don't want any trouble. I just want your watch."

"I'll give you mine," Yoori offered diplomatically, extending her wrist to offer the silver Rolex Tae Hyun gifted her.

"A lot of people want what I have," Tae Hyun growled, gently pushing Yoori's extended arm down while keeping his eyes on the attempted mugger. He inched closer to him, his eyes becoming scarier. He only stopped when the cuffs anchored him to Yoori. Tae Hyun did not appear less intimidating with the handcuffs. If anything, he looked like a ferocious, caged lion that could attack at any moment. "You should know that no one ever gets to have what I have."

The guy stared fearfully at the handcuffs.

"What . . . What is that?" he asked unsteadily, clearly wishing he held someone else up.

"Couples' bracelet," said Yoori while Tae Hyun said, "Handcuffs."

The guy became shakier. Despite his obvious fear of Tae Hyun, his curiosity won out. "Why . . . Why are you guys wearing handcuffs?"

"Shoot me," Tae Hyun said instead, not deigning to answer the guy.

The attempted mugger's voice rose to a high-pitched sound. *"What?"*

"What?" cried Yoori as well, tugging at Tae Hyun's wrist. "Did the ice cream give you a brain freeze? What's wrong with you? Why would you say that?"

"Shoot me," ordered Tae Hyun, staring unblinkingly at the attempted mugger. "I will give you one shot. If you get a bullet in me, I'll give you my watch. If not, I will wrap my hand around your neck, squeeze the life out of you, and just when you think you're going to die, I'm going to let go. Then,

I'm going to rip your flesh off with my bare hands, and when I'm done, I will break off your bones and pick my teeth with it."

A wash of silence hung over them.

For a long time, all that could be heard was the sound of falling snow.

A long pause later, Tae Hyun straightened his back and finally said, "Do you still want my watch?"

The teenager shook his head, looking like he couldn't have regretted being born more. He did not know who Tae Hyun was, but he now knew he wasn't someone to mug.

Tae Hyun nodded, still holding his ice cream. Throughout this entire scene, never once did the ice cream ruin his authoritative stature. If anything, it made him look more psychotic.

"Now get the fuck out of our sight," he commanded. He pointed a warning finger at the guy. "And if I see you holding anyone else at gunpoint, I *will* kill you. I will find out where you live, I will throw you in a coffin with hungry rats, I will stand by and listen to them devour your flesh, and then I will end your life. Got it?"

The boy nodded with a bow before taking off like the wind.

Throughout this speech, all Yoori could do was stare in awe.

After a gust of wind hurdled past them, she said, "That was so cool!" She took a step forward while licking her ice cream. Her eyes glistened in admiration for how her Snob handled this situation. Although he looked like a crazy fucker, it was awesome that he didn't resort to violence. "How'd you get so cool?"

"I can't believe I just got held up at gunpoint," Tae Hyun muttered to himself, still not over this embarrassing fact. He looked at the ice cream in his possession. He swayed his head in disbelief. He clearly hated his life right now. "I can't believe I just got held up at gunpoint while holding an ice cream cone."

Yoori laughed, pressing herself into him. "You handled yourself well."

"I threatened to kill him," Tae Hyun corrected blandly.

"Yeah, normal people do that," she said with another laugh. She paused. "Well, actually normal people put their safety first and give up their watch, but when it comes to you, I suppose the most normal thing was to scare the mugger shitless." She tugged at his arm, very pleased that this did not ruin their night. "Shall we continue this wonderfully normal day?"

Tae Hyun groaned, and Yoori tugged him on, disregarding his petulant moans. She got right back to their innocuous conversation before they were so rudely interrupted.

"You know what this night reminds me of?" Yoori asked nostalgically, trying to get Tae Hyun's mind off the mugger.

"What?" he asked, taking one huge bite of his ice cream before contorting his face at the iciness the little dessert offered. He was struggling to eat it (and forget about the mugger) to help make her day perfect, and he couldn't have looked more adorable doing so.

"Oh goodness, it felt like ages ago," Yoori shared whimsically, remembering the memory that left her warm with fondness. Her face lit up with delight. "But this night reminds me of the night where this insanely hot gang leader came into my life and pretty much handcuffed me and abducted me from my own home."

She smirked to herself while taking a bite of her ice cream.

"But he had such a bad attitude." Yoori was on a roll, earning a frown of discontent from the "hot gang leader" beside her. He was offended that she dared to speak so badly about him.

She plowed on like the energizer bunny. "You should've met this guy, Tae Hyun. You would've wanted to beat his ass down—just like that mugger you scared shitless. I had to sequester myself in my own apartment for eight days because I was waiting for him to come to my apartment with machine guns. It was kind of lame if you think about it. I should've just ran out of town—"

"Eight days?" Tae Hyun asked incredulously.

Yoori realized that she had never shared with Tae Hyun her thoughts on what happened those nights after she ran away from him.

She nodded to confirm.

"You paranoid freak," he said with adoration. He took the last bite of his ice cream in delight. Thoughts of the mugger vanquished from his mind. Being enlightened with her side of the story obviously made him happy. "I can't believe you hid yourself in your apartment for eight days." He gazed down at her with hilarity gleaming in his eyes. "How did it all work out for you, smart one?"

"It didn't." She feigned sourness while she lifted her ice cream up to his lips, silently instructing him to help her finish it.

She was imparted with a sour frown, one to which she smiled sweetly at before he leaned down and took a huge bite for her. He motioned for her to continue. It didn't even seem like he was cold anymore. He was too entertained and eager to hear her side of the story.

Yoori finished her own ice cream before continuing with her tale. "When I finally let my guard down, he came on the eighth day and proceeded to sit on the toilet cover while I showered. He pretty much threw a bathrobe at my face, packed up my stuff, pulled me out into the cold with nothing but a pink bathrobe on and abducted me." Her face twisted into a scowl. "That insensitive jerk. That night was such a cold night too. I had just showered and I was

267

freezing. It didn't help that I looked like a prostitute being carted off to jail with the handcuffs."

Tae Hyun smiled to himself, reliving the same scene. "You must've been the prettiest sight in that pink bathrobe."

Yoori blushed at his words.

They had been a couple for a while, and even though he spoiled her rotten with his actions, he rarely spoiled her with his words. The simple act of him complimenting her with no sarcasm in his voice was enough to make Yoori treasure this little moment.

"What was going on through your mind that night?" she asked, wanting to switch roles. She was curious to learn his side of the story.

Tae Hyun's smile grew a bit wider as he recounted his own memories. "I was thinking that I must be going crazy because I was going to have an unwilling girl move into my apartment with me. The thing that worried me more was that I knew this particular girl was going to drive me crazy because she had so much spunk in her. I knew she was going to be trouble with a capital 'T.'" He gazed at her. "You didn't know it then, but I wasn't looking forward to being handcuffed to you. The handcuffs were just a scare tactic used to keep you from running. I actually really hated being cuffed to you because your lame ass insisted on sleeping on the floor. Do you know how uncomfortable it was to sleep with my hand dangling down the bed and not being able to move around freely?"

"Do you not know how uncomfortable it was to sleep on the cold tiles while your mean ass hogged all the blanket?" Yoori's eyes sparkled when she realized something else. "Okay so that next morning, I woke up and I was in bed with you . . . what really happened? Did I really get onto the bed like you said?"

His prideful smirk was all the answer she needed to know the truth. "No. I got sick of hearing you shiver so I went down, carried you in my arms, and pretty much threw you into bed with me."

"I knew it, you liar!" she gasped out. If that was a lie, then what about the other mysteries? "So, when I fainted and you told me I got down on the floor and slept with you . . . you were lying then too, weren't you?"

He shook his head. "No, you really did that. You murmured something in your sleep and got up. I thought you were awake and asked if you were getting better, but you didn't say anything. You just came down onto the floor, wrapped your arms around me, and then slept on my chest. It was actually kind of scary because you lifted up my shirt and kept smoothing your hands over my abs." A coy grin came over his lips, hinting to her that he didn't mind it so much that she was molesting him. "That was when I knew you had a thing for my stomach. You wouldn't stop caressing it until you fell asleep."

Fire burned on her cheeks. "Why . . . Why didn't you wake me up?"

Damn. How embarrassing was it that she was molesting a complete stranger in her sleep?

His powerful shoulders lifted in a shrug. "I felt bad for you because you seemed really sad, even when you were sleeping. I let you do it because it seemed to have calmed you down. That was why I got up early to make breakfast. I wanted to cheer you up. But then you wound up pissing me off, so I ate everything until I wanted to throw up."

Yoori inhaled blissfully when she replayed that moment where she said he was only being nice to her because he wanted to "experiment" his food on her to get other girls. It was so strange to talk about the past and see how far they had come since those days.

"Why were we cuffed together for so long if you didn't enjoy it, Tae Hyun?" she inquired seconds later.

Tae Hyun was quiet for a moment before he said, "I wanted an excuse to hold your hand."

He turned his eyes away from her for a fleeting moment, and Yoori saw a little blush take over his face as he said this. The weight of the object that had fast become their "couples' bracelet" moved against their wrists while their hands tightened around each other.

"Did you look forward to having me move in?"

He shook his head and laughed. "I never invite girls home so to have one live with me, especially an unwilling and mean one, was a dreadful prospect for me. There were a lot of things I had to change in the apartment to make it suitable for you. For instance, do you notice how much cleaner it is since you moved in? I actually pick up after myself now because I don't want to deal with hearing you complain while calling me a pig. Even though it's you who makes the mess."

Yoori laughed to herself. "What else did you have to modify in your daily routine, Tae Hyun?"

"I don't wear much clothing when I sleep."

Wheels screeched to a stop at this mind-blowing and scandalously sexy tidbit. Her eyes blossomed as she stopped walking.

"Like . . . shirtless and just shorts?"

Tae Hyun eyed her with those smoldering eyes, the ones laced with unrivaled carnality that left her with yearnings throughout her body.

Nude, Yoori answered in her mind.

God's gift to women sleeps without anything covering his perfect, naked body.

How the hell was it possible that she wasn't graced with this sight?

"Um . . ." Yoori began quietly, being reminded of what she wanted to do with him once their night was over. She might as well talk to him about it now.

"I know you may think that I'd be uncomfortable . . . but you can sleep however you want. If you want to dress less to bed then I won't mind . . ."

"But we spoon at night," he countered as if spooning while he was nude was an issue for her.

Exactly.

Yoori continued to feign casualness. "I could suffer through it for you."

He shook his head with another laugh. "I won't tease myself."

This was her opening line to get the conversation moving in terms of going to the next level of their relationship.

"Tae Hyun," she started shyly, swaying uncertainly in her stance. Feeling edgy over the conversation she was about to initiate, Yoori nervously played with the buttons on his jacket. She pressed against him suggestively.

"Uh, what are you doing?" Tae Hyun asked awkwardly, his eyes clearly wondering if she ate something wrong. It was evident her strange behavior was scaring him.

Still nervous, Yoori swayed from side to side while kicking air and avoiding eye contact with him.

"It's been a while since you . . . you know . . ."

"What?" Tae Hyun asked, genuinely not understanding her hint.

"You know . . ." she repeated, not bothering to clarify.

This proved to be a bad idea when dealing with an impatient guy like Tae Hyun.

"Damn it, you mumbler," Tae Hyun berated, annoyed that she wasn't making sense. "Did a duck bite your tongue or something? Do I look like a mind reader? Just tell me!"

You impatient fool! How dare you yell at me! She wanted to scream at him for killing the mood for her. She held in the fiery urge to lash out at him. The desire to get them into bed after the night ended was too prominent in her horny mind.

"Why don't you tease me with your towel anymore?" she finally voiced, still kicking air while tugging at the buttons on his jacket. Gathering some nerves, she lifted her eyes to meet his.

The dawning realization played in his eyes when it all made sense to him.

Yoori continued on. "You did it once and I know I didn't pull it off, but you know . . ." She blushed immensely while staring into his beguiling brown eyes. "You know . . . I think we've been together long enough where I'm ready to . . . you know . . ."

Pull it off and maybe more, Yoori added bashfully in her head.

Tae Hyun smirked at her in absolute amusement. Sighing, he placed a hand underneath her chin and lifted her gaze to meet his when she tried to turn away from him. Her breath stalled once she saw his eyes again. There was a dark, carnal sexuality in his stare that had Yoori going weak in the knees.

"Are you really ready?" he asked while regarding her with uncertainty.

"You think I'm not?"

"I don't think we're ready."

Humiliation seared her cheeks. After trying so hard to get into her pants, he was rejecting her now?

"You thought we were ready when you seduced me like a porn star and pretty much told me that I owned your body," she told him with scorn. "Remember? 'This is all yours . . .'"

How could he say she pretty much owned his body when he wouldn't give it to her when she wanted it?

"I was impatient then, but I've seen things clearer now," he explained. "I don't think we're ready."

Yoori snorted.

How could they not be ready? They were twenty-four-year-olds with the biggest sexual tension surrounding them. How could they *not* be ready?

"So, you just don't want to?" she confronted, though deep down, she knew he wanted her.

He chuckled bitterly. "If only you knew how much I want you, how much I want to give you all the pleasures in the world and listen to your voice as you scream out my name." He looked at her. "But we're not ready to fully appreciate any of that."

She was still flabbergasted. "When will we be ready then?"

"When everything's perfect."

Okay. He just set the impossible bar, and this did not make her happy. She was trying to be a positive person, but she wasn't naïve anymore.

"Nothing in this world is perfect, Tae Hyun," she said sadly.

"I'll give you perfection," he told her with conviction in his voice. "When the time is right, I'll give you no less than perfection."

"How will you know when the time is right?"

"When you find what you're looking for, Nemo."

Yoori felt the balloons in her mind deflate at the knowledge that she wasn't getting "any" tonight.

Having no more to say, she begrudgingly accepted his stupid postponement and continued to walk with him. Five minutes later, they stopped by a flower shop to pick up some roses for Chae Young before they went to visit her and Jae Won. After she made the call to Hae Jin to have her and Kang Min come over to Chae Young's apartment to hang out, Yoori noticed that Tae Hyun was unusually quiet and sad while he held Chae Young's bouquet of flowers.

"What the hell are you pouting about?" Yoori confronted, not using her nice voice. She was too sexually frustrated to be *nice*.

"I just rejected sex with you," he groaned out, misery consuming his entire stature. He looked just like a brokenhearted kid. "Fuck. This isn't good for the sexual frustration," he muttered before reclining his head up to the sky and cursing the fates. It wasn't until he lowered his head and looked at her hesitantly did Yoori realized how frustrated Tae Hyun was that he wasn't getting "any" tonight as well.

"Do you still want to —?"

"No," Yoori snapped, though her body was cursing her for denying it the presence of his touch. "You just rejected me, asshole. You can suffer in sexual frustration hell for all I care."

"Fuck," he muttered again. "You're the only one I would endure all of this for."

A small smile tugged at Yoori's lips when she heard this.

A fleeting moment of silence perused between them as they both calmed down from the conversation they had.

"The . . . you know . . . better be worth it if we're waiting this long," said Yoori, breaching the silence to gaze at Tae Hyun. All bitterness aside, she still felt blessed to be with someone who was willing to wait for a perfect moment — if that moment ever existed — to have sex with her. If it ever happened, she knew it would be more than perfect if it were with him.

Tae Hyun's next words corroborated her belief that he was going to blow her mind when they finally made love.

"I'll give you the stars and the moon, Princess. And maybe even a city to go along with it."

In that suspended breath, that was all he needed to say for Yoori to feel like the world had just kneeled to the floor in her presence. The look on his face was one filled with love. She felt herself melt. Kwon Tae Hyun had the uncanny ability to make her feel like the most beautiful woman in the world. He made her feel like she deserved all the happiness in the world and that if he could, he would give her the world on its knees.

With no warning, he pulled her to a quiet corner, placed Chae Young's bouquet on the ground, and cupped her face into his palms.

Her heart palpitated in anticipation as his soft lips covered hers. His kiss was slow and sensual. It pressed against hers with perfect pressure. It had her so weak in the knees that she would've fallen over if he hadn't held on to her with care.

Cars whizzed by, people sauntered past them, and bicyclists fluttered past, yet the only one left in her world was Tae Hyun, the one giving her the kiss that was overflowing with hope, promise, and love. She would die a happy woman if she could kiss him like this for the rest of her time on earth.

"I wish," he began tenderly, resting his forehead against hers while they breathed in the cool night's air. "I wish I could've introduced you to my parents. They would've loved you."

A terrible sense of guilt splashed over her when she was reminded of his parents—or more specifically, his mother. The entire day was spent ignoring her problems. Tae Hyun did a fantastic job of not mentioning anything else, but he didn't realize that the biggest problem she was trying to avoid was the one he brought up. Yoori was horrified, yet she couldn't deny the happiness that reigned over her to hear Tae Hyun speak such words. How odd it was to be simultaneously happy and depressed at the same time.

"Really?" She stared deep into his eyes for assurance. "You really think they would've liked me?"

He nodded, his eyes softer than she had ever seen it when he thought about his deceased parents. She could see the love he had for them and it broke her heart.

"My dad always told me that the only woman who would be capable of stealing my heart would be the type of woman who would put me in my place and humble me so much that I would feel as though the sun rises only when she appears." He chuckled warmly. "He would be so damn happy to know he was right." His smile grew wider. "And my mom . . . God, she would've loved you. She had the exact same personality as Hae Jin, and my baby sister is completely in love with you. I can only imagine how enamored my mother would've been with you. If anything, she would've encouraged your little spunky attitude and spoiled you rotten with affection."

"I wish . . . I wish I could've met them too," Yoori told him honestly, feeling the air expel from her chest. "I wish that both of them were alive now . . ."

A looming sense of remorse choked her chest. In that instant, as she stared up at her boyfriend, Yoori knew she could no longer keep the fact that she had something to do with his mother's death a secret. She was afraid to tell him, but she did not want any secrets to fester between them, especially after all that he had done for her. She could no longer keep this to herself.

"Tae Hyun, I—"

Yoori was interrupted by the sound of boots hitting the floor.

Thinking that her brother had finally come for her, Yoori jumped in her stance while a vigilant Tae Hyun protectively held her against him. His cold eyes locked onto the two intruders.

The vigilance in his eyes diminished.

It was his two Cobras: the blonde girl by the name of Sue and the eye-patched guy by the name of Rae. They were kneeling on one knee with their heads bowed down before Tae Hyun and Yoori.

"Boss," they greeted with the respectful tone they always gave to Tae Hyun. Even to an outsider like Yoori, she knew that these Cobras would give up their lives for him without hesitation. That was how far their loyalty went.

"Have you found her?" Tae Hyun asked at once.

Beside him, Yoori's blood pumped in exhilaration.

If they appeared, then that meant that they must've found . . .

"We have her," Sue confirmed, quelling the anxiety running through Yoori. "We have Seo Jin Ae."

Finally, the vengeful demon in the core of Yoori's gut breathed out, pushing the innocence in Yoori aside. *Let's give Chae Young the vengeance she deserves.*

And just like that, the heavenly fragment of Yoori's day ended while the beginnings of hell began.

"In our society, parasites must be punished..."

21: Bloodlust

Fresh from being kidnapped, Seo Jin Ae was kept prisoner in the one place Yoori had never anticipated to return to: the warehouse where Tae Hyun and Ji Hoon had battled one another and the place where she first met Ji Hoon. It was ironic because all of that also happened on the same day Jin Ae and her bodyguards had attacked Yoori. Yoori never thought she'd revisit this warehouse, but now that she had, it felt like a homecoming of some sort. Everything was coming full circle in Yoori's life, and she looked forward to bestowing Jin Ae with the same cruelty she had shown Yoori and her loved ones.

Darkness draped the warehouse like an ominous shadow, yet it elicited no fear from Yoori. All she felt was eagerness and excitement. She wanted to evoke misery from Jin Ae; she wanted to torture the girl. The tightness that once beleaguered her heart was liberated at the prospect of finally being able to destroy the last of the monsters that tormented Chae Young. Tonight was a long time coming. She looked forward to being the one to bring all this vengeance to fruition.

"I get to be the one who deals with her," Yoori declared to Tae Hyun.

After stepping out of the black SUV that Sue and Rae drove, Yoori and Tae Hyun marched toward the towering warehouse, the air between them drastically different from the blissful smiles they enjoyed earlier. Their handcuffs had been taken off, and for whatever reason, Yoori unknowingly distanced herself from Tae Hyun as they walked side by side in the cold night.

Her earmuffs and white coat were no longer present. All she wore were a black long sleeve sweater and black jeans. She could feel this foreign energy spread through her, bringing the deepest parts of her to life. She felt untouchable; it was as though she could take on the world.

Tae Hyun turned to her without saying a word, something setting off in his eyes. Since he caught the murderous flare in her eyes, he had been giving

275

her cautious looks throughout their car ride. Yoori did not deign to return his gaze. Instead, she kept her eyes solidified on the door that led into the warehouse. Although she did not make eye contact, she could feel the unease emitting from him. She sensed that Tae Hyun was looking at her quite differently, like he heard someone else's voice when she spoke to him. And truthfully, if the uncomfortable coiling in her gut was any indication, then she could also surmise that Tae Hyun was deeply unsettled by it.

Regardless of what Yoori may have detected from Tae Hyun, she was too distracted to trouble herself with the myriad of emotions that flashed in his eyes.

All that mattered to her at that moment was Jin Ae.

The bloodlust that coursed through her veins pulsated with impatience; it was an eruption of hunger that could only be extinguished by the feel of Jin Ae's blood on her hands. The recollection of Chae Young, Chae Young's father, and Jae Won suffering surfaced in Yoori's mind, acting as the fuel to ignite the fire that roared like a lion in her chest. She could not wait to annihilate Jin Ae.

As they drew closer, Yoori could scarcely make out the Cobras that guarded the door. They blended in with the darkness, which meant that Yoori couldn't identify their faces. All she could discern were their silhouettes bowing to Tae Hyun and opening the door for him, allowing a speck of light from the warehouse to sprinkle into the murky night. Sue and Rae stood guard with the other two Cobras while Tae Hyun and Yoori walked in, both very tense for very different reasons.

Lights embroidered the ceilings, yet the warehouse was considerably dark. The cold winter breeze continued to move through the room, intermixing with the dust that hovered in the air. It was an ominous, imposing space that held no hospitality for what was about to take place.

In front of her, Yoori could see Mina and three other Cobras lingering in the shadows. The three Cobras surrounded a black figure that kneeled on the ground while Mina stood a little further out, her arms crossed together as she supervised the scene before them. The only Cobra missing was Ace, who was given the task of keeping them updated on the whereabouts of Ju Won. Tae Hyun had told Yoori that they should anticipate Ju Won's response. After finding out that his niece had been kidnapped, there would be no doubt he would send out his soldiers to find Jin Ae.

"Let me go, you fuckers! How dare you do this to me? Don't you know who I am?"

The fury within Yoori boiled like lava once she heard the unmistakable voice of Jin Ae.

Sensing new presence in the room, Jin Ae lifted her face in Tae Hyun's direction.

Jin Ae's anger dissolved when her eyes found Tae Hyun. She sat up a little higher, her black pants, red silk top, and long black hair sullied from the dust. Regardless of such offending maladies, she still looked gorgeous. Her brown eyes held his. Whether it was love or infatuation, the adulation that Jin Ae had for Tae Hyun was the one thing that soothed her nerves as she stared up at him. Yoori recalled quickly that Jin Ae and Tae Hyun were an item before she met him, and that remembrance only pissed her off more.

"How could you do this to me?" Jin Ae asked Tae Hyun, her voice melancholic when Tae Hyun and Yoori stopped a few feet away from where she kneeled. Her beautiful face was marred with hurt.

Instead of answering her right away, Tae Hyun gave a stiff nod to his Cobras, a silent command for them to stand in the back. Their work was done for the time being. The Cobras bowed, understanding the wordless order and stood in a sequential line behind Mina.

Now, the stage belonged to Tae Hyun and Jin Ae.

Yoori's patience was deteriorating, but she would let Tae Hyun and Jin Ae have their moment. Although it enraged her that they were even speaking to one another, Yoori remained composed. Jin Ae would feel her presence soon enough.

"I told you after Yoori's initiation to stay away from her or I'd have your head," Tae Hyun finally voiced to Jin Ae, his eyes boring down on hers. "I wanted to kill you for tasking your men to try and rape Yoori—rape *my* girlfriend. I let you go because she forgave you, but you went too far this time."

The ire in his voice was subtly eclipsed by the regret streaming from his stance. Yoori could sense then that although Tae Hyun did not want to kill Jin Ae, he knew there was no other choice.

"You can't go unpunished for what you did, Jin Ae," he continued heavily. "You have to pay for what happened to Chae Young. You have to pay for the hell you put her through."

"What . . . What did I do? Who the hell is Chae Young?" Jin Ae cried with confusion. She narrowed her eyes onto Yoori. The adoration she once displayed for Tae Hyun evaporated.

They glared at one another, despising each other's existence.

"You bitch!" Jin Ae seethed to Yoori. Her voice amplified with raw, unfiltered hatred. "I knew you were just hiding behind that innocent act when you 'forgave' me after my uncle made me kneel before you. I should've known it was you who tricked Tae Hyun and set this whole thing up!"

That was all Yoori needed to convince her that patience was no longer her virtue. The despicable accusations that Jin Ae hurled at Yoori lit her fuse.

Her awaiting monster burst out and nothing but the thirst for blood blinded its existence.

"You're a waste of life, you disgusting whore!" Yoori screamed, speeding toward her and kicking Jin Ae right in the nose with all the force that she had.

Crack!

The sound of Jin Ae's nose breaking rang into the dusty air as her neck snapped backward.

Blood trickled down Jin Ae's nose as she cursed at Yoori. "I'm going to kill you, you fucking bitch!"

"Untie her now," Yoori ordered to one of the Cobras.

The Cobra with the pixie haircut carried out her commands as if Yoori were Tae Hyun.

"I'll punish you fairly. I'll *kill* you fairly," she spat at Jin Ae while the female Cobra sliced Jin Ae's rope with a single cut and retreated back to the other Cobras.

"Yoori—"

"Stay out of this," Yoori snapped at Tae Hyun, who was regarding her with unease in his eyes. She did not acknowledge the disquiet in his gaze. All she knew was that he was trying to stop her from punishing Jin Ae. For this, she was furious with him. "I listened to you when you told me to wait, but now this arena is mine."

"You must think you're so special," Jin Ae interrupted, standing up and glaring at Yoori. She mopped the blood from her nose with the back of her hand. Her fists clenched together in a fighting form. "Just because you have Tae Hyun and Ji Hoon in the palm of your hand, you think you can take away what's mine?"

Yoori's taunting laughter reverberated throughout the warehouse. She canted her head, moving away from Tae Hyun and approaching Jin Ae like a predator in the night.

"What is yours, Jin Ae?" she asked mockingly.

"The Underworld," Jin Ae replied without missing a beat. "If you hadn't appeared then the two most powerful Kings would've been in the palm of *my* hand. Tae Hyun would've taken me back if you hadn't appeared in our world. I would've been able to rule this world with him if it wasn't for you!"

Another derisive laugh escaped Yoori's lips.

"The Underworld has not and will never belong to you, little girl," Yoori seethed, knowing then that it was the An Soo Jin in her that found hilarity in Jin Ae's words. She no longer had control over her wrath. "It was mine, it continues to be mine, and it will *always* be mine."

Jin Ae appeared in front of Yoori in that instant, elbowing her across the face and then delivering a painful punch that connected with her cheek. Yoori's head snapped to the side, nearly causing her to plunge to the ground.

"Stay out of this!" Yoori warned, fighting to stay balanced once she saw Tae Hyun make a move to intervene.

After saying this, a furious Yoori caught the fist that Jin Ae threw, lifted it up, and twisted her wrist with a snap, causing Jin Ae's eyes to enlarge in agony as she let out an anguished scream.

"How could you do this to another woman?" Yoori screamed, reminded of why she wanted Jin Ae's head in the first place.

She thought about Chae Young and the pain that had devoured her life. Yoori grew angrier.

Clenching her fists together, Yoori delivered blow after blow across Jin Ae's face, her chest, and her stomach. Whenever Jin Ae tried to fight back, Yoori would just snap bones apart, simultaneously surprising and horrifying Jin Ae. She realized then that there was more to Yoori than what meets the eye.

"Do *what*?" Jin Ae uttered, screaming once blood began to engulf her face. Agony throbbed in her small voice.

"Stop denying it!" Yoori growled, becoming more heated. "If you did it, then have the balls to say that you did!"

"Stop . . . Stop lying!" Jin Ae cried, coughing and choking on her own blood. An uppercut was imparted to her, nearly breaking her jaw. "I . . . I didn't do anything!"

The denial only brought Yoori more anger.

"You sent those eleven gang members to rape Chae Young! You were there!" she shouted, wanting Jin Ae to admit her involvement before she killed her. She continued to punch her like Jin Ae was her personal boxing bag. "You wanted to get to me, and you allowed those scumbags to rape the one friend who had been there for me since I moved to this godforsaken city!"

"I didn't!" Jin Ae sobbed, groaning horrifically as blood consumed every inch of her skin. She was no match for Yoori's fury—Soo Jin's fury—and she was beginning to realize that she wasn't fighting with a girl. She was fighting with a skilled and merciless killer.

Her desperate and swollen eyes rolled over to Tae Hyun, who was staring at the whole scene before him in shock, horror, and disgust.

"Tae Hyun! Please!" Jin Ae sobbed, terror causing her body to shake like a leaf. "She's lying! I didn't do anything! I don't even know who Chae Young is or what she's talking about!" Her cries grew louder. "Please, *please help me!*"

"Stop lying!" Yoori roared, kicking Jin Ae across the face.

An already weak Jin Ae tumbled to the ground at the force of the kick and slammed her head against the wall behind her. Her breathing was faint, helpless.

Fuming with the clouds of rage that blinded her senses, Yoori chased after Jin Ae with no more desire to punish her. She simply wanted to end things once and for all. She banged the sole of her black boot against Jin Ae's neck, using all the power she had to officially snap Jin Ae's neck apart and end her pitiful life.

"Yoori, stop!"

It was Tae Hyun's interference that saved Jin Ae from losing the one crucial whiff of air that would kill her, and it was Tae Hyun's intrusion that infuriated Yoori.

She tried to fight against his hold, but he was much stronger.

He forcefully dragged her away until they were several feet from Jin Ae's fallen body.

"Does it hurt you to watch me beat your precious little whore?" Yoori spat out, unable to control her anger for his betrayal. She pulled her arm out of his grip in disgust. Why? Why was he stopping her? Did he still have feelings for Jin Ae? Did he still have feelings for that worthless piece of shit?

"*Don't*," Tae Hyun warned severely, quelling the psychotic rage that seared in Yoori's soul. His eyes burned with ire. "There has been no other woman, and I don't want any other woman. I've been nothing but faithful to you, and you know how much you mean to me. Don't you fucking insult me like this."

"Why are you stopping me then?" Yoori breathed out heatedly. "You told me that once we get her, I could have her head!"

"That was only when I thought she was the one who orchestrated the rape!" he shouted before taking a deep breath to calm down. He shook his head, staring at Jin Ae with regret. His eyes found Yoori's. "I know you're angry. I want nothing more than to ease that anger by giving you the vengeance you want, but I don't think you'll get it from Jin Ae. What if she's telling the truth? What if she wasn't even involved? What if someone framed her, and you're now getting ready to kill someone who has nothing to do with this? Can you live with that Yoori? Can you live with killing the wrong person if she's telling the truth?"

"She's not!" Yoori combated psychotically, breathing in roughly while she glared at Tae Hyun with animosity. "She's not, and you're being a fucking idiot for believing her!"

"Look at yourself!" Tae Hyun roared back, shaking her shoulders with his hands. "Do you see what you've turned into? Do you not hear yourself right now? Do you not hear *Soo Jin*?"

Silence collapsed over Yoori as his voice acted as the splash of cold water she needed. The violent fire that blazed through her cooled. It wasn't so much the fact that he was yelling at her, but it was because his face was marred with alarm for her. Only then did Yoori feel the weight of the blood on her hands. It terrified her because despite the concern in Tae Hyun's eyes, she still wanted to slaughter Jin Ae. It was only when a tentative voice interrupted them that the course of their night changed.

"Jin Ae has been training in China since Ms. Choi's initiation," Mina spoke up, her eyes widening with disbelief when she finally processed what was happening.

"What?" Yoori and Tae Hyun asked, both turning to Mina.

The Cobras were ordered to find Jin Ae, but they were never given a specific reason as to *why* Jin Ae had to be found. Yoori could only assume that they believed they had to find Jin Ae because of the rivalry that existed between herself and Jin Ae.

"After Ms. Choi's initiation, Ju Won sent Jin Ae to train in China," Mina provided, her gaze apologetic that she didn't tell them this sooner. "We just found out tonight. That was why she wasn't at his masquerade ball. That was also why we had such trouble finding her. She hasn't been in Seoul for weeks. She just arrived today."

Yoori went cold.

Her ears blurred out Mina's apology for not speaking up about this sooner, that she didn't know what it was Yoori and Tae Hyun wanted to punish Jin Ae for.

Yoori felt like a ton of bricks had fallen on her.

Jin Ae was lying motionless on the floor, her face barely recognizable through the blood that stained her features. She was broken. Yoori had successfully broken her, but only for the wrong reason.

Through the veil of hatred that once covered her eyes, Yoori found her sensibility. Something in her clicked. It was *never* Jin Ae who orchestrated Chae Young's rape. Jin Ae was framed, and the one who was behind it had escaped Yoori's wrath all along.

Jin Ae was actually the victim right now.

An undeserved victim of Yoori's uncontained rage.

"Boss!" Ace called, running into the warehouse and interrupting their trains of thought. His expression was one of panic. "Word has gotten out about Jin Ae being kidnapped, and Ju Won's men are searching all over the city for her. Some of them are in the area, and they'll arrive soon. If you need to kill her, then you'll have to do it now."

"Take her to the hospital," Yoori said brokenly, finding it impossible to even make eye contact with the girl she had just savagely beaten. There was no way Yoori would allow anyone to kill Jin Ae, especially for crimes that she never committed. "Get her to the hospital now and help her."

Ace hesitated, looking at Tae Hyun. "If we kill her, then we can erase all evidence that we were the ones who had her. If we let her live, then Ju Won will know what happened. He will come after you—"

"When Yoori tells you to do something, you do it," Tae Hyun reprimanded Ace, who still had a worried expression on his face. Tae Hyun eyed Mina and his Cobras, all of whom were waiting for further orders. "Take her to the hospital, give them my name, and have Dr. Han take care of her. Get her help . . . *Now.*"

Standing motionless while staring down at the crimson blood on her hands, Yoori's lungs constricted when she heard Jin Ae whimper in pain. The Cobras scooped her limp body up and swept her out of the warehouse, leaving Yoori alone with Tae Hyun.

Yoori felt numb. It seemed as though she was hovering in a sea of fire. She was so angry that her blood boiled, and this fact alone scared her. She wasn't supposed to be this angry. She was supposed to be in control. What happened to her?

She stared up and saw how Tae Hyun was gazing at her. For the first time, she saw caution against her in his eyes.

"I will never allow another situation where you could do this again, Yoori," he said to her, guardedness now fully present in his gaze. It pained her to see this, to see him watch her like she was a bomb that was ready to detonate at any moment.

"What?" she asked, shaking while she took in what he just said. How could he not let this happen again? The culprit was still out there. Yoori still had to punish that person!

"I wasn't there with you when you killed those eleven gang members. I've never been there when Soo Jin 'comes out' of you." He walked closer to her, concern etching across his vigilant eyes. His gaze broke her heart. It seemed like he realized he was losing someone—*her*.

"When I walked in, I was prepared to have my Cobras kill Jin Ae because my hands had already been tainted countless times, and it was a demon that I could live with. I only imagined that you would come in here, slap her, punch her a couple of times, and leave the rest up to my Cobras, but the murderous look in your eyes when you reveled in the spill of her blood . . . this isn't you, Yoori." He stared into her eyes. "I don't like seeing you like this. I promised you once before that I would always protect you, and I've never felt the need more than at this moment. I see now what a threat Soo Jin is . . . how much she could devour your soul." He sighed painstakingly. "Did you even hear me when I called out for you to stop? Do you even see yourself right now?"

"So, you're finally disgusted with her, aren't you?" she asked, her voice smaller than it had ever been.

Yoori felt fragmented, lost between a world of anger and a world of morals. She did not want to be a killer, but she wanted to punish the fucker who brought this hell upon Chae Young. She wanted to just be Yoori, but she realized then that she was losing her control over Soo Jin's killer instincts. She felt like shit. Fragmented shit, and it didn't help that her boyfriend was staring at her with a multitude of concern, disgust, and fear. While he wasn't afraid of her, he was damn well afraid of losing her.

"Only because I can protect you from anyone else who presents any harm to you," Tae Hyun replied moments later, confirming Yoori's belief of how he felt. There was defeat in his eyes, defeat that Yoori was used to seeing in herself, and defeat that Tae Hyun wasn't used to admitting. His voice became lower, sadder. "But I don't know how to protect you from Soo Jin."

Reverberations of footsteps encroaching upon them silenced their lips.

Tae Hyun turned. Once he saw that it was one of his Cobras, the tenseness in his body left him. Ace had returned from outside, his face still fixed with mystification.

"Boss, I don't understand," he said honestly, stopping beside them. "We've spent weeks tracking her down, and now that we've finally found her, you're letting her go?"

"She wasn't the culprit," Tae Hyun answered without thinking, forgetting that Ace wasn't privy to the news that he and Yoori wanted Jin Ae because of what happened at the diner. "She wasn't the one who sent those eleven gang members that Yoori killed."

Something then illuminated in Ace's eyes. "Are you talking about what happened in the alley?"

"What are you talking about, Ace?" Tae Hyun asked swiftly, his eyes boring into Ace's. "There's only a few who know what happened, and you shouldn't be one of them."

As Yoori listened to Ace, she began to resent that Tae Hyun's Cobras were so loyal to him. They did not question anything he asked of them; they simply did it because their King had commanded it. If only one of them had asked Tae Hyun why he wanted to punish Jin Ae, then they wouldn't have wasted so much time going after Jin Ae, whom was never involved in the first place.

"When I came back to Seoul, I was in the area doing some business, trying to find out valuable information for you so that we would be able to rejoin the gang," he said to Tae Hyun before looking at both of them. "I was on the roof and heard a loud noise. I went over to the edge to see what the

283

commotion was. That was when I got my first sighting of Ms. Choi, and that was how I knew she was An Soo Jin. When I saw her take on those eleven gang members, I knew she was the Queen that we failed to kill. I was ready to drop down there and fight her myself, but then I realized she was the one rumored to be your new girlfriend. This was confirmed when I saw you come to her aid after her fight was over. That was when I followed both of you and waited for the opportune moment for her to be alone before letting the other Cobras know."

He forged on, his face regretful that he didn't share this sooner.

"It didn't matter to me then because this little detail was irrelevant. I have no idea if it matters now, but I saw someone get out of their car during your fight with the rest of the gang members. They got a glimpse of you killing the rest of the gang members while Ms. Choi hid behind the dead corpses."

"Who did you see, Ace?" Yoori inquired, her instincts blaring as if telling her that whoever it was he saw must be the one behind it all.

Ace inhaled deeply.

After a long moment, he answered.

"Lee Ji Hoon. I saw Lee Ji Hoon."

The air escaped Yoori's chest. She felt like she was knocked in the stomach with a large sledgehammer at this revelation. Something struck her when she remembered a small and insignificant part of the conversation she had with Ji Hoon outside of the restaurant after she and Tae Hyun had broken up.

"I heard about the eleven gang members you killed," he whispered, earning silence from her. He saw her eyes widen and continued to speak. "We both know that only Soo Jin has enough power to do all of that."

"You said that Ji Hoon came *as* Tae Hyun started killing the other gang members in the alley?"

Ace nodded, causing the invisible blow to her stomach to worsen in pain.

While bewilderment and rage besieged her, the fog lifted and the world became clearer to Yoori as she mindlessly spoke. "There were other gang members who were killed that morning. He could not have known it was eleven gang members I killed unless he was the one who sent the *specific* number."

This realization exacerbated the flames that already occupied her body. She clenched her bloodied fists, never feeling more furious in her life.

The truth was finally out.

It was Ji Hoon who sent those eleven gang members to rape Chae Young.

It was Ji Hoon all along.

"They must be exterminated."

22: Chasing Skulls

"You're not going after him!" Tae Hyun argued with Yoori after they reached their apartment.

Since leaving the warehouse, Tae Hyun and Yoori had been at each other's throats about their next course of action. Yoori, who felt blindsided and betrayed by the revelation that it was Ji Hoon who orchestrated Chae Young's rape, wanted nothing more than to find him and skin him alive. Tae Hyun, who was also furious that it had been Ji Hoon all along, wasn't receptive to that plan. He wanted to kill Ji Hoon, but he refused to allow Yoori to endanger herself. His refusal was the beginning of their heated quarrel.

They stormed into the crowded living room, both shaking from so much rage that even the dozens of Serpents, who had been called in for reinforcements, were gazing at them with wariness in their eyes. Tae Hyun shot a death glare to anyone who was staring, and they averted their eyes in terror. Breathing heavily, he pushed Yoori past the crowd and gave them some semblance of privacy by slamming the door shut.

"I want his head!" Yoori snarled after the door closed shut. She held in her wrath because they had company outside, but she was done with the politeness now. She was fuming and needed to kill Ji Hoon to extinguish the rage inside her. The fact that Tae Hyun was making this endeavor harder was the last straw for her.

"You're no match for him!" Tae Hyun snapped back. The same fury that had ignited an inferno inside her erupted from his body. "If there's anyone who could kill Ji Hoon, then it would be me. I gave you Jin Ae because I knew that I could watch over you, but I'm not letting you near Ji Hoon."

"Kwon Tae Hyun!" she screamed, wanting to wring his neck. His stubbornness may have been charming to her in the past, but in a moment like this, when she was at the end of her patience, it was nothing more than a hindrance that she resented.

She exhaled angrily. Any follow up words she wanted to scream out were abruptly stopped when his voice towered over hers.

"Choi Yoori, you're not going after him."

His eyes on her were firmer than steel.

Cursing to herself, Yoori whirled around and indignantly slammed her hand against the door. She glowered at him, feeling the animosity sweep through her.

For anything else, it was likely that Tae Hyun would be more flexible in terms of giving her what she wanted. However, when it came to allowing her to run off to fight Ji Hoon, Tae Hyun was bound and determined to stop her in every way that he could. He did not believe she could survive a battle with Ji Hoon, and he did not even want to entertain the idea of her trying to fight him. In that heated moment, it was a rationality that Yoori despised him for.

"Ji Hoon isn't some measly gang leader off the streets," he explained when he saw the resentment for him on her face. "He did not become the King of Skulls because of his blood right alone. He's been trained by the best, and he is as good as me. Don't be a fool and think that you can take him on because you'd have to pay for that mistake with your life."

Yoori wanted to tell him to fuck off—it didn't matter if he didn't believe she could handle Ji Hoon. The murderous killer in her was livid. *She* believed that she could kill him. At the going rate, her wrath was strong enough to annihilate an entire army if she chose to. She wanted to tell him this, but much like everything else that happened tonight, another interruption barreled through them.

Tae Hyun's Blackberry sounded off.

"What?" Tae Hyun barked impatiently, not even looking at his screen. An expression of regret spread over his face once the voice on the other line deluged like bombs through the receiver.

"Kwon Tae Hyun! What the hell are you thinking?"

It was Dong Min's voice and for the first time, he had lost all control.

Yoori felt several nerves in her body twitch in fear by simply listening to his voice. In the past, she had seen Jung Min and Ju Won lose their control, but Dong Min had been the sole Advisor who was able to retain his cool. Unfortunately for this night, it seemed like everyone was losing their sanity.

Tae Hyun grimaced in irritation. Yoori was already lashing out at him; the last thing he needed was to be chastised by his Advisor. "I'm not in the mood for this right now—"

"Three *fucking* years!" Dong Min bellowed out, dismissing what Tae Hyun was getting ready to say. His voice elevated with every irate word. "Three *fucking* years we've worked toward this moment and now we're two weeks away from Ju Won's 65th birthday, the day he chooses his fucking heir, and you not only kidnap his niece, but you beat her to the point where she had to go to the fucking hospital?!"

Outrage.

Nothing but outrage scorched his voice.

"It was me!" Yoori shouted from the background. She was angry with Tae Hyun, but his safety was still a priority for her. He should not take the fall for what she did. "I was the one who beat her! If you want to blame anyone, then blame me—"

"Shut up!" Tae Hyun hissed, severely pissed off that she even remotely mentioned her involvement in hurting Ju Won's beloved niece. It was apparent that Yoori's safety was the sole priority on Tae Hyun's list.

"It was me," he said into the phone. "She had nothing to do with it."

He took the blame for it without hesitation.

His gallant words fell on deaf ears.

"I should've known," she heard Dong Min state with spitefulness.

If he was standing before her, then she was sure Dong Min would've beheaded her with a butcher knife. She did not blame him. If she had someone who was screwing with her advisee's future—especially when this advisee was Tae Hyun—she would behead that person as well.

"Tae Hyun, come over to the mansion now," he ordered, manufacturing a calmer voice to better get his point across. Dong Min was raised to be a crime lord, but he was a politician by nature. He was acutely aware that the only way to get anything done was to remain levelheaded. There were times to be enraged and there were times to get things resolved. Tonight was a night to get things resolved. "Ju Won will be there, and he always has a soft spot for you. Talk to him and keep him calm until his damn party."

"I'm not apologizing to him."

"You *will*," Dong Min told him with simple resolution. Residual anger throbbed in his voice. He kept the fury contained, but only barely. "You know as much as I do that power is the only thing that will save you and that girl of yours. You've placed her above everything else; now you have to do everything in your power to keep her alive. Giving Ju Won the opportunity to turn the Underworld against you will not help in that endeavor. And trust me, he *will* turn everyone against you unless you fix things. So come right now, humor him while acting like you care enough to calm him down, and *then* we'll figure out the rest."

Without waiting for Tae Hyun to utter a response, Dong Min hung up.

The moment Tae Hyun smothered a curse under his breath, Yoori knew that it meant he was planning to go. If they had killed Jin Ae, then they wouldn't have had to deal with this. Since they both chose to keep her alive, the consequence was graver for them. It was a consequence that Tae Hyun had to mend if he wanted to keep power in his corner and keep Yoori safe by his side.

He tucked the phone into his jacket and locked his eyes with her firm ones. The inferno from his gaze dispersed like fire under water. If the conversation with Dong Min was useful for one thing, it was reminding Tae Hyun of his priority when it came to her safety.

He placed a gentle hand under her chin and lifted it up.

"I know how angry you are right now," he pacified, having simmered down since his conversation with Dong Min, "but you're not going after Ji Hoon. Jin Ae was one thing, but Ji Hoon is a completely different ballgame. I won't risk anything happening to you. I can't and I won't."

Yoori could barely contain her scoff. The concern she had for him was replaced with scorn. Her rage was still at an all-time high and she was getting tired of being told what to do—especially by him. He was her boyfriend; not her master. She refused to be ordered around like he was her King. "I'm going and you can't stop me."

Tae Hyun expressed no indication to back down. "We will deal with everything when I come back. In the meantime, you will stay here."

Yoori raised her chin up in defiance. Her grave expression dared him to challenge her. "You can't make me."

"I'm making you." His voice on her was still tender, but she did not miss the ominous undercurrent in his tone. He was dangerously powerful. Even the deep core of her body knew that Tae Hyun would easily overpower Soo Jin's fighting instincts if he chose to. "I'm giving the orders to Kang Min and the rest of the Serpents. None of them will let you go without my command."

"Bastard," she cursed when she saw that all the roads had been blocked now. Tae Hyun was a force to be reckoned with when he was on your side, but he was a much bigger force to be reckoned with when he wasn't. Unfortunately for Yoori, on this matter, Tae Hyun wasn't on her side. He was the principal roadblock in her way.

"That's enough, Yoori," said Tae Hyun, knowing well that between the two of them, he had to be the coolheaded one. There was controlled strain in his voice. It was a rarity for Tae Hyun to demonstrate this much restraint, especially considering that he was accustomed to people bending to his will at the snap of a finger. Yoori was his exception and his only weakness.

Attempting to make things right between them before he departed, Tae Hyun sighed and wrapped one arm around her waist. He pulled her closer to his body. He stroked her cheek with his fingers, his eyes searching for hers. It was a caring gesture that earned nothing but a glare from an embittered Yoori. In spite of her ire, he continued to show his affections.

"I'm leaving now," he whispered, trying to get through to her before he made his exit. He did not want to end this conversation with her begrudging him. "We'll talk about it when I come back. Until then, get some rest. I'll be back soon."

Desperate for a heartfelt remembrance of her before he left, Tae Hyun leaned in for a kiss. Yoori heaved her head back, giving him the cold shoulder while denying his kiss. It saddened Yoori to do this because she wanted to kiss him too. Nevertheless, she was too incensed to succumb to it. He needed to be punished for not giving her what she wanted. If she couldn't punish him by beating the fuck out of him, then she would punish him by giving him the cold shoulder. She knew what hurt him more and it was not the prospect of getting beaten.

A modicum of pain reflected on his face before it became shadowed with stubbornness of his own. His voiceless stare said it all: he wasn't giving in even if she was planning on not talking to him for the days to come. For her safety, he would endure her punishments.

With no more to discuss, he gave her one last lingering look before he unhooked her from his arms, pulled his once caressing fingers back, and then disappeared out of their bedroom.

She could hear him give firm orders to his Serpents to keep her safe in the apartment and then heard the door slam shut.

Just like that, he was gone.

■ ■ ■

It took Yoori a little over thirty minutes to soak in that room alone.

The only thing that existed in her world was the need for answers and the desire to rip off Ji Hoon's head. She buried her face in her hands, feeling her sanity disintegrate. Her frantic mind ran over the prospect of Ji Hoon being the mastermind behind Chae Young's rape. She could not fathom how someone she placed so much trust in could do something so deplorable. He had been nothing but kind to her since they met. Why would he do such a thing? What did he have to gain from getting eleven gang members to rape her friend? Yoori felt herself tremble. Despite her anger, a huge part of her hoped that it wasn't him. She hoped that somehow, he wasn't involved in it. It was a hopeful wish that did little to quench the uncontrollable firestorm within her body. A dark and violent cancer had spread through her, and Yoori could no longer contain it.

She lifted her head up, her resolve set.

Fuck waiting around.

She had no time to marinate in her own thoughts. The only way to get answers (and vengeance) was to go after it.

Yoori pulled the door open.

She knew what to do to leave this apartment.

"Kang Min," Yoori called out from the bedroom.

Kang Min, who was wearing a black t-shirt and brown pants, was sitting on the living room couch with a dozen other Serpents. He popped his head up after hearing her voice. He rose from his seat, maneuvered himself around the crowd, and came to the door. He barely stopped to greet her before Yoori dragged him in and closed the door behind her.

"Boss?" Kang Min asked, noting how odd she was behaving. His eyes glimpsed over at the dried splatters of blood on her body. He knew the blood didn't belong to her.

"I need to leave now," she informed him at once.

His brows lowered in apprehension. He already regretted coming into this room. "Boss Kwon doesn't permit it."

"Tae Hyun doesn't own me," Yoori bit out, the urge to leave mounting inside her. It did not help that her anger was on the verge of rising as well. Kang Min reminding her of Tae Hyun's "orders" only worsened her mood. "I can do as I please."

"He's protecting you," Kang Min respectfully disagreed.

"He's keeping me caged."

Yoori could see the confliction in his eyes. Kang Min wanted to adhere to her wishes, but he also wanted to adhere to Tae Hyun's commands.

"Boss, he'll be back soon," Kang Min started to compromise. "We can deal with it then—"

"*I'm* your boss," she snapped, surprising both Kang Min and herself with her authoritative tone of voice. She had never used that tone with Kang Min before, but it could not be helped. She was sick and tired of people telling her what to do. She was not going to allow Kang Min to dictate what she could or couldn't do, even if he was only doing it as a proxy of Tae Hyun's. "Not Tae Hyun. My orders will always supersede his." She pointed at the door, prepared to set her plan into motion. "Now we're going to walk out together and you're going to tell the Serpents out there that you're taking me to see Tae Hyun. After that, when we're in the clear, I'm going to leave in the Mercedes and you're going to leave me alone."

"Boss," he continued, concern for her lining his voice. He was hesitant, not because he was afraid of Tae Hyun, but because to him, her plan was pretty much to endanger herself. "Whatever it is you're doing, it's not safe—"

"How far does your loyalty go, Kang Min?"

It was a question that Yoori dreaded asking. She knew how far Kang Min's loyalty went. It was infinite. If worse came to worst, he would die for her without hesitation. This was why her heart ached when she asked him that horrible question. The look on his face was one that spoke of shock and hurt that she'd even ask such a question. Yoori felt awful, but it was what worked on him—it was what broke him and convinced him to adhere to her every command.

Pretty soon, they were walking out in the darkness, and Yoori was feeling free. Free to do what she wanted; free to allow her murderous rage to run amuck. She sprinted for the Mercedes, mindlessly thanking Kang Min and telling him that he could go.

Before she could get far, his hand clamped over her arm.

"Boss, I'm not afraid of death," Kang Min told her, the confliction never leaving his eyes. Wind roared in resistance, brushing their hair every which way. He was still troubled that he disregarded Tae Hyun's orders and followed hers. "I told you once before that my loyalty for An Soo Jin—for you—will supersede my loyalty for Boss Kwon. But my job is to protect you and in a time like this, Boss Kwon is the only one who could keep you safe." He cast a sideways glance at the car and then returned his curious eyes back to her. His gaze questioned her motivation for acting so bizarrely tonight. "Why are you doing this? What is so important that you have to leave now? Why can't you wait for him to come back?"

Yoori considered lying to him. She swiftly decided against it. So many people had lied to her, and it broke her. She did not want to perpetuate this cycle with Kang Min. He had a right to know why she was so against Tae Hyun tonight and why she had to leave in such an underhanded fashion.

"I have to find Ji Hoon," Yoori replied, no longer finding it necessary to hide things from him.

Bewilderment stole his face. He did not expect to hear this answer. "Why?"

"He sent those eleven gang members to rape Chae Young," she revealed bluntly, her impatience berating her to just leave and go find Ji Hoon. However, the desire to tell Kang Min the truth eclipsed her bloodlust. It was only right that Kang Min knew who had been torturing his older brother and his older brother's girlfriend. It was only right that she left with him understanding why all of this was happening. She wasn't losing her mind; she was seeking retribution.

The conflagration that flared in his gaze mirrored that of Yoori's.

"What?" he asked even though he heard exactly what she said.

"He was behind it all," she elaborated, growing angrier with every spoken word, every reminder of what a bastard Ji Hoon was. "At first, Tae Hyun and I thought it was Jin Ae because Chae Young mentioned that a girl was there at the diner. It turned out Ji Hoon was framing Jin Ae. It was him. It was Ji Hoon all along, and I have to find him. I have to find out why and I have to make him pay."

The rage that engulfed Kang Min's baby-like face was chilling. He no longer cared about following Tae Hyun's orders. The only thing he cared about was revenge. "I'm going with you."

"No!" Yoori objected, only expecting him to stay behind and understand her reasoning. The last thing she wanted was for him to come along and endanger his life. She believed that she had a fighting chance with Ji Hoon. Kang Min, on the other hand, was no match for him. "You're not going with me."

"If you're not waiting for Boss Kwon, then I'm going with you," he said resolutely. "I don't care what you say."

Her face hardened like steel. "Don't you dare—"

"Chae Young is like a sister to me!" Kang Min shouted, finally losing his cool with her. The muscles in his jaw bunched while his breathing grew harsher. "Do you think you're the only one affected by all of this, boss? Do you think you're the only one who wants vengeance for her?" He raked a hand through his hair and breathed out in slow breaths, trying to regulate his overwhelming anger. Once he calmed, he clasped his hands together and gazed at Yoori with angst in his eyes. "I know you killed all those gang members, and I pray to God everyday that I could have my chance with one of them so I could avenge Chae Young and my brother. This whole thing broke them. It broke Chae Young and my older brother. Jae Won should be the one to go after Ji Hoon. But since he's not here, I'm going for him. I'm going for Chae Young, and I'm going for you. It would only help you if I'm there with you."

There was a protective part of her that wanted to refuse him. She wanted to tell him to stay. The heaviness in her heart was the only thing that prevented her from making him stay behind. Kang Min was right. Jae Won was the one who should be here. Since he wasn't, Yoori and Kang Min would go in his place. Though every protective instinct in her gut was telling her to leave Kang Min there—where it was safe—she nodded anyway because she was too blinded by ire to know better. If she was waging war on Ji Hoon, then she needed a soldier by her side.

"Do you know where to go?" Kang Min asked, buckling his seatbelt from the passenger side. The Mercedes had been fixed and it was as good as new. It was perfect for Yoori to prowl the violent night with.

"Yes," Yoori confirmed, staring straight ahead. She floored the gas pedal with the sole of her boot and allowed her instincts to take over. "I know where to go."

■ ■ ■

292

How she knew exactly where he was, Yoori wasn't sure.

While driving the Mercedes and updating Kang Min on what had been going on in terms of her beating Jin Ae, Jin Ae being hospitalized, and Jin Ae ultimately being framed, she just allowed her instincts, or perhaps Soo Jin's instincts, to take over. Sure enough, after running through a series of red lights, they arrived at Fever, a bar that Ji Hoon owned.

It was early morning and Yoori knew, judging by the other black Mercedes that sat near the curb, that Ji Hoon was at the bar, possibly using it as his private office because the bar was already long closed.

Anticipation mounted in Yoori's body after she and Kang Min stepped out of the car. She was intensely aware that she wasn't being herself tonight. If anything, she was far from her usual self. She could feel a splitting headache form in her mind. It was as if a part of her was fighting another part of her, fighting to take over. Despite the internal war inside her, all that continued to prevail was the need to find Ji Hoon. She felt like a predator tracking its prey. She was hungry for blood and that blood was Ji Hoon's.

"Kang Min," she prompted quietly, pointing at a group of people standing outside the bar. There were five Skulls guarding the door.

She was about to conjure up a plan on how they should proceed into the club—perhaps starting with her beating the five men into submission—when gunshots went off from beside her. The next second, all five Skulls became nothing but mere memories as they collapsed onto the cement, their eyes wide open while life flickered out of their gazes.

Yoori peered at Kang Min, who was holding his black gun out. Fresh steam fluttered from the barrel of his gun.

The expression on his face conveyed that he wasn't in the mood to deal with politics. His typically composed demeanor was gone. At the moment, he was rash, just like Yoori.

Good, Yoori thought. The less time that was wasted before she got to rip Ji Hoon's gut out, the better.

"Did you hear that?" echoed the screams of panic from inside the bar. "Get up! Grab your fucking guns!"

The battle had started.

Yoori and Kang Min exchanged one last look with one another. She felt him drop an object into the palm of her hand. The throbbing of her migraine lessened as she held the weight of Soo Jin's precious gold gun in her grasp.

A torrent of blissful air flowed through her. It felt like the deep, abysmal part of her had finally taken a breath from the prison she held it in. She had always kept her fighting instincts buried deep inside her, afraid that just one ounce of lost control would release the killer from her body. She released that fighter, if only remotely, when she fought with Jin Ae and now, as she burst into the brightly lit bar with Kang Min, she knew that her control was slipping.

She wanted to destroy Ji Hoon but, by God, she hoped she wouldn't destroy herself in the process.

"Get Lee Ji Hoon out here or I'll pump metal into your brains!" Kang Min shouted to the dozen of Skulls members in the bar.

They had heard the gunshots outside and fashioned a circular formation throughout the bar to protect their King. Each held black guns in their hands. All the guns were aimed at Yoori and Kang Min.

Edgy silence manifested in the room, hanging over the bar like rain clouds. The tension was only broken when the man of the hour spoke.

"Yoori?"

And there he appeared.

Striding out of the private hall, dressed in a navy blue dress shirt and black pants, puzzlement ruffled Ji Hoon's face when he took in the scene before him. He surveyed the room, almost not believing his eyes. He had not expected Yoori at the bar, much less pointing a gun at him. He looked between her and Kang Min. Both still had their guns raised, ready to shoot everyone in the bar to get to him.

Yoori watched him carefully. She watched him stare at her with concern washed over his face. His eyes ran over her gold gun. There was a slight flicker of annoyance in his eyes as he moved toward her and Kang Min.

"What are you doing, Yoori?" he asked carefully, stopping a few feet away from them.

In a room filled with armed and dangerous people, Ji Hoon was the only one who was unarmed and the only one who displayed no fear. He had good reason. He was arguably the strongest person in the room. Tae Hyun's words replayed in her mind, reminding Yoori of how dangerous the man in front of her was. Ji Hoon did not become a King by birthright alone. He may not have been armed, but he was the deadliest weapon in this room.

Yoori wanted to shoot him then, to assuage her bloodlust and avenge Chae Young. An apprehensive part of her prevented her from doing so. The wheels of her mind started turning while her eyes roamed over him. Memories of the care she had for him invaded her thoughts. She briefly wondered if she had jumped to conclusions too quickly. The small doubt acted as a change agent in her mind, releasing a flood of other doubts. What if it wasn't him? What if this was all a mistake? What if *he* was framed? The bigger part of her told her that none of this was a mistake though. He had been the monster all along—a monster that she needed to kill before it was too late. She struggled with herself, the gun still held firm in her possession.

"It was you all along," Yoori confronted, aiming her gun at him. She did not know what to believe. She only knew that she had to get her answers now.

There was no better way to get an answer than to point a gun at someone. "It was you all along, wasn't it?"

If it was possible, Ji Hoon's visage became even more mystified. Yoori would even daresay he was hurt that she was talking to him in such a spiteful manner.

"Yoori," he started delicately, "what are you talking about?" Before allowing her to answer, he turned to his men. There was severity in his eyes for them. He was livid that they were pointing their guns at her. "Didn't we have this lesson before? Lower your guns in her presence."

Sounds of Skulls, very unhappily, lowering their guns resounded in the tense atmosphere of the bar.

Yoori and Kang Min, however, kept theirs up.

Ji Hoon faced Kang Min. The severity in his eyes remained. "Lower that gun, Kang Min. My men don't take it lightly when a gun is pointed in my direction."

"Fuck you, asshole," Kang Min spat out, holding firm on to his gun.

Ji Hoon clenched his jaw. He tolerated the spitefulness from Yoori, but not from a simple soldier in the Underworld.

"There are a dozen guns here and two that belong to you and Yoori," he went on patiently, his voice becoming sterner. "You were Soo Jin's right-hand man, Kang Min. She trained you to know better than this. You know your odds. Would you risk yours and Yoori's life when you know I'd evade your bullets anyway?"

Kang Min considered his words. Though uncertainty strained his face, Kang Min listened to logic and cautiously lowered his gun. He was angry, but his anger took a backseat to Yoori's safety.

Yoori did not follow suit.

She kept her gun up while Ji Hoon angled his head to his men and said, "Leave."

"But boss . . ." one began with worry.

"Leave," he interrupted. His gaze returned its attention to Yoori. He looked past the gun she had aimed on him. His expression became softer when trained on hers. "I want to be alone with them."

Knowing that it was futile to argue, Ji Hoon's men gave distrustful growls. They scowled at Kang Min and Yoori for a moment before piling out of the bar. After they were gone, Ji Hoon continued his conversation with Yoori.

"To what do I owe the pleasure?" he inquired, making an effort to get closer to Yoori. Though it was blatant that Ji Hoon was not pleased with her still aiming a gun at him, he said nothing of the matter.

"Stay . . . Stay back!" Yoori warned, panicking at his growing proximity.

She trembled while holding the gun in her hands. She didn't know why she was afraid all of a sudden. At first, she was so angry and so sure that he did it. She couldn't wait to kill him. But after seeing him, she felt uncertain. She did not know what to think—or what to believe.

"Why are you doing this, Yoori? Did Tae Hyun put you up to this?" Ji Hoon asked. He was almost near her when Kang Min pulled her behind him, protecting her with the wall of his body.

She had enough with her own cowardice. Yoori pushed Kang Min out of the way and faced Ji Hoon. One way or another, she had to settle things and set everything straight.

"It was you, wasn't it?" she accused, allowing everything to flood out of her. All of her bottled up emotions poured out into the bar. "*You* were the one who sent those eleven gang members to the diner and had them rape my friend. *You* tried to frame Jin Ae, but you were spotted getting out of the car and going right into the alley where Tae Hyun and I were. You were going to check up on your men, weren't you?"

Ji Hoon's expression was a veil of disbelief. He looked like he couldn't believe the peculiar situation he was in.

"I . . . I have no idea what you're talking about, Yoori," he sputtered out seconds later.

"Stop lying, motherfucker!" Kang Min snarled from the side, his body prepared to lunge at Ji Hoon.

Yoori placed her hand on Kang Min's chest, silently telling him to calm down.

Despite being unhappy with the direction of the conversation, Ji Hoon looked directly in her eyes. "Look," he placated, logically going through all her accusations. "I was in the area when I heard gunshots. I went to see what was going on and I saw everything. I wanted to go in and help, but I saw that Tae Hyun already had a handle on things. I didn't feel it was necessary to butt in, even though I wanted to help save you." He exhaled breathily, shaking his head. "But I have no idea what else you're talking about. I don't know who your friend is, and I had no part in what happened to her."

"How did you know there were eleven gang members that I killed?" Yoori interrogated, not ready to rule him out yet. "When you came, Tae Hyun was already there and he was already killing more than the eleven gang members that I killed. There was no possible way you could've known the *exact* number."

"I know how you kill," he answered easily. "I know how *both* of you kill your enemies. I knew you killed those eleven gang members while Tae Hyun killed the rest of the gang members that came after. You both have your own signature of killing. Of course I'd know who killed who."

Yoori paused, pondering his words. She was at a loss of what to say next. Shit.

What he said made sense.

If Young Jae and Anna knew Yoori was alive because of how those gang members were killed, then this also gave Ji Hoon credibility.

"Who told you all of this?" he asked firmly, his expression scrutinizing.

"Ace," Yoori answered, not knowing where to go from there. Did she jump to the wrong conclusion again?

A hostile smirk overtook Ji Hoon's lips. "The lead Cobra? Tae Hyun's right-hand man?"

Yoori could hear it in his tone. Ji Hoon was insinuating that Ace had an ulterior motive. For a fleeting moment, she wondered if that was plausible as well. Ace attempted to kill her only weeks before. Maybe he wasn't as over it as she thought he was. Perhaps this was just another grandiose plot to get her killed.

"Your right-hand soldier is Yen," Kang Min confronted, knowing where Ji Hoon was planning on veering the conversation. He would not allow the diversion. His suspicions were purely on Ji Hoon. "There was a woman at the diner."

"And Tae Hyun's right-hand is also a woman," Ji Hoon supplied, verbalizing what Yoori was thinking. "Mina, as I recall."

Disjointed with the holes in her puzzle, Yoori tried to make sense of everything that was occurring. Was it possible? Was Ace playing her the entire time? Was it possible that it was Ace and Mina who did this, and Mina was actually the woman at the diner? Were they trying to pit her against Ji Hoon or was it the truth the entire time? That it was actually Ji Hoon who orchestrated this entire thing?

"You're so quick to assume it was me, but what if it was Tae Hyun the entire time?" Ji Hoon spoke up, feeding on the confusion eating away at Yoori. "What if he's up to something, Yoori? Have you thought of that?"

"Boss, don't let him get inside your head," Kang Min said before any further damage could be performed. He could see that she was doubting everything she discovered tonight. "Tae Hyun loves you. He's not that type of person. He would never hurt anyone you love."

"Tae Hyun is a revered crime lord, Yoori," Ji Hoon continued to instigate. He drew closer to Yoori in her numb, distracted state. "He's a manipulative King and a very good actor. Right now, he could be playing you and you would be none the wiser."

He brought his hand up and held her pale cheek in his palm, staring deep into her confounded eyes. Yoori lowered her gun while he did this, giving him the opportunity to pull her closer to him. She felt so fragmented. She didn't know what to believe anymore. Her mind couldn't make sense of anything.

"Don't doubt me, Yoori," he whispered, his visage pleading for her to believe him. "I wouldn't lie to you about this. What happened to Chae Young was horrific, but I'm not involved. You have to believe me. I would never do something like this."

Yoori didn't know what to do or who to believe.

She was confused.

She was so confused until Kang Min's voice swam into her psyche and settled everything once and for all.

". . . We never mentioned Chae Young's name."

And then there was no more doubt in Yoori's mind.

Ji Hoon's previous words echoed in her head.

"But I have no idea what else you're talking about. I don't know who your friend is, and I had no part in what happened to her."

He lied.

He knew exactly who Chae Young was and what happened to her . . . because he was the one behind all of this.

After hearing Kang Min's words and seeing the change of anger in Yoori's eyes, Ji Hoon's once warm eyes transformed into dark, icy eyes.

There was no more acting on his part.

He realized he had slipped up and had been caught.

A cold smirk swept over his lips, and Yoori knew that confronting him would be the easy part. Getting out of this bar alive would be the hard part.

"Remember that the next time you become tempted..."

23: The Beginning of the End

Ji Hoon did not allot them time to prepare for his attack.

Before Yoori could even think to do anything, Ji Hoon violently knocked her to the side.

Unable to balance herself, she tumbled backward against a barstool. Her head collided against the marble of the bar before falling to the ground with a loud crash. Stars exploded in her darkened vision while pain acted as a jackhammer puncturing into her skull. She could scarcely breathe from the sudden attack.

While Yoori lay on the floor, struggling to see past the blurry vision that left her unable to stand up, Ji Hoon's knee connected against Kang Min's gut. Kang Min tried to raise his gun and shoot at him, but it was too late. A pained gasp tore out from Kang Min as Ji Hoon followed his attack with a punch across the face. Blood spurted from Kang Min's mouth. Unable to maintain his grip on the gun, Kang Min's hand involuntarily tossed the gun into the air. It flew across the room, rendering it useless to Kang Min, who was too inexperienced when compared to a powerful King like Ji Hoon.

Ji Hoon smirked, following after Kang Min.

Kang Min was staggering to keep himself balanced. Blood drizzled from his swollen mouth. Though hurt, he was still resilient.

"Soo Jin had always been so proud of her two favorite Scorpions," said Ji Hoon, stalking after Kang Min like a lion. "I should've known if anyone were to catch on to the small details, it would be you."

"You bastard," Kang Min retorted with revulsion, spitting out blood from his mouth. "I knew it was you as soon as I heard that your name was involved in this."

Ji Hoon laughed with mocking amusement.

"Why do you give a fuck anyway, Kang Min?" He walked in circles around Kang Min like the predator that he was. "Lee Chae Young belonged to

Jae Won, not you. As far as I'm concerned, she shouldn't have been worth it for you to come here and fight against me of all people."

"First of all, she's my brother's girlfriend. She doesn't belong to him. Secondly, I love my older brother. You don't touch anyone my brother loves. *That's* why she's worth it, you piece of shit!" Kang Min yelled, suddenly lunging toward Ji Hoon.

He attempted to deliver a punch across the face, but Ji Hoon was quick to block. Unperturbed, Kang Min jabbed an uppercut and then punched him in the eye before grabbing Ji Hoon's neck and locking his hand around it. He bashed Ji Hoon's head against the small round table behind them. The table fractured under the attack, nearly breaking apart.

Rage seared in Ji Hoon's eyes.

"Then you can die for them, you naïve fuck," Ji Hoon sneered, enraged that Kang Min had managed to get a few punches in.

Growling, Ji Hoon placed his hands under the table and proceeded to flip it. He allowed his body to plunge to the ground while jabbing the rough edges of the table's feet against Kang Min's solar plexus, leaving him to stumble across the room at the sudden force.

Flinging the table aside, Ji Hoon charged at Kang Min, his eyes hungry for blood.

He was near Kang Min until . . .

Boom!

The force of wood crushed against Ji Hoon's back, causing him to crumple to the floor, only inches from Kang Min and inches from Yoori, who had just broken a barstool over him.

Wrath cloaked her eyes. She was hurting herself, but the adrenaline and determination to hurt Ji Hoon distracted her from the otherwise unbearable pain.

Only keeping the broken wooden leg, she discarded what was left of the barstool. Yoori rocketed toward him at full speed and kneed him across the face before he was able to spring up. She followed suit by propelling the wooden leg into his gut. When he groaned in pain, she flipped the leg in midair, caught it with her opposite hand, and delivered an uppercut against his chin with it. Though she was quick, Ji Hoon was quicker. He lifted his chin up before the wood could pierce through his head.

Pissed off at the presence of another fighter, Ji Hoon seized Yoori's wrist and slammed her hand against a wall. Yoori screamed, losing her grip on the wooden leg. When her weapon slipped from her grasp, he pushed her away and then skirted around her.

He had someone else to take care of before he dealt with Yoori.

He charged for Kang Min like a bull. Kang Min stood his ground, rallying everything he had to fight. He proved to be no match for Ji Hoon. With a merciless kick, Kang Min was sent whirling across the edge of the room. He flew straight toward an alcohol shelf behind him.

"No!" Yoori screamed.

Kang Min never saw it coming.

Ji Hoon was as quick as a bolt of lighting. He hooked his hand behind the heavy black shelf and pushed it forward, aiming it toward Kang Min. The gargantuan alcohol bottles from the shelf tumbled forward, breaking upon Kang Min's skull with loud cracks. The shelf came with it, eventually landing on Kang Min with a thundering crash.

Boom!

Silence emanated from Kang Min as he lay buried beneath the shelf.

Only Ji Hoon and Yoori were left standing.

Panting for breath, Ji Hoon's cold eyes met Yoori's.

A firestorm of fury engulfed Yoori as she gazed at Kang Min's motionless body.

"You fucking bastard!" she screamed, spotting her gold gun on the floor. She was going to kill Ji Hoon. She was going to kill the motherfucker!

Her fingers were an inch away from the gun when his leather shoe kicked the gun away. Having one option taken out, Yoori leapt up and attempted to punch him across the face. He easily blocked her attack. He held up her wrists and then pushed her against the wall, leaving her unable to do anything while his cruel eyes bore into her.

"This is all your fault. If you want to blame someone, then you should blame yourself," he told her, finally showing his true colors. There was no adoration in his voice or gaze. He was sick and tired of her.

"Why? Why did you do this to Chae Young? What the fuck is wrong with you?" she screamed. Unfiltered hatred swept through her and she was sure she would die from it.

She tried to fight him, but he denied her efforts and kept her pinned against the wall.

He stared at her without guilt. "I had those scums go after your friend because I knew she was the only one capable of luring you out alone—without Tae Hyun. I figured if you came in time to see them rape her, then you'd be helpless and I could swoop in to save you. But your friend . . ." He shook his head disbelievingly. "Your fucking friend was so loyal to you. She wouldn't call you in fear of them hurting you, so she endured the raping and all the abuse, just so she didn't have to call you. I knew then that I had to resort to Plan B, which was to have them rape her all night long and leave her alive so that you would be able to see the damage . . . so you could break, free that anger, and allow Soo Jin to come out while you tried to find her rapists."

301

He shrugged with apathy. "And of course, I framed Jin Ae because she was the obvious suspect. If I had known that Tae Hyun's Cobras were scattered around Seoul, then I would've never shown my face at the alley to check up on those gang members. The plan got fucked up when you came later that morning to find your friend and became even more fucked up when Ace apparently spotted me." He leisurely canted his head to the side to stretch his neck. "I suppose it's for the best. I was getting tired of playing the lovesick puppy."

He elicited a sigh, lowering his hands and placing them on her hips.

Yoori wanted to throw up once he started to touch her, molest her.

"It's pretty amusing to see you attempt to come at me, as if you had the physical capabilities to fight me." His laughter ridiculed her. "You're no match for me, baby. The only reason why your head isn't ripped off by now is because I still have hope that you'll remember everything soon and that Soo Jin will come into play."

"You wanted . . ." Yoori started brokenly, not believing how cruel this person in front of her was. "You wanted me to regain my memories the entire time?"

"I didn't want you to in the beginning, when I thought for sure that it was going to be an easy task to pull you away from Tae Hyun." His voice grew angrier while he tightened his grip around her throat. His eyes became more menacing. "You fucking bitch. I hate losing anything and I hate it even more when I lose to Kwon Tae Hyun. It fucking killed me to see you with him when all I wanted to do was take you back for myself. I spoiled you rotten with affection, yet even with all the charm I threw at you, you never once faltered from him." Scorn poured into his voice. "You were so resilient, so in love with Tae Hyun that you didn't even give me the time of day. I didn't want you to remember in the beginning because I didn't want to deal with that stupid plan of yours." He shook his head. "But after it was clear that I'd be losing you for good if I didn't pull some other tricks out of my sleeve, I knew what I had to do. I had to bring Soo Jin back and what better way to do that than to piss Choi Yoori off and bring out that little killer instinct that you keep locked away?"

His disgusting words dispensed over her, but Yoori couldn't hear most of what he was saying. Her mind was only on Chae Young now. She still couldn't believe it.

"You had them rape her . . . one by one . . . while she begged for death . . . so you could get me back in the end? You ruined her life . . . just so Soo Jin would come back . . . just so you could reclaim your prized possession?"

It was when she peered into his emotionless eyes did Yoori grasp how wrong she had been. What a fool she had been. All these months, she felt sorry for him because she felt guilty that he had lost the one he loved. But as she stared at him, disgust heaved in her stomach. Lee Ji Hoon may think he loved Soo Jin, but he never truly did. He merely saw her as a possession and a trophy. What human being would send eleven gang members to rape an innocent girl for their own selfish needs? And why did he do that? So he could continue to play the part of the brokenhearted prince and steal her away from the only one who mattered to her? Just so he could resort to "Plan B" and provoke Soo Jin to come out of her?

"You bastard. You *fucking* bastard," she gritted out, repulsed that she was in the presence of someone so revolting. Yoori could not fathom how she allowed him to fool her for so long. "I should've known. I should've known you were a fucking bastard when we were on that roof. I should've known how morally fucked up you were when you spoke ill about Tae Hyun's father and continued to taunt Tae Hyun about what you did with his sister!"

"This is all your fault," Ji Hoon told her with conviction. "With any other stupid bitch, all I had to do was smile and they would eat up everything I say. All I had to do was speak and they would get on their knees and worship me like I walked on water." He glared at her. "But you . . . all you see is fucking Kwon Tae Hyun. I'm twice the man that bastard is and you can't even spare a fucking glance in my direction whenever he's around!"

Yoori shook as she thought about him and Tae Hyun. For so long, this world had tried to embed in her mind the difference between the two—that Ji Hoon was the brokenhearted Prince Charming while Tae Hyun was the sadistic monster who would sacrifice anything for his own benefit.

She saw it all clearly now.

She recalled all those moments where Ji Hoon played his part well, where he pretended to be heartbroken, like he was the innocent one in all of this. Tae Hyun was right. Ji Hoon was truly more ruthless than him. Instead of being the type of man that Tae Hyun was, Ji Hoon resorted to pretending to be weak, pretending to be human so that people in the Underworld would underestimate him. It was a genius plan because he had the element of surprise. When he finally showed his true colors, the ones deceived would never see it coming.

Ji Hoon was the best actor there was, and judging by the lack of regret in his eyes, he really didn't care about the well-being of Chae Young. He didn't care that he would've been "kinder" if he killed Chae Young instead of allowing eleven men, one after the other, to rape and torture her. He didn't even care about breaking Yoori. He didn't care about anyone but himself.

He was unlike Tae Hyun, who had to endure all the bullshit because he saw Ji Hoon's true colors. He had to endure Yoori being stupid and constantly giving Ji Hoon chances. He had to endure her listening to Ji Hoon's instigations and alienating herself from him. He had to endure being labeled as the "other guy." He had to endure taking care of her while Ji Hoon broke her soul apart. He had to endure so much, and it was all because of Ji Hoon.

It was all because of that fucking monster.

She replayed all those times where Ji Hoon spoke ill of Tae Hyun, and she lost it.

How dare he? How dare he compare himself to Tae Hyun? How dare he say he was twice the man that Tae Hyun was? How dare he even put his name and Tae Hyun's name in the same sentence?

"You disgusting pig!" she shouted at the top of her lungs, leaning down to grab a big alcohol bottle from the table beside her. She whirled it into him with brute force. "You'll never be half the man he is!"

Bam!

"Fuck!" Ji Hoon cried once the weight of the alcohol bottle broke over the side of his head.

He looked at her in scorn.

"You stupid bitch!" he snapped, slapping her face with the back of his hand.

"You're nothing compared to him!" Yoori screamed, fighting against his hold and slowly losing under his strength. Her cheek stung from the slap.

"Shut up!" he growled.

"Why do you think I can't even look at you when he's around?" she went on, shouting hysterically. "All this time, you've played the victim when I should've seen your true colors all along. But I was fucking blinded because of my stupid girl mentality that everything you do should be excused because you were in love with Soo Jin. I felt sorry for you because she was taken from you, but all along, you were never the victim you played. You're nothing but a sick bastard. A girl doesn't want you, and you go to such lengths as to having her friend raped so that you could continue to appear like Prince Charming and save her? You disgust me. You're fucked up in the head! You need help! Do you think Tae Hyun would ever resort to any of this? No, because he doesn't have to! Because he's better than you in every way! He's twice the man you are!"

"Shut the fuck up!"

"Everyone in this world knows how great he is. *That's* why he is so revered. If Soo Jin was here, do you think she would even look at you? You think your precious Queen wouldn't be infatuated with him?" Seeing the pain in his angry eyes, she continued to taunt him. "Soo Jin never loved you. If she did, do you think I'd even fall for Tae Hyun? You're a monster, Ji Hoon! Nothing but a disgusting monster!"

"You're one to talk," Ji Hoon sneered, grabbing her by the collar and literally lifting her up the wall. "You're the disgusting one who was ready to betray her own brother to become a gang leader herself. You were the one who killed thirty-four innocent people, including a mother and her twins."

He broke into a sadistic smile.

"We're one of a kind, baby," he continued mercilessly. "You and me, we're alike in every way. That was why this world loved us when we were together, because we were the epitome of what an Underworld couple should be. That's why they hate the relationship you have with Tae Hyun, because you make each other human while Soo Jin and I made one another Gods!"

"Shut up!"

Ji Hoon grinned at the pain that immersed her face. "You think your King is so great, but you'll rethink that when you're on the other side, when you're the one who is fighting him."

He laughed before finally adding something that stopped her cold.

"Does he even know that you killed his mother?"

The blood pumping in Yoori halted. "I didn't—"

"You killed her," Ji Hoon told her with much amusement, enlightening Yoori with her worst fear. He fed on her anguish. "She was drunk and miserable, yes, but you were the one who snuck into the Serpents' mansion. You were the one who bypassed all the security, and you were the one who pulled her into the bathroom and proceeded to kill her."

"Stop it! You're lying!" she shouted, but deep in her heart, she knew he wasn't.

"Broken bottles, baby," he told her proudly. "That was how they found her. She 'committed suicide' in the bathtub with the water running. She slit her wrists with the jagged edges of a broken alcohol bottle." He laughed. "And as I recall, killing people with broken bottles is *your* signature move."

Ji Hoon smirked at her stunned silence upon realizing how Tae Hyun's mother actually died—that it was Soo Jin who had murdered her all along.

"That's when I knew I had to have you. You were a fucking genius. You didn't take the credit for it. You allowed the family to think she committed suicide because you knew it would break them and fuck them up even more as a family. If you took credit, they would unite against you. If you allowed them to think she killed herself, they would disband and hate each other." His taunting smile broadened while his voice lowered in gravity. "How do you think your precious King will react when he finds out? Remember, Yoori . . . Kwon Tae Hyun hates me more than life itself because I was the one who killed his father. How do you think he'll feel about you when he finds out that it was you who killed his beloved mother? Do you think you'll see him as the perfect man then? Better yet, do you still think you'll be in love with him when you regain your memories?"

"I won't—"

"You will. I can see it in your eyes that the time is near." Hatred saturated his eyes. "I love Soo Jin, but I despise you, Yoori. I know that you're the one keeping Soo Jin locked in there so you can fuck around with Tae Hyun. But the one good thing out of all of this is that I can't wait for her to come out and trap you in your own body. Isn't that how it works, Yoori? You'll be powerless, and I'll love it because you know that Soo Jin is coming back to me. She won't give a damn about what I did to Chae Young and she'll come back to me because she belongs with me. Doesn't that kill you, Yoori? The fact that no matter what happens tonight, you'll eventually be mine again?"

"I'll never be yours!" Yoori shrieked, dreading the day she may cease to exist in this world, dreading the day she may possibly fall back into Ji Hoon's arms, and dreading the day Tae Hyun finds out the truth about his mother.

With tears of rage concealing her eyes, her migraine worsened. It was only when she started to shake uncontrollably did Yoori realized that she had been holding a jagged edge of the broken bottle the entire time.

Hope glittered in her path. She had to get away. She had to kill Ji Hoon, and she had to get away from here. She wasted no more time.

"Go to hell, you son of a bitch!"

She stabbed the jagged edge into his arm and used all the strength she had to pierce it as deep as she could. Then, she twisted it.

"Ahhhhh!" Ji Hoon roared when the glass buried itself into his arm.

When he released his hold on her, Yoori used this opportunity to sling the broken bottle across his face, intending to cut his skin apart. She was deterred when Ji Hoon raised his leg. The ruthless kick that was delivered to the side of her face caused Yoori to fly to the other end of the room.

She crashed into a clutter of barstools.

Yoori groaned as pain coursed through her. She blindly reached around and felt something cold underneath her fingers. Hope surged through her when she realized what it could be. She looked down and sure enough, there was her gold gun resting beside her.

In the background, Ji Hoon was still groaning. He clutched on to his arm, applying pressure to keep blood from pouring out of the deep wound.

Without fear, hesitation, or anymore doubt in her mind that he should be killed, Yoori seized her gold gun and aimed it at Ji Hoon.

His eyes bloomed at the sight of her gun.

She pulled the trigger.

Boom!

He tried to run, but he wasn't quick enough. Her first shot was a through and through.

"Ahhh!"

The bullet went into his arm, causing him to groan louder while rivulets of sweat formed on his forehead. His eyes blazed with knowledge that he wasn't just dealing with Yoori's fighting instincts; he was also dealing with the killer instincts of Soo Jin.

Satisfaction hummed in her chest, and Yoori's eyes became merciless. She wanted more. She wanted his blood and she wanted Ji Hoon to die on the floor beneath her feet. She pulled the trigger again and the hungry bullets flew out, exploding into the bar.

If Yoori were shooting at a normal gang member, the shots would have gone into her prey's head every time. Unfortunately, Ji Hoon was a skilled Underworld King. Though her shots were impressive, it didn't match his speed as he ran across the room, jumping on tables while sending chairs flying in her direction to distract Yoori as he ran straight for the back exit.

Undeterred, she stalked across the room and followed him.

Just as she was sure the last of her bullet would finally land in his head, Ji Hoon gave her one last venomous look that promised her she hadn't seen the last of him.

Then, he did the unthinkable . . .

He smiled.

It was a smile that sent chills up Yoori's spine.

His face was pleased that she was fighting him, that she was more than ready to kill him.

"I guess Soo Jin is more alive in you than the both of us could imagine, right, Yoori?" he groaned, blood secreting from his arms while the grin remained. He sighed in pleasure. "I'll relish the moment she comes back and shoots Kwon Tae Hyun down like this. What a great day that'll be."

Before Yoori could pull the final shot, she realized that she had run out of bullets. There was no time to reload because, just then, Ji Hoon jumped out of the back window, breaking through the glass while leaving a trail of blood behind him.

He was gone.

Yoori wanted to chase Ji Hoon down and kill him with her bare hands.

It was the groaning in the background that jolted her back to reality.

Oh no.

Horror struck her when she remembered that Kang Min had been buried underneath the shelf and was badly hurt.

She whirled around to help him.

"Kang Min!" Yoori called, sprinting to where he was. Her hands latched on to the shelf that hung above him. "Kang Min! I'm here! I'm here! I'll get you out soon! Hold on!"

Yoori lifted the enormous shelf with all the strength she had, nearly straining her muscles as she did so. It was heavy, but the power and adrenaline pumping through her was more than a match for the shelf. Groaning, Yoori dug her feet into the floor to help push against the shelf.

She could see Kang Min lying underneath, blood and glass pooling around his body.

Frantic with the need to get him to a hospital, Yoori groaned again and exerted one final push that did the job. The shelf collapsed onto an open space beside Kang Min with a loud, thundering crash.

Yoori placed a hand above his chest. She was thankful she could feel his heartbeat. Determined to get him help, Yoori grabbed Kang Min, sat him up, placed one arm over her shoulder, and used all the power left in her to carry him out.

"Boss . . ." Kang Min croaked out, his swollen and bloodied eyes trying to make her out. It was obvious to Yoori that he was fighting between being conscious and unconscious. In spite of his grave situation, his main concern was her. "Are you okay?"

"Yes, and you're going to be okay as well," she told him, wanting to tear up as she examined his assaulted state. It broke her heart to see him like this.

"Everything hurts . . ." he murmured, his face contorting in pain.

She struggled to walk out of the bar, holding him tight against her.

"I know," Yoori told him faintly, kicking down the entrance of the bar door. They struggled to walk into the cold winter darkness. "It won't hurt for long, Kang Min. I'll get you to the hospital soon. Just hold on, okay? Think of Hae Jin and hold on!"

Kang Min bobbed his head; his face grew more determined at the thought of his girlfriend.

It was only when a cold thrash of wind hit her did Yoori realize there was someone else breathing in their presence . . .

Sometimes in life, there are no ways to explain where we gather the strength in our deepest cores when it feels like the end is near. In the morning, Yoori woke up and gathered the last of her strength to live her life as happily as she could. Yet, there were also times in life where we realize that there is no more strength for us to gather because all the hope that we had in life had been vanquished.

For Yoori, all of her hope in life vanquished the moment she stepped outside with Kang Min and caught sight of someone who had more than enough power to turn her world upside down. He had more than enough power to mend her and more than enough power to break her.

Yoori's heart stopped beating at the sight of him.

Standing beside a black Jaguar car was Tae Hyun. His cold eyes were firmly solidified on her. There was no love in them. There was only hurt, disbelief, rage, and unfathomable pain.

It was then that she knew the end had come.
He heard.
Kwon Tae Hyun had heard everything.

"Remember the stories you've heard of all the legends that fell from grace."

24: The Silence of Paris

Before the changing of tides, there is always silence.

A long foreboding silence that chills the flow of blood, a prolonged silence that steals breaths, and an ominous silence that promises a flood unlike any other once the calm clears.

Such unbearable silence hovered like rain clouds over Yoori and Tae Hyun.

The ticking clock of life seemingly froze in its position while her eyes latched onto his. The cold night bit at her skin, yet it offered no distraction to Yoori, for the bigger chill she experienced was from Tae Hyun's stare. It was a damning moment for her.

There was no doubt in her mind that Tae Hyun had heard everything Ji Hoon said about Soo Jin killing his mother.

The stunned silence deriving from Tae Hyun wouldn't merit any other possibility than the fact that he came just in time to hear Ji Hoon announce that his mother's death was not a suicide, but a murder. He couldn't have come any moment before that because if so, he would've gone in and saved her immediately. No, Yoori thought in pained realization. By how he was acting, she could envision Tae Hyun driving past the limits of acceleration to get to her. She could envision him running out of the car, ready and willing to kill Ji Hoon once and for all—until he heard those unspeakable words.

She remembered Ji Hoon's smile before he ran out from the opposite side of the building, away from where Tae Hyun stood, and she now understood why Ji Hoon smiled.

He knew.

He knew all along that Tae Hyun had arrived. That was why he said all those things. He wanted to destroy Yoori, and what better way to destroy her than by ripping Tae Hyun away from her—the one strong anchor holding her to the soils of life?

Her stomach twisted in violent motions. She agonized over the fact that Ji Hoon had not only managed to betray her, but the disgusting bastard also managed to put an ax through the one good thing in her life. He wanted to tear her from Tae Hyun. If he couldn't do it by wooing her, then he would do it by spilling out Soo Jin's dirty secret.

Yoori withered where she stood, never hating being in her own skin more. She regretted it so much. She should've listened to Tae Hyun and stayed in the apartment, but she was stupid and reckless. Now both of them were paying for her careless mistake.

Tae Hyun.

Her aggrieved eyes searched his.

A million different emotions flickered in his dazed eyes. The most prominent of emotions were pain, anger, and disbelief.

The sight tore at Yoori's insides.

She had never seen Tae Hyun, with all the glory that surrounded him as the King of Serpents, so helpless. It pained her because she could feel the hurt emitting from him, as well as the anger coursing out of him. It was only when she felt the fury prevail over the hurt did Yoori's heart crack. There was no love in his eyes, not even a flicker. He was angry. He was so angry with her.

I'm sorry. I'm so sorry, Tae Hyun. I didn't know . . .

She parted her lips to speak. Her apprehensive silence was eclipsed by the sound of Kang Min's groans. Instantaneously, Yoori was brought to reality when she recalled that she was still holding on to Kang Min who was still in excruciating pain.

Snapping out of his stupor after hearing Kang Min's groans, the heat (and arguably hate) in Tae Hyun's eyes transformed into alarm when he finally processed the scene before him: Yoori carrying an injured Kang Min who was badly assaulted and needed to be hospitalized immediately.

Tae Hyun ran over to them without saying anything to her. He relieved Kang Min from Yoori's shoulder and lifted Kang Min's numb arm over his own shoulder. In a matter of seconds, Tae Hyun was beside his Jaguar and was already carefully stuffing Kang Min into the passenger seat.

They had no time to deal with their mess; they had more important life and death matters to tend to.

Though she received no invitation to enter Tae Hyun's car, a frazzled and worried Yoori didn't think twice about waiting for permission. She instinctively jumped into the backseat of the car to help watch Kang Min from the back.

The velocity of the Jaguar picked up in unmatchable speed. Within seconds, they were zooming past the blurs of the city lights.

Her eyes lingering on Tae Hyun, Yoori did well to keep Kang Min awake by speaking to him and asking him innocuous questions about Hae Jin. It was the only subject that brought life to Kang Min's tired eyes. While she spoke to him, she prayed for the fates to spare Kang Min's life. She prayed for Kang Min's life, and she prayed for Tae Hyun to just look at her, speak to her even if it were just to scream at her. She simply wanted him to acknowledge her. Being ignored by Tae Hyun never merited any good outcomes. Yoori feared his silence only equated to his contemplation about leaving her.

The thought tormented her.

Please . . . just talk to me, she begged in her mind, wanting some sort of confirmation that he would at least open himself to her instead of shutting her out.

The silent request fell on fate's deaf ears.

He did not speak to her.

He did not speak to her when the paramedics wheeled Kang Min into the emergency room. He did not acknowledge her when he used his connections to get Kang Min the best doctor in Seoul. He did not talk to her when Hae Jin, Jae Won, and Chae Young came rushing into the hospital (Hae Jin in tears while Jae Won and Chae Young were as pale as ghosts). He did not look at her as he took Jae Won to the side and explained to him everything that pertained to why Kang Min was hurt, and who was the one who orchestrated Chae Young's rape. He did not stand by her while Yoori and Chae Young comforted Hae Jin or while Jae Won brooded in anger, worrying dearly for his brother's life. The whole time, as the three of them refused to tell Hae Jin and Chae Young how Kang Min got hurt (in fear of Hae Jin acting rash or Chae Young being pulled into things that would take away from her recovery), Tae Hyun did not speak or deign to cast his gaze in Yoori's direction.

It was as if he was already ready to kick her out of his life and move on.

Momentary reprieve washed over Yoori when the doctor finally came out hours later and informed them that although Kang Min was badly hurt, his body was still resilient. As long as he rested in the hospital for several days and took it easy, he was going to be fine.

Sighs of relief swam into the air.

It didn't take long for Hae Jin, Jae Won, and Chae Young to rush into Kang Min's hospital room once he was able to have visitors. This act left Yoori and Tae Hyun alone with nothing but silence emitting from their clamped lips.

The hall was busy with hospital workers, yet the liveliness of the hall was nothing but faded background noise to Yoori. All that garnered her attention was Tae Hyun. His eyes were staring at an undetected area of the floor tiles, his mind clearly in a deep contemplation mode. He still wouldn't look at her.

Their time together in the morning, when they hung out and did normal, heartwarming couple activities, seemed like a lifetime ago. The warm memories only acted as salt to the wound that was elongating in Yoori's heart.

Though she didn't exactly know what to say to Tae Hyun (what could you really say when your boyfriend finds out that it was you who killed his mother?), Yoori was desperate enough to hear his voice that she was willing to say anything to have him talk to her again.

"Tae Hyun—"

The glare that was cast in her direction was what caused her breath to still in her constricted chest.

Yoori clamped her lips shut, taken aback by the emotions reveling in his eyes.

There was an indisputable potency of rage, betrayal, and hurt that materialized in the warm brown eyes that used to hold so much love and adoration for her. The way he looked at her cut her like scalding knives. His eyes said it all: he did not want to talk to her or hear her voice. The only thing he wanted was to get far away from her, and he did just that.

He turned on his heels and walked away, leaving a dejected Yoori to stare helplessly at his back. He turned the corner and disappeared out of sight.

Every part of Yoori's body screamed at her, shouted at her to chase after him. Her heart jumped in her chest as if willing her to follow him so they wouldn't lose him. Alas, the bigger part of her rationale knew that although it saddened her to have him treat her like this, she also understood that he had every right to be angry with her. He had every right to want to distance himself from her. How could she expect him to absorb the fact that in her past life, she was the one who murdered his mother? Someone he loved so much that he would've given anything to introduce Yoori to her?

Yoori weakly folded her arms across her chest to keep from crying. She succumbed to the weakening of her legs and allowed her back to hit the wall behind her. It went against the well-being of her desperate heart to let him walk away, but for Yoori, it was Tae Hyun's well-being that mattered more than hers. He needed time to himself; he needed time to take in all of this. All she could do was wait for him to come back to her and pray the time he had to himself would work in her favor instead of against her.

Yoori waited for him to come home that night. He didn't, and a part of her strength cracked. She waited the day after while visiting Kang Min. He still didn't come, and she felt her willpower grow fainter. She waited the week after when Kang Min, much to everyone's relief, was finally released from the hospital. Tae Hyun still didn't appear, and she felt her heart whimper in torture. Yoori waited and waited for two weeks, her abating soul hanging on by mere strings. She wasn't mentally strong to begin with, and the punishment she received from Tae Hyun was slowly pushing her over the edge of desperation. She was in the process of falling over the edge when the door to their bedroom finally clicked open.

Yoori lifted her head up and felt the world vibrate with colors and jump to life when she saw him.

"Hi," Yoori said briskly, standing up from the bed. She inattentively straightened her black silk blouse over her faded blue jeans. Even subconsciously, she wanted to look good for him. It had been two weeks since she had seen him, and she didn't want to appear unkempt.

She wore a timid smile on her face while conflicted emotions surged through her like a freight train. On one hand, she was miserable after all that had taken place in her life, but on the other hand, she couldn't feel more elated to finally see Tae Hyun standing before her. After two weeks of no contact, only hearing about how he was doing through the brothers, he was finally with her, and Yoori couldn't help but feel satisfied with his presence.

Her weary eyes scanned him greedily, soaking in the very image of the man who stole every inch of her once stubborn heart.

Tae Hyun was dressed in a tuxedo with a black bow tie, looking like the most gorgeous man she had ever laid eyes on. He looked like he owned the world. And as she recalled, that particular night was finally Ju Won's 65th birthday. If everything went according to plan, then Tae Hyun would undoubtedly own the world before the night was over.

Judging by the time, Yoori gathered that Tae Hyun was late. This fact alone was what sent shivers down her spine.

Her gaze reached his eyes. She did not miss the severity of his silent gaze on her.

There was a dangerous presence to him, one that Yoori had never encountered and one that pained her to encounter. They stood close, yet he was distant. There was love in her eyes, yet his eyes were indifferent, stagnant of emotions that she couldn't decipher. He was cold to her, and it hurt her beyond all measures. However, it didn't dissuade her from wanting to hold on to him. Despite all the obstacles that were in her path, she did not want to give up on the one amazing thing in her life. She did not want to give up Tae Hyun.

"Are you going to Ju Won's birthday right now?" she asked dimly, nervously playing with her fingers. She knew the answer, but all she cared about was getting him to talk to her. She missed his presence, his voice, his warmth, and him.

Fortunately for Yoori, Tae Hyun was willing to talk, but unfortunately for her, the conversation went straight into the topic that she was afraid of.

"That night," he began steadily, showing no emotions in his dark eyes. His tone was business-like, detached. "When I was with you in the bathtub, you held on to me and asked me not to fault you for the things Soo Jin did in the past. You knew then that she killed my mother, didn't you?"

The foundation of the little strength she stood on fractured under his question. How he asked this and how he looked at her, every part of her knew then that this was going to be the start of the worst conversation she would ever have in her life.

Swallowing uncomfortably, refusing to allow any tears to form in her eyes, Yoori stared at his impassive eyes and said, "I . . . I had a suspicion that she did, but I didn't know for sure until Ji Hoon told—"

"Why didn't you say anything to me?" he cut her off, not even remotely interested in what her excuse was. It was evident he was reminded of how he found out this information when she mentioned Ji Hoon's name; this recollection only made him angrier. "For the days that followed," he persisted scornfully, hints of fire blazing in his eyes, "all those times where I stayed by your side, held on to you, embraced you, and took care of you . . . you didn't deign it was necessary to let me know that there was a possibility that Soo Jin had something to do with my mother's death?"

"I wanted to tell you two weeks ago," Yoori responded in a quiet voice, wilting like a dying rose under the wrath of the unforgiving sun. Little by little, her hope that he would understand her quandary faded. She had never felt so small and vulnerable when she stood next to him. But now, as he towered over her, his strong body emanating so much power and control, she truly felt like she was in the presence of a God, not her silly and teasing boyfriend who gave her piggyback rides in the park and berated her for making a cute fat kid cry.

"When we were walking in the street, I wanted to tell you after you mentioned your parents and how you would've loved to introduce me to them . . . I wanted to tell you then . . ."

"But you didn't," he finished for her. "You didn't tell me anything. Instead, you waited it out until I found out everything from the one bastard I hate the most. I was at my wit's end, worried for my girlfriend's safety, and before I could even run into the bar, I had to *casually* find out that the girl who I was willing to give up my life for . . . was actually the one who took my mother's life?"

The control on her strength faded when he broke her with this.

"I'm sorry . . ." Yoori apologized sorrowfully, knowing that Tae Hyun had every right in the world to be angry with her. He had every right in the world to be tired of her and hate her.

"I'm sorry, I'm so sorry. I wish I listened to you. I wish I stayed in the apartment. I wish it was me who told you instead of that heartless bastard." Her voice suppressed the tears that were fighting to get past the lump in her

315

throat. "I didn't know how to tell you, Tae Hyun. How was I supposed to tell you something like this? How was I supposed to gather up the courage to tell you that I think I had something to do with your mother's death?" She inhaled painfully. "I was afraid . . . I was afraid of losing you."

There was no empathy in his eyes for her dilemma, and he made no effort to assure her that she wasn't going to lose him. It appeared that over the course of the last two weeks, Tae Hyun had already concluded that there wasn't anything Yoori could say to excuse her from her faults—or Soo Jin's faults. This fact alone chafed like coals to her skin. She couldn't help but take a step forward, her desolate eyes imploring his cold ones for a sense of warmness. He wasn't looking at her like she was Yoori; he was looking at her like she was Soo Jin, and this realization was the breaking point for her.

"You told me once that Soo Jin and I are completely different people and that you don't see us as the same person, that what she did has no reflection on me . . ." She gazed at him despairingly, wondering how it was possible that the eyes that used to gaze at her with so much love could be so cold and hateful. "Do you not remember saying that to me?"

Tae Hyun shook his head to himself, smirking but never once allowing any warmth to seep into his eyes.

"I've been telling myself that for the past two weeks," he told her, his handsome face morphing into a look of hurt. "Yet the memory of my mother, lying dead in the bathtub overshadows any justification I could make."

He eyed her, erasing the once pained expression on his face with resolution.

"I can't be with you," he went on uncaringly, leaving Yoori to press her hands into her stomach to mitigate the pain that was beginning to unravel in the core of her gut. Like cancer, the pain was spreading everywhere . . .

"I can't be with the one who took part in helping to destroy my family, and I can't be with the one who killed my mother." His face was now paled with unreadable emotions. "I owe my parents—*my mother*—too much to put my needs above my respect and love for her. The simple fact that I'm doing what I'm about to do is already spitting on her grave. I can't do more than that."

Yoori's lips trembled while puzzlement filled her gaze. "Do what?" What was he about to do?

And at last, a speck of emotion flickered in Tae Hyun's eyes. "I kicked Kang Min and Jae Won out of the gang."

Her eyes widened with incredulity. "What?"

"They're out of the gang," he repeated simply. There were finally pained emotions in his eyes and she knew that the emotions he felt weren't due to kicking the brothers out of his gang.

"Why?"

Tae Hyun stared at her poignantly. ". . . You will leave the country tonight."

His words acted as a sledgehammer that pummeled every nerve in her body into smithereens. Subconsciously, a part of her knew it would come to this, but that didn't mean it was easier to listen to it. It didn't mean it was easier to fight through the unrelenting need to fall to her knees in agony and experience it.

Her heart clenched while he continued to speak. Yoori tried to shut him out, but she heard and felt everything. She heard him and she felt every part of her body shatter upon hearing him speak about her leaving for good.

"I've arranged everything for you . . . all three of you. I've transferred all the money you'll ever need into your accounts. I've placed calls to my contacts all over the world as a favor for them to watch over you. They can't protect you, but they'll do what they can for you so you have to be smart about where you go and where you are seen."

Yoori shook her head, unable to contain the cancer-like flood ravaging within her. "Tae Hyun, don't do this—"

"By the time I return from Ju Won's party, I expect every shred of your existence in my life to be gone," he persisted, ignoring her plea. "Never come back to Korea, and wherever you choose to go, if you hear that I'm near, then you'll be smart to keep out of my sight. Because the next time I see you, I'm bypassing the courtesies and I'll take care of you as I should take care of you."

Yoori knew what he meant by that and despite all the coldness and hatred he was shooting her way, she was certain he would never be capable of even laying a finger on her. It was clear to her what he was trying to do.

"Could you really kill me?"

There was skepticism in her voice. It was a skepticism that Tae Hyun caught and one that pissed him off.

"I've killed my own brother for raping my baby sister," he told her coldly, his eyes overflowing with hostility. "What makes you think I won't kill you for killing my mother? What makes you think that you're worth anything to me that I won't pump bullets into your skull?"

"Why are you having me leave the country then? Why not kill me now?"

His posture stiffened at her question. "I once promised to protect you with all that I had." There was regret in his voice. "This is the first time I'm eating my own words, and I'm doing what I can for you. Take advantage of this moment and get out of my sight before I change my mind."

Breathing past the aches in her chest, Yoori approached him, her eyes never straying from his. He didn't move from where he stood, but she could feel his body go rigid in her near presence. It was as though he was bunching his muscles to keep from reaching out to her, perhaps to hold her in his arms like he always did. She ignored this hopeful thought and kept approaching him.

When she reached him, Yoori felt the warmth radiate from his impassive and hard body. Gathering her breath, she reached behind him, lifted his suit up, and pulled out one of his silver guns. The dangerous coldness of the weapon frosted her skin.

"Kill me now," she urged, placing the gun in the palm of his hand. She gazed up at him challengingly, calling out his bluff. "Finish it now and make it easier for the both of us."

"You think I wouldn't?"

With lightning reflexes, Tae Hyun grabbed her shoulder and pushed her up against the wall, holding the barrel of the gun underneath her chin. His face contorted with rage that she was stupid enough to even dare him to kill her.

"You think you have me in the palm of your hand, don't you? That I could never hurt you because you mean something to me?" He smirked and then laughed cynically to himself. "Guys make idiotic girls believe that, Choi Yoori. When they want to fuck you senseless, they make you believe that so they could get into your pants. I'm no different from Lee Ji Hoon; I'm as much of a ruthless bastard as he is. You were stupid enough to believe he was a good person, so what makes you think you won't make the same mistake with me?" His words stabbed her like knives. "What makes you think that none of this is an act and that I'm not lying to you like I lied to you the last time, when I used you because of your 'resemblance' to Soo Jin? What makes you think I'm not making a fool out of you again?"

Seeing the sting that enveloped her eyes at the reminder of how he broke her the first time around, Tae Hyun went on, pushing the gun tighter against her chin to show her how serious he was being. Though the force of his hold on her was strong, she could feel Tae Hyun straining his muscles and using all the willpower he had to not use his full strength on her. Despite the threatening tone in his voice, she could still sense his unwillingness to hurt her. She could still sense his instincts to protect her.

"Don't push me," he growled. Rage tormented his irises while he stared down into her brown eyes. "You have no idea of the things I'm capable of. I'm letting you go now, and if you're smart, you'll stay away from this world, and you'll stay away from me."

Yoori was silent while she searched his eyes with hers. "This is all I'm worth to you?"

"You're worth *nothing* to me," he corrected tightly, his body for some reasoning stiffening, as if in disagreement with what he said. "You've been nothing but a distraction for me, but I'm seeing things clearer now. The only thing that matters is my throne in the Underworld. Fairytale endings with a stupid, naive girl didn't mean anything and will never mean anything to me."

"Prove it," she challenged, unfazed by his words. Yoori pressed her chin onto the barrel of the gun underneath her. She didn't believe a single word he said. "Show me how worthless I am to you."

Confliction marred his eyes while the muscles in his jaw bunched up with tension. His breathing grew heavier, yet he didn't allow any outward expressions to betray how he felt.

"Close your eyes," he finally said. "Close your eyes now, and I'll take care of it."

Yoori did as she was told and closed her eyes.

The last sight of Tae Hyun's cold eyes became imprinted in her mind.

Soon, silence cascaded over them.

Yoori felt him press the gun closer against her skin. The coldness of the weapon stole any warmth within her, and she could hear his finger trailing over the trigger, as if counting down the seconds to finally shoot her.

Then, she heard him curse at himself for what he was about to do.

In a swift instant, the coldness that canvassed over her was replaced with warmth, blissful warmth that rocked every cell in her body. A bang occurred, but it wasn't from the gun. It came from an impulsive Tae Hyun who relinquished his control and finally allowed his emotions to run free as his lips nipped hers with indisputable love.

He pulled her tight against him, holding her with such care that Yoori knew he only threatened to kill her so that she would leave him. Tae Hyun was angry, there was no denying that. He was angry at Soo Jin, but he was angrier at himself for not being able to hate Yoori. She had broken him and she knew that. He may have wanted to hate her, but that didn't mean he truly did.

In a fluid motion, his strong hands framed her jaw and then feathered over her cheeks. Yearning filled him and enraptured her. His caresses soothed her while his sensuous lips pressed against hers, mending all the pain she felt while white-hot flames riddled over her body.

They kissed like lovers once separated; they kissed like lovers about to be separated.

It was so heavenly that she wanted to cry. Breathing felt like a waste of time as she nipped his delicious lips with hers, seeking to make their moment last forever.

Pain became intermingled with bliss while they kissed. If she ever had any doubts in her mind about how much he loved her, then it was all squashed by the ecstasy he scattered over her in his kiss. A man wouldn't kiss the way Tae Hyun kissed her unless he was in love. Yoori knew, despite how he tried to fight it, that Tae Hyun was unquestionably in love with her, just as she was with him.

"God, this wasn't supposed to happen."

Yoori could've sworn she heard Tae Hyun say this, but the knowledge of whether he voiced this or not was lost when he picked her up and threw her onto the soft bed. His desperate lips continued to seek her aching ones. He leaned on his elbows while she wrapped her arms around his neck, pulling him down to her. Even under the confines of the suit, she could still feel his hard muscles ripple underneath the expensive fabric, every nerve of his enticing body bunching in approval of her touch.

A multitude of emotions stampeded over her, yet the forerunners were the love and pain she felt while he kissed her. There was so much hopelessness and ardor in his kiss that it broke her. In that moment, she could feel his frustration, his unsounded desperation, and worse of all—his heartache.

Tae Hyun did not kiss her like she was worth nothing to him; he kissed her like she was worth everything to him. He kissed her like a man who was about to lose everything.

Unable to maintain her composure, Yoori finally permitted her emotions to wash out with his. She desperately kissed him and held on to him. She didn't allow tears to fall, yet inwardly, she was crying like there was no tomorrow.

"I'm sorry," Yoori uttered through her misery. She opened her eyes. "I'm so sorry about what she did—what I did."

He moved his lips to her collarbone, traced kisses up the column of her neck, and then kissed the soft skin of her chin, as if apologizing for even daring to place a gun there.

Tae Hyun did not say anything while she spoke, but she could feel the torture he felt while her words came over him. She could feel the lingering ache in his fading kisses, yet he continued to hold her close to him. It was as though he was savoring the sensation of loving her body one last time.

"Anyone else can punish me for what Soo Jin did, but please don't punish me. Please don't punish me for things I can't control. Please don't leave me over this," she begged breathlessly, knowing what he was doing while he kissed her like a man possessed.

He was letting her go.

He was using this moment as the last one to remember her by and he was letting her go.

It was a kiss between fire and water, one that exploded with passion and one that would fade into nothing but heartache once the flames died out.

"Please," she begged, unable to fathom going through the rest of her days without her partner-in-crime by her side. Who was she going to bicker with? Who was she going to laugh with? Who would she joke around and wear handcuffs with? Who else would be there and talk to her from night until midmorning? Who else would hold her in his arms and make her feel like it was the safest place in the world to be? Who else would steal her heart if he already had every inch of it?

"Please, Snob," she whispered in a broken voice, never wanting to lose the one person who made her love her life so much. "Please don't do this to us."

At her plea, Tae Hyun stopped kissing her.

He no longer allowed himself to be lost in the moment.

She felt him exhale excruciatingly after hearing her use his nickname. Agonized and torn with himself, Tae Hyun refused to make eye contact with her while he nuzzled his cheek against the side of her neck like a brokenhearted wolf.

His breath lingered on her skin.

Tae Hyun did not speak, but she could hear his words and feel his pain by the way he breathed. He did not want to kill her, nor did he have the heart to hurt her. Yet, what saddened her was the fact that despite all of this, despite his feelings for her and regardless of how much pain he felt, he was still leaving her.

Then, what killed her more was the fact that when he pressed his cheek against her neck, she could feel a single teardrop transfer over from his skin to hers. Yoori began to shake. Every nerve in her body screamed out in tears at the thought of him, the revered King of the Underworld, the chosen God of this ruthless society, finally becoming human for her.

She lost it as well.

Tae Hyun would only cry if he lost someone he loved. She imagined he had only cried three times in his life—once for his father's death, once for his mother's death, and once for his brother's death. And now, the fourth time was for her; because even after becoming human for her, he had to become a God again and give her up.

Yoori lost it and allowed her tears to run free. She cried for herself, she cried for him, she cried for them, and she cried for everything they stood to lose because they fell for each other. She cried because it was evident he had made his decision.

". . . Find someone else, Yoori," he said long moments later, confirming her worst fears. He lifted himself up while finally staring into her eyes. "Go somewhere where no one knows you, find a man who has no connections to the Underworld, be with him, marry him, have a family with him, and lead the life you were always meant to lead—a long, safe . . . and happy one."

The ache in his voice from knowing that he couldn't be this man for her tortured Yoori.

"I don't want anyone else," she argued desperately, feeling like he was ripping her heart from her chest. "I want you. I only want you."

Tae Hyun did not say anything when she voiced this. He merely stared at her, a million different emotions plaguing his features. There was unbridled grief in his gaze; it was one that mirrored every inch of hers. The only difference was that there were no remnants of tears in his eyes. He had kissed her to hide his pain; he had kissed her until his own tears dried before he allowed his wounded gaze to meet hers.

Then slowly, reluctantly, he brought a hand to her cheek and caressed it with his fingers, relishing in the feel of her warm skin before the end.

"Kang Min and Jae Won are waiting for you beside the elevator," Tae Hun finally said, swallowing tightly while pulling his hand from the warmth of her cheek.

"No! Don't do this!" Yoori cried, getting up with him while trying to grab his arm. She couldn't let him leave. Oh God, how could she let him leave like this?

"Once you leave, never contact me again," he continued, closing his eyes in brief pain while whipping his arm away from her grasp. "We're done."

He was heading for the door when she broke apart and finally shouted out, "You told me that it would be worth it!"

Tae Hyun paused in his position at her scream.

His back was faced toward her, and it was clear he was listening to every word.

Yoori went on, never feeling more broken as she stood beside the bed, hot tears embellishing her eyes.

"I told you I didn't want to be with you because I knew it wasn't going to be easy, but you told me it would be worth it!"

Pain rippled through her while she shook and shook. This wasn't how it was supposed to end. They were supposed to be stronger than this. They were supposed to fight through this. They were supposed to make it through this.

"How could you do this now? How could you give up on us after all that you promised me?"

"I was a fool then," Tae Hyun answered her, his voice softer and more miserable than she had ever heard it. "I should've never told you that I would never fault you for the things Soo Jin did when I didn't know that my own mother was murdered by her. I should've never promised you the world when I'm bound by the laws of this world—by the laws of my gang—to avenge my family if anyone dares to kill them. I should've never told you that it would be worth it when I didn't know how impossible it was going to be."

He lowered his head and stared at the ground, misery enveloping the powerful aura that continued to radiate from him.

"No matter how much I try to tell myself that you and Soo Jin are completely separate entities, I know deep down that you're one in the same.

This couldn't have been more obvious with how you acted at the warehouse, when you fought Jin Ae. This couldn't have been more obvious when we came back to the apartment and you began to stare at me like I was an obstacle in your way, like I was your enemy." He took in an excruciating breath. "She's part of you, just as you're a part of her. And the simple fact is, she killed my mother. I'll never forget that; I'll never forgive that. It doesn't matter how much I want you. It'll never matter because in the end . . . I'll never love Soo Jin."

Yoori's soul ripped apart while her world shattered at the enormity of his last words.

"I'll never love Soo Jin."

It repeated in her mind and slashed at all the remaining hope in her already weak body.

Every nerve, cell, and atom in her body felt the pain and reality from his words. The mind-numbing pain was released and Yoori began to drown within it.

In the past, she had always tried to separate herself from Soo Jin. Yet after hearing his words, it was clear now how impossible that task was. No matter how much she hated her past self, the ultimate truth was that she was still Soo Jin in every possible way.

It was impossible; it was impossible for them to be together now and she realized that.

How could she continue to fight it when her past self was the one who hurt him first? How could she fight it when her past self was the one who murdered his mother and took part in destroying his family? How could she force him to stay with her when he didn't want to be near Soo Jin?

It was the one obstacle they couldn't overcome.

Soo Jin.

They could never overcome Soo Jin.

With one lingering stare on her, as if to catalog the memory of her in his mind, Tae Hyun inhaled deeply, relinquishing all the emotions he showed her in this room while reverting his expression back to the emotionless visage he walked in with.

He had a party to attend, a world to rule over, and a future to save.

He had no more time to be distracted with her.

"Make it easier for us," he said to her with finality, pain displaying one last time in his eyes before he turned away from her. "Just leave and don't come back."

Helpless and destroyed, Yoori watched in silence as he stalked into the hallway, treaded into the living room, and then left the apartment without another word to her.

They were done.

They were *done*.

It was only after she heard the door click close did Yoori renounce the last of her strength and collapsed to the ground, finally allowing her violent sobs to tear from her chest. She shook and covered her face with her quivering hands, finding it harder and harder to breathe.

He wasn't coming back; he was never coming back.

"Please stop crying," Yoori brokenly whispered to herself. "Please stop crying,"

The tears refused to stop.

If she thought she went through hell before when he left her the first time, then she didn't know what hell was because the agonizing throbbing that ripped through her was one that stole every breath from her lungs. Yoori had to struggle to breathe through her heart-wrenching sobs.

Oh God, this can't be happening, she thought to herself, praying that all of this was merely a nightmare.

Except she was miserably aware that it wasn't.

The pain . . . the mind-numbing pain was too real and too unbearable to be a dream.

Make it easier for him, a shattered voice whispered in her mind. *Stop distracting him. All he has left is his Underworld. Just leave and let him find someone else who would give him the life you could never give him. You never listen to him . . . well, listen to him now and just leave . . .*

Though dazed with heartache, Yoori listened to her own rationale.

She had never listened to him, but she would listen to him now. Yoori would leave him alone; she would take Soo Jin far away from him. It was the least she could do for him.

Using all the strength she had, Yoori crawled up. She ignored the potent pain engulfing her insides and ran to the closet. Grabbing all that belonged to her, she threw clothes after clothes into an opened luggage while tear after tear continued to shed from her eyes.

Yoori only stopped crying after she threw the last of her clothes into the luggage and happened across a familiar article of clothing in the closet.

Tae Hyun's black hoodie stood in her line of vision.

Yoori held her breath as she pulled the hoodie off the hanger. Her aching heart lifted marginally. Yoori cradled the garment close to her chest like she had found a hidden treasure. He would never miss this, she told herself while she hugged the hoodie, remembering the scent of his cologne and how he was always the one who kept her warm. She had to keep a memory of him, a memory of their good times while she tried to live past the misery that awaited her.

With the hoodie held against her chest, she scanned the room one last time. Yoori tried to ignore the anguished realization that she was no longer welcomed in the room that had come to belong to her as well. She placed that pain aside and rummaged through all the drawers to make sure she had everything. Yoori wanted to do what Tae Hyun asked of her. She wanted to get rid of every shred of her existence before he came back.

After finding some things in the drawers, Yoori, who was having a hard time seeing through the tears blurring her vision, was ready to pack up and leave when she mindlessly opened the drawer to the desk and saw two particular items stare up at her.

It was the jade knife and the silver heart necklace that belonged to Soo Jin.

Chills formed on her skin while Yoori stared back at the innocuous, yet mocking items. Items that meant nothing to her, but meant everything to Soo Jin.

Her eyes zeroed in on the necklace.

Yoori closed her fingers around it and held up the silver chain. Anger undulated within her, and she glared at the heart pendant.

The engraving taunted her eyes: "To my daughter, the best are never distracted."

Disgust heaved inside her while Yoori's eyes became consumed with hate. She was being put through hell, she couldn't be with the man she loved, and she couldn't lead a normal life because of her . . . because of An Soo Jin and the mistakes she made in her past.

And Soo Jin justified her actions with this fucking engraving.

Rage engulfed Yoori.

That fucking monster justified killing Tae Hyun's mother, she justified killing innocent people, and she justified ruining Yoori's life with this fucking necklace.

Shaking, she screamed in anger and suddenly flung the necklace across the room.

Crack!

The pendant slammed into the wall with unforgiving force and broke apart, falling down to the tiles like broken wings. Yoori should've felt relief to see Soo Jin's treasured keepsake break so easily, but no such relief befell her as she stared at the two broken pieces of the pendant.

One half was broken with a hollow space in the center while the other half had something sticking out of it.

It had something that looked like . . . a USB stick.

Yoori's eyes enlarged at the sight. She walked over to it and picked it up, not believing her eyes. All along, the necklace had hidden a USB stick.

She quickly examined it and gasped in her mind when she realized the USB stick contained information that could answer all her questions. Everything she had ever wondered about Soo Jin, it could all be answered in this very USB stick. Her pulse raced frantically. She had no more time to waste.

In a flash, Yoori ran over to Tae Hyun's desk, pulled out his laptop, and stuck the USB stick into the portal of the laptop. Still holding Tae Hyun's hoodie to her chest, Yoori's heart drummed feverishly while she waited for the folder in the USB stick to load.

The world breathed in quiet anticipation when the folder finally popped up, revealing a single icon that marked the file as a video file.

Mindlessly and almost brokenly, Yoori moved the mouse over to the icon and clicked on it. She was too curious and too unprepared for what appeared on the screen.

"Oh God . . ."

A gasp escaped her lips when the media player opened up, revealing a still shot of someone who looked deathly familiar to her.

It was Soo Jin.

The video was a self-recording of An Soo Jin.

Shaking with bewilderment, not even realizing what she was doing, Yoori clicked the play icon and felt her world tilt on its axis when the voice and live image of her alter ego, the infamous Queen of the Underworld, came to life before her.

"The best are never distracted . . ." An Soo Jin whispered, sending fear up Yoori's spine. The acceleration of her weak heart ran rampant at the sight of herself—her past self.

After so long, she finally got to meet Soo Jin. She finally got to meet the one who was singlehandedly responsible for the current wretchedness that befell her life.

Soo Jin was sitting across the camera with a white wall behind her. She wore a sleeveless brown silk blouse that complimented her porcelain skin. With her long beautiful curls gathered to one side of her shoulder, Soo Jin couldn't have encompassed more beauty or power to Yoori. There was an air of wonder to Soo Jin.

Even under the restrictions of a video recording, Soo Jin still radiated power, knowledge, and beauty. They were the same person, yet outwardly, Yoori knew that because of all the power and grace Soo Jin emanated, Soo Jin was much more beautiful than her. There was such confidence, such strength, and such ability to control her emotions that even under a video file, Soo Jin overpowered her in many ways.

"A face of an angel and the morals of the Devil."

These words replayed in her mind while Yoori stared unblinkingly at the laptop screen, still not believing that after so long, she was finally face to face with the one who left such a mark in the Underworld, and left such a mark on her life.

So, this was the girl who held the Underworld in the palm of her hand. This was the girl who yielded as much power as Tae Hyun over a society that only revered the best. This was the girl who killed Tae Hyun's mother and destroyed Yoori's relationship with him.

"If you're watching this right now, then it must mean that you're broken again—that you're afraid of doing what has to be done," Soo Jin continued, her pale face emitting a reserved pain that Yoori couldn't decipher the cause from. The video was grainy, not very clear as the lighting was limited, but Yoori could make out how tired Soo Jin was when she recorded this video.

Soo Jin went on, staring into the camera as if staring into Yoori's soul.

"But I'll remind you," Soo Jin assured, her cold eyes swarming with resolution.

It was then that Yoori knew why Soo Jin made this video. Soo Jin didn't make this video specifically anticipating getting amnesia; she made this video to remind herself why she had to be a God in the face of human weaknesses. She made it to remind herself why she had to be ruthless in the face of morals and fear.

Yoori's assumptions were confirmed as Soo Jin pressed on, anger teeming in her deadly eyes. "I'll remind you of everything that led to this moment and I'll remind you why you can no longer be broken, why we have to finish what we started. I'll remind you why we can't be human, why you were always meant to be a God—"

"Oh God . . ."

Unable to listen, Yoori clicked "Pause," freezing Soo Jin and the knowledge she held.

Yoori covered her mouth in dreadfulness.

Silence prevailed over her.

She stared into Soo Jin's eyes—her own eyes—like it was an ocean. An ocean of knowledge meant for her to drown in.

This was it.

Fear coursed through Yoori.

She knew, while her stomach coiled like a hungry snake, that listening to the finalities of this video would be her trigger. She could feel it in her tormented soul that listening to Soo Jin's words would be the thing that would finish her—kill her. Yoori knew with all her instincts that she should turn off the laptop, rip the USB stick out, and flush it down the toilet to keep the demons from consuming her. She was aware that this was the thing to destroy if she wanted to keep Soo Jin's memory from overpowering her.

Yoori wanted to do that, but as she felt the weight of Tae Hyun's hoodie in her grasp, she remembered all the pain she was going through.

The heartache came back, the sobs that filled her chest came back, and the dark future ahead of her came back to her mind.

What was the point of fighting to be Yoori . . . if there was no more strength left within her? What was the point of being Yoori if she couldn't withstand the guilt? What was the point of being Yoori if she no longer wanted to live through all the guilt of Soo Jin's past and live through the knowledge that she could never be with the man she loved? What was the point of fighting . . . when she was never meant to exist in the first place?

Yoori was no longer strong enough for this world.

This world was never meant for her. It was always meant for Soo Jin and it was only obvious now, with how broken Yoori had become, that there was no more hope for her.

She had finally fallen over the edge and nothing but a vortex of misery awaited her. Nothing but agony awaited her weakened soul. Nothing but pain awaited her, unless she allowed An Soo Jin to quell her pain.

Yoori thought of Tae Hyun, remembered his confliction with wanting to save her, and remembered his confliction with wanting to kill Soo Jin to avenge his mother.

She wanted to help give him that.

Tae Hyun would never be able to kill her because he loved her, but if she were no longer here, if she were no longer Yoori, then he could kill Soo Jin and get the justice he so rightfully deserved for his mother. That way, she would be put out of her misery, Soo Jin would finally get the fate she deserved, and Tae Hyun could move on. He could get rid of Soo Jin and it would be as if she died three years ago—when she was supposed to.

Yoori nodded inwardly, never more afraid to end her life until this very moment, when she realized *she* was the one pushing herself over the edge.

Biting her quivering lips, she lifted up Tae Hyun's hoodie and embraced it, pretending to herself that she was embracing Tae Hyun for the last time. Yoori buried her face into the fabric and allowed her tears to drip into it. God, she was going to miss him.

"I'm sorry . . . I'm sorry that you had to meet me," she sobbed through her tears, hating herself for causing him so much pain. The agony she felt was excruciating. "I'll make it easier for us . . . I'll leave."

The last of her tears dripped onto the black hoodie while she finally lifted her face from the garment and clicked "Play," thereby unleashing the Pandora's Box.

Silence came for her.

An Soo Jin spoke . . . The secrets of her past became unveiled, and the changing of tides occurred. The world around Yoori darkened as An Soo Jin's memories came over her, took over her, and drowned the last of her existence on earth.

Little by little, the tears dried up, the pain became erased, and all that was left were the memories of what happened in her past. All that was left was a world reverted to three years prior.

All that was left was the end for Choi Yoori . . . and the beginning for An Soo Jin.

"If you go against our bylaws..."

25: An Soo Jin

Three Years Prior . . .

"Kneel."

Much like the wind that coursed through the veil of the night, the command was simple and melodic. There was no threatening force behind the soft voice, no malice. Yet, because it was delivered by an entity who struck unparalleled fear into the hearts of men, the simple request moved mountains and within moments, the sound of surrendering knees hitting the damp grass resounded into the air.

Standing atop the highest balcony that oversaw the backyard of the luxurious Scorpions' estate she grew up in, the young woman smiled in delight at the scene before her.

She was surrounded by her two dozen Scorpions, men and women alike in their twenties, all of whom she grew up with and personally trained to become the outstanding and feared soldiers they are today. All were standing on the surrounding balconies that made up a vast circle, barricading the massive lawn like an arena for gladiators. Some sat comfortably on the edge of the white railings, others pressed their backs against the wall, while the rest simply stood with their arms crossed. Despite their differing vantage points, all eyes were trained on the scene below them.

Their amused expressions mirrored that of their boss's—the very boss who defied boundaries and managed to become the most revered woman in their elite society.

The Queen of the Underworld.

It was an epithet that was instilled into the blood of An Soo Jin on the night of her birth.

A descendent from the prestigious bloodline of a powerful South Korean crime family from her father's side, she was also a descendant of the renowned Royal bloodline of the Japanese Underworld from her mother's side. Soo Jin, much like her older brother, was meant for greatness the moment she inhaled her first breath.

Her mother's death shortly after her birth marked the beginning of Soo Jin's stringent, unforgiving, and ultimately historic upbringing.

Though her father loved her deeply, he was also a prideful man who wanted the best for his children. While his son, An Young Jae, trained with the best of the Japanese Underworld to become the heir to the Scorpions' throne, the former King of Scorpions also made sure his daughter received esteemed training that would catapult her status in a society dominated by men. Most Underworld fathers encouraged their daughters to be trained to be a part of the 1st or 2nd layer of the Underworld pyramid, but Soo Jin's father was an exception. He believed that his daughter was meant for something more and he did everything in his power to have that come to fruition.

Having been very close to the highly respected Advisor, Seo Ju Won, her father arranged for his young daughter to be trained by the three most powerful Advisors of the 2nd layer. Though she had one of the severest upbringings a child could ever imagine having—especially for a young girl trying to prove herself in a male-dominated world—she couldn't have been more thankful for her father's insistence that she trained with the best.

She "sold" her soul to the Devil shortly after she reached the age of ten and everything was history from then on.

An Soo Jin's name became synonymous with reverence even before she made her official debut in the Underworld. Whispers of a second-born heir being trained by all three Advisors ran rampant in the Underworld and when she finally made her much awaited appearance in this powerful society, her name became legendary. The skilled, cunning, and powerful Queen indisputably became the pride of the Scorpions, the pride of the elder Advisors, and the pride of the Underworld, who welcomed her with open arms. The growth of her power and reverence had only elevated since and Soo Jin couldn't have felt more pride with her station in life. She was a Queen amongst Kings, a God amongst Royals.

Closing her eyes to enjoy the fresh air that curled around them, Soo Jin instinctively pressed her small body against the chest of her boyfriend of two years, Lee Ji Hoon. He was also watching the scene before them with an entertained expression.

Soo Jin wore a pubescent, white, sleeveless dress that swam over her perfect body and ended just below her thighs. Behind her, Ji Hoon wore a crisp white shirt with a black tie and black pants. The rest of her Scorpions wore black ensembles that allowed them to blend in with the shadows of the night.

In this dark picture, she was the epitome of an angel; it was the malevolent spark in her cruel eyes that made her look like the Devil.

An amused smirk lined her lips while her brown eyes stared down at the thirty kneeling men whose faces had been beaten to a pulp. Blood stained their facial features, streaked onto their skin, blinded their eyes, tattooed their tattered clothes, and encircled their wrists and necks, which were previously bound together with ropes and chains. There were even some who had their ears personally cut off by her and were now bleeding incessantly because of that.

They were trembling.

They were all trembling with desperation and fear.

It was a glorious and entertaining scene for Soo Jin.

She rejoiced in the sight of their broken bodies, the smell of their streaming blood, and the taste of their unbridled fear. The splendor of the scene was only elevated with the additional enjoyment she received from punishing the one group of people she hated the most—the Serpents.

"Knives," she then said, her serene voice disrupting the silence.

From all around the neighboring balconies, a slew of twinkling silver knives flew into the air like arrows, momentarily streaking and covering the rays of the moon before they fell to the ground and landed in front of the Serpents.

Shudders stole the Serpents' breaths.

They quivered and gaped at the knives that winked at them in the cold and unforgiving night. Silence and horror overtook them. They gazed at one another, glimpsed at the knives, and then stared up at her. Their eyes dawned with cursed knowledge with what they were going to have to do with the weapons.

"I'm sure all of you have heard about me and the things I enjoy watching," Soo Jin began in a whimsical and carefree tone. It sounded like the most tranquil music in a storm-filled night.

As the wind came and blew the curls of her long beautiful hair to one side, she felt Ji Hoon wrap his arms tighter around her, pulling her closer. She could feel his smile against her neck as well as the drumming of his heart. It was racing in anticipation for the show to come. It matched the drumming of her own excited heart.

"Five minutes," she announced concisely.

Several of her Scorpions shifted their positions on the balconies while she spoke. Some leaned their arms on the white railings while others joined their fellow Scorpions, hung their legs over the railings and sat comfortably, awaiting what was to come. While this occurred, Soo Jin's own dark eyes gleamed in exhilaration. She was going to enjoy torturing the very men who were serving the bastard who killed her father.

"You will have five minutes to pick up those knives, fight one another, and attempt to ride out the remaining five minutes with your lives intact," she went on, noting that the air in the vicinity matched that of a coliseum for fighting gladiators.

Terror emanated from the "performers" while excitement radiated from the audience. Bloodlust waltzed in the air.

Soo Jin continued to set the law of the game like the Queen she was.

"After which, I'll let you go and you'll live to see another day. You can gloat to your fellow Serpents about surviving after being captured by the Queen of the Underworld herself." She took a moment to laugh. "I typically join in on the fights and rip a few limbs, but as you can see . . ." She spread out her hands to showcase her white dress. "I'm wearing a very pretty dress tonight. I'm about to have dinner with my boyfriend, so I'm not interested in getting it stained."

She lowered her hands while Ji Hoon laughed at the last bit.

"Having said that, I think you should all count your blessings that I'm not jumping in there with you. There's actually a very good chance that several of you will walk out of here alive."

"So, all we have to do is fight each other in the span of the next five minutes and you'll let us out of here . . . alive?" one of the captives asked from below. His gruff voice was strained with hope and speculation. He was hopeful, but the "easiness" of the task at hand unnerved him. He clearly knew nothing in the Underworld would ever be this easy.

A few chuckles bounced off the balconies where Soo Jin's Scorpions stood. Soo Jin's lips lifted in hilarity at the naive inquiry.

"Give us a good show, survive the next five minutes, and I promise I'll let you walk out of here," Soo Jin confirmed, earning a few exhalations of relief from the Serpents kneeling on the lawn.

All were eyeing the knives as if they were their tickets to freedom.

"Right now, you're no longer Serpents. You're merely men on the brink of death," Ji Hoon reminded them, though the tone in his voice indicated that he had no faith these Serpents would adhere to the oath they took to protect one another in the face of their approaching death. "If we see you going easy on each other, I'll jump down there myself and personally finish you off."

"Ji Hoon, there's no need," Soo Jin appeased, squeezing his hand as if she was the most kindhearted one of the night. "Our performers know what type of audience we are. I'm sure they'll give us a good show."

With this, Soo Jin inclined her head at a female Scorpion who stood on the adjacent balcony to the right of hers. The female, by the name of Anna, bowed at Soo Jin and extracted a black gun from behind her back. She raised it into the air like rising curtains before an exquisite opera show.

"Five . . ." Anna began to count down as the bodies of the captive Serpents stiffened in preparation.

"You're very cruel," Ji Hoon purred into Soo Jin's left ear.

Two shadows appeared from behind them after Anna's voice infiltrated the air.

Soo Jin smiled, both at his assessment and the knowledge that her two favorite Scorpions had appeared by her side.

"'Heartless' is the commonly used term," Soo Jin corrected with the same amusement.

"Four . . ."

"Do they know that you'll be participating?" Ji Hoon asked while Anna continued with her countdown.

Laughter issued from her lips. "They will soon."

"Three . . ."

She extended her hands out and within seconds, Jae Won and Kang Min were by her side as they took out the tools Soo Jin would be using to participate in the show ahead.

"Two . . ."

As the world beneath them became overrun with the desperation for survival, Jae Won and Kang Min dutifully placed the renowned gold guns in the palms of her hands. At the feel of the gold surface kissing her skin, Soo Jin breathed in delight. She enfolded her grip on the guns, feeling as though her pets had been reunited with her. A gush of power flooded through her. She was ready to start her fun.

"One . . ."

In each of her hands, Soo Jin held the judge, jury, and executioner for the lives of the humans below her.

She smirked, loving her godlike status in life.

It was the way it should be.

"Go," Anna announced, firing a bullet into the moonlit skies.

Cheers reverberated from the audience above, and the show began.

Desperate to walk out of the Scorpions' estate alive, each of the Serpents scrambled for knives. They wasted no time in cutting off the flesh of the one they used to call "brother"; there was no more brotherhood left. All that remained was savagery and the need to save one's own skin.

"You should know," Soo Jin started, her voice dying out under the guttural screams, the echoes of ripping skin, and the spurting of blood from the world beneath her, "that in the course of the next five minutes . . . I'll be firing at all of you as well."

None of the men heard her.

Her amusement persevered. Their lack of acknowledgement did not faze her.

Soo Jin knew they'd hear her soon enough.

All eyes of the Scorpions were on her when she cocked her two guns and aimed at the Serpents beneath her.

Before their five minutes were up, each and every one of the Serpents would hear her.

■ ■ ■

"Isaac Asimov once said, 'Life is pleasant. Death is peaceful. It's the transition that's troublesome.' When you kill someone, Kang Min, you have to make the transition as troublesome and as unbearable as possible . . ."

While speaking, Soo Jin kicked the newly amputated fingers aside with her red stiletto heels. She took the bloodied knife from Kang Min, who was still trembling as he stared down at the moaning gang member. The lowly street gang member, who was kneeling before them, had no association with the top gangs in the Underworld. However, as he was a convenient "tool" for Soo Jin to teach Kang Min the ways of the world, he had become an unlucky guinea pig.

"Humans respond well to death, but not to torture," she continued to lecture, tossing the now useless knife into the distance. "It doesn't take much to break a human being and it doesn't take much to own their souls."

After having Kang Min snatch the boy, who had been in the process of beating a girl for not having enough money to pay off her debt, Soo Jin ordered Kang Min, who was still hesitant when it came to hurting people who had done no wrong to him, to torture the boy by cutting off his fingers. To further harden his emotions, she also ordered Kang Min to stab the boy sixteen times. Despite his pleas to Kang Min to just kill him, Soo Jin ordered Kang Min to keep him alive.

The boy was barely able to kneel straight. The assortment of stab wounds on his body had blood pouring out of him in every which way. His white t-shirt was stained crimson red and his jeans were soaked with blood.

Soo Jin laughed faintly, not even the least bit affected by the sight of the young boy quivering in his stance. He continued to kneel before them, his eyes, though dimmed with pain, gleamed slightly as if hopeful that somehow, some way, it was possible that his captors would have enough heart to end his misery.

"It's just a matter of one being ruthless enough to go through all the necessary stages to make them beg for death." Soo Jin squatted down beside the boy, the fabric of her long black slacks bending at her knees. Her red, cuff-sleeved blazer glowed under the dissipating rays of the late afternoon sun. Soo

Jin's beautiful and angelic face drew close to the boy's paling one. "Because when they do that, that's when you know you own their soul."

She reached out her hand and tilted her head. The shiny curls of her long hair wavered to one side while she inspected his face. He didn't look older than sixteen. He was young, but that did little to inspire any sympathy from Soo Jin. She regarded him with condescending pity.

"I'm sure you regret defying your mother's wishes by joining some lowly street gang now, don't you?" she asked coolly, mocking the fear that secreted from him.

The boy nodded hopelessly. Tears mixed with his own blood as they glided down his eyes. The weight of the world's regret laid in his eyes, yet it evoked no pity from Soo Jin, who was all but used to seeing pathetic humans cry when their lives hung in the balance.

She stroked a finger up and down his bloodied cheeks, her manicured nails collecting the blood. The boy shuddered and tried to move away from her, but when she applied pressure into the touch, the boy stopped moving. Possibly in fear that Soo Jin would rip his cheek apart if he inched away from her, he stayed rooted in his position.

Satisfied with his submission, Soo Jin continued to speak, her voice elevated with slight annoyance. His existence reminded her of how much she hated parasites like him. "To you, all you see about the world of gangs is that we're a lowly world who lives in alleys, surrounds ourselves with drugs, and do drive by shootings for the hell of it. You join your lowly street gangs thinking that you'll be a part of a highly elite world and you do nothing but embarrass the very society that you pretend to be a part of."

She smirked dryly, digging her nails into the open wound on his face, making him shudder even more from agony. He was pleading her to stop, yet with each plea, she dug her long nails deeper into the open flesh.

"The media is cruel to you kids. You think you know about the world of gangs through your movies, your books, and the pathetic outlet you call your news. You know nothing about my exclusive world, yet you call yourself a gang member, reel in the rewards of being a soldier in the Underworld, and come out as nothing but a spineless fool when you meet the real deal." Anger outlined her once calm face. "I despise little leeches like you. You embarrass my people and taint our names with your inferiority, and if I had more time, I'd pick off each and every one of you like the worthless pieces of shit you are."

She had always hated being in alleys for the simple fact that they were synonymous with the media's stereotypical view of gangs. There were smaller gangs who were actually a part of the Underworld and parasitic street gangs who were nothing but trash to her exclusive society. Unfortunately, the outside world was only familiar with the parasitic street gangs because they were the only ones who were unskilled enough to be caught by the law.

It was an unknown history to the outside world that street gangs actually derived from the Underworld gangs. As the story goes, unqualified gang members who were kicked out from the elite society formed street gangs of their own. It was a commonly misguided assumption that the Underworld crime lords were similar to the street gangs that were popularly portrayed in the media. For a prideful Queen like Soo Jin, as well as many other Royals in the Underworld, such notions offended them greatly because the ways of their world were more extravagant, business-like, orderly, and so much more superior and complex than the world of parasitic street gangs.

The "Royals," as some had termed this powerful group, in the Underworld were fans of drug trafficking, money laundering, and territorial wars, but their favorite pastime was controlling how the outside world worked. In short, the society resembled that of kingdoms in the modern world. Kings and Queens fought for boundless power while concurrently being politically charming enough to garner support from the other citizens in the Underworld. It was a complex structure that had all layers working together when needed. All of this ultimately led to profits that were economically pleasing to their bank accounts, flexible laws that were obedient to their way of life, power to please their pride, and finally, sustenance to uphold the bylaws of the secret society.

As far as Soo Jin was concerned, the only ones who stood on the same level as the Underworld in Korea were the "Royals" in the Italian, Chinese, Japanese, and American Underworlds, alongside any other country that had the Underworld pyramid. They were the only other secret societies that covertly ran the lives of the people in their country and they were the only peers outside of her society that she would give any reverence to. Any others impersonating the "gang" notion from her world were leeches to her. She would love to exterminate them fully if she had enough time to do so.

Soo Jin expelled a breath, pushing these scornful thoughts back. She focused her attention on the young boy who represented everything she was infuriated with.

More tears flowed from his eyes. A breath later, a shuddering sob exploded from his brutally assaulted body. His own blood began to form a big pool around him, drenching him and the heels of her stilettos with his impending death.

Her annoyance with his existence mounted, but the calmness in her demeanor remained.

"But you should count your blessings, little one," she appeased, pulling her nails out of the open flesh while wiping his tears away with her bloodstained fingers. "It is a rare occurrence for a parasite like you to meet someone like me and it is an even rarer occurrence for someone like you to receive any mercy from me. Yet, every dog has his days and today is yours."

She motioned for him to stare up at Kang Min, who was dressed in a brown jacket and black pants. The rays of the sun moved behind him, making him appear divine. He was still peering down at the young boy with profound anguish in his eyes.

"Standing there is your God. The moment he tortured you was the moment he took your soul. He now holds your life in his hands." She leaned in closer to the boy, who was staring pleadingly at Kang Min. "Beg your God, little one. Beg your God for death and he will grant it to you."

She spoke . . . and he listened.

"Please . . ." the young boy implored, having no more desire to live. "Please just kill me."

"Kang Min," Soo Jin called. She could sense his apprehension and she didn't like it one bit. "End it . . . *now*."

Although trembling faintly, Kang Min was unable to disobey any command given by the boss who saved his life and raised him. After taking a deep breath to calm his nerves, Kang Min stepped forward, gazed down into the boy's eyes, placed his hands on either side of the boy's head and then, with the speed of lightning, snapped apart the boy's neck like it was a dry twig.

The cracking of bones jumped in the air and evaporated in the wind, leaving nothing behind but the soft thud of the boy's lifeless body falling to the alleyway pavement.

"You did well, Kang Min."

Soo Jin rose up and stood beside a fifteen-year-old Kang Min, who was no longer shaking, but chalk white. They stared at the lifeless body of the boy who was breathing only moments prior. She folded her arms. It had always amazed Soo Jin how thin the veil was between the world of living and death. Such realizations only further conveyed to her how thankful she was to be the person she had been trained to become. A Queen amongst humans . . .

Sucks to be you, little one, she thought, gazing one last time at the boy before returning her attention to the eighteen-year-old Jae Won, who was still defying gravity by jumping off the alleyway walls while the scene before them took place.

She averted her eyes to Kang Min and frowned when she caught the remorse that exalted from his breathing.

"You should never feel remorse in this world," Soo Jin lectured swiftly, unhappy with his weakness.

Kang Min, like his older brother, had always been a talented and fast learner. If Soo Jin was the pride of the Advisors, then the brothers were her pride. They were fast learners, but the one aspect of training that they had yet

338

to master, all of which the rest of the Scorpions she trained had excelled in, was the ability to place their emotions aside and actually become Gods amongst humans.

"The only loyalty you owe is to your own blood and your trusted alliances," Soo Jin went on, the coldness of her eyes burying into Kang Min's young and innocent ones. "Everyone else is just a casualty in this world and is worthless to you. They do not deserve your remorse. You save what's left of your humanity for your brother and the gang that raised you."

Kang Min nodded quietly, understanding this logic, yet always having trouble executing it.

Soo Jin tilted her head at him when she caught another line of regret that penetrated his eyes. The guilt did not arise for the one he just killed. It arose from the disappointment that he had upset her. The thought of him chastising himself thawed Soo Jin's typically cold heart. She was strict with their training because she wanted to protect them. As emotionally vulnerable as they were, the loyalty the brothers had shown her over the years was unmatched by any other. It was one that would instill their values in her heart forever. The bond the three shared was untouchable and it was one that helped keep Soo Jin sane in such a sadistic world. She loved them like they were her family members.

The grave rigor in her eyes alleviated on Kang Min like an older sister would for her little brother. She wanted to tell him to not feel ashamed, that it took a while to eradicate one's soul. All it took was practice in killing. She wanted to tell him that she wasn't disappointed with him.

Her thoughts were interrupted when his brother's voice peeled her from her reverie.

"We have a lot to learn, boss," Jae Won commented from behind, overhearing enough of the conversation even while he was busy training. His panting voice edged closer to them before she heard a pained moan emit from him.

Soo Jin whipped her attention to him. When her eyes fastened onto Jae Won's limping leg, displeasure bubbled in her chest. There were splatters of dirt stuck to his black jacket and pants from the training he did. His one singular blemish that always enraged Soo Jin was that he wore his weakness on his sleeves.

Ever since his initiation into the Scorpions, where her ten-year-old self had initiated him and Kang Min (who were eight and five respectively) and broken countless bones in their bodies, Jae Won always had weak legs. Soo Jin refused to allow this setback from his initiation to hinder his training. She continued to push his body while forcing him to use other means to bypass his Achilles' heel. Training on alleyway walls had always acted as a good warm-up for Soo Jin and the brothers. Jae Won, who required this type of training the most, would have never been able to withstand her rigorous evening trainings had it not been for this exercise. She wanted the best for the brothers. This was why it pissed her off to no end whenever they showed the world their weaknesses.

"The next time you groan in pain, stop your training without my orders, and limp pathetically in front of me while showing everyone how weak your legs are, I'll bury you alive in a coffin for five days as your punishment," Soo Jin warned severely, her irate eyes set on Jae Won.

Blood drained from Jae Won's face at the thought of being buried alive in a coffin.

She had never punished him in such a manner, but Soo Jin was more than willing to if he continued to expose his weakness like this. At this rate, it would be better to bury him alive to eliminate any bad habits. If this bad habit of showing people how weak his lower body was continued, then she was certain it would put him in an early grave later on. She would do everything in her power to prevent that fate for him.

"I'm sorry, boss," Jae Won responded quickly. His tone was respectful. He understood that she was looking out for him. "I won't let it happen again."

"Good," Soo Jin approved, knowing that Jae Won would do good on his word. The only one who should see his weakness was her, no one else.

She gazed down at her bloodied manicure and the alley they were in. She had had enough of this disgusting area. It was time to head back to her true Underworld home.

Soo Jin gestured a wave with her hand. "Now let's get out of here before I throw up from disgust."

"You will never be the exception."

26: The War of Kingdoms

The sun had settled behind the darkening dusk, leaving behind the last stream of its glorious rays after Soo Jin and the brothers washed up and made their way through the streets. Their eyes reflected the view of the sky that hung over the block they were on.

The remainders of the luminescent rays were caked between layers of purple, pink, and dark blue hues that brought the vibrancy of life to the canvas in the skies. The heavens above were beautiful, but the beauty it possessed did little to reflect onto its parallel counterpart. The world beneath it looked like a blemish on a picturesque painting.

On every corner of the block Soo Jin and the brothers walked on, there were prostitutes, drug addicts, homeless people, muggers, rapists, and parasitic street gangs who loitered the streets 24/7. It was a filthy area that disgusted Soo Jin, but one that she saw great use for. As with any parasitic world, these areas fulfilled their use by becoming the perfect "classrooms" for Soo Jin to teach her protégé trainees on how to kill and torture someone without regard to their feelings. What better place to train someone to be a soldier in the Underworld than to have him or her practice on already worthless human beings? There was good and bad in everything and in this case, the usefulness of the good superseded the bad.

"Boss," Jae Won prompted as they continued to tread down the sidewalk.

Soo Jin turned to him, her patient eyes silently urging him to continue with his query.

"There are rumors circulating that the three elder Advisors are in discussion with the rest of the Advisors in the 2nd layer to merge the layers in the Underworld under one King—one direct Lord to rule over all the layers. They want to do that in order to unify our efforts to extend power throughout the regions of the world."

By now, even Kang Min was paying close attention while his brother continued.

"Have you heard about this?" Jae Won finished.

A knowing smile graced Soo Jin's lips. Jae Won's words did not faze her. She was already privy to this information from her brother, Ji Hoon, and the Advisors themselves.

"Of course I've heard," she stated apathetically. "I am the Queen of this world, aren't I?"

Jae Won nodded in concurrence, expecting no less from his boss.

"Who would you support as the new Lord?" Kang Min inquired at once.

The guilt that once plagued him faded from his innocent eyes as the three fell back into the normalcy of their conversations with one another — that was how liberating the trio's relationship could be. Even under dire circumstances, they could always alleviate each other's guilt and stress, just as brothers and sisters would for each other.

"I don't know," Soo Jin mused out loud, the heels of her stilettos piercing the blood splattered cement that seemed to always decorate the sidewalk in this part of town.

She beamed at the reminder of Ji Hoon. She hadn't seen her boyfriend in several days and the reminder made her miss him terribly.

"The new Lord can be my brother or my boyfriend. Either way, my title as the Queen of the Underworld remains." She heaved a breath when they stepped over a dead body on the street as if it was trash. "But if I have to choose, my support will always go to my brother." She pursed her lips when another thought came to her mind. "But then again, I wouldn't mind if Ji Hoon got the position."

"Do you love Lee Ji Hoon, boss?" Kang Min suddenly asked, his countenance already twisting with disapproval while Jae Won's was cloaked with annoyance at the mention of Ji Hoon's name.

"I do," she replied without hesitation. Soo Jin mentally noted the awkwardness that surrounded the air between her and the brothers. She noticed that such awkwardness always appeared whenever Ji Hoon's name was mentioned. It bothered her, but not enough for her to demand to know what the brothers had against her boyfriend. "He's everything I could want in a man, and the fact that he spoils the hell out of me, promises me the world, and adores me is an added bonus. What more could a girl ask for?"

And she meant every word of it.

Ji Hoon was good-looking, charming, ruthless, and powerful. He was the exact replica of her and she loved every bit of it.

"We don't trust him," Jae Won blurted out, immediately earning a look of displeasure from Soo Jin. "He allows his Skulls to rape their enemies' women for sport. There's even rumors that he encourages them to do this to ruin the lives of anyone who has gone against him. Kang Min and I know that our world isn't exactly the most moralistic one, but for someone to have the audacity to do stuff like that—"

"I really couldn't care less," Soo Jin dismissed, exasperation igniting a fire in her voice. "What my boyfriend does to others is no concern of mine. I don't know those people and I couldn't care less what happens to them."

Jae Won tried to conceal his disappointment. Her cruel words about not caring about the welfare of innocent people bothered him. He looked like he wanted to address it, but gave up on the endeavor. He had other things he wanted to bring to her attention. "But there's something off about him, boss. He doesn't deserve you."

"Yeah," Kang Min agreed vehemently. "You can do better than him—"

"Who would be better than him in this world?" Soo Jin interjected impatiently, earning quiet responses from the brothers. "My brother is an omitted option, Kwon Ho Young is a piece of shit that I'm waiting to kill, and I think that pretty much narrows down the choices of men who are worthy of me. At least from a power standpoint." She glared at them. "Now drop it. I won't tolerate listening to this anymore."

Biting back a curse, they shook their heads in frustration, but clamped their lips shut. After growing up by her side for ten years, they knew how hardheaded Soo Jin could be. Even though they knew when to shut up, they also knew when to subtly add their two cents without pissing her off.

"One day, you'll find someone who is better than him," Jae Won persisted coolly. The soft wind blew through their dark outfits when he said this. There was a smile on his face; it was clear he was anticipating this day with great hope.

"And when you do," Kang Min added with just as much care, "we'll be the first to give you our approvals."

Soo Jin laughed and hid a bittersweet smile at the brothers' determination to prove their point. Conversations like this made Soo Jin wonder if the brothers truly belonged in her world. They were killers, yet in many ways, they were still too innocent—too human.

She wanted to tell them that she had grown up faster than any other young girls her age. She stopped believing in fairytale stories where the man of her dreams would appear out of nowhere, sweep her off her feet, sail off with her into the sunset, whisk her away to a foreign city, and steal every inch of her stubborn heart. Soo Jin had long given up on that daydream and doubted she would ever waste her time on such fantasies again. Ji Hoon was her world and she loved him a lot. It was only the notion of being "in" love with him that seemed questionable for her. Regardless, this wasn't something she was about to verbalize to the brothers.

Before she could further mull over the matter, the awareness of a familiar presence snatched Soo Jin out of her immediate thoughts and alerted every instinct in her body.

An enemy was in close range.

Her observant eyes moved like a hawk's. They fastened onto their target and sure enough, she sighted the one who caused her skin to crawl in disgust.

He was across the street standing by his car, staring right at her. Darkness surrounded him, but she could see the amusement on his face. It mocked and taunted her.

"Go home," she ordered the brothers without further explanation.

"Boss?" they began, perplexed at her abrupt order.

It didn't take them long to follow her gaze. Their eyes expanded once they spotted the person who currently commanded Soo Jin's unyielding attention.

"But—"

"*Now*," she snarled through gritted teeth.

Soo Jin did not make eye contact with them, but she knew they could feel her fury and impatience. She wanted to be alone with this enemy and she needed the brothers to stay as far away as possible just in case anything went down. They were trained well, but they were still too young to fight against a King in the Underworld.

It was only her who could go against Kings.

Helpless whenever Soo Jin gave a direct order, the brothers shot one more worried glance at the silhouette across the street and then bowed towards Soo Jin before retreating, having no choice but to adhere to their boss's order. They didn't like it, but their loyalty superseded their feelings. They left without another word.

"An Soo Jin," the deep male voice pleasantly greeted when she stepped foot into the quiet street that housed only parked cars, herself, and the crime lord who stood yards away from her.

"Kwon Ho Young," she greeted in the same manner, yet the undercurrent in her voice revealed an aversion that was simply uncontainable. All the different variations of anger chased after one another in the blood inside her veins. The bastard who killed her father was standing there before her . . . so casually, so nonchalantly, and so alive that it irritated every nerve in her murderous soul.

Wearing a black suit with a cigar between his lips, Ho Young blew out a puff of smoke while his figure glowed under the flickering orange street light that was prematurely lit, despite the still presence of the morose sunset. The hue of the flickering light mirrored that of his lit cigar, which appeared to be glowing every sporadic second. Soo Jin scrutinized the bloody stains on his fingers. She was positive the blood was not his.

"Hasn't your older brother warned you not to stand in the streets all by your lonesome, little one?" Ho Young asked, taking a seat on the hood of the black Mercedes convertible behind him. The license plate was new, indicating to Soo Jin that he had just made the purchase. "Especially when powerful Kings such as myself are lurking around?"

"My older brother is not my babysitter," Soo Jin retorted, furious that he was using such a patronizing tone with her.

The only one she would tolerate calling her "little one" was her brother and that was only because he was her older brother. The thought of Ho Young calling her a nickname that was specifically reserved for her brother offended Soo Jin. She inhaled, making sure to keep her hot-headedness in check. It was a well-known fact that she could never maintain her temper around Ho Young and, of course, the bastard ate it up and ridiculed her with it. Even though she wanted to kill him, she was restricted by her brother's orders.

"I can take care of myself," she gritted out.

"It's the cocky ones who die first," he warned, another cloud of smoke escaping from his lips.

"The ones who go against my gang die first."

She was slowly losing her patience. Oh, how she wanted to simply run up to him, beat his ass, plunge her fist into the depths of his throat, and rip out his buzz-cut hair by the roots on his skull.

Soo Jin was known to be a highly skilled fighter, but what made her so feared in the Underworld was the viciousness of her soul. She had the ability to torture people moments before their death and she showed no remorse in doing so. Soo Jin loved treating the ones she hated like animals. She had no qualms about killing people and she definitely had no problem torturing them to death. And at that moment, every torture device Soo Jin had ever employed in her life was a torture device that she wanted to bequeath unto Ho Young. She could still remember the still image of her father's dead body lying on the ground. It was a sight that would forever break what was left of her soul, and it was a sight that made her the Queen she was today: ruthless, powerful, and vengeful.

"Oh yes," Ho Young voiced, unhappiness penetrating his eyes at the reminder of who she had killed. "You've been having some fun with kidnapping and torturing my Serpents, haven't you?"

"Lots of fun," she confirmed haughtily, trying to provoke him to fight her.

She had made a promise to her brother to never go after Ho Young unless he attacked her first. It was a promise she thought was easy to keep until she had to employ it. Whenever the bastard was in her sight, he was a temptation to her violent instincts, a taunting red cape to the murderous bull within her that wanted nothing more than to pummel him into oblivion. The only thing that prevented her from going after Ho Young was the promise she made to her brother. Yet, Soo Jin also knew the ways in which flexibility could be used with keeping one's word. She never promised her brother that she wouldn't provoke Ho Young to fight her first.

"Who needs pets when I have the cowardly Serpents acting as my fighting dogs?"

Soo Jin was condescending, but not enough to break Ho Young's cool exterior.

He chuckled, shaking his head at her and not in the least bit provoked.

That was the thing about Kwon Ho Young. For one reason or the other, he was always calm with her and never made any efforts to attack or hurt her. This inaction on his part infuriated Soo Jin who was just itching for an excuse to kill him.

"The Serpents' empire is on the rise, Soo Jin," he told her gently, the patience in his voice constant while he addressed her. "It doesn't matter how many of my men you kill because four more will come and take their places. Just give it a rest. You know that in the end, my Serpents and I will be the ones ruling over this layer. Be the smart girl you are and stop pissing me off. You'll need my favor to keep your title once I'm crowned the Lord of our world."

Now it was Soo Jin's turn to laugh mockingly. "As I distinctly recall, my brother and Ji Hoon are in the process of merging their gangs together. And the simple fact that they have me is sure to get them some points with the Advisors, as well as with the rest of the layers. One of *them* will be the new Lord." She smirked. "What do you have Ho Young? The scavengers you call your gang members? You think your legion of leeches will catapult you into the role as the Lord of our world?"

Ho Young laughed. "You forget, Soo Jin, that in addition to all the power I have in this layer, I also have my little brother by my side."

Soo Jin stiffened at the reminder of his younger brother.

Ho Young's smile grew even wider at her reaction.

He inhaled another puff of smoke before blowing it out and breathing in the cold air.

"As I recall, the two of you have never met, but I'm sure you've heard of him." Pride canvassed his voice at the mention of his brother. "The chosen Prince and the new expected ruler of the 1st layer."

Soo Jin clenched her fists in restrained fury.

Yes, she had heard of Kwon Tae Hyun.

The second son of the Kwon family; the one who won the mentorship from the top crime lords in the 1st layer, had the friendships of some of the most powerful heirs in the palm of his hand, had Shin Dong Min—one of the three elder Advisors—as his personal Advisor, a feat unheard of for any Prince in the 1st layer, and was irrefutably the pride of the exclusive 1st layer.

The politicians, business tycoons, and heavy media influencers were known to be "snobbish" when it came to dealing with their more powerful counterparts and had always been distant to the Kings of the 3rd layer. Garnering support from the majority of the 1st layer had always appeared to be an unfeasible feat . . . that was until the Prince of Serpents came along and dazzled everyone with his charms, cunningness, superiority, impressive fighting skills that was said to have rivaled Kings and, of course, the unrivaled good looks that were said to have stolen the hearts of any woman he came across.

Soo Jin scoffed in skepticism at the last bit about how much of an eye-candy he was.

She had never met the guy, nor had the pleasure of seeing how good-looking he was, but just hearing the rave reviews from the typically hard to impress 1st layer crowd irritated her. She hated the bastard for the simple reason that he was Ho Young's baby brother, and she hated it more that there was someone out there, who wasn't an heir to the 3rd layer throne like her, receiving the same type of reverence as her. Granted her status was still higher, it was no secret that the revered Prince of the 1st layer was becoming stronger and stronger. She was willing to bet that it would only be a matter of time before the spoiled 1st layer bastard yielded as much power as she did. He was a force to be reckoned with and having him by Ho Young's side only meant that there was a higher chance that the favor of the Underworld would tilt in their direction, thereby meaning that the distribution of power would eventually be theirs.

The prospect enraged Soo Jin.

She made a mental note to kill off the "good-looking and charming" bastard for the simple fact that his existence offended her and boiled her competitive blood.

"An Soo Jin," Ho Young mocked, finding hilarity in the obvious anger resonating from the revered Queen, "your jealousy over Tae Hyun's growing reverence is toxic. I swear, I'm about to keel over from the steam that comes out of you whenever you think of him."

Jealousy was never a great color on her.

"Fuck you, you worthless pig," Soo Jin snapped, unable to contain her rage. She clenched her fists. She wanted nothing more than to rip his guts out with her bare hands. She had done it before with others and would love to do it to him.

"You're not my type," Ho Young taunted, inhaling another round of smoke that seemed to reach the pit of his lungs before extricating itself with the current of the wind.

She grew angrier with his careless demeanor.

Then, she lost it because she knew what his type was. "I dare you to laugh once I cut off your dick and shove it down your throat, you disgusting piece of shi—"

"Don't you have other things to do than stand here and piss off my sister?" a deep male voice interrupted just as Soo Jin was preparing to lunge at Ho Young and kill him once and for all.

Soo Jin turned and was annoyed when her brother, An Young Jae, moved beside her. His eyes were firmly set on Ho Young. The appearance of her brother meant one thing: she would not be able to fight with Kwon Ho Young.

They stared at one another, both Kings fearless in spite of the other.

Tension saturated the air, and Soo Jin could've sworn they were having a silent conversation with each other before Ho Young broke the silence and smiled mockingly at Young Jae's comment.

His expression said it all: he was ready to leave anyway.

Allowing one last puff of smoke to curl away from his lips, he threw the cigar away and killed the light with the sole of his expensive black leather shoe.

"Yes, now that you've mentioned it, I believe it is time to send this new car over to my little brother before he comes back to visit our fair city." His unreadable eyes moved on to Young Jae. He held it there for a brief moment before his gaze journeyed on to Soo Jin. His lips lifted into a patronizing grin. Then, he said words that he knew would make her blood simmer. "It's been a pleasure, my Queen."

There was no respect with how he addressed her. He said it with such ridicule that it became the last straw for Soo Jin.

Fucking bastard.

Unable to stand it, Soo Jin released her inhibitions and made a move to chase after Ho Young. She was stopped in her tracks when her brother's hand encircled her arm like a vise. His grip on her was unforgiving. It was sure to leave a bruise, but Soo Jin didn't even flinch at the pain. She was too focused on Ho Young.

In her bout of anger, she decided to open Pandora's Box.

"I saw you that night, Ho Young," she uttered, knowing just what to say to knock him off his high horse.

She no longer wanted to keep a secret what she'd known about Ho Young for the past two years. She did not care about keeping her word to her brother and keeping this information to herself. All she wanted to do was to hurt Ho Young and take credit in the glory of what happened to his family.

Ho Young's eyes grew firm on her. "What are you talking about?"

"Soo Jin," Young Jae said gravely, tightening his grip on her arm. Her brother wasn't an idiot. He knew what she was trying to do; he knew she was trying to provoke Ho Young. "Don't you dare."

His severe voice did little to dissuade Soo Jin who, although was loyal enough to her brother, was spoiled enough by him that she just didn't care to adhere to his strict call. That was the thing about Soo Jin, her pride and hot temper surpassed even her loyalty to her brother.

"The night of your mother's death," she whispered despite her brother's warning to shut up. "I saw you walking out of your baby sister's room, buttoning the last button of your shirt before you went back to your room."

She laughed when she saw the dawning light of knowledge in Ho Young's eyes. He looked gobsmacked that there had been a witness to that scene.

Soo Jin went on, feeding on his stricken state. "How proud your mother must be in death to realize that her eldest son has been raping his baby sister all along." A savage laugh flooded from her. "I wonder how that little brother of yours will feel if he ever finds out what you've been doing to her? I'm sure that little tidbit would ruin the great brotherhood shared between the two of you, don't you think?"

"When . . . were you in the Serpents' estate?" he asked instead, not even bothering to deny her accusations.

Ho Young, like her brother, was one of the more intelligent men that she had met. It was a quality that all the Kings of the Underworld had to possess. He knew immediately that Soo Jin wasn't simply telling him that she knew he had been raping his sister; he knew she was also insinuating something else. And if the darkness that overtook his eyes was any indication, then he already had a hunch that this bomb would be a big one.

The memory of that night came vividly to her mind and she slowly unraveled it to him.

"I was . . . visiting your mother." She purposely made the indifference in her tone of voice as cruel as possible. "Brought her some alcohol bottles to help her along with her misery." Soo Jin feigned a disappointed sigh, which earned a growl from her older brother. He was infuriated that she even dared to reveal this against his orders. "It's a crying shame what happened to her. What a senseless death."

Ho Young's eyes enlarged at this admission. He did not need to hear her actual confession to know what she was implying. "It was you all along . . ."

The patience that once enamored him evaporated with the last rays of the setting sun. A powerful and dangerous aura took over instead. He was angry, livid. All this fury was directed at Soo Jin, who more than welcomed his hatred.

"Ho Young," Young Jae said tightly, tightening his grip on Soo Jin.

He pulled her behind him with a force that Soo Jin could've fought, but chose not to for she knew she had not only pushed Ho Young's patience over the edge, but his as well. However, as aggravated as Young Jae was with her, the brotherly protection he had for her overshadowed his own irritation.

His indiscernible eyes buried into Ho Young's. "Any fight you want to get justice for begins and ends with me. I'm sure you haven't forgotten that agreement we made, the one that states we leave our sisters out of our war? You *do* care about your sister enough to protect her, right?"

The tone in which Young Jae asked this question hit a nerve in Ho Young.

Anger dispelled out of his eyes at Young Jae's reminder of his sister.

Soo Jin smirked. So, that was the reason why Ho Young never tried to hurt her, because they made an agreement to not hurt each other's sisters. The logic seemed odd to her, as she required no protection, but it seemed to be a pact that Ho Young took seriously because the fury that once veiled over him vanished with the desire to protect his sister.

"It is lucky for both of you that I'm busy right now," he said with finality, remnants of darkness still coloring his voice. "And to be brief, I hope you don't mind that I ordered my Cobras to kill two dozen of your Scorpions to even the score for killing my men the other night. The bodies are laying on your estate's lawn as we speak."

Soo Jin stiffened in anger at this knowledge.

Ho Young grinned as if he was telling them he had just left a care package at their home. "And just for how our meeting progressed tonight, I'll send out the orders to have two dozen more sent your way." He inclined his head toward Soo Jin. Residual malice treaded on his features. "You should be more careful from this point on. One day, your disillusioned pride will get you killed. Take care . . . little one."

On that note, Ho Young pulled the door to the Mercedes open. He seated himself in the car just as Soo Jin made a move to run after him for giving her that subtle threat.

"Stay where you are, lil sis," Young Jae commanded simply, his eyes on Ho Young as he started the engine.

Soo Jin didn't even realize she was still steps away from chasing after him until her brother's voice stopped her. She did as she was told, for she knew her disobedience of her brother's orders was capped for the night. Everyone had their limits; she did not want to push his.

"Oppa, please," Soo Jin pleaded through clenched teeth, watching Ho Young drive away in the car he just bought his younger brother. "Let me go after him. I can't stand seeing him breathe after what he did to our father. Let me have the honor of killing him. I don't know how much longer I can obey your commands and wait for you to kill him. You're taking too long and it's making me wonder if you ever will."

She didn't hide the resentment in her voice as she watched Ho Young drive away.

Young Jae did not miss the insinuation of her words. The cold eyes she received from him told her there was no way in hell he was giving her the glory of killing Ho Young. Simply put, it was clear he was getting pretty damn tired of her disobedience.

"Don't you dare question me and my plans. We have spoken about this. Ho Young's head belongs to me," Young Jae warned sternly, his eyes challenging her to further disobey his orders. "I know you want him dead. Trust me, so do I. But we need patience, Soo Jin. There is killing and there is torturing. I want him when my power is highest, when the Underworld kneels before me. I want him when he has nothing, when he is kneeling before me in misery, begging for his life. I want to watch the tears flow down his eyes as I skin him alive. I want to win during a war, not a simple battle. That revenge will be sweeter than killing him now, in the middle of the evening where we would never be able to savor his death and our victory."

The mental image that manifested in her mind at her brother's words did little to repress her rage. It was all in the future and it was all too long for her to wait. She did not want to wait any further. Soo Jin parted her lips to argue, but was again silenced by Young Jae. He had already anticipated her rebuttal.

"Do you really have any loyalty to me if you can't even listen to my orders?!" he screamed.

Soo Jin clamped her mouth shut, her lips twitching in embarrassment. She could feel the heart-shaped necklace her father gave her burn a mark into her chest.

This was one of the few times he yelled at her, and she knew she had pushed him over the edge. Yet, as her angry eyes averted from the space Ho Young once stood in, the animosity she felt when she laid her eyes on Young Jae was one that fueled another fire in her soul.

Soo Jin pondered the irony of her station in life.

She was a Queen before others, yet still a lowly soldier when in the presence of her brother.

How pathetic she felt to have her powers so confined, how angry she felt that he was the one curbing the potential of her power, and how bitter she felt to know that he was the one who stood in her way on the path to ultimate power.

Soo Jin closed her eyes, biting back thoughts about what life would be like if he was gone, if she could be the one to rule over the Scorpions. However, she stowed away such thoughts for she knew nothing good would come out of tempting herself with a power that she should never seek. She loved her brother and despite her love for power, she wasn't willing to allow her thoughts to venture on to the possibility of her betraying him.

"Yes, oppa," Soo Jin relented, bowing as her show of adherence to his orders. "I'll stay away from him."

She wasn't happy with what she said, but prideful entities were rarely happy when they took commands from others.

Satisfied, Young Jae smiled at her cooperation. He placed a hand on her shoulder to show how much he appreciated her compliance. "It is better this way, lil sis. Just trust me on this. It's better this way."

She nodded, not fully registering his words.

Although his gaze on her was kind, she could also see a restless fatigue in his eyes. He had just returned from doing something and he did not look settled. She glanced down at his hands and saw that there was blood marring his fists. He had just hit something.

"Something is bothering you," Soo Jin noted, concern replacing the bitterness. Her brother rarely had his feathers ruffled and if he did, then it meant a disconcertion had occurred.

"I've heard some . . . .unsettling news," he confirmed.

Soo Jin furrowed her brows. "What is it?"

"Hwang Tony . . . has been spotted."

It was Soo Jin's turn to be rattled.

"Hwang . . . Hwang Tony?" Her eyes blossomed at this information. "Hwang Hee Jun's younger brother? But I thought he died when you raided the Siberian Tigers' estate and killed the lineage?"

"Somehow, some way, he made it out alive and he's in Seoul. When we killed them, we eradicated the Siberian Tigers' lineage, but not the extended family. Hwang Hee Jun's girlfriend, her children, and some of his extended family continue to live, and I believe they have been housing Tony."

"What do you want me to do?" Soo Jin asked, knowing already that this type of problem was something that her brother always personally went to her for.

"What you do best," he said slowly, his intent clear. "Kidnap the family, bring them to Club Pure, and do what I need you to do there. My reputation hangs on the line. We need to find Tony and kill him immediately. We also need to silence any necessary people who are threats to ruining the reign of my throne."

"Of course," she replied. Her strict eyes softened slightly when a specific tidbit came to her mind. She recalled that Hwang Hee Jun had a girlfriend who had two children of her own. "What about the children?"

"I would like it," Young Jae began, his eyes softening at the thought of the children, "if the mother and her children would be spared. If they don't know too much, then I would prefer for them to be spared."

Soo Jin nodded, understanding the reluctance on her brother's part to hurt a mother and her children. Out of the two siblings, Young Jae was always the kinder one.

"If everything goes well, then I think we can arrange that."

"And Soo Jin?"

"Yes, oppa?"

"There will be four other selected Scorpions with us," he shared carefully. "None of our other Scorpions, or anyone else, will be involved. We'll keep this quiet. I don't want anyone to know about Tony still being alive and what we're about to do."

Soo Jin nodded, understanding what he was implying.

"When we're through with them," she assured, knowing well the controversial line that was drawn in the Underworld between Kings killing gang members and "innocents." Her brother could never be involved in this tryst if he wanted to keep the honor in his reputation intact. "No one would know why they were there in the first place."

He smiled in approval of her answer. "Can you get this taken care of now?"

"Soon," she promised. "I'll get it all set up, but before that, I have a meeting with Ju Won. It'll only take a few moments. In the meantime, I'll make sure to give the orders to the four Scorpions to scope out the homes before we abduct the extended family."

Young Jae nodded at what she said, his mind already venturing elsewhere. "What does Ju Won want?"

"With him, who knows," Soo Jin said honestly. All she knew was that if Ju Won wanted to see her, then he would get his way. That was how much loyalty and admiration she had for the eldest Advisor who helped her become the Queen she was today.

"Be careful with him, lil sis," Young Jae admonished as she prepared to leave. He had never liked Ju Won. "He is a ruthless bastard and he can't be trusted. I don't want you to place so much trust in him and be betrayed in the end."

Soo Jin felt the weight of her two gold guns behind her back as she backed away from her brother and headed over to the precious black Lamborghini that awaited her down the street.

"You forget, big brother, that I was personally trained by him," she said with much amusement, not knowing then how the simple meeting with Ju Won would be the changing of tides that would alter the course of her life forever.

"If any type of betrayal occurs . . . then it will be on my part."

"You will be made an example of. . ."

27: The Betrayal of Scorpions

The giant infrastructure stood as an innocuous home owned by the sublimely powerful. When one stepped out of their car and laid eyes upon it, nothing but wonder would suspend over them.

For Soo Jin, as she stepped away from her black Lamborghini, she merely viewed it as a training ground that had acted as her second home when she was growing up. It was a place that welcomed her as a young child, made her inhuman during her teen years, and molded her into a Queen as she became a woman. It was heaven, hell, and the Underworld all rolled into one.

There were cars parked on the streets, and she knew from her heightened sense of hearing that there were bodyguards hiding within the vehicles. She could hear Ju Won's many bodyguards patrol the grounds, their breathing silent to many, but obvious to her. She could even see the shadows of snipers looming on the roof. If another naked eye were asked to stare in the same direction, they would see no trace of human entities. Soo Jin knew better. She grew up with these bodyguards and she knew the ins and outs of this mansion like she knew the back of her hand.

From its exterior, Ju Won's mansion appeared perfectly safe and ordinary. But for those who knew better, for those who knew the type of people who resided within this vicinity, they were well aware that this "innocuous" place was a death trap in every sense of the word. If you were invited, it would welcome you with respect. If you were summoned, it would perceive you with caution. If you were uninvited, it would kill you without hesitation.

Striding onto the property with her head held high and her heels digging into the perfectly manicured walkway, Soo Jin wore a fearless expression. The silence of the property welcomed her. The estate may be a perilous place for some, but in Soo Jin's case, *she* would always be the executioner. She was the ultimate death trap.

Unafraid of the killers that surrounded her, she proceeded into the mansion as she always did and advanced into the enormous hall. She casually grazed her fingers over the sleek white wall before finally entering the rectangular room that was large enough to fit the entire Underworld. The room, which doubled as a colossal arena, was well lit, a deviation from the shadows that usually draped over the room. Strangely enough, Soo Jin also noticed that there were no snipers above her.

How odd, she mused as her stilettos made her presence known to the room.

The snipers typically hid within the structure of the elaborate ceiling, waiting like guardians to protect the Advisors if need be. It was peculiar to her that none of the snipers were in the room. In fact, it didn't seem like anyone else was in the room but her and the eldest Advisor.

Soo Jin shrugged, stowing away those thoughts and concluding that they were probably out training in the gardens.

She continued to move deeper into the room.

So many memories . . .

Soo Jin felt like she had stepped back into time. While walking, she could see a gold coffin laying in the darker right corner of the room. The insides of her gut coiled at the unpleasant flashbacks the coffin brought. Although the exterior was made out of gold, the interior of the coffin was made out of wood. Soo Jin recalled asking Ju Won why this was the case. The answer he gave her still haunted her to this day. He said that he simply loved the sound people made when they were clawing at the wood, doing everything in their power to escape. He said he loved it even more when they screamed out in anguish upon realizing that there was no way out of the coffin. Clawing at the wood may have given them some semblance of hope, but reaching the gold surface only reinforced the horror in knowing that they have finally reached the end of their rope.

"There is nothing more beautiful than the sound of people giving up on their control in life, giving up on hope," he once told her before throwing her into that same coffin and locking her in after her first night of training.

Memories of her fingers, filled with wooden splinters, bleeding from attempting to scrape her way out of the claustrophobic coffin invaded her mind. The Advisors had used that as her punishment during her training. Every night she failed as a God, they would toss her into that coffin and lock her in for the night. The memories thrashed into her mind like ocean waves, making it hard for her to breathe. Even then, when Soo Jin knew there was no way out of the coffin once she was sealed in, she continued to claw at the wood because it was against every survival instinct in her body to lie there and do nothing. Soo Jin would never forget how powerless she felt. She was grateful to no longer be in that pathetic state again.

Soo Jin dragged her gaze away from the coffin. She wanted to block out that terrible stage of her life. Her journey to becoming a God was an excruciating one, and now that it was over, it was time to move on.

Her eyes swept the room for her Advisor. Her focus lingered on the three familiar chairs at the far end of the room. The seats resembled that of thrones. Ju Won's center seat sat roughly two inches higher than Shin Dong Min's and Shin Jung Min's. It was a throne she had always wanted to sit in. The Advisors always looked so comfortable, so powerful when they watched her fight dozens of people twice her size and barked orders at her on how to properly fight back. Many other memories from her years of training came back to her, both the triumphant and soul-ripping ones. They all reminded her of how far she had come, all the power she acquired, and all the power that awaited her in the future. The very remembrance of this calmed her before she finally spotted Ju Won.

He was standing in front of the windows with his back turned to her. His black suit blended in with the darkness of the impending night sky.

"Uncle," she greeted with a small bow.

Soo Jin stood beside him and followed his gaze. She stared out the floor-to-ceiling window that overlooked his grandiose backyard and the city lights behind it.

"Soo Jin," he greeted, his tone warm. Albeit his focus was still on the city, she could feel the smile in his eyes at her arrival.

As much as she loathed her upbringing, Soo Jin couldn't deny that she was happy to see her Advisor. He had always been strict with her when he trained her—the Shin Elders as well. In the same token, they were also like father figures to her—Ju Won being the primary one. He did everything in his power to make her a lethal weapon in this cruel society. For that, she could never resent him.

"Have you been well?" she asked politely, a tone she rarely used with anyone else but the Advisors, her brother, and her father.

"Do you remember when I stood here with you when you were ten?" he launched reminiscently, lightly dismissing her question. His eyes were still fastened on the darkening skies. "I told you that for the next seven to eight years, you would know nothing but hardship. While other Princesses of the Underworld would be preoccupied with being pampered by their parents, their older siblings, or their prospective boyfriends, you would be placed through a world of hell where your body, mind, and soul would rip apart under unimaginable circumstances."

A dry smile tilted on Soo Jin's lips.

It was impossible not to recall those memories when she was in the very training ground that molded her into the Queen she was today.

Soo Jin sighed, reminiscing with her Advisor. "There were fifty-six times during the course of training where I laid in a pile of my own blood, writhing in so much pain that I thought I was going to die. Fifty-six times up until I reached the age of fifteen, and then I lost count."

While other prospective Kings trained with revered mentors from every country imaginable, Soo Jin was shown the malice of the world in Ju Won's mansion. She was sealed in a room with pedophiles, rapists, and murderers who were promised exemption from Underworld punishment if they could torture and ultimately kill her. This cruelty was bestowed to her as training to toughen her up in a world dominated by men. It was also used to show her how worthless and deserving of death some people were. She was taught survival at a young age. Even as a child, Soo Jin knew her relationship with her adversaries was an inverse one. If she wanted to live, then they must die. Kill or be killed.

So everyday, throughout the course of her training, she lunged across walls, snapped necks apart, tortured people with her knives, luxuriated in their screams, and relished in her victories over worthless human beings who were never worthy of life. Soo Jin killed and became so desensitized that blood merely resembled water to her. Screams of agony became mere whispers in the wind while the sight of life evaporating from peoples' eyes became entertainment to her. She was molded to be better than human, and by the time her training was over, all she knew was power. To her, there was no better feeling than to be feared and venerated like a God.

"That ten-year-old girl seems to be a part of another world," Soo Jin murmured, vaguely remembering the events of her life prior to training. It all felt like a dream from another world, like the innocence she once had never existed.

Ju Won permitted himself a small smile. "Everyone wondered why out of all the chosen heirs of the Underworld, I chose you . . . the second born daughter who was never meant to be an heir. Everyone wondered why out of all the young princes I could've picked to carry on my lineage, I chose you." He chuckled, finally casting his gaze to her. He was an old man, yet the power that continued to exude from him was awe-inspiring. Even after ten years of being trained by him, Soo Jin couldn't help but feel honored to stand in his company. She felt privileged to be the protégé he chose to carry on his lineage.

"You were always meant for greatness, Soo Jin," he told her proudly.

It was at this point that Soo Jin caught the insinuating undertone in his voice. It was very subtle, but she caught it all the same. Soo Jin regarded him strangely, curious of his motives. This meeting with him wasn't a normal one. He had asked her to come here for a reason.

Ju Won confirmed her suspicions by forging on. "That was why I chose you and that is the reason why I'm meeting with you now. I want to discuss your future."

Soo Jin raised an inquisitive brow. "My future?"

Though she grew up with Ju Won and admired him like a second father, Soo Jin wasn't a fool. She knew how ruthless Ju Won could be, and despite the honor she received from being around him, she also knew she had to be cautious with him at all times.

"The Kings reign over the 3rd layer, Soo Jin," he began, his own eyes scrutinizing her, "but ultimately, it is a God who will rule over this world. There are big things coming, and this society needs a Lord who will catapult it to great heights, to bring us higher than we've ever been."

"What are you saying?"

"An Young Jae, Kwon Ho Young, and Lee Ji Hoon are great and powerful leaders, but they are all missing a certain quality that makes them God material. They are not legendary enough." Pride permeated his warm eyes. "But you . . . everything that embodies you is legendary. Everything that personifies you is epic. You are the one, Soo Jin. You are the one who should rule this world. Not as a Queen by the side of a great King, but as a Queen who rivals the great Kings to become a God—our Lord."

"I will not fight my brother or Ji Hoon for the throne," Soo Jin snapped swiftly, though she knew a big part of her was only saying what she felt she *should* say. Did she really mean it? In the depths of her broken soul, she wasn't sure.

And Ju Won could read this.

He knew she didn't mean it.

"Ji Hoon will give you whatever you want. We both know that," Ju Won shrewdly noted. "The only one you would have to fight is your brother. He's the only one standing in your way, the only shadow that you are stuck underneath."

Rage swarmed over her like a firestorm.

Whether it was because she hated Ju Won for trying to pit her against her own brother or the fact that the greedy part of her was considering this betrayal, she wasn't sure. All she knew was that she was furious with Ju Won for eliciting this emotion from her.

"I will not betray my own brother," she declared again, although she couldn't deny how tempting it all sounded.

That was her flaw.

Power had always been her drug of strength . . . and weakness.

Ju Won's face began to line with irritation.

"Young Jae is a pathetic excuse for a King," he sneered angrily, losing his cool with her. The tone in his voice was venomous. It was blatantly clear he hated her older brother.

"He is my brother," Soo Jin retaliated, a sudden protectiveness surging through her when Ju Won spoke so negatively about Young Jae. Her voice elevated with conviction. She could feel the guns behind her back burn with wrath. "I am ruthless Ju Won, very much so. But not to my own brother, not to the only flesh and blood I have left, and certainly not to the one I vowed my undying loyalty to."

"Your loyalty belongs with your father first and foremost!" Ju Won countered, and that was the last straw for Soo Jin.

She had enough with the old man badmouthing her brother and bringing up her father's name in the process. It was simply unacceptable.

"My patience is dwindling, Ju Won," Soo Jin warned gravely, suddenly whipping out her gold gun and pressing it underneath his chin.

Murder drenched her eyes.

Ju Won intimidated her, but she certainly wasn't afraid to do what was necessary. After years of training, she had picked up her own fighting skills and had mastered the art of using weapons all on her own. She was a skilled fighter and knew that if she wanted to, she could snap Ju Won's neck like a twig. Ju Won raised her to be a Queen, and now that she was one, she would make sure he knew damn well who had the most power in this room and who would kneel before whom.

"I grew up being raised by you firsthand; I know how you are. I know you find entertainment in pitting people against one another. I allowed you to get away with things in the past because you are my Advisor and I owe so much to you. But don't test my patience when it comes to betraying my own brother—my own gang. I will blow your fucking head off before I become your puppet and betray my own family."

"You speak of loyalty," Ju Won uttered coolly, unfazed by what Soo Jin was doing to him. There was no fear that exuded from him. It was as if he had expected this reaction from her. He knew just what to say to quell the anger. "But what about your brother's betrayal?"

Chills chased after chills in her body once he said this.

Soo Jin pressed the gun harder into him.

"What," she demanded slowly, disturbed by his insinuation, "are you talking about?"

"You heard about his raid on the Siberian Tigers' estate. You heard about him exterminating the bloodline that was supposed to succeed the Siberian Tigers' throne, but do you know why he insisted on killing the *entire* lineage?"

"For his throne," Soo Jin answered, though her own instincts were beginning to doubt the answer she offered. There was something in the tone of Ju Won's voice that rocked her to her very core. Her grip on the gun was already slackening as she stared at him.

Ju Won chuckled faintly. He slowly reached his hand into his jacket pocket and pulled out a remote. He casually handed it to her.

"To keep his secret intact," he enlightened.

Shortly after, sounds of whirling descended into the room. A 60-inch, flat screen TV cascaded from the ceiling and lowered itself just above the three "thrones." When the TV reached its position, it stopped moving, turned on, and displayed a blue screen.

An unnatural chill crept over her. In shocked silence, Soo Jin stared at the TV like she would at the tides, right before the winds brought forth a monstrous typhoon that would destroy anything in its path.

Watch the screen, her inner voice instructed her.

Her heart thundered in her chest as though begging her to disregard her mind's advisement. She was conflicted because she knew that whatever it was Ju Won wanted to show her, it was going to be bad. She mulled over it for several more seconds before she released her grip on the gun and pulled it away from Ju Won's chin.

It was an instinctive decision.

Instead of shooting him, she took the remote he offered her. It took an elongated moment, which felt like eternities to the nerves inhabiting Soo Jin's body, before she breathed past the anticipation and finally pressed the "Play" button.

A kaleidoscope of colors displayed on the screen in blurs before a film took its place on the TV.

It was a video recording.

The film was grainy, a bit shaky, and the zoomed in features were difficult to see. The roaring of the violent wind was prominent in the video. It looked like someone was shooting the scene from the top of a building somewhere. The recording wasn't the best quality, but it showed enough for the viewer to see everything clearly.

The lens of the camera focused on a warehouse that was beside a seaport of sorts. Soo Jin could see the railings that separated the concrete land from the sea of water beside it. The ground was empty, vacant of any breathing entities. Soo Jin examined it, suddenly feeling familiarity to the area. It gradually occurred to her why it looked familiar.

It was a seaport warehouse that her family owned. Her father used it during his reign as the King of Scorpions for his shipping business.

The calm before the storm, the voice cryptically said in her mind.

And it was.

It was calm . . . quiet . . . until she felt her world tilt after her father walked onto the screen. The weight of the beloved necklace her father gifted her increased in mass around her neck. It had been so long since Soo Jin had seen him. Her heart clenched at the sight of her father, not only because of his sudden appearance on the screen, but also because he was wearing the same gray suit she last saw him in — the one he was murdered in. Oxygen became lodged in her chest.

His eight bodyguards surrounded him, and he looked as powerful as she last remembered him. His men encased him in a V-formation, protecting him as they ventured out of the warehouse. They were heading to a black town car to leave the premises. Before they reached the car, however, an ambush occurred as a sniper shot four of her father's men down.

The hand that held her gun went limp.

It hit Soo Jin that she was watching the very recording of her father's murder.

Besieged with horror, she mindlessly stumbled forward, her face paling as she continued to watch the film. Sounds of gunshots filled the large room she was in, causing her own heart to race thunderously.

Four of the bodyguards, despite the wounds that marred their chests, raced to cover her father, blocking him as countless more bullets continued to infiltrate their bodies. In front of them, the remaining four began to fire shots all around, shooting at the sniper who was burying metal into their bodies.

In the course of all this, her father withdrew two guns of his own and began to shoot. His efforts were halted when a single bullet came speeding toward him, entering through his elbow, and then puncturing into the neck of the bodyguard protecting him. Shortly after that, another bullet was fired, penetrating her father's kneecap and causing him to plunge to the floor.

Unfathomable pain ripped through her when this occurred.

And then, all was lost.

One by one, his men were shot down, their bodies twitching incessantly before the life dissipated from them. Her father was left all alone, struggling to stand up despite the bullet that was lodged in his kneecap. He was alone . . . until Kwon Ho Young, who was dressed in a black pinstriped suit, walked into the screen with a black gun in his hand.

The way he walked was triumphant and mocking.

The grip Soo Jin had on her gun tightened; she would give anything to be there to save her father.

Ho Young kicked her father's guns away. She could see that Ho Young was laughing at him. His back was turned to the camera, but she could discern that he was laughing and ridiculing her father.

Her father, despite the fact that he had been shot twice, tried to fight Ho Young. His efforts proved to be fruitless. He could scarcely get a punch in before he was shot again in the back. The bullet came from the exact direction of where the warehouse stood.

Then, the world froze.

From the area in which the most recent shot was fired, her brother—Young Jae—stepped into the range of the screen. He was holding a gun of his own.

Her extremities went cold, her eyes unblinking.

The betrayal that marked her father's face was undeniable when he collapsed to the ground. Blood flooded from his body, yet none of that pain equated to the agony in his eyes as he stared up at his son and realized that he had been betrayed by his own flesh and blood.

He was there . . . he was there all along, she thought horrifically.

An Young Jae wasn't protecting their father.

He had just shot him in the back.

He had just *helped* Kwon Ho Young.

There was no regret in Young Jae's emotionless face. It did not hurt him to see his father staring up at him with anguish in his eyes. To make the betrayal worse, he had the audacity to kick their father's stomach while he was already down. Soo Jin's fury reached new heights when Young Jae lifted his foot and proceeded to press the sole of his boot into her father's neck. Her father struggled underneath, desperately trying to push his foot off so he could breathe. Young Jae did not budge. Instead, he motioned for Ho Young to come forward. Ho Young inched closer, and without hesitation, he slammed his foot onto her father's mouth. Coagulated blood spurted from her father's mouth. It was only then did Young Jae release his foot from her father's neck.

Soo Jin was shaking.

She was shaking with so much shock that she couldn't even breathe. It felt like her world was collapsing all around her. Her mind grappled with the realization that her older brother—the one she adored and promised her undying loyalty to—was the one behind her father's demise. She would not have believed this travesty if she had not witnessed it with her own eyes. Soo Jin swallowed tightly, unshed tears beginning to gleam in her eyes. Her heart was racing beyond all levels of acceleration, and then, just like that, her heart stopped pounding when the horror occurred.

The seconds before her father's death . . .

Young Jae and Ho Young, both of whom were standing above her father's fallen body, lifted up their guns. They stared straight into her father's widened eyes. No hesitation marked the nerves in their bodies. Simultaneously, they pulled the trigger.

Boom! Boom!

Two earth-shattering bangs thundered into the quiet room, causing Soo Jin's eyes to ripple with tears.

Soo Jin remembered that day perfectly. She remembered how her father looked, how his body was bleeding every which way. Two bullets laid where his eyes should've been, forever ridiculing him even in death. His mouth was parted open from shock, dismay, and hurt.

As if dying with her father's last breath, the recording stopped. Darkness ensued, and then a blue screen took over, informing Soo Jin that there was no more footage to display.

"How long have you had this video?" Soo Jin asked long seconds later, her tear-cloaked eyes still staring unblinkingly at the TV screen. She was so incredibly stunned that she couldn't even discern her emotions at that point. The images of her father's death replayed in her mind, tormenting her with every passing moment.

"Last night," Ju Won answered. In a rare display of emotions, his own eyes were also shrouded with pain. It was clear that the death of Soo Jin's father, one of his few good friends in the Underworld, devastated him tremendously. "It was given to me last night."

"Who gave it to you?"

"Who do you think?"

Soo Jin brokenly pondered over the answer. If what Ju Won said about her brother was true — that there was an ulterior reason why he chose to exterminate the entire Siberian Tigers' lineage — then there was only one person who could've given Ju Won that tape.

"Tony," she stated, never feeling more rage and hurt course through her.

Ju Won nodded, and Soo Jin's congested mind continued to ponder over memories that didn't make sense before, but made perfect sense now.

"He didn't ask me to help kill them that night," she ruminated slowly, recalling how odd it felt to her when Young Jae decided to attack the Siberian Tigers' estate. He did not even recruit her to help him. "He said he didn't want me involved in it."

"Because he had Ho Young's help," Ju Won supplied. "The only reason why Young Jae was able to infiltrate the estate and kill nearly the entire lineage was because Ho Young joined forces with him and helped him that night."

"Somehow," Soo Jin reasoned, the pieces of the puzzle coming together for her, "they knew that the Siberian Tigers had the tape."

Ju Won nodded again. "That was why Young Jae and Ho Young raided the estate." Disgust cloaked his voice. "It wasn't to kill the lineage so Young Jae would succeed the Scorpions' throne — he could've done that by just killing Hee Jun. It was because the lineage had a video recording of the conspiracy that showed his partnership with Ho Young. It was because they had footage that showed Young Jae's betrayal. If anyone else saw that tape, their reputations would be tarnished because everyone would know that they helped each other become Kings."

"My reputation hangs on the line. We need to find Tony and kill him immediately. We also need to silence any necessary people who are threats to ruining the reign of my throne."

Her brother's words resounded in her mind, reminding her of the situation they were in.

"How did Tony survive?" Soo Jin finally asked.

"Ho Young and Young Jae were messy. The Siberian Tigers' estate wasn't an easy place to raid, and they were too distracted with finding the tape. They killed Hee Jun and assumed Tony was dead since they shot him several times. Fortunately for Tony, one of his men found him in time. He was hospitalized and sent to the Philippines for two years to recover. He was on the brink of death before he was able to regain some strength and return to Korea. His extended family provided a home for him and helped him find me. Young Jae and Ho Young found one tape, but they didn't realize there was another one. They also didn't realize Tony was in possession of it. I didn't know he was alive until he appeared on my doorstep last night, telling me that he had something to show me and that he needed you to watch this."

Soo Jin inhaled slowly, still fragmented with all that was happening. "Where is he now?"

"Missing," Ju Won answered at once. A long pause stole his lips before he said, "Young Jae has him, Soo Jin."

"Not possible," she dismissed, replaying the conversation she had with her brother earlier. "Why would he have me kidnap an entire family if he has—"

Soo Jin stopped speaking when the sudden realization dawned on her.

"Young Jae isn't the type of person he pretends to be," Ju Won said to her, aware of what was running through her mind. His wise eyes held the same knowledge. "Why do you think he's having you kidnap an entire family if he already has Tony? What do you think he's going to do to them once you bring them to him? Why do you think he's giving you the task of retrieving the family?"

For the first time in her life, Soo Jin was speechless.

She knew exactly where Ju Won was headed with this logic, for it was the same road her logic paved for her. Slowly, the shock that swept over her became replaced with unfathomable rage. She clenched her fists, her animosity for her brother mounting as she listened to Ju Won's words.

"You will be the one who kills them, Soo Jin," he told her. "Somehow, some way, you will be the one to kill them all. Young Jae is a bastard, but he's a smart bastard nonetheless. He knows the politics involved in our world. We are ruthless, yes, but we're also honorable when we need to be. He killed an entire lineage because he didn't want it known that he colluded with his enemy to kill his own father. He's having you kidnap an entire family because he wants them all dead, and he wants you to take the fall for it."

Ju Won stood closer to her, cupping her cheek with the palm of his hand like a father would for his daughter.

"All these years, you've stayed in his shadow and served him with your life. Yet all along, he never once offered you the loyalty you've shown him. What do you do in this situation, Soo Jin? What have I taught you, my child?"

"I will *not* kill him in his sleep," Soo Jin breathed out, the tears that once blurred her vision drying up under the immeasurable anger she felt. Even the coldness of the room did little to pacify the volcanic lava erupting through her. "I used rat poison to defeat others when I was ten, but I am no longer a child. I cannot stoop that low."

"No, I taught you greatness," Ju Won said vehemently. "If you want revenge, you will bring a war upon him."

"I have no soldiers," she said at once. No matter how much Soo Jin wanted a war, she wasn't a fool either. She had the loyalty of the Scorpions she personally trained and the loyalty of the Skulls as Ji Hoon would always stay by her side, yes, but that was it. The fact that Young Jae and Ho Young had an alliance meant that the war she intended to wage against her brother would not be a war — it would be a massacre of the people on her side. Ho Young and Young Jae were too strong compared to her and Ji Hoon. Even though she was a revered Queen, she wasn't a crime lord. She had no commanding power over the Scorpions who would give up their lives for her older brother if he asked them to. Her numbers just weren't strong enough to go against his.

"Tony wants to give you power over his gang, Soo Jin. He wants to give you his soldiers."

She narrowed her eyes onto Ju Won. "The Siberian Tigers are dead."

He shook his head. "The lineage is dead, but the gang is just inactive. They are waiting for the chosen one to resurrect their gang, and you're going to be that new power." Before she could protest, he went on. "I've already spoken to Tony. His arms are no longer the same. He will never be able to fight again. In this war, he knows that he will merely be a tool for you to seek revenge for his family, and he's willing to give you reign over his throne. He's willing to give you his Siberian Tigers."

"How?" she inquired, seeing no hope in this matter. If it was true that her brother had Tony, then all of this was futile. "How would I lead his gang if my brother has him?"

"The Siberian Tigers' jade knife," Ju Won told her instantly. "Before his death, Hee Jun gave the jade knife to his girlfriend, Eve. He gave it to her for safekeeping, to protect it for Tony until he succeeded the throne. In order to lead the Siberian Tigers, their bylaws mandate that the new Siberian Tigers' King must possess the jade knife. The new King must also perform a ritual based on a riddle that had been passed down from the Siberian Tigers' forefathers. All the Siberian Tigers know about this ritual. Unfortunately, Tony did not give me the riddle. He wanted to personally give it to you. But now Young Jae has him, and Eve still has the jade knife." He regarded her, his face swarming with conviction. "Your only saving grace is Eve. She not only has the knife, but she also knows the riddle. You must get both from her."

A skeptical scoff escaped Soo Jin. There were so many holes in his plan that she could not even begin to take it seriously. "How would I do that? There are Scorpions watching her every move, waiting to kidnap her. I would never be able to get close to her without arousing suspicion."

"There's only one thing you can do in this situation that doesn't give anything away."

Soo Jin slanted her head and stared at Ju Won in disbelief. She knew what he was suggesting. "You want me to torture them for the information once my brother's men bring them to the club?"

"You and I know that the extended family is dead the moment Young Jae sets his eyes on them. He doesn't know how many of them know about the tape and the conspiracy, which means he's going to kill all of them to keep his secret and his reputation intact. They are merely living on borrowed time right now, and if you can't get the information from Eve, then you will miss your chance for your war. You can attempt to kill him one on one, but we both know that victory is only sweet if you get your vengeance during a war—when you're making history at the same time. And after this, I will give you my empire. This alone will show our society the unending support I have for you. It will also show the trust I have that you will lead this world well. In addition to your revenge, you will also be the top candidate to become the Lord of the Underworld."

Soo Jin could not conceal the glint that twinkled in her eyes.

Lord of the Underworld.

What a powerful name.

Ju Won smiled, looking at her with promise. "What do you say, Soo Jin? Are you willing to do what it takes to avenge your father? Are you willing to become what it takes to get your vengeance? Will you become the God you were always meant to be?" The air grew stern as he asked the last words that would seal her fate for the years to come. "Are you in, or are you out?"

Soo Jin thought back to the video she watched, the very evidence that proved what a ruthless bastard her brother truly was. All along, he conspired with Ho Young to kill their father. All along, he had been lying to her, using her. Her mind ventured on to the family he wanted her to kidnap. She realized now that the reason why he gave her this task was because he was throwing her under the bus. He wanted her to take the blame for the family that he was going to kill. He didn't care about her father and he most certainly didn't care about her.

A volcanic eruption exploded in her body.

A decade of constant training, a decade of killings, and a decade with a deteriorating soul washed over Soo Jin. It acted as the catalyst for the unfathomable rage that engulfed her very being.

Young Jae was never fit to be the King of Scorpions—a part of her had always known this. And now, with all that she discovered, she also knew he no longer deserved her loyalty. He deserved nothing but a cruel and painful death—the very same one bestowed upon her father.

He deserved a war.

Soo Jin said nothing for a long time.

Her eyes involuntarily roamed the room before they zeroed in on the gold coffin—her gold coffin. An unstoppable inferno raged inside her, bringing forth images of all the blood, sweat, and tears she sacrificed to become the Queen of the Underworld. Her gaze migrated to the throne-like chair in the room. Hope heaved through her. She had the title, but now, she wanted a Kingdom befitting of her moniker.

With her ambition as her guide and her hatred for Young Jae as her motivator, Soo Jin made an unspoken promise to Ju Won. She utilized a method commonly used by the Kings in the Underworld to give their unbreakable word and effectively sealed her fate in this world.

Fire blazed in her eyes as she handed her gold gun to Ju Won.

Simply and resolutely, she said, "In."

"You will be punished..."

28: The Changing of Tides

An Soo Jin was just like any other mountain that stood amongst the heavens, its peak reigning over its inferior inhabitants.

When untouched, she stands with towering pride and strikes fear into anyone who dares to cross her. However, when a certain tide changes and she feels that change, she fights viciously to hold on to the remainder of her inhumanity that had catapulted within her short, yet elongated lifespan. This was her therapy; this was An Soo Jin's decade-long secret for her survival in a world so cruel that even monstrous beasts whimper before the society in fear. She lived and breathed power. She lived and breathed pride. She lived and breathed battles.

To fight the occasional crippling human emotions that plagued her, Soo Jin would, without fail, resort to killing people without mercy or battling a worthy opponent who would give her the fight of her life. These two tactics had always worked because they made her feel inhumane; they made her feel better than human. It had always worked, but now, as the current magnitude of human emotions pelted over her, Soo Jin couldn't help but feel a bit more human than she had ever felt in ten years.

She didn't like the pit-like feeling that made a home in her gut. She wasn't fond of the headaches torturing her, and she sure as hell didn't like that she was prone to tearing up whenever she thought of her father's death and her brother's ultimate betrayal. She was feeling a bit too human for her own taste and being this weak was simply intolerable for her.

Others from the outside looking in would be fools to assume that discovering her brother's betrayal would mean that she would become the "good guy" in this equation—that somehow, a decade of killing and being heartless would dissipate and she would see the errors of her ways.

The mere thought was comical to her.

Soo Jin was loyal—fiercely so. Nevertheless, her one good trait was violently overshadowed by the fact that she was also self-serving, power hungry, vindictive, and cold-blooded. She did not spend years perfecting her skills and sacrificing her blood to have it all fall to ruin. She did not give up her soul to become a God just to become a feeble human again. All of that was simply . . . unacceptable.

She had to fix it.

She had to rectify it if she wanted any chance of saving herself.

Her decision was set two nights later.

At eight that evening, Soo Jin led four other Scorpions into the various homes inhabited by the extended Siberian Tigers' family. While she shot at innocent people and brutally dragged them from their homes, the conversation between herself and Ju Won invaded her mind.

"How are you going to play this out, Soo Jin?" Ju Won had asked moments after Soo Jin made the agreement to bring war upon Young Jae. "What are your plans?"

"I need time to resurrect the Siberian Tigers," Soo Jin answered, already formulating her strategy. There was determined conviction in the eyes that used to be blurred with fragile tears. She was a woman on a mission. To be distracted with human emotions was not something she would allow. Too much was riding on this very moment.

"It's been two years, and they have dispersed throughout the regions of this country." She stared at Ju Won, fierce resolve shrouding her visage. "I'm going to need time to regroup them. In this timeframe, I also want my trusted trainees to leave the Scorpions and either form their own gangs or infiltrate other ones. I want more numbers on my side, and I want to break apart other gangs when everything comes full circle . . ."

"Get the fuck over here!" Soo Jin shouted, grabbing on to the collar of a seventy-year-old man who was trying to tend to his fallen wife. Soo Jin had just punched him in the gut and elbowed him in the face.

His wife, a frail little old lady, was coughing up blood as she writhed on the floor. Soo Jin stood with dominance in a white semi-truck that they were piling the family members into. In the background, other Scorpions were beating and tying the family members up as well.

As she barked orders at the Scorpions in the truck, her mind continued to relive her conversation with Ju Won.

"How are you going to do all this without arousing suspicion from Young Jae?" Ju Won had asked her.

"I will not be around to be suspicious," she shared, already thinking this part through. "My brother is a smart man. If I'm under his rule, then there's not much I can hide if I'm trying to resurrect a gang of my own. He'll kill me before he gives me that chance." Something glowed in her eyes, a glint that hinted at her motives. "My only way out is to disappear under his hands and his hands alone."

Ju Won's eyes narrowed onto her. "You're going to fake your death?"

"Please!" the old man in the semi-truck cried. He dropped to his knees before Soo Jin. "Please, why are you doing this?"

Soo Jin did not respond. She merely pulled his collar, dragged him up, and then threw him hard on to the floor beside his wife. Once his head collided with the wall of the truck, Soo Jin took out her gold gun and pointed it at him.

"Tie her up," she commanded, throwing him the ropes to do it.

When the old man hesitated, an impatient Soo Jin, who was not willing to use up her bullets yet, took out her knife. She sped over to him. With great force, she snatched his hand and viciously sliced off two of his fingers. A portion of his pinky and the tip of his middle finger plunged on to the floor.

His guttural screams drenched the truck while Soo Jin smirked. Shaking her head without remorse, she said, "I asked you nicely before, but don't fuck with me, old man. Now hurry and tie her up before I cut off the rest of your fingers."

Her own words to Ju Won echoed in her mind as the man painfully did as he was told.

"When we were younger, I always told him that if I were to kill myself, then it would be through injecting myself with a drug to die. I wanted to die in the cleanest of ways, without foam coming out of my mouth and without blood seeping out of me. He has to be the one to do it to keep my plan intact; he has to inject the poison into me if I want to fully disappear without him trying to track me down."

Concern entered Ju Won's gaze. "What would the Queen of the Underworld commit suicide over?"

Soo Jin thought about the age-old curse that had plagued humans since the beginning of time. In every killer's life, there is said to be a moment in time when, after years upon years of killing, an altering of tides occur in which the cruelty you lived by fades under the return of a soul once given up to become inhuman. This moment is said to be the downfall of killers who find themselves falling to ruins when their soul—their humanity—returns to them and demands retribution for all the lives they cruelly stole.

Soo Jin had heard stories of this curse falling upon the once "immortal legends" of this world and about the radical state these former legends spiral into when they had to face the curse of a lifetime.

This curse had never happened to her (and for this, she was thankful). However, she imagined it would be the perfect excuse to give and the perfect road to take if she wanted to be absolutely believable to her brother. She knew enough about the standards of limitations when it came to fucking around with one's humanity, and she knew what to use as her "breaking point."

She was going to use the Siberian Tigers' extended family, namely the mother and her two children, and she was going to perform the human equivalent of the unforgivable: killing innocents and killing children.

The genius of her plan brought pride to her sadistic eyes.

They were it—they were the ones who would help her on the road to glory. They were the ones who would help keep her inhumanity—and ultimately her power—intact.

Killing two birds with one stone, Soo Jin thought triumphantly, feeling no dread in the evil she was about to commit.

The Queen of the Underworld would commit suicide because she became embarrassingly "human" again . . . *Genius*.

Standing inside the moving truck, while keeping her eyes on the family members who were now sobbing together, Soo Jin felt nothing but anticipation for what was to come.

She had no reservations about killing innocent people prior to finding out about her brother's betrayal and continued to have no problem killing them with or without that information. As far as Soo Jin was concerned, they were merely casualties in order to obtain information about taking over the Siberian Tigers' throne. They were simply tools used to make her brother believe the act she was about to pull.

Soo Jin waved her blood-hungry knife and slashed off the ears of any of the family members who dared to fight her while they were being transported to the club.

Wiping off blood splatters from her face, her emotionless eyes involuntarily shifted over to Eve and her two children, all of whom were hiding in the back corner of the truck, shaking relentlessly. Eve was tied up and bound with sturdy ropes while the small boys, the only ones untouched by the Scorpions and herself, were tending to their mother. Their innocent brown eyes were wide with fright while they looked at their aunts and uncles. The extended family may not have been related to the children by blood, but it was clear to Soo Jin in the way they would whisper comforting words to the boys that they loved them nonetheless. It was also obvious to Soo Jin that the boys were fighting between the need to stay with their mother and the desire to run over to one of their aunts and uncles to help tend to their wounds as well.

Their fear of Soo Jin when she raised her bloodied knife to motion for them to sit still, however, cemented them in their positions. Helpless, they wrapped their small arms around their mother, shaking with her while she cried at the sight of her deceased lover's family getting beaten to death by the Scorpions who stood behind Soo Jin.

Remember to "cry" when you kill those three, Soo Jin reminded herself when the truck came to a halt.

The terror in the enclosed space thickened when the entryway of the truck was wheeled up. The cold night's breeze crawled in. A collective hush came over the truck. Everyone knew what was to come. They were going to meet the one behind all of this.

Young Jae.

Standing before them, dressed in one of his impeccable black suits, Young Jae had on his signature expression. It was an expression that held severity, yet also hiding a hint of warmth as if to fabricate the verity of his true intentions. Even under the eyes of his soon-to-be victims and his Scorpions, he was still acting it up for them. It was a wonder to Soo Jin that she only now caught up with his act.

Though less than thrilled with seeing him, Soo Jin manufactured a smile and silently greeted him with a wave of the knife.

Pleased that he had the entire extended family in his grasp, Young Jae gave Soo Jin an approving look before he motioned with his fingers for the Scorpions to bring the family members forward and take them into the club.

"I want to kill two birds with one stone and do something else while we're here," Soo Jin said, jumping out of the truck. The rest of the family members had quietly been filed in. It was just Soo Jin and her brother standing out on the desolate street.

Young Jae didn't appear to be paying attention.

"We'll discuss it later," he said distractedly. He lifted a knife that he was holding by the blade and handed it to her. "But before that, torture them and find me Tony. After that, you can do whatever you want."

A smile graced Soo Jin's lips. She was ecstatic to hear her predicted answer from him. Soo Jin grabbed the knife by the blade and walked into the club with her guns behind her back. The end justified the means, and if torturing them meant she would become the Lord of the Underworld, then she was all too happy to bestow hell on to them.

An hour and a half was how long it took for Soo Jin to singlehandedly torture thirty-one family members, kill sixteen, and then leave the remaining fifteen to writhe on the floor like dying worms. The three left—the mother and her two children—sat in the corner unharmed. But not for long.

"I don't trust him," Young Jae whispered. His eyes roamed the room from the balcony while he spoke to her.

The floor was littered with blood, amputated fingers, disembodied flesh, and corpses.

After finding out Tony's location—useless information given that her brother was the one who had him—Soo Jin went up to the balcony. She brought up finding a "prized" heirloom for Ju Won in order to get his favor on their side. It was a lie that she started to perpetuate while she was torturing the family members by asking them where the infamous jade knife was. Unfortunately for Soo Jin, Young Jae had never gotten along with Ju Won. He was anything but cooperative when it came to procuring something for the eldest Advisor. But fortunately, Soo Jin was a cunning and persuasive individual. If she wanted something, then there were few who could deny her.

"What could it hurt if we continued to torture them?" she placated diplomatically. Splatters of blood stained the jeans and black jacket she wore.

Soo Jin would be damned if she couldn't get the jade knife and the riddle. She had to get to the mother and the two children. She knew that the only option was to openly interrogate them in front of her brother. It was the only way to avoid suspicion.

"Nothing matters anymore," she continued, her mind already wheeling the plan into motion. "The moment they stepped foot in here, they were going to die anyway. Why not try to find out something for Ju Won while we're at it?"

The vindictiveness of her own words made her proud.

What a blessing to be above crippling human emotions.

"You trust him too much, lil sis," said Young Jae. His eyes on her were severe. "Ju Won is a snake and the worst possible kind. Nothing he offers you should be taken lightly."

"He's offering our family his empire, oppa," Soo Jin lied, raising her voice, yet keeping it respectful to avoid pissing him off. "You know the pendulum of power that comes with that exchange. The Serpents are becoming stronger. Kwon Ho Young not only has the support of China's Underworld, but he also has a trump card—his younger brother. His brother is on his way to ruling over the 1st layer. You know how influential that layer is when the Corporate Crime Lords are united. If we don't move Ju Won over to our side, then all the power will shift to the Serpents. Is that what you want? For this world to kneel under the rule of the Serpents? The fuckers who murdered our father?"

There was poignancy in her eyes that flickered for a split second. It was one that almost betrayed her knowledge that it was her brother who killed their father.

"Don't speak to me as if our father's death affected you more than it affected me," Young Jae warned, detecting her bitterness even when she tried so hard to hide it. "You have no idea what I'm going through."

Soo Jin bowed her head as her apology, mentally chastising herself for giving her emotions away. "I'm sorry," she lied. "You know how much I hate them whenever I think about our father." She persevered, refusing to give up. "Our world is changing, oppa. The three gangs are growing stronger and stronger everyday, but there's a shifting of power now. Pretty soon, once things are in order, there will only be one Lord of the Underworld to rule over this entire layer and the two layers above it. I can't stand here and allow the Serpents to have that power, especially when all we have to do is find out whatever it is Ju Won wants from the family below."

Her eyes fastened onto the floor where the unharmed mother and twins sat huddled in the corner, their faces paled from fear. She had been eyeing them the entire night with dwindling patience. She had to get information and she had to get it from them now.

"You're not touching them, Soo Jin," Young Jae warned softly, though she knew by the dark undertone of his voice that he wanted her to. He wanted her to kill them, he wanted her to take the blame, and he wanted her to kill the entire family for the sake of his reputation.

In that moment, the stage was set with two performers: An Young Jae and An Soo Jin.

Soo Jin was determined to be the best performer of the two.

"Look at how they shake," she directed coldly. "That woman was Hwang Hee Jun's girlfriend, and although the children aren't his, I'm sure he loved them like his own. From the fear in their eyes, how they shudder, and how they looked at me when I tortured and shot those sixteen people, I know that they are the ones who have the answers we're looking for."

"You're entertaining the idea of torturing a mother and her two children?"

"In every war there are casualties," said Soo Jin. The emotions in her eyes were unreadable because she made it that way. "I plan on interrogating them, and I'll do what's necessary if they refuse to tell me the truth." She turned to him. "Have the others leave, oppa," she told him, wanting as few people in the room as possible. She didn't want to risk the other Scorpions being in close range. "It should only be the two of us who hear any of this."

"You're not invincible, baby sister," said Young Jae, though he made no effort to physically stop her from going after them. "Murdering gang members is very different from hurting innocent people."

Or killing our father? She wanted to add, but bit down the urge.

Instead, she passively said, "She should've known better than to get involved with the King of Siberian Tigers then." Soo Jin held his eyes with hers, knowing exactly what to say to get him to give in. "What happens tonight will be placed under my name and my name alone. I killed those sixteen people, and I'll finish the rest. What I do to the mother and her children will have no effect on you. I don't want to do this either, but if it's for the good of our gang, then I'll torture them all night if I have to."

375

Young Jae took a long, thoughtful moment to deliberate everything. He acted as if he cared, yet she could see it all so clearly now. He wasn't deliberating—he was rejoicing.

"Don't hurt them too badly."

"You were always the kindest of the two of us." It disgusted her to say this because she had once truly believed it. She knew better now. As she jumped over the balcony, prepared to do what was necessary to be the one standing in the end, she was more than willing to be the more ruthless out of the two.

Her boots landed on the floor, crushing two amputated fingers beneath her before she raced over to the mother and children.

And then . . . it began.

"Get the fuck over here," Soo Jin growled, grabbing the mother by the curls of her black hair. She forcefully dragged her over to the corner of the club where stairs and a white pillar stood.

Something set off in Soo Jin the moment she heard Eve shriek in pain. A tormented scream from a distant past played in the backdrop of her memory, reminding her of a life before her reign as a Queen. Agonizing flashes of Ju Won ruthlessly pulling her hair while she cried and begged him for mercy on the first night of her training swarmed her mind, nearly causing her to collapse where she stood. She had to take a preparatory breath before the images dispersed from her mind, bringing her back to the present.

Soo Jin swallowed uneasily, unnerved from this awful memory of her lowest point in life. Though thunderstruck by this peculiar event, she struggled to focus on the task at hand. It was an endeavor that proved to be a difficult task. While she continued to drag Eve across the room, the blood that pumped in her veins wasn't that of usual excitement from hurting people. Strangely enough, it was one of dread. Dread of hurting an innocent person; dread of hurting someone who was as innocent as her before she lost her soul to the Underworld. It was an emotion she did everything in her power to suppress, no matter how nauseous she was beginning to feel. She had a job to do, a plan to keep, and a future to maintain.

Eve screamed while her children chased after her and Soo Jin. Eve tried to resist, but found it was futile, as her hands and legs were bound with sturdy ropes. In order to put on a believable show, Soo Jin decided that she had to give the mother more hell than the others. She knew this, but somehow, in addition to the unease she suddenly felt, this logic was not executed so easily.

The weight of her arms and legs seemed to have increased in mass. This was something that had not happened since her earlier training days. It took a great deal of effort to lift them, making it nearly impossible to use them. It felt like weights had curled itself around her leg when she raised it up to kick the mother across the face. The wail of pain that escaped from Eve tormented Soo Jin. She was flabbergasted that it took effort to not only listen to the mother wail in agony, but to also watch her children crawl beside her to try and tend to her. Something in her heart cracked at the sight, but she had to push through it.

Soo Jin narrowed her eyes on the children. She couldn't have the kids distracting their mother. She would never get the information if they were there to distract her. Knowing that Young Jae was watching the scene closely, she was careful with keeping her act up. The kids didn't get too far with tending to their mother before she kicked them both out of the way. Breath stalled in Soo Jin's chest when she heard their small, delicate bodies hit the floor.

Eve screamed out for her babies, worsening the headache forming in Soo Jin's head. She inhaled painfully to gather her nerves for her next set of actions. Running up to Eve, she seized her by the collar of her dress. Soo Jin was growing impatient—and apparently losing her wits. She had to get this done as soon as possible because it was killing her mentally and physically to be in the same room as the mother and children. Being heartless was no longer easy for her; it was no longer second nature to her. She couldn't comprehend what was happening to her. Why the hell were the memories from her past coming back to her, and why was she trembling at a moment like this? Nothing made sense to her but the daunting task at hand. The only thing that made sense was getting the answers from Eve and closing the chapter on this bizarre night. Perhaps when it all ended, she would return to normal.

"I need your help," Soo Jin quickly whispered, her hushed voice betraying her eagerness to finish what she started. She pressed Eve's skull against the pillar and faked a chokehold against her neck. The strain in her voice surprised Soo Jin herself. It was the first time in a very long time where she felt like she was losing control. It wasn't a sensation that she enjoyed, especially at a time like this where her very future hung on the balance. "Nothing is what it seems here. I'm not your enemy. I'm on your side and I need your help."

"L-liar," Eve struggled to say.

Soo Jin could hear her fighting to breathe. Even by holding her, Soo Jin could feel her pain. This fact alone scared the hell out of her. She did not want to feel anyone's pain, least of all a woman who had a death sentence hanging over her head. She was a God. She did not want to feel pain.

"I'm not lying," Soo Jin growled under her breath, applying more pressure against Eve's neck to show her how serious she was being. Time was limited and she had to hurry. "Tony wasn't killed. He was in the Philippines for two years before he finally came back to Seoul."

Eve stilled noticeably.

Feeding on this reaction, Soo Jin hastened to add, "Tony went to Ju Won to share in his plans. He wanted me on his side; he wanted to give me his Siberian Tigers."

Eve laughed through her pain. She glared at Soo Jin with open suspicion. "You really expect me to believe that Tony wanted to give you his Siberian Tigers? Fuck you, bitch. I should let that bastard brother of yours know about your betrayal."

Panic set in Soo Jin's nerves like acid. Before Eve could say anything, Soo Jin elbowed her across the face, causing the back of her head to slam against the pillar.

"No, no, no! Please stop hurting mommy!" the boys screamed while the family members in the background shouted, "You bitch! Leave them alone! They don't know anything!"

Within the commotion, Young Jae ordered his Scorpions to leave. He was utterly distracted, and Soo Jin used that moment to get through to Eve one last time.

"Eve," she began, staring straight into the woman's eyes. "He has Tony. Young Jae *already* has Tony."

Soo Jin rushed to finish when Eve fell silent. "You and I both know that the moment you walked in here, you were never going to leave — you or your children. If you saw the tape that Hee Jun and Tony had, then you know what Young Jae's capable of."

Tears soaked Eve's eyes. She also knew that Young Jae was never going to spare her children.

"Help me, Eve," Soo Jin implored. "In death, people never get their revenge. You have no more people left on your side. Young Jae has killed everyone you love. But right now, you have your chance to change things. Help me. Help me deceive him, help me get the jade knife, and give me the riddle." By now, the children were kneeling before Soo Jin, crying incessantly and begging her to stop hurting their mother. She stared at Eve dead in the eyes while their cries continued in the background. "Will you help me?"

Eve took a second to mull over Soo Jin's words, perhaps to detect if Soo Jin was even being authentic. Soo Jin was honestly astonished when Eve actually blinked in confirmation. Thrown off by the absolute trust that she garnered, Soo Jin pulled herself together and gave the show of her life.

"Just tell me where it is! I know that you know it!" Soo Jin shrieked. She opened Eve's mouth and stuck the blade of the knife in, threateningly holding it there. "I know that Hee Jun trusted you," she continued, slicing the palm of her own hand to make it appear like she was cutting the insides of Eve's mouth. "He couldn't be sure that he would survive, and I know that of all people, he told you."

"I really don't know!" Eve cried manically, Soo Jin's blood spurting out from her mouth. While pretending to choke on the blood, Eve whispered, "The knife . . ."

She glanced at her two children. They were still kneeling beside them and crying for mercy. Soo Jin followed her lead. Her eyes widened once she saw a shadow of a green, glimmering hue under the yellow t-shirt one of the children wore. The jade knife. It was with the kid all along.

Excitement blared inside her.

She had to get to them now.

"Would your sons know?" Soo Jin asked, carefully withdrawing the knife from Eve's mouth.

She wheeled around. She snatched both the kids by their collars, ripping the necklace—the jade knife—away in the heat of the moment before throwing them like ragged dolls toward Eve. While doing this, she also threw the jade knife behind the pillar next to them. She continued with her acting.

Now she needed the riddle and the answer.

"Did Hee Jun tell them instead?"

"No! No! Please, don't touch them. Don't hurt my babies!" Eve begged, tears gleaming in her eyes. Eve was acting for Young Jae, but she knew Eve's pain was real, especially when the boys' cries grew louder.

"Please!" one of the boys screamed, his voice choking on his tears. "Please don't kill us or our mommy!"

"Shut up! Shut up! Shut up!" Soo Jin spat out. Her face blanched at the sight of them crying. She closed her eyes in frustration, her breathing growing hoarse. The children's incessant crying was driving her crazy. Moreover, it was ripping her heart apart. She couldn't fathom all these emotions brewing like a storm inside her. What the hell was happening to her?

Desperate to keep herself from falling apart, Soo Jin raced to get the riddle from Eve so that she could end this once and for all. "Tell me now because I have no more fucking patience. I'll start cutting off their fingers if you don't start talking."

"Soo Jin, that's enough," Young Jae ordered, the sounds of the kids crying seemingly driving him crazy with guilt as well.

Soo Jin pretended to not hear him.

"Now tell me," she whispered to Eve, who was already beginning to fall apart from listening to her children's wails, "what is the riddle?"

Crying as her voice became submerged under the tears of her children, Eve closed her eyes and struggled to answer against her own disjointed thoughts. Before giving Soo Jin the riddle, she gave her something else first. "The answer to the riddle is '57.'"

This was where everything went wrong.

"57!" the boys cried out, thinking that Soo Jin couldn't hear their mother. Even under the veil of young age, they still knew enough—and were desperate enough—to do anything to save their mother's life. "57!"

"I told you to fucking stop crying!" Soo Jin shouted heatedly, panic burying into her when she realized they were giving everything away. With instinct, she slapped them across the cheeks to shut them up. It did not work. Slapping them only made the pain within her ache more. "Shut up!"

They did not listen. They continued to cry and continued to shout out the number. They continued to shout it out and in a moment of dread, she knew they were going to ruin everything. With emotions she didn't understand hitting her like a tsunami, Soo Jin turned to Eve, her silent eyes apologizing for what she was about to do.

"I have to," she whispered brokenly.

Eve returned the gaze, tears already bubbling in her own eyes. She also knew that they were ruining everything; she also knew what had to be done so their inevitable deaths wouldn't be in vain.

With the weight of the world resting on her lids, Eve closed her eyes, allowing her tears to drip free as her silent confirmation swam heartbrokenly to Soo Jin. Their cries grew louder and as they made the motions of running over to Young Jae for help, Soo Jin reluctantly pulled her gun out and did the unthinkable . . .

Boom! Boom!

Two gunshots were fired, and the crying stopped instantly.

A deafening hush collapsed on to the room, only to be broken when two small, lifeless bodies fell onto the floor.

"Nooooooooo!" the club erupted in screams of horror from the family members and from Eve, who was shaking uncontrollably from the sobs that exploded from her chest.

It took all of Soo Jin's strength not to keel over as something started blurring her eyes. She blinked and was horrified when a single teardrop slid down. Tears. She gasped, not believing that she was actually crying. She swallowed convulsively and ran over to Eve. She couldn't be distracted, not when she was so close to getting what she wanted tonight.

"Now!" Soo Jin shouted through her tears, her gun shaking violently. "Tell me now. Tell me something, and I'll let you go with them. If not, I won't even let you die. I'll keep you alive and have you stare at them until they begin to rot away!"

Eve's tears mixed with the blood on her face. She gazed at Soo Jin, silently begging her to kill her.

"On the left side of the Siberian Tigers' estate," she whispered, staring at Soo Jin dead in the eyes. It was a look Soo Jin would never forget; it was a look that condemned Soo Jin to kill Young Jae for the hell he placed them through, "buried deep in the ground under the red roses. What you're looking for, you'll find it there."

Soo Jin knew she should've asked for the procedure so she wouldn't waste time trying to decipher the riddle, but she couldn't find it in her heart to prolong Eve's misery. Her two babies had been shot right in front of her. She was begging Soo Jin to kill her, and for the first time, Soo Jin chose compassion over her own greed. She would figure out the rest of the answers herself, but right now, it was time for mercy.

Boom!

The next bullet that left her gun and speared through Eve's forehead was fast and quick, just like the misery that etched itself in her chest when she finally stumbled up on her legs and peered up at her brother. He was staring at her in disbelief. Whether it was because he was shocked that she actually killed the children and mother or because she had tears in her eyes, she wasn't sure. All that she knew was that his breath seemed to have stilled in his chest as well.

Wails and curses stormed the room from the remaining family members. Aware that she couldn't allow any of them to live any longer, Soo Jin sucked in another heavy breath and began to shoot at the remaining family members, silencing them once and for all.

"You . . . You shouldn't be here any longer, oppa," Soo Jin stuttered to Young Jae once the only breathing entities in the room were herself and her brother. She had to get him away from the club so that she could come back alone to retrieve the jade knife. "Let's leave now. We have to find the jade knife. I'll come back myself later tonight to clean this mess up. We can't risk your reputation, remember?"

Young Jae stared at her cautiously. If she didn't know what a bastard he was, she might even say he looked worried. "Are you okay — ?"

"Let's leave," she interrupted, making sure she didn't register the concern in his eyes before she ran out of the club and sought a jade knife that was never buried under the red roses.

■ ■ ■

The silence that embalmed her was an unfamiliar sensation. It came over like a flood when she walked into the carnage she singlehandedly created. The club was as dark as they had left it, and she didn't bother to turn on the lights. Something in her dreaded looking at all the bodies that died under her hands. It was better to leave them buried in the dark than for her to face them in the light.

As expected, the exploration to find the jade knife at the Siberian Tigers' estate was useless. They searched the premises for hours and found nothing.

Young Jae was looking impatient, and Soo Jin knew he didn't give a damn about finding the jade knife for Ju Won. He only cared about using the information they recovered from the family members as an excuse to "find" Tony. She suspected Young Jae was eager to get back to wherever he was holding Tony. And in truth, in that particular moment, her mind was too hazy to care. All she wanted to do was return to the club and retrieve the jade knife. It was only after she entered the club did her blurred mind finally comprehend what was happening to her.

It seemed that the curse she never wanted—a curse she never thought she'd receive—was the only entity that surrounded her while she stared around the club. Her chest tightened and she could swear she felt her heart clench as she inhaled the scent of gunpowder, blood, and the residual fear that was beginning to die out in the club. It was the most anguish she ever experienced. She couldn't stop shaking. It was happening. It was actually happening. After a decade of killing, of being surrounded by death, and having no soul, she could no longer escape from the inevitable. All it took was one scream, one cursed memory from the past, and the flood came. A decade's worth of misplaced emotions returned like a tsunami and Soo Jin became inundated.

The silence came, the tides changed, and then the mountain inevitably moved . . .

She didn't know if the tears in her eyes came because she was overwhelmed with betraying her own brother, if she was subconsciously acting, or if it was because she actually felt remorse for killing all of them. Her lower lip quivered. This was never supposed to happen to her. She was never supposed to feel remorse. She was never supposed to feel remorse for any of them. They were all supposed to be worthless. They weren't supposed to mean anything to her. This was never supposed to happen . . . yet it did.

Against all the orders that came out of her prideful body, and against a decade of fighting to be a God, her knees buckled and for the first time in her life, the great Queen fell to her knees and kneeled. She kneeled before the dead victims who surrounded her. Despite the screams that resonated from the better part of her prideful mind, a dazed Soo Jin could only focus on the silent part of her that stood in the corner of her mind. It was a quiet part of her that she had locked away and hadn't let out since her inception into the Underworld—the human part of her that would forever be her weakness.

"Only for a moment," the quiet and grief-stricken voice begged. "Stop being a monster and please let me out for a moment. Please let us do what's right. Please."

For that suspended moment, Soo Jin listened to no one else but her human counterpart. For that frozen moment, as she bowed her head in respect for those she cruelly killed, Soo Jin allowed her human emotions to run free.

The pain held in her chest exuded out and the tears began to blur her eyes once more.

"I'm sorry," she whispered, kneeling and bowing down to the blood-soaked ground. "I'm so sorry for everything."

She kneeled and bowed thirty-four times, the pain elevating every time the number increased. Her despondent eyes settled onto Eve and her two children, the ones who were the catalyst for all of this and the ones who haunted her most. The look in Eve's eyes . . . the voices of the two children . . . and the fatal gunshots . . . they all tormented her.

"I will make things right," Soo Jin promised, bowing three more times in apology to them. Resolution flooded into her eyes. The pain, as crippling as it was becoming, was not going to be a deterrent for her. She still had a plan to enact. In honor of them. In respect for them.

Soo Jin rose to her feet. The soles of her boots pressed into the puddles of blood while she walked around the dozens of dead bodies in the room. She maneuvered around the bodies of the dead children and reached down behind the pillar where the jade knife lay.

With the knife in her hand, she numbly went to a corner where she could initiate the second part of her plan. She hid the knife in her pocket, took out her cell phone, and dialed Ji Hoon's number.

In the Underworld, for every King, there were different politics that one had to abide by to establish themselves as legendary, feared, and respected. Young Jae wasn't a King who could take credit for killing an innocent family because his reputation had always been that he was the "kindest" out of all the Kings. He couldn't break out of this mold without losing the support of those who stood beside him because of this reputation. Ho Young, who could kill innocents without blinking an eye, was seen as the most ruthless one. He could do anything and his reputation would not be compromised because the people who supported him loved for him to be ruthless. And finally there was Ji Hoon. Although he had always been viewed as a powerful King, he was also seen as a heavily distracted one. He adored Soo Jin and this society knew that.

Soo Jin was also aware that "love" would never be widely popularized in their world. Ji Hoon would always be punished for being "distracted"—that was unless she made their love notorious. Even in her semi-broken state, Soo Jin was clearheaded enough to watch out for her boyfriend. She planned to make things right for him. Ji Hoon was all she had left and she would be damned if she didn't help turn him into one of the most powerful and notorious Kings in this world, and thereby help them as a couple. She was going to make them infamous in the Underworld.

"Ji Hoon?" The message she left him was one that she had never left anyone before. She had never felt so weak and so human in her life as she sat there, waiting for him to come and get her. By this time, she knew that gang members were out stalking the streets, loitering about, and she wanted them to see Ji Hoon and herself come out of the club. For this crime, she wanted to give Ji Hoon the credit.

While she waited, Soo Jin couldn't help but hear the screams in her head. Oh God, the screams. They were getting louder and louder in her head. She couldn't hear anything else. She couldn't control anything. She couldn't control her tears, couldn't control her misery, and couldn't control her inhumanity. She struggled to maintain her sanity. Why? Why was it so hard for her to be inhuman right now? Why the fuck was it so hard all of a sudden?

She smirked morosely to herself.

This was her price to pay for allowing her humanity to shine through. This was her punishment for being weak and this was her ultimate punishment for becoming human again. The Gods reside in heaven and humans go to hell. *This* was her hell.

Soo Jin was so lost in her thoughts that she didn't even realize Ji Hoon had arrived until he was right in front of her, holding her to his chest while he stared at her. He was saying things she couldn't hear because she was so overcome with the screams. She wasn't sure what she said to him, but she knew it probably sounded crazy. The bewilderment on his face told her he was perplexed by her unusual behavior.

"It's okay, baby. I'm here," he whispered despite his confusion.

He held her close to his arms and without a moment of delay, they were inside his car and driving off. Ji Hoon only stiffened when he spotted some gang members peeking into the club from his rearview mirror. He knew that they saw them leave the club. He made a move to stop the car and reverse back to kill them, to stop them from spreading rumors until Soo Jin, who had enough sense to snap out of her daze, lifted her hand up and held a firm grip on his wrist.

"They must spread the rumors," she told him with conviction. The confusion in his eyes did not cause her resolve to falter. "Your reputation has been tarnished in this world because of your love for me, Ji Hoon. But I'm making things right. After tonight, when people hear of your 'involvement' in the Club Massacre, you will be the most infamous King this world has ever known. We have to let them live; we have to let them spread the rumors."

"Soo Jin, what's going on?" he asked, bewildered.

Unable to lie to him, she told him everything. She told him about Tony. She told him about the tape. She told him about the jade knife. She told him about the Siberian Tigers. She told him about what happened in the club and finally, she told him about her plans and how she needed him to give her a formula that would help fake her death.

"Have you lost your mind?" Ji Hoon asked after she was done talking. His eyes scrutinized hers. "Your brother? After all that you told me about what the fucker did, you want him to be the one who injects you with the formula?"

"It's the only way!" Soo Jin gritted out as thunder started to rumble outside. "I need to disappear, and I need time to resurrect the Siberian Tigers!"

"How fucking hard is it?" cried Ji Hoon. "I'll kill Young Jae, and we'll get this over with! You don't have to risk your life!"

"Young Jae will be *my* kill!" she snarled through clenched teeth, infuriated that he couldn't see where she was coming from. "He will be *my* kill in the war that *I'm* bringing him! I want him to feel the same betrayal he gave to our father when he murdered him, and you can go fuck yourself if you think you're getting in the way of that!"

"You expect me to sit here, listen to your ridiculous plan, and help give you the very formula that may actually cause you to die?"

"I don't have time for this," Soo Jin uttered impatiently. She still had to figure out a place to hide the jade knife. Everything was time sensitive now. She didn't have time to convince Ji Hoon.

"You're making a mistake," he told her, watching the stubbornness sweep out of her.

"No," she contended. "My mistake would be going through all this shit and not having Young Jae's head and my own throne to make me feel better. In the span of the last few hours, I've become so fucking human that I feel like I'm going crazy. I did not just cry and feel the effects of hell just to let this epic moment pass me by." She stopped to breathe and gather her wits. She momentarily calmed down, knowing that he was only trying to watch out for her. "You're all I have left, Ji Hoon. I need this right now. I need this revenge and I need you to help me get it."

When he opened his mouth to combat her wishes, she interrupted him by opening the door and storming out.

"You think about it and let me know," she stated, not wanting to hear him oppose her plans.

She slammed the door shut, leaving him to stare at her in disbelief.

Despite being broken and arguing with her boyfriend, Soo Jin was unwilling to allow any of this to thwart her plans. She refused to experience hell without coming out with her plan being intact.

Hide the jade knife, she told herself as she began to walk away, feeling disgusted with everything the knife represented. *Hide it and let's set the plan in motion . . .*

"And you will regret ever being born."

29: The Human Queen

"Oppa!" the young girl screamed when her older brother tugged at her arm. He proceeded to drag her through the sea of dancing people at the masquerade ball they were attending. "Oppa! No, no, no!" she repeatedly shouted. "I don't want to dance with you! You're so weird! I want to dance with that cute boy I saw!"

A newly turned ten-year-old Soo Jin, who was dressed in one of the prettiest pink princess gowns for her Uncle Ju Won's party, looked around vividly, searching for the cute boy she saw. Her heart fluttered when she spotted him in the corner with a teacup in hand. He was so handsome. She wanted to run after him and talk to him, but her stupid big brother wouldn't stop dragging her away from the cutie.

"Come on, you dumb-dumb!" the young Young Jae shouted. He was dressed in a black tuxedo of his own. He continued to tug her into the middle of the dancing crowd. "I need to practice so I can dance with my future wifey! After that, you can go find your future husband and dance with him."

"Why me?" Soo Jin whined petulantly. "Why do I have to dance with you?"

"Because you're my baby sister. That's what siblings do for each other!"

"Do what?"

"Have each other's back!" Young Jae preached like a shepherd on a mission. "I got yours and you got mine!"

He laughed, pinching his baby sister's nose who, despite her own bitterness, would do this stupid favor for him and dance with him. He was, after all, her brother and she loved him.

"You got my back right, lil sis?"

■■■

"What I'm about to share, you will speak about to no one else. If you dare to breathe a word of it to anyone, then I will hunt you down and make you pay for everything," Soo Jin said sternly, standing in a private room filled with over two dozen of her Scorpions, all of whom were personally trained by her.

Jae Won and Kang Min were standing in the crowd, staring at her with immense curiosity.

"We understand, boss," one of the Scorpions conceded. "You have our word. We won't repeat what goes on here."

Other voices murmured in agreement, assuring her that she had their unwavering loyalty.

It had been days since the "Club Massacre" and the rumors had already circulated about her and Ji Hoon. The rumors were whispers of horror and fascination with the couple who were deemed as the most notorious couple in Underworld history.

During this timespan, Soo Jin avoided calls from Ji Hoon because she no longer wanted to hear how much he hated her plans. To everyone else, she made a point to show how "broken" she was. In truth, that didn't take much acting on her part because she was actually feeling depressed. She could not stop thinking about what happened at the club. Remorse continued to pelt over her like rain. Such a feeling was becoming unbearable for her. It was so crippling that she didn't know how to stow it away and reclaim the inhumane side that she loved so much. It also didn't help that, even after countless hours of deciphering, she still couldn't figure out what the riddle Eve gave her meant.

With the inability to control her own feelings and figure out the riddle aside, Soo Jin was still a force to be reckoned with in terms of executing her plans. She was well aware of how important it was that all branches of her grand plan went accordingly. The first of which would have to start with moving her trusted Scorpions out of the gang they grew up in.

"I have . . . an important task for all of you," she started faintly, already deciding that she couldn't tell them her full plans until after the fact. Just in case anything went awry, she did not want to give away too much information to certain individuals all at once. She was the only one who could see the big picture; no one else could know what her grand plan was. "I have spoken to my brother and we decided that in order to expand the gang without anyone truly knowing, we have to do it silently so our rivals will be none the wiser." She gazed at each and every one of them. "The task I have is for you to leave the Scorpions gang without saying another word to anyone or talking about this with each other. I want all of you to go out into the Underworld, form your own gangs, infiltrate other gangs, and essentially invest your time in there to mold the best and bring them with you when I call for you."

Her chest ached with unease. It troubled her that she had to lie to the group of people who have risked their lives for her. They were the ones she trusted the most.

"Please know that there is no set time for how long you are to stay out there. You will be seen as traitors amongst the gang you grew up in. You should also know that what I'm asking you to do will be one of the hardest things you'll have to do in your life. My brother will openly say that he is unaware of this plan. If it goes haywire, it'll be your heads on the line." She sighed, looking at all the brave faces of the ones she trained. They didn't even flinch in fear for what she wanted them to do. This was why she had so much pride in them. They were a reflection of her, and she loved that they represented the best of her. "But if there's any group of people whom I trust more than anything to do this right, then it's all of you. I trust that if anyone can withstand this hardship and come out triumphant, it's all of you."

"We're all under your debt, boss," Anna spoke up from the back, earning nods from the rest of the Scorpions who would give up their lives for her. "Whatever you and our King need us to do, we'll all do it without any inhibitions or questions."

Soo Jin nodded favorably at Anna and the rest of her trainees. "Your loyalty will not be forgotten. I promise that when the time comes for me to retrieve all of you, I will not forget what you've done." She motioned for them to look at the white piece of paper she gave to each of them. "In your hands, you hold a letter that tells you of the gang I want you to infiltrate or the region of the country where I want you to form new gangs. Go back to your rooms, read the paper, and after you're done, burn it and leave no trace of it. Over the course of the next few weeks, you will all leave accordingly. Do not say goodbye to anyone and remember to not breathe a word of this once you leave this room. When we're ready, I'll come back for all of you."

"Yes, boss," the Scorpions replied before filing out of the meeting room.

The only ones left were Jae Won and Kang Min, both of who broke her heart as they stood before her. She trusted them with her life and had never felt guiltier for keeping such a big plan from them. She told herself it was better this way. The less anyone else knew, the better.

"Boss?" Jae Won asked, holding his piece of paper in his hand.

"Yes?"

"Kang Min and I should stay and protect you."

Soo Jin permitted a small smile to grace her lips. She should have known they would do this. "I do not need your protection."

"But—"

"I do not need your protection," she repeated when Kang Min made an effort to combat her commands. She looked at the pieces of paper they held in their hands. Her chest tightened uneasily. Jae Won was given the task of forming a gang of his own in Seoul while Kang Min was given the task of infiltrating into the Serpents gang. It was the two most dangerous jobs.

"Boss," Kang Min started hesitantly. His gentle gaze noted the swollenness of her eyes, which were the aftereffects of crying. "We've been worried about you. Are you sure you're okay?"

"I know that the two of you will do well," she said quickly, disregarding his concern. The last thing she wanted to do was to talk about her feelings. She may have been plagued with human emotions, but that did not mean she wanted to talk about it. "Now go get ready and remember to take care of yourselves."

Soo Jin left them with a heavy heart and ventured back into the hall to find her brother. The time was coming near. She had played the broken one long enough. It was time to talk to her brother about helping her commit "suicide."

Scorpions bowed to her in respect as she walked down the hall. Soo Jin was close to veering into her brother's office before she nearly collided with someone who just walked out.

She knitted her brows when she saw that it was Anna.

"What are you doing here?" Soo Jin asked instinctively, taking inventory of Anna's sudden nervousness when she saw that it was Soo Jin she nearly crashed into.

Anna's face blanched. "I . . . I just—"

"I called her in," Young Jae answered, stepping out of his office with a black suit on. He looked from Anna to Soo Jin. "Is there a problem?"

"No," replied Soo Jin, still glancing at Anna peculiarly. "I just need to talk to you."

"Great," said Young Jae, wearing a big smile. "You've come just in time then. I was about to have Anna go look for you. Come out to the balconies with me. I have something to show you."

Soo Jin disregarded her fleeting confusion before she nodded at Young Jae, who was already turning to Anna with a smile still on his face.

"Thank you, Anna . . . for all your help."

"No problem," Anna replied before bowing to both Soo Jin and Young Jae, and then leaving in a flash.

Restlessness briefly rustled in the pit of Soo Jin's stomach. She was distracted from that feeling when Young Jae wrapped an arm around her and warmly pulled her into his office. They strode across the brightly lit room and headed straight for the connecting balcony. As they walked, she noticed that subtle tension exuded out of him. She had the impression he was perturbed about something.

"You look upset," she observed, resenting how comforting it still felt to be walking beside her older brother.

It would take time to cut off ties when it pertains to blood, she reflected to herself.

"I've heard some . . . upsetting news," he shared, his eyes displaying discomfort that she was able to read him. "I recently found out that a partner I've been working with for quite some time has been ruining some parts of my business behind my back. I'm . . . disappointed."

"Anyone I know?"

"An associate in Japan," Young Jae stated briskly. "Plus, I'm upset because I've been worried about you. You've been different since the incident at the club. Are you alright?"

"That's what I wanted to talk to you about," Soo Jin said delicately, unable to subdue the pain at the remembrance. "I need to be somewhere alone with you. I need you to meet me—"

It was the groaning that shut Soo Jin up.

Eyes enlarged, Soo Jin raced to the balcony. Air left her chest when she saw what was on the lawn where most of their killings and massacres took place.

Someone was tied up to a lamppost, shirtless while only wearing black pants. His pale face was beyond recognizable as blood ate at his skin. His hair looked like it had been recently shaved off. His body, mainly his chest area, was covered with stab wounds that had blood continuously flowing from it. Every inch of him was covered with blood. It did not take long for Soo Jin to surmise who this person was.

Hwang Tony.

He was thinner than an Underworld Prince should be. He looked emaciated, like he hadn't eaten for weeks. She could see the outlining of his ribcage, and she could see that he was no longer an Underworld Royal. Now, because of her brother, he was just a man on the brink of death.

After days of detaining him, Young Jae finally decided that it was time to show Soo Jin that he had "found" Tony.

With a triumphant smile on his face, Young Jae swung his legs over the railing of the balcony. He jumped down onto the wet lawn, easily landing on the soles of his leather shoes. Feeling disjointed and trying hard not to appear suspicious, Soo Jin jumped down after him. Her fall wasn't nearly as graceful. After years of landing flawlessly on her feet, Soo Jin broke her perfect record when she nearly stumbled to the side. She stood upright, her stupefied eyes still rested on a battered Tony.

Her chest started to ache again. Fuck, this was terrible. She was already starting to feel empathetic and she didn't even know the guy. It was official.

Her "I'm human again" condition was worse than she thought it to be. Fear enraptured her. She did not want to be here and deal with another person dying, especially the last remaining heir of the Siberian Tigers.

"We found him earlier today," Young Jae began to lie. His eyes did not waver from Tony as they approached him. "With the information you gathered from the family members. And now, I want to reward you for that. I want to reward you for all that you did."

An ice-cold feeling canvassed her body. Soo Jin turned to see that Young Jae had bent down to retrieve a long, bloodied knife that sat serenely on the grass. Staring straight into her eyes, he handed it to her.

"You wanted the honor of killing Ho Young, I didn't give it to you. Now, I want to give you the honor of killing someone else." He moved the knife closer to her, his eyes unblinking. "Exterminate the last remaining bloodline of the Siberian Tigers and end any chance of their reign for the centuries to come. That's your honor, baby sister. That's the honor you get for everything that you've done for me."

Though the migraine that started to thunder in her head was deafening, Soo Jin tried to ignore it and quietly took the knife. She turned, held the knife up, and stared at Tony. It eluded her why it was difficult to look at this guy when days ago, she couldn't care less whether he lived or died. Something had changed inside her. It was a damning thing for Soo Jin to accept that she was no longer the ruthless bitch she used to be—she was no longer the Queen she wanted to be. She was now someone she was afraid to be: a cursed human.

When he lifted his lids, Tony's eyes were merely slits when they regarded her. His eyes were etched with blood, and when he parted his mouth slightly, she realized that her brother had cut his tongue out, rendering him unable to speak. Soo Jin gave her brother credit where it was due. Young Jae was smart. He was careful with eradicating the possibility of Tony slipping any incriminating information to her.

Tony stared at her, his eyes seemingly piercing into her soul. She deduced that Young Jae had told him everything that transpired in the club. She was certain he was aware that she was the one who killed his last remaining family members. In addition to this, she also surmised that Tony knew she was on his side. She could tell by the look in his eyes as he did not look at her with hatred. He looked at her with hope. He knew that she would be the one to avenge him and his family.

The riddle, she tried to emphasize through her eyes. *I can't solve the riddle alone. Please help me solve it.*

He was quiet.

She wasn't sure if he understood her silent request until he parted his lips and mouthed something along the lines of "57." Then, he suddenly tilted his left cheek onto his shoulder.

That was all he did; it was all he could do.

Soo Jin wanted to request further help, but when she felt Young Jae's towering presence behind her, she stopped. She could feel her brother's curious eyes on her. He was more than likely wondering what she was doing and why she was taking so long.

"I'm sorry," she silently said as she swallowed to push back the distress that was rising through her. Soo Jin looked at Tony one last time. She knew the look in his eyes said, *"Avenge us."*

Closing her eyes in confirmation, Soo Jin lifted the knife that seemed to have held the weight of the world on it. She positioned the blade across his throat and then, with bated breath, she sliced the flesh, holding back her own screams as Tony's dying blood squirted onto her face.

A multitude of knives seemingly stabbed her stomach when the warm blood dripped from her face. Shaking from trauma, Soo Jin turned and lifted her eyes up to her older brother. She was surprised again because her vision was blurred, thereby meaning that the tears had found her once more. She smirked cynically. How easy it was to cry these days . . .

Yet, what shocked her wasn't the fact that she had tears in her eyes. What blindsided her was that she saw tears in her brother's eyes as well.

Were her eyes playing tricks on her?

Why was he crying with her?

Holding a hand to her left cheek, Young Jae moved closer to her. His warmth reminded her of all the times when he forced her to practice dancing with him, all the times when they ran around together, and all the times he protected her. The memories tortured her. No one ever said that killing your own brother would be easy. She just didn't think it was going to be this difficult.

"Are you okay?" he asked, his voice genuinely concerned.

Soo Jin nodded with great effort, her tears increasing. Now, she wasn't crying because she had killed thirty-four innocent people and just killed another. She was crying for her brother. She was crying for the bond they once shared, she was crying for the only flesh and blood she had left, and she was crying for the one who brought forth this cursed moment to her.

"I . . . I need you to meet me in an alley the night after tomorrow," she told him past the blurs in her eyes. "I have to talk to you about my future here." She was quiet for a long moment before she added, "I . . . I don't think I can do this anymore."

There was no black and white in the world, just shades of gray. And when she stared at her brother, feeling his warmth and love seep from his hand and onto her cheek, she could feel her heart grow heavier in misery. She wished planning to kill him was more black and white. She wished it would be easier.

"I'll meet you wherever you need me to meet you," he confirmed gently, his expression becoming unreadable. "But before that, please get some rest. I think all of this is beginning to take a toll on you."

"Thank you, oppa," Soo Jin said, relieved that she could leave. She could no longer handle being around him.

"And little sis?" her brother added before she walked out. She stopped in her tracks and awaited his reply. She became further broken when she heard him say, "You know that I love you, right?"

The authenticity in his voice was undeniable, and this was where the world fell apart for her. Her legs picked up and she sped out, her mind running in rampant circles.

Shutting the door to her massive room in the Scorpions' estate, Soo Jin buried her face into her hands. She groaned with aggravation. Broken. It was then that Soo Jin knew, as the inhumane part of her was fighting with the humane part of her, that she was broken.

What was she going to do?

How was she supposed to bring war upon him when she couldn't even think straight?

It was only when she looked down and saw her dangling locket, her father's gift that secretly doubled as a USB stick, springing out from her blouse did she know what she had to do. She had to remind herself . . . she had to remind herself of what led to this moment and why she had to go on with her plans.

It was her one last chance to get her act together before she met her brother in the alley. She prayed that it would work.

■■■

"'The best are never distracted,'" Soo Jin whispered, sitting across the camcorder with a white wall behind her. She didn't care how foolish or pathetic she looked. She needed this moment to vent out her feelings; she needed this moment to find some therapeutic solace by making a goddamn video to remind herself, and her future broken self, why she had to be a God in this world.

With that thought in mind, she persevered, staring into the camera as if she was talking to her future self. "If you're watching this right now, then it must mean that you're broken again—that you're afraid of doing what has to be done. But I'll remind you," she assured, her eyes growing cold with resolution when the image of her father being killed by Young Jae and Ho Young invaded her mind. Anger shrouded her eyes. "I'll remind you of everything that led to this moment and I'll remind you why you can no longer be broken, why we have to finish what we started. I'll remind you why we can't be human, why you were always meant to be a God, and why these feelings of remorse and guilt are purely unacceptable."

With a heavy heart, she began to recite all that happened. Pain and anger intermingled themselves into her memories, torturing her mental state. Her brother's impending death was merited, but it did not mean it was going to be easy. It also didn't help that her human emotions were going haywire while she spoke. A hole in her had been punctured, and it seemed that all the emotions that she had pushed aside were fighting to get through, as if eager to finally swim in her body after all those years of being suppressed. It was drowning Soo Jin, it was suffocating her, and it was overwhelming her.

She wanted to control it, yet she couldn't.

Soo Jin knew she couldn't, and she knew she couldn't make a pathetic self-help recording, especially if her present self wasn't even strong enough to see *why* she had to continue to fight through all of this and be a God.

"Fuck," Soo Jin growled under her breath, tugging the camera over to her and turning it off. This was useless. Why was she wasting time with a video recording when she should be figuring out the riddle? For days, the answer to the riddle evaded her understanding. Even with Tony's help, it did not make sense to her. Without the procedure, how was she going to resurrect the Siberian Tigers? How was she going to bring forth a war? How was she going to become a true God again?

Soo Jin was confounded.

Desperate for a change of scenery, and the drink that always calmed her nerves, Soo Jin knew where she had to go in order to get her mind back on track. She vacated her room and went to the very place where the riddle was first given to her.

Soo Jin had no idea then how much that choice was going to affect her in the future—that the moment she walked out of her room, her life was going to be intertwined with someone who would play the greatest and most pivotal role in her life.

"This is a world where Gods walk amongst humans."

30: Once-in-a-Lifetime Duel

Exasperated.

That was how the great An Soo Jin felt as she stood in the dark club that had been cleaned up. There were no more dead bodies on the floor, just a pristine looking establishment worthy of the "Club Pure" name.

Soo Jin sighed as she recited the riddle in her mind and wondered how on earth she was supposed to move on from here. Her time was up. She had set a night to meet with her brother to "kill" herself and had already given instructions to her trusted Scorpions to leave the gang by either infiltrating rival gangs or creating new gangs of their own. Everything had been set into motion, but there was still one holdback. She still couldn't figure out the damn riddle that was the key to her succession into the Siberian Tigers' throne.

With her favorite tea in hand, Soo Jin lifted up the styrofoam cup and gulped down the drink she created herself. Queen of Babylon white tea, mixed with rooibos rose garden tea with a small pinch of German rock cane sugar danced in her mouth and glided down her throat, acting as the stimulant she needed. She hadn't eaten all day and drinking this heavenly tea was the only thing that soothed her mind while she tried to decode the riddle. It was the only thing that pushed away thoughts of the people she killed, thoughts of her brother, and thoughts of her fucked up "I'm human again" dilemma.

"On the left side of the Siberian Tigers' estate, buried deep in the ground under the red roses. What you're looking for, you'll find it there."

Soo Jin had always been an independent person. Her intelligence and strength spoke for themselves. There were few things that stumped her and even fewer things that she couldn't conquer. Nevertheless, as she stood dumbfounded in the club, she was beginning to wish for a partner-in-crime to help her decipher this riddle. She debated on calling Ji Hoon, but for some reason, decided at the last second that she didn't want him involved in this portion of her plan.

Soo Jin placed her cup on the floor and crouched down on her knees. She looked around the club, wishing that she would get a blast of inspiration that would tell her what the true answer was. Soo Jin didn't get too far with her thoughts before she heard voices coming closer from the outside.

Not intent on being caught here in case her brother sent any Scorpions her way, Soo Jin easily bounced onto a table, kicked the nearby wall for support, and jumped into the air. She reached out and hung her hands in the space between the balcony rails of the club. Suspending herself there for a second before she swung herself up, she did a backflip in the air and flew toward the balcony. Soo Jin landed effortlessly on the balls of her feet just as the new company walked in.

Through the endless darkness, she could see the ten figures walk in, and though she had never met them, she already knew who they were.

Ho Young's Cobras.

There was a certain air that surrounded them, one filled with so much arrogance and superiority that she knew these were the trophy assassins who had been making an infamous name for themselves around the Underworld.

Fight them, a voice in her head prompted. *Fight the ones who work for Ho Young, kill them, and reset the balance. Bring back our cruelty, our ruthlessness, and our inhumanity. Make us better than human again.*

But another voice in her head told her to not bother.

We could kill them all too easily. There is no challenge. They are not the worthy mountains we seek to fight.

Soo Jin was debating. She was in the process of debating while the assassins explored the club in the darkness.

Fighting them would most likely bring some remnants of her old self back—if not her entire self. But she didn't have time. She had things to do, a future to still set in motion. Her time to solve the riddle was running up, and she feared she would never solve it at this rate. Soo Jin was still deliberating over her next course of action when she glanced down and saw that a female Cobra, one who had a tight brown ponytail and a pierced gold ring on her nose, approach the cup of tea she had forgotten. The girl bent down to pick it up.

Soo Jin clenched her fists. *Crap.*

While this occurred, her dazed mind repeated the riddle one last time, and then, the answer illuminated like a light bulb in her mind.

It all finally made sense to her.

Voices screaming out the number "57" hurled into her mind while the image of Tony moving his left cheek over his shoulder stood out to her like neon lights.

"On the left side of the Siberian Tigers' estate, buried deep in the ground under the red roses. What you're looking for, you'll find it there."

It all finally made sense.

The number "57" was supposed to resemble "S.T." in physical appearance. And finally, "S.T." stood as the acronym for the "Siberian Tigers."

"Buried deep in the ground under the red roses," she whispered quietly, knowledge dawning in her eyes.

At long last, she had finally solved the riddle—the procedure.

She had to scar someone's body.

If the new succeeding leader wanted to resurrect the gang, then he or she would have to scar the number "57," the number representing the pride of the Siberian Tigers, on someone else's body as a message that only the Siberian Tigers would understand. And she had to scar the left cheek of someone to send out this message . . .

A wicked glint sparkled in Soo Jin's eyes. She fastened her gaze onto the Cobras, who now seemed like the unlikely saviors who had just helped her solve the riddle. They were her unlikely saviors and her unsuspecting new victims.

Below, the female Cobra lifted the cup, checked the temperature of the tea, and found that it was still warm. Soo Jin jumped over the balcony just as the female Cobra announced, "Someone else is in here."

Seconds later, Soo Jin landed elegantly on her feet, standing in front of them with a predatory smile on her face. She was elated to have solved the riddle and that these Cobras were going to give her one hell of a fight. She had fallen to ruins these past few days, and it felt great to feel the God within her return. Her heart raced as she stood before them in the same manner she would have stood before anyone else in the Underworld—like a Queen. This moment was a longtime coming, and she was ecstatic it was finally here.

Just as she already knew they were the Cobras prior to meeting them, Soo Jin knew by the look in their eyes that they, too, knew who she was. If their thrill was anything to judge by, they were excited with the possibility of dueling her as well.

"Cobras," Soo Jin greeted with a nod, feeling more of her old self return. She stalked across the room like a lion. She made sure to make eye contact with every single one of them before she stopped beside the stairs next to the pillar. "The very pride of the Serpents," she continued in a whimsical tone. She sized them all up before smirking. "I take it all of you are here to gather information for your boss on what happened the other night, correct?"

They didn't answer her question.

Instead, the female leader, the one who stumbled upon the tea said, "It's an honor to finally meet the celebrated Queen of our world."

The woman's eyes were gleaming at the thought of challenging someone so revered. The rest of the Cobras shared this excitement, and it sparked a fire inside Soo Jin. It was the very fire that pumped in her veins when her ruthlessness was present. Soo Jin could see in their gazes that it no longer mattered why they were sent to the club and what their mission was. The only thing that concerned them was that they had stumbled upon the Queen herself. They were exhilarated for the opportunity to finally fight someone who held such a torch over their world.

"It would be a bigger honor to challenge you," the male leader spoke, his eyes fearless. His voice shared the anticipation of his fellow assassins. "We've heard such legendary things about you."

"That and the simple fact that our Serpents brothers were recently slaughtered by you makes this meeting a big treat for us," another male with a Mohawk spoke. Anger was prominent in his voice.

This made Soo Jin laugh. For the first time in days, she genuinely laughed. The Cobras telling her that they wanted revenge was akin to hearing a child tell you they were going to beat you to death. It was too comical. "Oh, so you want revenge? Is that it?" she teased.

Offended by her laughter and her flippant demeanor, the sternness in their faces darkened.

"Our boss would be pleased if he finds out the assassins he trained were able to kill such a celebrated Queen," the male leader spoke, pride already reveling in his voice.

The blood in her veins seared at the knowledge that they were doing this for Ho Young. It was never a good idea for someone to bring up Ho Young to her, and it was a far worse idea for anyone to challenge her.

Soo Jin would be lying if she said she also wasn't pleased. It had been so long since she last challenged a group of highly trained fighters, and she had missed it so. The thought of what she had to do with the "57" scar entered her mind while her eyes assessed each of them. It would be fun to mix work and play together.

"Let's play then," she cajoled, cracking her neck in preparation for the fun she was about to have. Planning a war against her brother aside, Soo Jin lived for the thrills that came with fighting skilled soldiers and conquering them. It was sustenance to her pride and stimulation for her entertainment. It was wonderful, it was magical, it was distracting, and it was fun as hell. She couldn't wait.

"One on one?" the female leader spoke. Despite the enthusiasm they all shared, she also wanted to be fair. This was a quality that Soo Jin respected; it wasn't enough to convince Soo Jin to go soft on the little snakes, but it was enough for her to view them as formidable opponents.

"Let's be fair," Soo Jin proposed carelessly, knowing that her skills far exceeded theirs. "Ten on one."

The battle that ensued between Soo Jin and the Cobras was one that she didn't anticipate to be so . . . enjoyable. As she lurched over tables, broke chairs apart to use as weapons, jumped onto balconies while fighting assassins in midair, An Soo Jin had never felt more exhilarated and challenged in her life. She performed backflips and spin kicks that left some opponents flying into the air while simultaneously head-butting and throwing some down on the tables with force.

The Cobras were no match for her, but they were the best group of assassins she ever had the pleasure of fighting. They were so skilled, so full of agility, and so strong that she actually had to double the effort she usually used whenever she fought with her opponents. The ones she had fought rarely, if ever, had the same fighting abilities as her. She was thoroughly impressed that these Cobras lived up to their reputations and more. The joy it brought her was drug-like.

Soo Jin gave them a break from her beatings and crouched on a nearby table. She watched them writhe on the floor, still trying to gather their inner strengths to fight her again. In that second, it was evident to her that Ho Young wasn't the master who trained these skilled killers. She knew how Ho Young fought, and it wasn't possible that he was the one who trained them.

It was someone else who was more skilled and powerful.

"Ho Young wasn't the one who trained you," Soo Jin stated, looking at them shrewdly. Curiosity marked her features. She wondered who this formidable person could be. "Who trained you?"

When they spoke the name, Soo Jin saw the light at the end of her once dark tunnel.

Though many were trying to regain their strength and their breaths, one gave her a hostile look and said, "The Prince."

Life invaded her body and her eyes broadened in delight.

"Kwon Tae Hyun," she thought out loud.

In every society, there are always individuals who are gifted with the ability to anticipate the future before anyone else. In that select group, there are also elites who could orchestrate future events. For Soo Jin, as she scanned the group of the best and most skilled assassins she had ever had the honor of fighting, she saw in them the God who created them.

She now understood what Ju Won meant when he said that Young Jae, Ho Young, and even Ji Hoon did not have what it took to be a Lord. They simply weren't legendary enough. Despite her love for Ji Hoon and the bias she wanted to have for him, this was a statement that she not only agreed on, but also one she finally understood.

Only a legend can foresee the future of another legend.

This quality was exactly why Ju Won chose Soo Jin to be his first advisee; this was why he chose to personally train her. As a revered legend, he saw the indescribable quality that he knew would lead her to everlasting greatness.

The revered Queen understood it all too clearly as the Prince of Serpents invaded her mind.

No matter his current station in life, no matter how unknown he was compared to the rest of the Kings, and no matter how distant he seemed, Soo Jin knew as easily as she knew the wonders that awaited her future that he was going to turn this world upside down. Ji Hoon may stand beside her, Young Jae and Ho Young may be casualties of her war, but Kwon Tae Hyun would be the last thing standing between her throne and her immortality as a legend in this world.

Because he was it—he was the one she spent years training for. He was that one other mountain who was meant for the same greatness as her, and he was the one who would give her the fight of their lives when their confrontation came to a head. Soo Jin smiled, feeling remnants of her human side fading under the touch of competitiveness that was overtaking her body, reminding her again why she had to be a God in the face of human limitations.

Her biggest enemy in the future became her biggest savior because the prospect of his greatness reminded her of her own. Her smile grew wider as she felt the vitality of life return to her, the pathetic human emotions leaving her.

The duel of the century, she thought with excitement before she fought, overpowered, and sliced the number "57" onto his beloved Cobras' cheeks. For good measure, she even killed the youngest Cobra to set off the hatred she needed the future King to have for her. She wanted him livid, at his deepest rage, when they would finally meet face to face and battle one another.

Soo Jin was so delighted that she had finally met her match that she couldn't even focus. Adrenaline and excitement revved up inside her as she carelessly dumped the young girl's corpse from her grasp. She strode out of the club feeling like a God again. Her heart was pumping erratically, and she had never felt more alive, more ready to do what she needed to do to get the Siberian Tigers' throne and finish Young Jae off. She was more than ready to face the one King who would give her the battle she had been dying to have since she was ten—a legendary duel.

Eager to set something else in motion, Soo Jin dialed the number to one of her associates in the States once she got into her Lamborghini.

"I want Kwon Tae Hyun to come home," she told the man. Although she couldn't see him, she knew he was furrowing his brows in bewilderment. He was thrown off by her unexpected orders.

"By force?"

"No," Soo Jin answered with a cunning smile. She already knew what to do to get him to come home on his own will. "Get your associates and start the whispers in America: Kwon Ho Young has been raping his baby sister. Spread it, make sure it floats over to him, and Kwon Tae Hyun will come running."

"Why do you want him to come home, boss?" her associate asked curiously.

The memory of her father and how he died flashed in her mind. Young Jae was going to receive the same betrayal from her. And Ho Young . . . Ho Young needed the same betrayal, and she wanted his younger brother to be the one who bequeathed it upon him. She was killing two birds with one stone because she also wanted to ensure a future for Tae Hyun.

"I want him to kill Ho Young," she said blithely. She additionally added in her mind: *And I want him to be the new King of Serpents.*

She wanted him to get this position.

She wanted him to rise to power.

She wanted him to be the candidate to become the Lord of the Underworld, and when everything was ready, she wanted to fight him for it.

Soo Jin laughed to herself, thinking about the irony of her life as she went back home and finished recording the tape to commemorate this wonderful turn of event.

In the face of human emotions, how ironic was it that Kwon Tae Hyun, someone she had never met, was the only one powerful enough to make her want to fight through all of this turmoil and become a God? How ironic was it that he was the only one who was able to save her life when she was about to be consumed by human emotions?

An Young Jae.

Kwon Ho Young.

Lee Ji Hoon.

None of the current Kings had ever given her such a reason to live, to want to fight for the throne.

But Kwon Tae Hyun . . . Kwon Tae Hyun was different.

Kwon Tae Hyun was going to be epic.

He was going to be powerful, and he was going to be a force to be reckoned with in this world. He would give her the battle of a lifetime, and he was going to make an immortal legend out of her—for conquering him and killing him would be the gift she gives herself when she stands amongst the heavens alone, without another towering mountain to overshadow her.

Soo Jin's calculating smile became lethal. She was going to enjoy meeting Tae Hyun, she was going to enjoy fighting him, and she was going to enjoy killing him.

Soo Jin had no idea as she finished her recording, imported the file into the USB stick, and returned to the Siberian Tigers' estate to hide it, how much her life was going to go astray after that night was over. She had no idea how wrong everything was going to turn out. That her brother had anticipated her betrayal because he was tipped off, that Ho Young had somehow saved her and hid her, and that she would get amnesia and forget all about Ji Hoon, all the while (much to her own horror) allowing her human counterpart to finally come out and breathe in the world for the three years to follow.

Everything after that night went wrong for her.

Everything went wrong except one thing: Tae Hyun.

The one she had never met, the one she didn't know, and the one who would become the most prominent person in her life . . . nearly everything she anticipated for him happened.

After hearing the rumors about his brother raping his younger sister, Tae Hyun did return home. He did kill Kwon Ho Young, and he did succeed the Serpents' throne. And just as she had predicted, he did become one of the most revered Kings in the Underworld. Not only that, but he also became the biggest contender for the Lord of the Underworld throne—the very same throne that she sought and the very same throne she was willing to fight to the death for.

"Future King of Serpents, I can't wait to meet you, conquer you, and kill you," she stated elatedly, reveling in the thought of being exposed to something so fun, so exciting, and so thrilling in the near future.

Soo Jin inhaled expectantly, turning off the camera and setting the next three years of her life into motion.

"We are going to give each other the once-in-a-lifetime duel that only Gods could dream of."

"Once you're in, the only exit is death."

31: Welcome Back to the Underworld

Before the changing of tides, there is always silence.

A prolonged silence to warn people about what's coming, an insufferable silence that promises pain, and an epic silence that guarantees an event that will carve itself into history.

This particular silence was one that washed over the brothers as they stood outside in the apartment hall.

It had been a couple of hours since Tae Hyun kicked them out of his gang, and it had also been a couple of hours since they waited for Yoori to walk out of the apartment with her bags in hand.

The silence that moved between the brothers was a somber one.

After Tae Hyun walked out of his apartment, his face cool with impassiveness, they tried to reason with him. They tried to convince Tae Hyun to allow Yoori, and themselves included, to stay in Korea. Their pleas fell on deaf ears. The stubbornness that emitted from Tae Hyun was a decisive one. It was well-known that once the King of Serpents made a decision, he stuck with it no matter what. This was a trait that the brothers were more than aware of.

Yes, the silence was somber . . . that was until a sudden change in atmosphere occurred.

The temperature didn't change, no one spoke, and no one was in their presence. Even so, they felt that change, that familiar feeling they only received when they were in the presence of one of the most important people in their lives.

The door to Tae Hyun's apartment swung open, revealing the catalyst for the changing of tides.

Stepping through the door, as expected, was Choi Yoori. She was dressed simply in black jeans, boots, and a black hoodie. Yet, an unexpected emanation of power streamed from her. It was the aura of an entity who could move mountains, and with the absence of Tae Hyun, there was only one other person who could evoke such power.

Jae Won and Kang Min's eyes enlarged. Their bodies froze in shock. They stared at her, their eyes unblinking as she walked down the hall. All that could be heard was the sound of her boots stabbing into the ground while she approached them. Her face was shrouded with determination, sternness, and reserved excitement.

The breath escaped their chests when she finally stood across from them. She thawed the once cool expression on her face and assessed the shock that consumed their eyes. Then, she smiled in a way that only their boss could give them.

"It's been a long time," she whispered, looking between Kang Min and Jae Won. She took in how tall they were and how much they had grown in her absence. "You two have grown."

Shocked gasps escaped their lips.

Disbelievingly, they said, "*Boss?*"

She didn't say anything, but when she extended her hands out, palm first, they knew who this woman was.

It was An Soo Jin.

An Soo Jin had finally returned.

Smiling uncontrollably, both in happiness and disbelief, the brothers whipped her beloved weapons out from behind their backs and placed the gold guns in the palms of her awaiting hands.

A wide, blissful smile danced across Soo Jin's beautiful face. She closed her eyes in delight, luxuriating in the feel of her guns after three years of absence. She inhaled deeply before staring down at the black hoodie she wore. The hoodie still had remnants of wet tears that had yet to dry up.

"I think it's time for me to be welcomed home at the party everyone seems to be at," Soo Jin began with much amusement.

The competitive blood inside her veins pumped ecstatically when she held the fabric of the black hoodie in her hand.

Her smile became vindictive.

Her long-awaited homecoming brought back a war, and there was only one Underworld King worthy of it.

"And I think it's time . . . for me to officially meet Kwon Tae Hyun."

ABOUT THE AUTHOR

Con Template currently resides in California. When she is not outside with her DSLR capturing reality, you can find her in between realities when she is writing about a "King," a "Prince of Hell," an "Architect," an "Ancient," and a "Titan."

She is working on the final book of the Welcome to the Underworld novels and introducing a new series, An Eternity of Eclipse.

You can follow her at *contemplate13.wordpress.com* or *twitter.com/contemplate13*.